The
Angel of
Twickenham

SCEPTRE

The Angel of Twickenham

URSULA BENTLEY

SCEPTRE

First published in 1997 by Hodder and Stoughton
A division of Hodder Headline PLC
A Sceptre book

10 9 8 7 6 5 4 3 2 1

British Library Cataloguing in Publication Data

Bentley, Ursula
  The angel of Twickenham
  1. English fiction – 20th century
  I. Title
  823.9'14 [F]

  ISBN 0 340 68582 4

Typeset by Palimpsest Book Production Limited,
Polmont, Stirlingshire
Printed and bound in Great Britain by
Mackays of Chatham PLC, Chatham, Kent

Hodder and Stoughton
A division of Hodder Headline PLC
338 Euston Road
London NW1 3BH

To Paul

ʃ

The great tide of wedding had receded. The happy couple were safely *en route* to a go-slow at Gatwick. It had been an unreconstructed British wedding. Not for them the all-night dance to an accordion band, the hilarious bits of business, congas through the *Stadthaus* flower-beds and dawn farewells with garlicky kisses. Instead they had sit-down chicken breasts and a cup of tea before the symbolic anticlimax.

'There's a knees-up later at the Star of Bengal,' said Dotty. 'On Thames.' Flushed with Spanish cuvée she lowered her carriage onto a chair and tried to locate her mouth in the mirror of the hotel's finest ladies' room – possibly the finest toilet facilities in the Southeast. 'The Fox and Entrails, as was. I ask you – knocking back chapatis in a place like that. It used to be the watering hole of Norbiton Rowing Club, you know.'

'They're only getting their own back, Dotty,' said Harriet. 'It's no worse than cucumber sandwiches in Jaipur.'

'But those people *wanted* to be British.'

'Oh Dotty, don't be silly.' Harriet leant her face on her hand. The Crushed Aubergine nails looked to advantage in a casual mélange with lowlights.

'All right, don't give me the Rights of Man lecture, I've got it on cassette. Tell you what, why don't you all come back to our place on the way home? You've never been, you know.'

She did. Harriet sat up straight. 'I think Warren will be anxious to relax. He's been awfully stressed since going to M25TV.'

'Americans are always stressed. That's no excuse to be anti-social.'

Harriet wopped Dotty playfully with her copy of the Marriage Service. 'Not fair. We've had you two over often enough.'

'Well, now's your chance to see how the other half lives. Oh, go on. He can do his market research while he's there. I'm the only one who watches M25TV. Even the budgie asks to be covered.'

'I watch it – when I'm not working.'

Dotty opened her mouth to question this codicil, then changed her mind. Although she and Harriet got on like fish and chips when they did meet, they were not close relations.

'By the way, did I tell you I could have had *Ashes and Broomsticks* at the Lyric last year? Post-modern *Cinderella*. Instead of the prince she wins first prize in a business incentive scheme and opens a Get In Shape shop. I didn't fancy it.'

'Aren't you a bit old for Cinders?' said Dotty.

'It was the Fairy Godmother. Or rather, small business advisor.'

'So you got to put your feet up for three days, did you?'

'Of course. Besides, I'm not happy about leaving Tiz with this au pair. She's so moody. The French ones aften are.'

'Why don't you get an English one then?'

'Oh Dotty.' Harriet sighed for her second cousin-in-law once removed. She was very fond of Dotty, and Dotty was one of us in the sense that she would never mistake a napkin ring for an arthritis bangle, but still—

A peach moiré marquee hurtled through the door. Her crown of stephanotis askew, Tiziana's eyes were also wild.

'Mummy! Mummy!'

Harriet stood up, with a farewell glance in the mirror. 'No need to shout, darling.'

'Mummy, guess what!'

'What?'

'Yoevil and Kean have been kidnapped!'

'Yoevil and Kean? Why? By whom?' She fell back on her chair.

'I don't believe it,' said Dotty. But she was pale and tottering – as who would not be at the abduction of Britain's skating monarchs.

'It's true! They were taken at gunpoint from an Ovaltine awards ceremony. They interrupted programmes to announce it.'

'In broad daylight? How frightful. Who would do such a thing?'

'Terrorists, of course. Afghans – no, Arcadians—'

'Armenians?'

'Yes, that's right. They think it's something to do with guns we sold them in 1910.'

'It makes you think twice about success, doesn't it?' said Dotty.

'Dotty, how can you be so heartless? Don't you *care*?' Tiziana sank onto the floor, obliging ladies who wanted to go to the lavatory to wade through her dress.

'Don't sit on the floor, darling. That thing's got to go back to the hire company.'

'It doesn't matter. It's so *awful*. Will they hurt them?'

'Oh well,' said Dotty. 'So much for *War and Peace on Ice*. I was looking forward to that.'

'Perhaps they'll just make one leg shorter than the other.'

'Mum!' Tiziana burst into tears.

Harriet took her daughter in her arms. 'Sorry, darling, that was bad taste. It *is* awful. Terrible. But don't cry. Kidnappers don't usually get away with it. Why, I should think they'd get the army out.'

'I'm glad the happy couple have left already,' said Dotty. 'It would have ruined the wedding. Now you dry your eyes. You're all coming back with Uncle Fin and me and I'll make banana pancakes.'

'Can I have chocolate on mine?'

Harriet groaned, but did not protest. In view of the national emergency, some exercise in solidarity seemed appropriate.

'Go and round up the boys, darling, and tell Semiramide we're going as well.'

'I haven't seen her for ages.'

'Try the bedrooms,' said Harriet darkly.

Warren had to be cranked up to an acceptable level of concern about Yoevil and Kean. He was even less interested in calling in at Dotty's on the way home.

'She's your relation,' chided Harriet. 'She'll be awfully hurt if we don't.'

Warren's cheek twitched with fatigue, and his eyes gave a hint of desperation to escape from his role as star turn at gatherings of ordinary folk. 'OK. But no more than a half-hour.'

Semiramide, the au pair, was tracked down to the hotel kitchen, where she had discovered a fellow Gaul in the pastry section. Her expression, as Tiziana dragged her through the swing door, would have moved the Rock of Gibraltar.

'Come *on*. You're holding everybody up and I'm starving.'

'I too,' said Semi. 'Ow can I eat quiche zat is wet?'

'You never eat anything but couscous anyway. Now come *on*.'

Semi refused to go in Fin and Dotty's car and folded her arms to signal that she was officially sulking. Harriet let her sit in the front as a treat. With Semi in a mood, and Warren cheated of his customary round of golf, the weekend had gone into a black hole. Harriet kept her eye on Semi for signs that she was still breathing.

Dotty and Fin lived in Twickenham in a sweep of Tudorbethan beach huts clearly designed to bring the Royal Crescent, Bath, to its knees. Japheth and Mungo laughed aloud as they drew up outside the half-timbered semi.

Harriet rounded on her sons, who were sitting in the rear of the Volvo, behind the dog guard.

'Now don't you two dare make any rude comments about Dotty's house. They're very proud of it.'

'We weren't going to!' protested Mungo, the younger and more mendacious. 'Anyway, what are we going to do here?'

'We aren't staying long enough to draw up a programme of activities. Just talk to Uncle Fin. I'm sure he'd appreciate the attention. God knows what he does all day now he's retired.'

'That's rude, Mum,' said Tiz.

'Sorry. You're right. Well just sit down and be quiet for a change.'

Warren was less scathing about the crescent. He looked about him with benign interest.

'Is this some kind of model village? It kinda – says something, don't you think?'

'Apart from "Tory Stronghold" no, I don't think it does. Come on, let's get it over with.'

They left Semiramide asleep in the car and trailed up the garden path. Tiz charted the course, jumping from one stone mushroom to the next, holding Harriet's hand.

'Are these sacred mushrooms, Mum?'

'Only to Dotty.'

'What does "sacred" mean?'

'Holy.'

'Why aren't they holy mushrooms then? English is stupid.'

Harriet sighed. There were times when she felt like shooting down her daughter's enquiring mind like an enemy aircraft.

Uncle Fin opened the door. He had already slipped into his cardigan.

'You found it all right, then?' he beamed.

'No,' said Mungo.

'Don't be rude, Mungo.' Harriet kissed Uncle Fin. 'Hey – where are you two going?'

The boys were up the stairs in a couple of strides. Japheth grinned at her through the bannisters.

'Exploring!'

'You can't explore a cubicle. Oh, sorry, Fin, I didn't mean—' Harriet ran up the stairs after them, but was brought up short by a dizzy reminder of her alcohol consumption. 'Now look, this isn't a climbing frame, it's Dotty's house.'

'We're only looking, Mum.'

'You should ask first.'

'Let them be, Harriet,' said Uncle Fin. 'They can't do any harm.' He smiled fondly at the boys.

Harriet gave up. There was no arguing with ignorance on that scale. The problem was repressing the gratification when it was exposed, as it always was to obtusely childless couples like Dotty and Fin.

'I'm just whipping up the batter, Tiz,' called Dotty from the kitchen. 'Do you want to come and help?'

'Tizzy, not in that dress—'

'I'll be careful, Mum.'

Uncle Fin ushered Warren and Harriet into the living room. The April chill was blasted by a ferocious gas fire that Harriet feared would strip the skin off her shins. Warren sank onto the miniature sofa and motioned Harriet to join him. Uncle Fin hovered.

'You two just make yourselves comfortable. Can I get you anything? Would you like the television on, Warren?'

'No thanks, Fin. It's not like my oxygen supply, OK?'

'No, right. Well, I think I'll just go and help Dotty.'

Warren closed his eyes and his head instinctively sought the clubland leather comforts of home. 'What are those two apeshits doing?'

Muffled thumps from upstairs told of the boys' successful attempt to amuse themselves, but experience had taught Harriet not to bother unless the light fitting fell down, or water came through the ceiling.

'I wish you wouldn't call them that.'

'I wish they wouldn't act like that.'

'Well, it certainly wasn't the object of their upbringing. I've spent my entire adult life trying to civilize them.'

'Sweetheart, that is a fucking lie. You were in Chichester for six months.'

'Will you shut up about Chichester! It was in 1975, for God's sake. The time I've spent working since doesn't amount to a long weekend. What was that?'

'What?'

'I thought I saw something fall past the window.'

'Did it have legs?'

'What's that noise?' There had followed an explosive squelch, and then another. 'It must be the boys. Why don't you go and deal with them for once?'

'Honey—' Warren lifted a heart-rending hand in protest.

'Oh God, all right—'

'I love you, sweetheart.'

'Bollocks.'

Harriet found Japheth and Mungo in the front bedroom. Her head of steam was almost diffused by the astonishing number of coordinated Spring Meadow furnishings, down to the Kleenex cover. The boys were hanging out of the window.

'What do you two think you're doing?'

'We don't think, Mum, as you're always telling us.'

'Why is the carpet wet? You are *not* on the water bombs again – Jesus – look at Dotty's carpet – don't you think you're a bit old for this infantile barbarism?'

'Obviously not, Mum.'

Harriet gagged on her frustration, not least because her inner sense of incoherence always failed to express itself, emerging instead in orderly clichés.

'I mean – why do you have to be so – mindless – *mental* – why can't you just not do *anything* for five minutes? Is that too much to ask?'

'Yup.'

Harriet took a swipe at Mungo, but he escaped over the bed.

'You're both complete idiots! Why we're paying for your education, God knows. You'll end up on the roof of Strangeways anyhow. Mungo, go and clear up the garden and Japh, you mop the bathroom – I can guess what state it's in.'

'Harriet!'

'Yes, Dotty?' Harriet produced a cheery note with professional ease.

'Tea's ready.'

'We'll be right down.' Her voice resumed its rasp. 'Now do as I say immediately or you can forget sailing camp.'

('Mum—'

('Mum—'

'I mean it. Then come and have some tea in *total silence*.'

'Bor-ing.'

'They don't even have a computer.'

'Enough!'

Harriet went down the stairs, which were dangerously narrow, obliging one to lock the feet into right angles for safety. Mungo jangled down in an overt display of truculence behind her. She pointed to the front door.

'Don't be long,' she hissed.

Dotty presided over a teatray laden with Assorted Biscuits. Fin handed them round, and Harriet accepted a lemon cream with a heave.

'How's the job going, Warren dear?' said Dotty. 'It's always difficult at first, isn't it?'

'What – running a TV station?'

'Any job. Fin could hardly sleep when they put him in charge of Dry Goods.'

'That's true. Mind you, it was the unions in those days. God bless Margaret Thatcher. She settled their hash all right, didn't she Dotty.'

'Yes indeed, dear. It's a pity she wasn't around in 1066.'

'Talking of the French, I hope Semi's all right,' said Harriet. 'Do you think I should go and look?'

('No.'

('No.'

('No.'

'Oh all right.'

'You were saying about the job, Warren. Fin, I don't think you should have any more biscuits.'

'Go on – just a gingernut.'

Fin balanced his teacup on his stomach and delicately dunked the gingernut in it. Harriet's poise faltered. The dunking of biscuits was a practice that took her mind straight back to an old-fashioned kitchen in her grandmother's house, where her mother's old nanny had initiated her into a habit which she reckoned brought her into communion with generations of poverty-stricken slum dwellers – gritty folk who dried their lock-knit combinations over the kitchen range, ate bread and dripping and knocked the hell out of Life in between their twelve-hour shifts. The romance of poverty had since left her, but she could still be cut with grief at the idea of that warm old woman under the cold sod. The thought occurred that her spirit lived in Dotty – the universal furnace, the human equivalent of the four-oven Aga.

'We don't have much trouble with the unions,' said Warren. 'Money's the main problem. We've got a couple of real funding bitches right now.'

'Funding?' said Fin. 'Don't the commercials pay for it all?'

'No way. We need sponsorship too.'

'Did you get Deutsche Rundfunk to come in on that project about Teutonic gloom?' said Harriet.

'I thought we had, but the Board wouldn't buy it. I'm keeping the Germans on the boil, though.'

'Why don't you make some programmes about England?' said Dotty.

'Sure, we could do that. *All Creatures Fat and Flabby*.'

Dotty puckled her lips. 'Well, *I* watch M25. But I don't know that I'd bother if you weren't my second cousin.'

'Thanks.'

Japheth and Mungo came in to the relief, for once, of all present. Dotty got them to sit on the floor. Mungo turned the fire off. Harriet was furious.

'Why did you do that? This isn't your house.'

'It was bursting my zits!'

'That's all right,' said Dotty. 'When Fin and I say make yourself at home, we mean it. I can't stand people who invite you into their house and then make you feel like a contestant on *Mastermind*.'

'You're not talking about us, I hope.'

'No, no,' said Dotty, lying. 'Are you OK, Fin?'

'Yes, I'm fine.' Fin had put down his biscuit and was frowning at the wall. He forced a smile. 'Now, you boys, tell us what you've been up to lately.'

'Nothing much.' Japheth lolled against his mother's knee. His blond hair, sleet straight, caught on her skirt in static wafts. Harriet sometimes resented his physical charms, though flawed enough, in the novelistic tradition, to make them interesting. It seemed to put a barrier between them that did not exist with the more homely, but presentable, Mungo. On her worst days she wondered if that six months in Chichester had anything to do with it – the feeling she now had that his physical closeness was a reproach rather than a reward.

'Don't be lazy, Japh.' She tweaked his hair. 'Tell Uncle Fin about that skiing trip. They went with the school. We nearly lost him.'

'It wasn't that exciting. We were just coming down a narrow ridge and the instructor was blown over the edge. There was a fantastic blizzard and we all had to lie face down in the snow on the edge of this cliff thing until we were rescued. He broke both his knees. It was great – we hated him anyway.'

'Good gracious,' said Dotty.

'You know, Mother, I'm thinking of giving up Chinese and doing Sport instead. It would only take me a couple of months.'

'For A-level?' said Fin.

'Yes.'

'You mean you can do Sport for A-Level? That's daft. No wonder this country's always in a crisis.'

'I don't know that Greek, British Constitution and Sport is a particularly useful combination, darling,' said Harriet. 'What do you think, Warren?'

'Don't ask me. I think they should both go to the States and get a rational education. Asking kids of sixteen to specialize in three subjects is like asking the dog to plan his diet.'

'Oh I say,' said Dotty. 'The proof of the pudding, Warren. The proof of the pudding.'

'What's that supposed to mean?'

Dotty adjusted her glasses. 'Well – our system works, doesn't it? Why do foreigners come and steal our academics, then? How many foreign lecturers are there at your Harvard then? How many British?'

'Quite a few, I guess, but—'

'You see! Two hundred and fifty million of you, and you can't even staff your own universities!'

Harriet smiled as Dotty's passion broke through the bonds of hospitality like King Kong.

'Now wait a minute.' Warren sat up. 'We're the only ones who can afford to buy the best, that's the size of it.'

'You think everything can be bought, no doubt,' sniffed Dotty.

'What's with this "you", Dotty? I chose to live here, OK? I'm not the fucking US ambassador.' But he spoke without rancour.

Dotty raised her eyebrows and looked down her nose. 'You're quite right. I apologize. Their loss is our gain, I'm sure. More tea?

'Harriet will have to get a job if all your lot are going to the university,' said Fin.

'I have a profession already, Fin.'

'Well, yes I know, love, but it's not like ready money, is it?'

'I'm very limited, having to work in London.'

'But you wouldn't want to traipse round smelly digs at your age, would you?' said Dotty.

'It's not smelly digs these days, it's all Holiday Inns and

convention centres. Anyhow, I couldn't leave Tiz with Semi. She's very clinging at the moment.'

Mungo yawned. 'Who do you think's going to win the World Cup, Uncle Fin?'

'Cameroon, I suppose.'

They laughed at his suicidal expression.

'Don't be like that, Fin,' said Harriet. 'The competition's good for us.'

'I tried to join the Black Section of the Epsom Labour Party,' said Japheth. 'To show solidarity with the ANC. Unfortunately there wasn't one.'

'Now what on earth did you want to do that for?' said Dotty.

'Why don't you just join the ANC?' suggested Warren.

'Thanks, Dad.' Japh's lip trembled. 'Don't worry, another six weeks and you can officially divorce me.'

'Oh baby—' He tousled Japh's hair. 'I was exactly the same at your age.'

'Then it's a pity you're not my age now.'

'Sor-ry.'

Tiziana pushed the door open with her bottom as she was licking her fingers. The peach moiré was covered with brown stains, of the kind one gingerly sniffs.

'Tiz, you are the limit. I told you not to cook chocolate in that dress.' She avoided looking at the real culprit – Dotty.

'I thought Tiz was supposed to be on a diet,' said Mungo. 'She looks like a parachute in that dress. Except a parachute has better legs.'

'Arsehole!'

'Tiz! How dare you talk like that.'

But the vengeful parachute had landed, on Mungo, and was pummelling his face in, 'Pig! Pig!' screamed Tiz.

'Stop it!' Harriet tried to grab her arms, but Tiz shook her off.

Dotty was pale. 'I've never seen Tiz like this.'

'She's over-excited,' said Harriet. 'She's never been a bridesmaid before.'

'I'm glad it doesn't affect everyone like that.'

Harriet was sweating as she grappled with Tiz's flailing arms. 'Stop it, Tiz. You'll hurt him.'

'Get her off me!' spluttered Mungo. His hips hiccoughed in an ineffectual attempt to dislodge her.

Japh, neatly perched on the arm of the sofa, looked on with real pleasure. 'Finish her off, Mungo. I thought you took Dolphin Management for GCSE.'

'What?' said Fin. 'I don't believe it.'

'He's joking,' said Warren. 'Tiz, honey, lay off. You've made your point.'

'Brilliant, Warren,' said Harriet. With a gasping wrench that split the peach moiré under the left arm Harriet pulled Tiz away and dragged her into the hall where the screams reached coconut-splitting registers as Harriet smacked her bare arm in a frenzied attack. Tiz called on Dotty to save her, and landed some well-placed blows on Harriet's bosom. At last Tiz broke away and ran back into the sitting room and Dotty's bewildered arms. Harriet fled up the stairs and locked herself into the cold turquoise bathroom. She leant against the door in a paroxysm of silent screams.

'I – hate – you – all,' she mouthed, and collapsed on the bath mat.

The paroxysms were eventually infiltrated by the observation that, for one so obsessed with hygiene, it was surprising that Dotty did not put the mat over the side of the bath when not in use. Harriet did not care to put her bathed foot on a mat contaminated by outdoor shoes and dog paws. The thought formed a walkway from the primal negative to the lesser ebb of sobbing shockwaves that followed it.

Presently she sat up, and took a long roll of loo paper to blow her nose. 'It's the demon drink,' she muttered. 'On the other hand, the children didn't have any.'

The sound of raised voices from downstairs distracted her. A lively inquest was in progess. It would lessen the impact of re-entry, but she was in no hurry to make it. That satisfaction when, despite her conventional efforts, the brutish side of child-rearing made an appearance in public, sustained her recovery from it.

She got up and inspected the damage in the mirror of the bathroom cabinet. Not too bad. The cabinet contained an inadequate repair kit: Boots No.7 liquid foundation, rosewater and glycerine also from Boots, and Boots Elderflower Eye Gel. What a pity, she thought, that Mr Boot had not been called something less sordid, like Honeywell. She took the comb from an unused packet of nit lotion, and when she had finished using it her nose had subsided sufficiently for her to go downstairs. There seemed to be quite a commotion down there. She could hear Warren on the phone. And somebody was crying.

Warren looked up as she came downstairs. His expression was serious.

'What is it?' said Harriet.

'Fin. He's had a heart attack or something. I just called an ambulance.'

The blood whirled out of Harriet's head. Tiz ran out of the sitting room and flung herself around Harriet's waist. They clung together, shaking.

'Mum – I'm sure he's dead.'

'N-no, darling, I'm sure he isn't. Sh-shall I have a look?'

'She may be right,' said Warren, with a look that said she was. 'Come with me, Tiz. We'd better go tell Semi. God, what a thing to happen.'

'I can't believe it,' said Harriet. She was accustomed to Life punishing her self-pity, but not with the swiftness of a karate chop.

Fin, slouched in the armchair with his eyes still open, was surrounded by an ikebana-style arrangement of bodies that cried out to be painted by Jacques-Louis David. Dotty was draped over one arm of the chair crying, and cuddling Fin in her arms. She murmured words of such tender pathos that Harriet wished for her sake that she had had no witnesses. Mungo stood behind her, patting her shoulder. Japheth knelt on the other side of Fin, stroking his arm and frowning into his face with what might have been scientific enquiry.

Mungo came and hugged her. 'I don't feel so good.'

'You did well, darling. It's all right. Go outside and get some fresh air. You too, Japh.'

She smiled at them as they quietly left the room with a last glance at Fin. Japh put a hierarchical arm around Tiz's shoulder. They were all right after all, she thought, when the plate armour of adolescence was stripped away. They would need much tender talking through, at least she hoped they would, to assimilate this first acquaintance with death. But Dotty's need was imperative. Harriet was glad that she had purged her own tension in the bathroom, not immediately connecting the boxing match and Fin's death. The good thing was that her own geyser had blown, leaving her in a relatively calm state to put at Dotty's disposal. Her training had given her profound respect for the effectiveness of the wordless gesture. She took Dotty in her arms, quietly hearing out the incoherent misery.

Outside Harriet saw, with difficulty through the ruched nylon nets and mullioned panes, that Warren had extracted Semi from the car and was explaining the situation to her, at the same time looking up and down the road for the ambulance. Tiz clung to his jacket. The boys had disappeared. The front door had been left open and a bitter current of air swept into the room. A couple of women appeared and spoke to Warren. They looked uneasily at the house where Death had scored while their own husbands were watching *Grandstand*.

Harriet eased Dotty off her and drew up a chair so that Dotty could sit beside Fin and hold his hand. She closed the door and put the fire on. The ball of flame threw her back on her heels and she bit on an oath.

'Would you like a small sherry, Dotty? It might calm you down.'

Dotty nodded. 'You're so good.' She crumpled again.

'Oh nonsense. Is it in the sideboard?' As she poured the drinks Harriet was pleased to notice that her hand was steady. Rising to an occasion was a cure for all ills. The sight of Dotty's swollen, and now multicoloured face, moved Harriet as she had not been moved since the birth of Tiziana. Pity for Dotty, and the momentum of the drama, gathered into a swell that lifted her generosity into a reckless reach.

'You mustn't worry about a thing, Dotty. You don't have to stay here. You must come back with us. We've got plenty of room.'

'Oh I couldn't, Harriet.'

'Why not? You can't stay here alone. You haven't got any – well – useful relatives except us, have you?'

'There's my – huh – sister.'

'But she's crippled with arthritis.'

'It's – huh – her own fault. She was always – huh – dieting. I told her she wasn't getting enough – huh – calcium. Look what happened to the – huh – Duchess of Windsor.'

'Not your problem, Dotty dear.'

'No.' Dotty sagged with gratitude at this kindly tease.

Harriet wished they could retire to another room, but the kitchen and downstairs loo were all that was on offer. While it was no strain to improvise a comforting monologue, the presence of the deceased made it singularly futile. She tried to persuade Dotty to lie down, call the doctor, pack a suitcase, but Dotty refused all suggestions.

'There is something you can do for me – huh – Harriet.'

'Anything, Dotty.'

'Could you say a – huh – prayer? I don't want him to go to that morgue place unblessed.'

'Ah. Right. Of course.' Even for Harriet, this was quite an assignment. Her childhood had been free of spiritual reference points. All she could think of was St Joan's agonized query to God as to when the world would be ready to receive His saints. It was a part she had taken over for six matinée performances at Greenwich in 1971. A peculiarly apt quotation, as she had never been asked to take over an evening performance. She clasped her hands and bowed her head.

'Oh Lord – hear my prayer and receive into the company of the saints the soul of thy dear departed husband – cousin – and friend – Finlay Outwood. Forgive him his sins and – grant him everlasting life and – sustain with your love – that looks on tempests and is never shaken – his loving wife, Dorothy – and grant them both peace and everlasting p—' No, not "peace" again. "—Salvation. Amen." Dotty was quiet. She heaved a shuddering sigh. 'That was beautiful.'

Harriet took her hand but could not speak for tears.

Three enormous men in waterproofs burst through the door, and murmurs of 'Mind the telephone seat' from the hall announced the arrival of the stretcher.

'Do you want to come with us, love?' bellowed the ambulance man tenderly.

Dotty shook her head. 'I'm all right here now.'

'Come into the kitchen, Dotty.'

Warren came in to supervise. 'I'm afraid there's a bit of a crowd outside, Dotty. You'd better stay here.'

It was bad enough witnessed from the kitchen. An upright piano argued insistently with the tight angles to be negotiated before the stretcher was carried out through the front door and down the path between the mushrooms. The doors of the ambulance closed and, after an exchange of particuars between Warren and the driver, it drove off. The crowd dispersed, apart from the two women, who hovered on the path. Warren suggested that Harriet stay the night and bring Dotty down the next day.

'Oh shit. The Cranleighs are coming for lunch.' Sir Hubert Cranleigh was on the board of M25TV, and not the sort of person one took for a ploughman's at the Three Pigeons.

'Bugger,' said Harriet. 'Can't you put them off?'

'Sure – but you know what it's like trying to fix dates with these people.'

'All right. I'll stay for a couple of hours and bring her home in a taxi.'

At Dotty's request Harriet went out to invite the two neighbours in, and to say goodbye to the children. Semiramide leapt back into the front seat and belted up at her approach. Harriet spoke to her through the window.

'I'm awfully sorry about this, Semi.'

'Iz OK. But I starving.'

'Yes, well, cook yourself something when you get home. Only please – not braised kidneys. We've got guests tomorrow. And look after Tiz, would you? She's very upset.'

'So are we,' said Mungo from the back seat.

'Yes, darling. We'll talk tomorrow.'

'You've got guests tomorrow,' Japheth reminded her.

Tiz was snug between them, for once. It was indeed an ill wind that blew nobody any good, thought Harriet, moved at the sight of this rare sibling solidarity.

'Will Uncle Fin be cremated?' said Tiz.

'I've no idea, darling. Don't think about it.'

'Why not? Dotty has to.'

'It's a bit premature, darling.'

'Will you come and tuck me up tonight?'

'And me,' said Mungo.

'Of course.' She was thrilled by their need, even though it would reduce still further the time available to prepare apricot filo pie with paw-paw coulis for tomorrow's lunch. Perhaps she could just beat some crystallized ginger into vanilla ice cream and use a free hand with the toffee brittle.

Harriet watched the car drive off, not waving, which seemed to strike the wrong note in the circumstances.

Back in the house Dotty was making tea in the kitchen. She had switched the radio on.

'I'll do that, Dotty. You go and sit down.'

'No, thank you. That's my friends in there and I'll look after them. Go and introduce yourself and I'll bring the tea in. We'll need a lot of lubricating while we're discussing the arrangements.'

Harriet put a hand on her arm. 'You're being so brave. I do admire you.'

Dotty's face squeezed into tears.

On the radio the news was announced that there was no clue as to the whereabouts of Yoevil and Kean. Dotty blew her nose.

'They were past their best anyway,' she said.

2 $\int$

The school holidays made Abutilon, formerly Windy Tops, an unsuitable residence for someone in the first throes of bereavement. Harriet hoped, however, that the pulse of young life scudding around Dotty like hand grenades would distract her for a while.

Dotty's comings and goings in the night made Harriet lie tense and wakeful. She was afraid that her wad of intimate sympathy with Dotty had been shot in the immediate crisis, and already it was inappropriate for her to get up and intrude on an agony in the bedroom that she could not share. The crisis had thrown them into a common junction of humanity, but when it was over they would resume on separate tracks. Not that she was uneasy at Dotty's presence in the house. Another body would scarcely be noticed. It sometimes made Harriet long for the lonely narrow beds and tinned food of her early days in digs, although she realized later that they had made her more receptive to Warren's proposal than she might otherwise have been. They had been madly in love, of course.

Some blissful years in Islington had followed. Marriage brought her luck. At one time she was simultaneously in a revival of *Showboat* in the West End, rehearsing Pinter in Bath and doing a voice-over for mouthwash. Then Warren had started to pine for golfing country – the Knickerbocker Belt, Harriet called it – on the grounds that Islington was giving him emphysema and that little Japheth, whom he had just installed in Harriet's uterus, numbered among his human rights the freedom to go to the candy store without an armed escort. This right Japheth never exercised until he was twelve, as the house was two miles from the village, and Harriet never let him out of her sight.

Warren had used a compass to draw a circle around Walton Heath Golf Club, and Abutilon lay fatefully within it. When they had cruised the area Harriet thought she would miscarry with laughter at the assortment of half-timbered mansions choked in rhododendrons called variously Chunters or Woodioke or Hydrangea House. She had grown up in faded chic in Barnes, in a cavernous Edwardian semi with her brother's oars stuck up in the hall. It was not Hampstead, but it was an urban village for which no one of taste or intellect need blush. Warren was obtuse on the distinction. Being American he was comfortable with wide private roads lined with mature trees, where the milk van seemed to make a political statement, but Harriet did not see how she could possibly live in such an isolated spot.

Windy Tops had other ideas. While mopping up the tears of mirth at the prospect of having such an address, the vibrations from the house itself hypnotized her objections. It was white, square-edged and elegant, built by a disciple of the Mackintosh school who had given as much thought to the drain covers as the front elevation. The opera singer Dame Carlotta Pastorino had once lived there. Inside it gleamed with light oak illuminated by narrow, or sturdy square windows. Woolly with the romance of pregnancy, dreams of Hampstead were set aside, together with practical objections like the five-mile walk to Tadworth station. When the baby was old enough life would resume as before, with the one-and-a-half-hour commute to London slipped into the programme without a ripple. The none-too-distant chunterings of JCBs carving out the M25 were a note of reassurance that they would still be within the purlieus of civilization.

On the day they picked up the keys from the estate agents' office a vision of the Hampstead of one's dreams glanced off the double-glazed bay window – its gracious tumble of Georgian ease, designer courtyards, plaques denoting the ghosts of the gifted, where all the leaves seemed to be a feathery pinnate lime, the better to flatter the smoke-grey brick. Said to terrify the novelist Iris Murdoch, its effect on Harriet's nerves was of quite a different order, more like the lure of Moscow to the Three Sisters.

But by the time Tiziana was stuck into Brownies and ballet with Miss Tracy, Harriet knew it was more than her life was worth to suggest a move. The boys would probably have enjoyed living in London – another pressing reason not to go. They worked off their energy on their BMXs and on Saturday night went to Sutton for a rumble at McDonald's.

Warren had persuaded Semi to cook lunch for Sir Hubert and his lady so that Harriet could have a long lie-in. They picked over their couscous with polite amazement.

'Mungo bashed the wing mirror on Sir Hubert's car,' said Tiz. 'They made one of those aerial slide thingies.'

'I'll get you later,' muttered Mungo.

'Oh, honestly,' said Harriet. 'I wondered why there was a rope hanging out of his window. I'm so sorry.'

Lady Kay swivelled her head stiffly towards Harriet. 'It's only cracked, dear. The insurance will pay.'

Dotty came in, and Sir Hubert rose to shake hands.

'I'm sorry I'm late. Stomach upset.'

'We were so sad to hear about your husband,' said Lady Kay. 'You're being awfully brave.'

'Thank you.' Dotty's voice broke with tears. 'I'm sorry.'

'No, don't be. One is too buttoned-up about these things.'

'Death, you mean?' said Tiz.

Dotty blew her nose as she sat down. 'It's just – after the wedding – huh – it seemed so cruel – after he'd had – huh – such a nice day.'

Harriet, allergic to non sequiturs, could not resist saying gently, 'It wouldn't have helped if he had spent the day breaking stones on a chain gang, Dotty dear.'

'Highly symbolic, really,' said Lady Kay. 'As Eliot said, Birth, Copulation and Death. That's all there is really.' She drained her Stony Hill Chardonnay with a quivering hand.

'What's copulation?' said Tiz.

'Bonking.'

'OK, Japh, cut it out,' said Warren. 'Lady Cranleigh was making a serious point, as you well know.'

'So-rry.'

'Mind you, I don't think Eliot would be much comfort to poor

Mrs Outwood. Have you got any Henry Vaughan in the house, Harriet?'

'What?' Harriet was thinking more on the line of Tums. 'Yes, probably. Could I have a drink, Warren?'

'Sorry, sweetheart. Dotty?'

'Just a drop.'

'I've always found Henry Vaughan frightfully steadying,' said Lady Kay to Dotty. 'Do try him.'

Dotty drained her glass. 'What, with my husband still warm?'

This unexpectedly resilient line took them by surprise. Lady Kay looked in vain at Harriet for guidance.

Sir Hubert spoke. 'Are you a musician, Mrs Outwood?'

'Not as such.'

'Because, really, opera's the only thing to take one completely out of oneself. *Ariadne auf Naxos*, that's the thing. Awe-inspiring. Don't you think so, Warren? It got me through Tanganyikan independence all right.'

'Oh, we *adored* Tanganyika,' said Lady Kay.

'My problems are pretty small compared to Tanganyikan independence,' sighed Dotty.

'But they're *your* problems, my dear. One mustn't pretend to get over them before one has.'

'One won't,' Dotty assured her.

'We'll look after you, Dotty.' Tiz hugged her arm. 'We're doing Help the Aged at school. You can be my community project.'

'Tiz—'

'It's all right, Harriet. She only meant it kindly. Can you spell "rehabilitation" Tiz?'

Semi started to clear the table. 'I suppose you are wanting ze *dessert* now.'

'Better get it over with,' said Mungo.

'Nothing for me, thank you,' said Dotty, eyeing the savaged pile of couscous.

Lady Kay smiled at Semi. 'Le repas etait formidable, ma petite.'

Semi gave her a frightened glance and hurried into the kitchen.

Harriet experienced a slight resentment that Dotty had pre-empted Semi's dessert. A flash forward of Dotty and Semi sharing the kitchen raised a frayed question mark.

'How wonderful to have a girl who can cook, Harriet,' said Lady Kay.

'She normally only cooks for herself. It doesn't leave me much time on the day bed, which was the original plan.'

'We could afford another au pair with our savings on the poll tax,' said Warren.

'Are you going to pay it?' said Sir Hubert.

'Sure. Aren't you?'

'Naturally one pays the wretched thing. That reminds me, Mrs Outwood, don't fall into the Direct Debit trap. If you pay in arrears you keep the interest yourself.'

'Fin and I never got into debt. We put a little aside every month for the gas and the water and—'

'The house must have been overrun with piggy banks,' said Harriet. 'What's this?'

Semi had just brought in a large platter with a bowl of something pink and wet, surrounded by smaller bowls of dried fruit and nuts.

'Yuch,' said Japheth. 'May we leave the table?'

'Would you mind?' Harriet appealed to the louche instincts of her guests, secretly kissing Japh's feet for remembering to ask.

The Cranleighs concurred and the children stampeded out of the room. Semi snorted in disgust and settled down to dissect a fig with a knife and fork.

'When I was at school we used to eat bananas with a knife and fork,' said Lady Kay with a sigh.

'Out of modesty, or what?' said Dotty.

'Probably!' Lady Kay laughed. 'I never thought of that.'

'I was stuck in a riot on Westminster Bridge the other day,' said Sir Hubert. 'Incovenient, of course, but I just hope it doesn't harden attitudes. To be honest, I don't give a toss about the poll tax. I'd just like to see this lot brought down. You see, the essence of the Tory Party is, it's a patrician party. And this lot – well, what can one say.'

'They're plain stupid if they think everyone will rush out to vote Conservative because we think they'll spend less. For one thing, so many people get rebates they won't give a sh—monkey's who's in power at the town hall.'

'And meanwhile,' said Lady Kay, 'they're demanding money with menaces from people who don't have any.'

'Exactly.' Harriet and Lady Kay clinked glasses.

'Harriet's a stage-door Socialist,' said Warren. 'She thinks everyone would be happy if artists ruled the world.'

Dotty was contemplating the dregs. 'Do you think we should all pay a different price for Mighty White?'

'Well, no, but surely, Dotty, blue as a laundry bag though you are, surely you don't think it's right that people with your—'

'Income?'

'Well – don't you mind that you pay the same as – us, for instance?'

'It'll only be half, now that Fin's gone. Any road, most of the money for local services goes on the police and education, neither of which, I'm happy to say, we've had any call for.'

Harriet stared at her. This was not only a swingeing attack on her offspring, but an outrage considering how nice Harriet had been to her lately.

'Don't be naive, Dotty. You can't put a red spot on the services you benefit from and refuse to pay for the others. You might as well say the healthy shouldn't subsidize the sick.'

Dotty looked up at this and pounded the table, waking up Semi's arrangement of dried nibbles.

'And why not? We're members of BUPA, you know. We've never used the National Health Service. We paid for every pill, cash down.'

'And what do you walk on when you go to the bank – water?'

Harriet and Dotty glared at each other for a moment, each doubting what they saw.

'Excuse me,' said Dotty. 'I think I'll go and help Semolina in the kitchen.'

Harriet covered her confusion with another drink and avoided Warren's eye. He looked as though he was on the point of emptying the water jug over her. The Cranleighs, however, were congenitally unperturbed by life in general, and rather pleased by Dotty. As a result of their wide experience organizing international bunfights they thought they understood her

better than Harriet did – wisdom, like intelligence, being transferable.

Lady Kay placed a hand on Harriet's arm. 'I think you ought
to try and be a little more selfish, my dear. There are times when
one feels torn apart by service to others.'

'It's no excuse for being rotten to Dotty at a time like this. Oh
– why did I say that?'

A flash of sunshine filled the room, bringing hints of exposure
and interrogation. It back-lit the smudged windows, the dregs
and spilt food, the hair in Warren's ears. A silverfish slithered
under the skirting board. Harriet was awash with hot panic. She
gripped the arm of the chair to stop herself running out of the
room. Then abruptly the clouds put out the light.

Warren stood up. 'Sir Hubert and I will take coffee in the den.
Then we'll get straight over to the club. Are you OK?'

'Yes – thank you. I didn't sleep well last night. I'm a beast when
I'm tired. I'm so sorry.'

They all assured her that she was as lively as a tuning fork.

Sir Hubert's last words were of care and concern in the community. 'Don't forget to remind Mrs Outwood that she can get
a rebate on the poll tax from the day of death.'

As arranged, Lady Kay took a siesta after lunch. Semi had
departed to see a French film. Dotty was scrubbing pans. The
boys had disappeared. Tiz was watching *Grease 2* on video. Harriet
circled for a bit, putting things away, making light conversation
with Dotty about the Cranleighs. Then, mindful of current theories of the importance of body contact, and well aware of how
the Princess of Wales would act in the circumstances, she went
to Dotty and put her arms around her. Dotty burst into tears.
Harriet was humbled. Dotty's grief made her own preoccupation
with the pointlessness of life seem trivial.

'I'm sorry, Dotty.' She patted the shuddering back as the sobs
went on and on.

The arrangements for Fin's funeral kept Harriet busy on the telephone and with much to-ing and fro-ing to Nonsuch Crescent.
Dotty insisted on going home the day after the Cranleighs' visit,
but Harriet was equally firm that she should return after the
funeral and stay for as long as she liked – or one week, whichever

was the greater. She did not say as much to Dotty, but, with the children back at school it was reasonable to suppose that Dotty would not want to stay long in a place where she knew no one.

It was unfortunate that the only convenient day for the crematorium was that on which Harriet was due to go and see a friend's performance in the hit musical, *Heartbreak Heath*, an adaptation of *King Lear*. Harriet was prepared to be stunned. Reviews had raised expectations that she would be blasted out of her seat by wind machines, awed by pop-up outcrops and a chorus of high-stepping Druids. Her friend played Regan.

Harriet was the first to admit that she was as excited by a trip to the theatre as any member of the public, and the thrill, tinged with envy, of seeing her friend's triumph, added a special piquancy. She would have put it off, but the show was booked out for eighteen months. As it was, she put off telling Dotty that she would have to go out on the evening of the funeral. When they set out for the Chapel of Ease in Ham, she had still not done so.

Warren had a conference with the Prix Italia committee, so Harriet was the only representative of the family. Dotty insisted she drove with her in the undertaker's limousine.

There were two surprises at the chapel: it was pink, and it was almost full. Harriet was struck by the number of people who had managed to take time off work, and that Dotty had so many relations and knew so many people, but it was on Harriet and Warren that the mantle of support had fallen. True, Dotty had given Warren a home for a while when he was a student. She supposed they owed Dotty a favour.

A curate from Dotty's parish church took the service, a bland young man who kept his hands clasped and his eyes on the ceiling. He went over the salient points of Fin's life on earth: his birth in Solihull; his apprenticeship, successfully completed, as an electrician; his membership of the Communist party – 'What!' shrieked Harriet silently – an early, if misguided example of Fin's concern for the disadvantaged, according to the curate. His service with the navy, learning to swim while stationed in Malta, wounded at the Battle of Matapan, meeting Dotty while she was a driver with the army in Palestine. 'Pull the other one!' thought Harriet, reeling. How come they had never mentioned these credentials? But nothing much had happened after the war, although the curate did his best to make their happy marriage, evening classes, steady employment and work for the Casualties Union sound like a non-stop razzle.

Dotty bore up well until the moment they were all dreading, when the rose-coloured curtain closed around the coffin as it was assigned to the flames. The curtain stuck. A young undertaker, like a discreet bridesmaid, came forward to release it. Dotty collapsed. Her noise, in the hushed atmosphere, was embarrassing, mainly because no one else joined in. At least I'll have a pewful of descendants bawling their heads off, thought Harriet. She pictured the scene – the children, friends from school, colleagues from the business, Sir Ian McKellen to elevate the occasion to one of national mourning. Before she knew what was happening she was groping for a handkerchief.

The rellies, from Northamptonshire, Hertfordshire and elsewhere, were ready to party. Harriet was repeatedly button-holed for an update on her life for the last twenty-five years, and diatribes about the shortcomings of M25TV. The meanness of dragging Dotty away from all this goodfellowship made Harriet anxious to get on with it. In the end Dotty was too squiffy to protest when Harriet urged the guests, on her behalf, to push off. The neighbours volunteered to clear up. It was already 4.30 and Harriet had to leave the house at 5.45.

'I expect you're looking forward to a quiet evening,' said Harriet, in a traffic jam at Tolworth Towers.

'Not particularly. I'll be having a lot of those in the years to come.'

'Well – the fact of the matter is – I have to go out this evening. I'm awfully sorry. I tried to get out of it, but it just wasn't possible. It's business, in a way.'

'Show business?' Dotty's tone was dry.

'Well – yes. I do feel bad about it, Dotty.' She paused to allow Dotty to leap in with her blessing. 'But you must be very tired. I'll make it up to you tomorrow. We'll have a nice dinner and – look through your photos, or something. Is that all right?'

'I can't wait,' said Dotty.

The sulphurous pall over London was evident long before the

train pulled in to Victoria. Harriet picked it up at East Croydon and, like a glue-sniffer returning to the fold, inhaled the acrid blend of filth and fumes. It was no wonder to Harriet that The Train as metaphor so often bore the heavy symbolism of Life's Journey – smelly, expensive, full of people one did not want to know and liable to be derailed by horizontal vegetation. On it, the aeons of motherhood uncoupled, and she was again the young hopeful who thought nothing of going to Barrow-in-Furness to play Peter Pan, rehearsing for fourteen hours in an aircraft hanger in Pinner, followed by five hours' waitressing, and who had the nerve to audition for parts that specified sword-swallowing skills.

The descent into the Underground was still more symbolic, as it drew her into London's nexus of grime, greed, grief, wheel-clamping and Culture. The carriage was so full of such a colourful spectrum of humanity it looked like the contents of God's stomach. Harriet adopted an air of gloom to show solidarity with the other passengers.

As she took her seat in the theatre Harriet made a note of any prominent persons present and unemployed acquaintances. A thought was spared for Dotty, no doubt being forced to watch *Strike It Lucky*, or perhaps volunteering to. She squashed her guilt with the thought that she would be there to provide support when the numbness had worn off, at the point where most friends and relatives retired with relief.

Lights dimmed. Drums rolled. Thunder bellowed through her body and trumpets lanced her bosom, St Theresa-style, as the towering gates of King Lear's castle smoothly retracted in their grooves. Surely this moment of arousal was one of the last thrills left to man, not counting take-off in Concorde. No professional sangfroid could prevent the programme going soggy in her hand. She prayed: Please God, do not cause Sam to crack on B flat or get her foot stuck in a revolving battlement. Amen. If it happened to the dipso leading lady that was another matter. There was an honourable tradition of drink-related mishaps on the stage, like the priestesses at a masque for James the First who poured jelly and custard over the Danish ambassador, 'So full of wine were their upper chambers.' But not, O Lord, tonight.

*　　*　　*

The stage door keeper recognized Harriet from a brief run at the Royal Court of a Czech play set in a state laundry. She had played the ghost of a resistance fighter who had no lines but occasionally wandered on with a bazooka. As it had been her last stage appearance her feelings were mixed as to the pleasure of seeing him again. Norman's laconic exterior could not quite conceal the odour of reflected glory.

'Fancy seeing you again, Harriet. Have you come to see Sam?'

'That's right.'

'Great, isn't she? Pity she's too old for Cordelia. That Romanie Whatsit couldn't sing her way out of a paper bag.'

'She's not that bad, but I wouldn't let her loose at a pig fair.'

Norman chuckled. 'You haven't changed. Been busy, have you?'

'Oh – this and that. I did some television—'

'That's right. I saw it. *Not in Front of the Hamster* wasn't it? Funny title, I thought.'

'Yes. Pity about the script.'

'Well, I'll just give Sam a call.'

Harriet interested herself in the noticeboard as members of the cast with trains to catch pushed past her. Among the lists for rehearsal calls, and rude messages from the wig department, was one from a Prince Igor, who wrote thusly: 'Calling all feelies. Lattie to share in Clapham. £50 a week all in. Nante trade, honest! Also to share barouche after the concert. Wallopers preferred.' She wondered if she had been out of circulation too long.

Her spirit lifted when the elderly actor playing Lear appeared. They had been on tour with The Strange Theatre Company in a harrowing play intended to reveal to factory workers what they had been feeling for the last few hundred years.

'Hello, Arthur. How are you?'

'So-so. I won £5,000 on the 1,000 Guineas at Newmarket last year. It came it at 7–2.'

'Still fluttering, then.'

'Yeah. Nice to see you, Harriet. Goodnight, Norman.'

There was something terribly matey about Arthur's total lack of interest in herself. Sam came down. They kissed and exchanged nice-to-see-yous, which Harriet, paranoid, sensed were more sincere on her part than Sam's.

'Sorry to keep you waiting, love. We've been having a go at the company manager about rehearsals. I mean, it's been every day this week. Half the cast got storm damage when that hack got into the computer.'

'Yes, I read about it. Were you injured?'

'No, I'm not in that scene. But then the banqueting table went berserk and knee-capped the other half. Now we've got to come in on Sunday because Romanie says she's got to have a sinus operation. Sinus, my arse. It's a lot lower down than that. Sorry, we're right at the top.'

Harriet panted up the narrow stairs, wearing a fixed smile. She could not help thinking that Sam was an unusual choice for Regan. A Yorkshire lass, round, rosy-cream prettiness surging from a tiny waist unthickened by childbirth, one looked at Sam and thought milk churns. She had the kind of energy usually associated with bursting out of corsets, which had been successfully harnessed to the powers of evil with the aid of a shaggy black wig and leather catsuit which left no doubt about her sadomasochistic relationship with the wimpish Duke of Cornwall. Harriet was confidant, she hoped without envy, that the difficult career hump had been negotiated, and that Sam might yet play Hedda Gabler – at somewhere like Southwold, perhaps.

Sam's dressing-room was at the far end of the prison-style corridor.

'Let's hope Maeve's gone.' She referred to Goneril, a faded blonde pop star who had been rehabilitated for the production. 'Did you notice she cut a song in Act Three? It was supposed to be a duet.'

But Maeve was huddled on the chaise-longue, tearful in her satin robe. On either side, poised like seraphim around the Ark of the Covenant, were two boy dancers, and a middle-aged man sat holding her hand. When he looked round they recognized each other immediately.

'Nick!'

'Harriet, my love!' He pulled her into a gorilla hug. 'Glasgow, 1971. *My brain is farting dewdrops.* How could I forget.'

'Therapy? It's good to see you, Nick.'

'Whatever happened to that young genius?'

'Last I heard he was writer in residence at a poly in Hull. Found his level, I'd say.'

'Harribitch! You know, I've really *missed* you. Let's look at you.' He cupped her chin in his hand and breathed heavy Campari fumes up her nostrils. 'Umm. You look marvellous. But your soul is in danger.'

'Why do you say that?'

'You have the look of a claustrophobic in a lift. Where is this lift?'

'Near Reigate.'

'Reigate. Christ. We must have a serious talk.'

'Leave her alone,' said Sam. 'She's come to see me.'

'Keep your wig on, I'm not poaching her. By the way, do you know Maeve, Harriet?'

'We've never met, no. Hello, Maeve. You were brilliant. I didn't notice a thing in Act Three, honestly.'

Maeve smiled, briefly. 'Thanks. It's my mum, you see.'

'Pardon?'

'My mum died last night.'

'No! How awful. I'm so sorry.'

Sam was aghast. 'Maeve! Why didn't you tell me?'

'Dunno.'

One of the seraphim spoke. 'She didn't trust herself, did she, Ferrars?'

'No. *Voce*'s the first thing to go.'

Maeve sobbed.

'You should have said.'

Nick was discomfited. 'We'd better go, Harriet. Give Sam and Maeve a moment alone.'

'Thanks,' said Sam. 'Wait for me downstairs, Harriet?'

'Of course.' They took pitying farewells of Maeve and gravely left the room.

Outside in the corridor Nick shook his head. 'Too bad. We were hoping the show would help her stay off the stuff.'

'Give her a chance. I would have thought being in work would help her get over it quicker than waiting by the phone.'

Nick linked her arm through his. 'Do I detect a personal note in that observation, Harriet?'

'I don't know. Shall I compare myself to a childless drug addict? OK – why not. Nick—' Harriet's pulse quickened. She was amazed at the insignificance her home life assumed when viewed from Nick's perspective. 'I haven't been doing much, actually. I got lazy. No – I lost my confidence, I think. In the nappy bucket. It happens to lots of women – not just us.'

'I know. But I wouldn't have thought it would happen to you.'

'You knew me before my brain fell out. But anyway, the kids are practically off my hands now.' So much for Tiziana's clinging phase. 'And something's come up – someone, actually – that's going to give me a lot more freedom. So – if you could bear me in mind—'

'What about whatsisname?'

'Warren? What about him?'

'Does he back you up on this?'

'I'm sure he will this time. To be honest, he didn't like me leaving the kids with an au pair – and they aren't given to staying in six nights a week anyhow. But Dot – this person is a distant cousin of his, so it's quite a different matter.' She quashed the thought that Warren could hardly take Dotty out to dine at Le Gavroche with foreign TV moguls and warped novelists, or fulfil any of her other functions apart from vigilante. 'I feel there's something of Fate in this conjunction of circumstances.'

'You'd never forgive yourself, etcetera.'

'Exactly. Oh, I've thought of putting it all behind me and retraining as a speech therapist or whatever people do, but it's not really what I want.'

'What's your voice like?'

'Er – why?'

'I'm casting a musical shortly. Get yourself a decent voice coach and things might happen. No promises. Usual conditions. Would you be prepared to audition?'

'Of course. What is it?' They had reached the stage door. The sinister warren of corridors behind them was dark and quiet, but Nick still lowered his voice.

'Have you heard about the new Perry Saddlesmith?'

'You're getting *that*!' Harriet was awestruck. Anyone directing a new Perry Saddlesmith was looking at a life insurance policy.

'Ssh. It's not in the bag. I'll know in a couple of weeks.'

'Oh Nick, how wonderful for you. For me!'

'Don't make any assumptions, Harriet. I'll do my best, that's all.'

'I know. What a coup – school fees – what school fees? What's it about?'

'The Battle of Ypres. And a few choruses before it, of course.'

'Who's doing the score?'

'A couple of Irish blokes.'

'I suppose it will be written for Elaine Paige. She'll be in one of those stingray headdresses—'

'In a moving love triangle with the wounded.'

'How are they going to fit dance routines into that?'

'Balls – memories—'

'Don't tell me they're going to have Baltic states prancing around singing "Your friend is my friend—"'

'This isn't funny, Harriet. This is megabucks.'

'I know. It isn't just *Oh What a Lovely War* mark two, is it?'

'Not really. That was satire. Very sixties. Preaching to the converted. This is a moving night out for the masses. Look, I'll keep in touch. I've got to run. Meeting my ex-wife for supper.'

'Which one?'

'*Miaow*. Love you.' He pecked her cheek. 'Auf wiedersehen!'

Sam was so taken aback at the idea that Harriet might also be in a West End musical that Harriet was, laughingly, obliged to warn her to keep her amazement within the bounds of politeness.

'What's the part, darling?'

'Actually, I forgot to ask. Probably won't get it. But I'll give it my best shot. Wouldn't it be marvellous if we are both in long runs up here?'

'Yes. Humungous. But is it really your thing?'

'Well, I'll have to work on the voice, but it sounds quite serious. Sort of post-modern – dissolving the barriers of past and present.'

'Alzheimer's does that.' They giggled into their Mersault. 'I'm having the lamb noisette with lavender sauce. How about you?'

Any lingering envy of her friend had dissolved in alcohol by the end of the evening, which saw Harriet transported to Victoria station in a state of euphoria she had not experienced for years. It was, for once, the fitting conversion of the anticipation with which she had faced the evening, so often prone to flutter and die in intangible discontent.

A discarded *Evening Standard* carried the news of the Blockade of Lithuania, a country which Harriet had always assumed was invented by Ivor Novello, and the death of Greta Garbo. Although the latter had not been seen for years, Harriet felt the world was just a little bit lonelier for her passing. She flipped through the pages for news of Yoevil and Kean, but the story had gone quiet, perhaps by arrangement with the police, who were no doubt indefatigably waiting for a member of the public to inform them of the couple's whereabouts.

The slats occasionally clattered for those travelling to Orpington or Portsmouth. It was now official departure time, and cold on the marbled floor. There were no British Rail operatives in sight, and a growing disquiet among passengers – mostly shifty-looking men and groups of couples from the suburbs clutching concert programmes. The circular seat was full. Not being an actress for nothing, Harriet boldly approached a tousle-haired youngish man sitting on it. She lowered her voice.

'Excuse me, I've just had a kidney transplant and I'm not supposed to stand up for long. Would you mind letting me sit down?'

His face, pleasant in a cheeky way, lit up.

'Sure.' He patted his lap. 'Make yourself comfortable.'

'What?'

A man on the other side of the seat said, without looking up from his paper, 'You can sit on mine, if you like.'

'Well – why not?' Harriet was fond of calling bluffs and, where possible, ramming them back down people's throats. Especially when she had been drinking. She sat down hard on the proffered knees. An old woman sitting next to the young man clutched her handbag even tighter.

'You be careful you don't catch nuffing, love.'

'I haven't got "nuffing",' the young man protested. 'I had to have the Aids test to go to Zimbabwe.' His accent was hard to place, but north of Watford.

'What did you get up to in Zimbabwe?' asked Harriet.

'Mind your own business. Just because you're sitting on my knee doesn't give you the right to know what I get up to in Zimbabwe.'

'Get down to, perhaps.'

The young man grinned. 'I like them sarcastic.' He joggled her up and down. 'Which kidney was it?'

'Stop it. The left.'

'Like hell. You wouldn't be half pissed if you'd just had a kidney transplant.'

'Are you calling me a liar?'

'Yeah.'

'Well you're right. But you'd better stop joggling me about or you'll get *noisettes d'agneau* down your shirt.'

'My sister had a kidney transplant,' said the old woman.

'Is she here?' asked the young man eagerly.

'It's not funny, young man. She's not allowed instant coffee. Or spinach. I have to keep a stock of those fruity teas for her – Wild Hibiscus – Rosehip and Burpalot – that sort of thing.'

'I would rather have no kidneys at all,' said Harriet, adapting a quote from *Peter Pan*. 'Did the surgeon bring it in a briefcase? They do, you know, if it's been filched.'

The old lady was offended. 'It was on the National Health.'

'Where's this fucking train, then?' The young man looked around for it. 'I'll go for a pee and see if I can find out what's happening. Watch my instrument, would you?' He indicated a bulbous black case on the ground.

'All right.'

He set off with a jaunty step, and Harriet settled down to a lengthy exposé of the old lady's relatives' operations. When they got to the one which involved sawing through a brother-in-law's breastbone she began to look out anxiously for the young man's return. The passengers had thinned out still further, although only one train had departed. Harriet, now coming out of the warm buzz of alcohol into the soggy shudders of sobriety, regretted that it was now too late to phone home and get someone out of bed to assure herself that they had not been burnt in it. Then a gentle plop from the departure board. 'Cancelled' was now official.

The old lady and most of the other passengers had disappeared. Clusters of irate concert-goers were fulminating their way to the taxi rank. One man, who had been standing on the same spot the whole time, flung his briefcase to the floor and kicked it right across the concourse. Harriet picked up the instrument case and paced up and down. Her first instinct was to smash the glass on the Information booth. This was immediately followed by an outburst of tears. She sniffed her way across the concourse and caught sight of the young man coming out of the Gents. His nose was bleeding.

'It's cancelled. The buggers. Are you going to Sutton too? Because if so, we're both stuck.'

'I am, as it happens. That's all I need.'

'What's the matter with your head?'

'There's a load of junkies in there beating up a kid. I tried to sort it out—'

'That was pretty stupid, wasn't it? Haven't you ever heard of market forces?'

'Bloody Thatcherite.'

'I am not a Thatcherite. I happen to believe in German-style social democracy.'

'German-style social democracy, my darling, only works because they're bloody Germans.'

'Look, could we sort out the political situation some other time? How are we going to get home?'

'Couldn't we stay in a hotel? You liked my knee. There's more where that came from.'

'Don't be ridiculous. Have you ever made love to a forty-eight-year-old sandwich? I'm prepared to share a taxi with you, but that's all.'

'My, you're loads of fun.'

'What's your name, by the way?'

'Damian de St Croix.'

'I'll bet.'

'It fucking is!'

'All right. It's unlikely enough to be true.'

In the People's Republic of Lambeth, Harriet learnt that Damian was a musician, currently playing the trombone in *Cats*. She was not in the least surprised. It was slightly harder to bracket him professionally with Mozart and von Karajan and other famous channels of the divine flow. But musicians often adopted a swaggering desperation which required the constant anaesthetic of booze and women. It was life-affirming in small doses, as it had doubtless been for victims of the Black Death to resort to flagellation routines. Harriet sympathized – with the pressures of live performance, at least. These days getting up in the morning had the same effect.

By Tolworth Towers they were on to his domestic arrangements. He lived in his girlfriend's flat in Reigate, because she was a cabin attendant with Dan Air and had to be near Gatwick. Yes, the commute was a drag, but the girlfriend, Pansy, a knockout, their sex life Reigate's answer to *The Naked Lunch*.

'I'm auditioning for a new musical myself, shortly. Perhaps we could travel home together – for security reasons.'

'I should have guessed you were an actress after all that garbage with the kidneys.'

'Thank you.'

'Er – I don't mean to be rude, but I don't think there's a bird in *Cats* over twenty-five.'

'No. Well this is going to be a grown-up musical. I probably won't get it, I've been out of circulation too long. But I have an instinct that now's the time to try and get back. Fate is holding up an idiot board to that effect.'

This was not meant as a description of Dotty, it just came out like it. As they slipped into the Green Belt, the prospect of informing Dotty of her new role made Harriet nervous.

Harriet asked Damian to drive her home, as she was too tired to pick up her car from Tadworth. Besides, she was not averse to this rakish piece of flotsam seeing Abutilon, her redoubt on the shifting sands.

The car churned up the pea shingle. He was duly impressed. 'Very nice. Very Sanderson.'

'I'll show you round some time. Wear flat shoes.'

They exchanged telephone numbers, and Harriet promised to let him know if she got the part. She tossed the number into the bin as soon as she got inside.

*   *   *

Warren lay with his customary precision under a smooth duvet. His navy blue nightshirt blended thoughtfully with the prevailing colour scheme. Harriet slid in onto her own posturepaedic mattress and stared at the pannelling.

The comfort of familiar things now mocked her flirtation with personal renewal. Worse, the very pelmets seemed to cry out 'Fool!' The Home, with all its dependants, responsibilities, its weight of habit-forming imperatives, descended on her like a dome over a cluttered cheese board. Hot tears hit the pillow. It was sheer buffoonery to imagine that Fin had died in order that Dotty would be willing and able to take over Harriet's role in the household. Warren rolled over.

'There you are. I was worried. I waited up till one.'

'Sorry. The train was cancelled. I had to get a taxi with a chap who plays the trombone in *Cats*. How was Dotty?'

'OK. She went to bed early. She's somewhat at a loss when you're not around.'

'Well she would be, the night of the funeral. At least I went.'

'Sweetheart, I couldn't get out of the Prix Italia thing.'

'I suppose it involved lunch with your bony novelist, too.' Harriet referred to Avelina Viper as the bony novelist, not only out of envy of her figure, but because Warren always came home afterwards spouting erudite twaddle about vertical time and romantic rationalism, until the fit worked itself out – like the runs.

'Among others, yes. Semi's ill, by the way.'

'Not choked on her hookah? again—'

'No. The usual food poisoning. I don't know why she doesn't go home.'

'I'll start making New England Boiled Dinner. That should do it.'

'She seems to have ganged up with the boys. They're always in a huddle talking about the World Cup.'

'At least there's someone in the family to share their enthusiasm.'

'It leaves Tiz out in the cold.'

'Perhaps they'll torment her less, then. She'll probably gang up with Dotty.'

'Dotty won't be around long enough – will she?'

'Probably not. I'm sure she'll be anxious to get back to Nonsuch Crescent and join the WVS.'

'Sweetheart, you know it's Tiz's birthday next week.'

'Yes. I would, wouldn't I?'

'She's been nagging me for a pony again.'

'Very droll. She must be desperate to try you.'

'That's because you're an unnatural mother, according to her.'

Harriet sat up. 'For God's sake! Don't you think I have enough to do?' She crash-landed back on the pillow. 'Anyway, there's nowhere to keep it.'

'She says Appalachia keeps hers in the yard.'

'Appalachia is an only child with two stepmothers.'

There was silence while they reflected on the logic of this statement.

At the same time, the demon Hope implanted the idea that if Harriet were to get the part, which would involve long hours and whole weekends away from home, then a pony would be an invaluable emotional prop for Tiziana. It would have to have the load-bearing skills of a pit prop too, in her case. Could ponies be reinforced with steel girders?

'You could train it to shit on the roses,' said Warren, in his most seductive tones.

'No. *You* could.'

'Sweetheart, I do have to work.'

Harriet flipped over like a sleeping fox surprised and thumped him in the ribs.

'Ouch! You're in a foul mood. Was Sam that good?'

Harriet lay motionless. Warren took her in his arms.

'I know what's bugging you, sweetheart. Hang in there. It won't be for ever.'

'Do you realize how few parts are written for people with Alzheimer's? As soon as you're "hard to place" they start talking as though you need the toilets adapted.'

Warren sighed, with difficulty restraining himself from the this-is-all-I-need-after-a-hard-day's-work routine. He compromised.

'I guess we need a vacation.'

'Of course. Without the kids. Have you been down to the marriage guidance bureau?'

They rolled back onto their own mattresses.

'Oh – Japheth's headmaster called. He says we have to go see him before the start of semester.'

'What about?'

'He wouldn't say.'

'Probably that geography teacher again. You know he asked Japh to go on holiday to New Zealand with him?'

'What the fuck for?'

'Oh, Warren. To count sheep, of course.'

Harriet feared that Dotty might make a habit of lying in, which would not be good for her, so she took up breakfast in bed at nine-fifteen.

Dotty lay huddled under the covers with her face to the wall. Her rounded planes, designed by nature for jollity, were plangent with grief. The false teeth in a Nutella jar, hinting of aborted embryos, added to the pathos.

'Oh, how kind,' said Dotty as she sat up. 'You shouldn't have bovvered. I'll be up in a minid.'

'No, no. You stay there as long as you like, Dotty. It's just that Semi's doing the kitchen floor this morning. If she's up to it, of course. Did you sleep well?'

'Nod really.' She put on her glasses and popped her teeth in. 'You've got noisy neighbours. I thought you said you were surrounded by old people's homes?'

'We are. Possibly the finest in the southeast. Perhaps they've got some young Turks working for them. We occasionally hear the call to evening prayer.'

'More foreigners. Don't tell me it's like the bloomin' League of Nations round here.'

'It's inevitable, Dotty. We're a melting pot society.'

Dotty sniffed. 'I prefer the word casserole myself.'

3 ∫

Baying through the fog at forty knots, Jelly and Custard ripped
Harriet past the newsagent. A placard outside the shop bore
the news that the last prisoner had been taken off the roof of
Strangeways, and that Yoevil and Kean had been sighted in
Uruguay. She felt the urge to buy a tabloid and read all about
it. The *Independent* was all very well for those with Chernobyl
and foetal research on the brain, but forced its weaker brethren
to deviant behaviour for sexier news. In fact 'I'm Too Sexy for my
Independent' was currently number one in the hit parade.

The dogs yanked her onto the common, where she released
them. She ran back across the road to phone her agent.

'Hello, George. I'm in a call box. We've got someone staying,
it's a bit embarrassing.'

'Harriet? I was going to call you actually.'

'Really? Did Nick Pollard contact you then? About a musical.'

'No. It's just a commercial, I'm afraid. If you're interested. Well
there's one that might be a bit much at your age, unless you fancy
being a Human Fly for the day. They're looking for a typical mum
– you know – to show that it's not just kids who enjoy being
catapulted upside down onto a Velcro wall.'

'Yuch. Nothing on Radio Three this month, George?'

'You're not interested then?'

'Couldn't they get Olga Korbut? No, I was just wondering if
you'd heard anything about the new Perry Saddlesmith production. Nick's doing it and he suggested I audition. It's called *Wipers!*
– you know, the Battle of Ypres.'

'In that case, what's in it for you, my love?'

'Ah, well it's set in a hospital behind the lines. I'd be the matron torn between her love for a legless captain and her ambition to open her own nursing school.'

'How's the voice? Give me a top A.'

'Cold turkey? Give us a break. Bugger.' She flattened herself against the telephone to avoid being seen by a friend who was after her to help run a karaoke night for the NSPCC.

'The thing is, I expect they'll be looking for someone—'

'Younger?'

'And more expensive, But I'll look into it if you're really keen.'

'I'm realistic, George. I just didn't want to upset Nick by not bothering to audition.'

'Have you got your domestic arrangements sorted?'

'Will have.'

'OK. Back to those scales. I'll call you if there's another ad.'

Dotty seized the *Daily Mail* as though it were a long-lost child.

'I thought that's what you'd read,' said Harriet. 'With your views on the poll tax.'

'Now, now, Harriet. Don't try and cover up that you were doing me a kindness. I appreciate it. But I'll fetch the paper myself in future, thanks all the same. I could fancy a walk to the shops of a morning.'

Dotty's *Daily Mail*, left open on the sofa, was to get on Harriet's nerves even before Dotty did.

The Cordwainers' Hospital School for Boys was a moving sight in the late April sunset. No parent could approach it without weeping at the cost of central heating alone.

The High Master's study was pitched at a psychological vantage point in the mock Tudor pile – at the head of several sweeping flights of polished stairs. Harriet, reminded of *Lift to the Scaffold*, clasped a clammy hand to her neck.

'Don't be nervous, sweetheart. We're customers, remember.'

'I'm not in a logical mood. After all, with Japheth's batting average, his position at the school should be unassailable.'

Doubt set in as the school secretary ushered them into the waiting room. The woman's smile was a mere reflex she had failed to control. Gone were the effusions that had greeted them after Cordwainers' beat St John's, Leatherhead, by eight wickets. They were left alone with the fading photographs and copies of the *Old Cordwainer*.

'This is calculated intimidation,' said Harriet. 'He can't possibly be busy in the holidays. I'm going to be sick.'

She was saved by the buzz from the High Master's office, and the secretary showed them in.

Dr Partridge did not come to the door to greet them. Instead Harriet's hand was warmly crushed over the desk. He had grown a beard, enhancing his image as admiral of the school fleet. His smile, too, was a warning, but Warren sat down and crossed a nonchalant leg.

Dr Partridge shuffled papers. 'Thank you for coming, Mr and Mrs – Funkel. You have two boys at the school, is that right?'

'Yes,' said Harriet. 'Japheth and Mungo.' As if he did not know.

'Ah yes, Mungo. Won the science prize in the second year. Very well-balanced child.'

The implications were obvious. 'You wanted to see us about Japheth, Dr Partridge.'

'Indeed.' He looked up, at Harriet. 'This isn't going to be easy, Mrs Funkel.'

'Dr Partridge, please come to the point.' A kaleidoscope of atrocities danced before Harriet's imagination. Had Japheth contracted Aids from a first year? Passed it on? Pushed the geography teacher down a pothole? Rogered Mrs Partridge?

'Calm down, sweetheart. Take your time, Dr Partridge.'

'Thank you. Did Japheth give you any idea why I asked to see you?'

'No. Actually we didn't tell him we were coming. You see, he's out a lot. He has a holiday job, running a football camp for the local yobs.'

'I'm delighted to hear it. He's a mercurial centre forward, of course.'

'Of course.'

Dr Partridge finally looked up, from one to the other.

'You have an au pair girl at home, I understand.'

'Yes,' said Harriet. 'What has she got to do with it?'

'A great deal, I'm afraid. The young lady is seminal to the case.'

'That expression has legal overtones,' said Warren.

'And biological ones,' said Harriet.

The great man sucked in his cheeks. 'How old is she?'

'Nineteen. Why?'

'Mrs Funkel, your son has been organizing a raffle.'

'That sounds innocent enough.'

'For a – prize.'

'They usually are.'

'There is nothing usual about the prize in this case. I understand that it was – carnal knowledge of this young lady. I'm sorry.'

Warren uncrossed his legs. Harriet's stomach slurped into her legs and she saw visions of green blobby men shifting on the desk.

'What?'

Dr Partridge, over the hump, sat back. 'I'm afraid the farcical, one might say Ealing comedy, nature of the offence, cannot disguise the fact that he was, in effect, pimping.'

'How can you be so sure of your facts?' said Warren.

'The young lady was smuggled into the Sixth Form Billiards Room during the Spring Roller Disco. I'm afraid it does not say much for the intelligence of our young people that they attracted attention to the proceedings with riotous war dances as the winner was announced.'

'Was there a second prize?' said Harriet.

'I beg your pardon?'

'Sorry. I can't quite take this in, Dr Partridge.'

'No, well I can understand your sense of shock. In many ways Japheth has been an ornament to the school. Particularly on the sporting field.'

Warren assumed an aggressive tone. 'Were they caught in the act? Anyhow, how come you're so sure Japh was behind it?'

'As to the first point, the winner was in the act of, as it were, claiming his prize. I admit that this had not proceeded beyond the ceremonial stage. As to the second, we interrogated the boys individually and, under the threat of suspension shortly before their A-Levels, it wasn't difficult to extract the truth.'

'So Japheth would have known why you wanted to see us,' said Harriet.

'Yes. I'm somewhat astonished that he made no mention of

it. Of course, I have no idea as to the nature of your family relationships, but it does suggest there is room for improvement, wouldn't you say?'

'Oh come on,' said Warren. 'He's eighteen years old. You can't supervise them like toddlers.'

'Indeed. However, I have to say, Mr Funkel, that your reaction is indicative of a problem. In my experience, deviant behaviour like this is usually a cry for help – for more intimate attention. I would not be so blunt if you showed more concern than you are doing.'

'Come off it, Dr Partridge. That kid has had a perfectly normal, supportive home life. You can't pin this on us. He's his own man, now.'

'Not as long as he's at this school. I must say, your attitude is most frustrating, Mr Funkel. A boy's behaviour is the result of his upbringing. Wouldn't you even admit that his moral values are, to say the least, confused? Exploiting a young woman, a guest in this country, for financial gain! I would have thought that you, Mrs Funkel, would have some repugnance, as a woman, to that aspect of the case.'

'I had no idea that his moral values had been activated at all. It's as much as I can do to get him out of bed in the morning.'

'Indeed. I wonder why?'

'Now look here—'

Warren half rose, but Harriet put a restraining hand on his arm.

'Dr Partridge, before you summon the vice squad to look into our domestic arrangements let me say I am *most* concerned. Well, as you see, I'm in shock. My husband naturally defends his son, but I have to say on his behalf, that he's actually had very little to do with Japheth's upbringing—'

'Harriet—'

'He's been too busy. You must know that's very common. It's not his fault. The responsibility is all mine.'

Dr Partridge, stranded on his upsurge of indignation, took a while to readjust.

'I'm not accusing you of neglect, Mrs Funkel.'

'Well, thank you. However, it's pretty clear where you stand on the question of nurture versus nature.'

'One can only go so far with nurture, I realize that. Look at the Royal Family. But nurture's purpose is to correct nature. That is as much the purpose of the school as the home.'

'I fully realize the implications for the school, Dr Partridge. Truly, I'm very, very sorry. And I would be grateful for your advice.'

'Well—'

'My husband is in shock, too. I'm sure when he's calmed down he'll help me do all we can to – to – do something about it. Japheth will be grounded, for a start.'

'With the young lady?'

'Oh dear – We'll think of something. I presume you also have some form of retribution in mind?'

'I was coming to that. May I suggest in passing, however, that you consider family therapy. I know it's a bore for the younger ones, but it has a proven track record with dysfunctional units.'

'Christ,' said Warren. 'The two-way mirror thing.'

'Now then. I have consulted with the governors, and their first reaction was that Japheth should be expelled immediately.'

'No!'

'I'm afraid so. But I managed to persuade them that, in the absence of forensic evidence, it would open the door to too many messy appeals, and ultimately not in the interest of the school.'

'Thank God for that.'

'Indeed. Nor do I favour suspension. Giving boys an extra holiday is not my idea of punishment.'

'Especially with the cricket season coming up,' said Warren.

'I hope you don't seriously think I would be influenced by such considerations, Mr Funkel.'

'Of course he doesn't. So what have you decided?'

'First of all, the profits from this venture will be confiscated and put towards the purchase of equipment for the Junior Science Block. Do you agree?'

'Absolutely. How much did they raise?'

'Approximately £2,000. Most of the boys bought several tickets.'

'I presume the gift will not be commemorated with a plaque.'

'Certainly not. And then we considered a form of community service order. The Staff Locker Room is in need of redecoration.

We suggest that the boys involved come in for a few days before the beginning of term and do it. And since Japheth was the ringleader, we thought it appropriate that he should organize them.'

'That seems fair enough. We'll pay for the paint, won't we, Warren?'

'Oh, sure.'

'Actually, we have the materials in stock. But – ah – if you did want to make an – ah – expatiatory contribution—'

'Matching funds?' suggested Warren.

'That would be entirely a matter for you to decide. We are launching an appeal to erect a dome over the swimming pool next term—No, please put your cheque book away, Mr Funkel.' He smiled. 'I am anxious to avoid the appearance of extortion.'

'What do you teach, Dr Partridge? Sophism?'

'*Please*, Warren. Unless you have any bombshells about Mungo up your sleeve, Dr Partridge, I think we'd like to go.'

'Certainly.'

The High Master accompanied them to the door. Warren shook hands and huffed off. Dr Partridge kept Harriet's hand in his for a moment longer.

'I think I see the problem, Mrs Funkel.'

'What do you mean?'

'I mean that your husband doth protest too much, methinks.'

'How much is enough? How would you react in the circumstances?'

'I don't know. But your husband's reaction has guilt written all over it.'

'You mean, he's been up to the same sort of thing?'

'No, no, no. Not necessarily. But – something – hmm? Wouldn't you say he feels guilty about something?'

Harriet's blood again plummeted out of her head, her one thought – Avelina Viper.

'I – I don't know. I'm not thinking straight at the moment.'

'Please forgive my being so personal, but it is sometimes easier for an outsider to see when there are problems brewing in a family. And don't worry too much about Japheth. I had to come down hard on him for the sake of the school, but, quite frankly, this country needs all the entrepreneurs it can get. Don't hesitate to get in touch if you want to discuss this further.' He squeezed her hand, now soggy as an ice-cream. 'It's often the parents one would most like to see who are most reluctant to come in.'

Warren's body language, as the car burnt rubber on the hapless school drive, shouted obscenities.

'What were you two talking about?'

'You. He obviously thinks you're at the bottom of it. Oh dear, this is no time for schoolboy humour.'

'You licked his arse.'

'So? Japheth's future is up it.'

'It's all crap. I don't believe a word of it.'

'What, you think it was a put-up job to get the Staff Locker Room redecorated?'

'Of course not. But Japh wouldn't do a thing like that. It's just their filthy minds.' The car ripped through a tube of hazel hedges, laughingly called the B1284. 'I mean, Christ, why would he be selling her off? If he was normal he'd be screwing her himself.'

'That's an odd thing to hold against him. Perhaps he is too.'

'I sure hope so.'

'Really, Warren. What would that make Semi? I mean, I know she's French, but she's not a whore. There's some would say you can't deal with Japheth's sexuality.'

'Can you? That's bollocks. It's the money thing that bugs me, that's all.'

'We should have given him more pocket money. You see, it is our fault.'

'He could've done a paper round like other kids.'

'I wouldn't let him. I was afraid he'd get mugged. I can't believe all this. Japheth was sicking up puréed carrots not so long ago. He seems to have grown up while I was in the bath, or something. Whatever will Dotty say? Nothing, probably, which will be worse. I know what she'll be thinking, though – 'Well, you wanted them.' She's such a back-seat child rearer.'

'Bugger Dotty,' was Warren's advice.

When told, Dotty duly formed her mouth into chrysanthemum formation, raised her eyebrows and, like Tom the Cabin Boy in *Captain Pugwash*, said – nothing. She offered to do some ironing.

Unfortunately Semi was already doing it, a sure sign, thought Harriet, that the girl was terrified out of her wits.

Dotty was scathing. 'What do the French know about ironing?'

Harriet was stumped.

All the children were out. Warren said he would just go over to the golf course, to fill in time until they got back.

'We can't raise the subject in front of Tiz,' said Harriet. 'It will have to be the full I-will-see-you-later-in-my-study bit.'

It was a great deal later, as Japheth phoned to say he had been given tickets for *Return to the Forbidden Planet*. Harriet found herself saying, 'Take a taxi from Sutton, darling. I'll pay.'

'Thanks, Mum. You're brill.'

The words reduced her innards to a grateful pulp.

By the time Japheth got home Harriet and Warren had drunk themselves into a near coma, only kept conscious by first-night nerves. There had not been a scene like this in the family since Mungo flushed a friend's gym bag down the loo, and sludge-gulpers from several counties had been required to retrieve it.

Warren told Japheth to fetch Semi into the den. Harriet had suggested the utility room as the laundry would deaden the noise, but Warren needed the cultural support of stuffed leather.

Harriet studied Semiramide as she sat down beside Japh on the sofa. On examination, it was impossible not to appreciate what people saw in her – the long olive body, legs like scaffolding in jeans, pale complexion and round pâté-coloured eyes, the whole framed in waist-length black hair that was too thick to brush but which had to be shampooed in Harriet's Wash-n-Go every day.

'I guess you know where we were today, Japh.'

'No, I don't. Could you get on with it, Dad, I'm tired.'

'*You're* tired! You don't even work.'

'I do, as a matter of fact.'

'Sorry, I forgot. You spend a week pushing wheelchairs round a field and all of a sudden we're on the same level.'

'They're not disabled. They're yobs. Anyhow, we never will be on the same level. It's called chronology, Dad.'

'OK, forget it.'

Harriet was huddled round her whisky glass. 'If you want it straight, Japh, Dr Partridge claims you organized a raffle. You organized a raffle. You organized—' Harriet gulped some more whisky. Why did this scene lack the drama of 'When Did You Last See Your Father'?

'Your needle's stuck, Mum. So what if I did?' His expression was helpful, but impatient.

'Oh for God's sake, Japh, you know what we're talking about. What have you got to say?'

Japh and Semi smiled at each other. 'I suppose he told you we were caught *in flagrante delicto*.' Harriet was incensed at the vocabulary of one who never read anything. 'That's crap. It wasn't like that at all.'

'Don't swear.'

'Dad does.'

'When you earn your own living you can do as you like.'

'Eh? You mean I can pay to swear?'

'What did happen then?' Warren already looked vindicated.

'Yes, I organized a raffle. It was only for a date. Timothy Al-Halab won it. He was a bit tight—'

'On Ecstasy, I suppose.'

'No, Mum. We don't do drugs.'

'Why not?'

'Because you don't score goals on drugs. You only think you do. Besides, I have no intention of keeping the Mafia in shoes.'

Despite herself, Harriet could not help thinking what a noble specimen of British Youth was here.

'So what did happen?'

'Well, the winner's kiss got a bit out of hand, that's all. And Mr Harrison came in and he was smashed out of his head as usual. He just got the wrong end of the stick.'

'We were going to give 'alf ze money to ze dolphins,' said Semi.

'So actually nothing – happened?'

'No.'

'You see,' said Warren. 'I told you.'

'Then how come Dr Partridge got the idea they had been promised – something more?'

'You mean sex? Why can't you say it, Mum? You're so hung up.'

'All right, Japh, don't give me the Old Fogies routine. I grew up in the sixties, remember.'

'Wild child! Anyway, I don't know why he got that idea. Perhaps he got the West Midlands Police Force to investigate them. Perhaps he got a turn-on from imagining it. Besides, his wife just ran off with a French engineer who was over here working on the Channel Tunnel. He's got a thing against Frogs. Oh, sorry, Semi.'

'Iz OK.'

Warren smiled. 'It was still pretty pathetic, Japh.'

'And in very poor taste,' said Harriet. 'You should be ashamed of yourselves.'

The ashamees shrugged. 'Right,' said Japh. 'I'm off to bed, then.'

'Hold on. Sit down,' said Warren. 'We're not going to leave it at that.'

'Don't get heavy, Dad. It doesn't suit you.'

'Japh, we're *paying* for that fucking school.'

'Ah! That'll be 10p, please.'

'You damn near got expelled. That'd be thirty thousand quid down the tubes. Now you go along with the good doctor's punishment or you can get out.'

'Of where?'

'Well – here. You're over eighteen now.'

'I love you too, Dad.'

'Dad doesn't mean that,' said Harriet. 'But you do have to organize your raffling friends to paint the Staff Locker Room.'

'What!'

'*And* – your mother and I have decided that Semi here should go back to France as soon as possible. I'm shorry, Shemi, but that's how it is.'

Semi looked mildly put out. 'I 'ave to go 'ome?'

Harriet felt herself blushing. 'We thought you would agree that things might be – awkward. In the circumstances.' And the prospect of no more chicken with cinnamon and chick peas had tipped the balance. 'You don't mind, do you? I rather assumed you'd be pleased.'

Semi shrugged. 'Iz OK.'

'No!' Japheth had spoken. He put a hand on Semi's knee. 'That's bloody unfair. If she goes, I go. Honestly, Mum, *you're* ashamed of *me*? In a few years time you'll be dining out on this incident, but Semi will feel like a criminal for the rest of her life if you chuck her out. I swear, if you do, I'll go with her. I'm over eighteen, as Dad just pointed out.'

'But – but—'

'But me no buts, Mum,' said Japheth. 'I'm going to stand by her. I don't have to make compromises with your *ancien regimes*.'

'Japheth, you're mad. What would you do in France?'

'Whatever I would do here, I suppose. For God's sake, Mum, we're going to be able to walk there soon.'

'Oh God—'

'Iz OK. I can go to different family.'

'That's not the point.'

The phone rang. Warren picked it up. 'It's for you, sweetheart. I think it's George.'

Harriet tried to get up. Warren brought the phone to her.

'George? It's one o'clock. What's the matter?'

'Is it? Christ, I thought it was around eleven. I've been at The Ivy.'

'That's nice. Japh, where are you going?'

'To bed, Mum. I'll talk to you in the morning.'

'Oh, all right. Goodnight, darling. Sorry, George.'

'I've just been talking to your Nick Pollard friend. Can you audition on Wednesday pm?'

'Yes. No. Where?'

'Apparently *Get Off My Tummy* is coming off in two weeks at the Prince Albert, so they're going in there. It's a bit small – they'll have to knock out the back of the stage but—'

'Two weeks!'

'No, no. Rehearsals start then – opening around June 20. Can you get there on Wednesday or not?'

'Of course.'

'Good. Two-thirty for three. Call me afterwards? And don't forget your music! What will you do?'

'I don't know. *Mack and Mabel* again, I suppose.'

'Harriet, this show is supposed to be a moving tribute to carnage—'

'*Miserables* then.'

'Great. You'd better get some sleep.'

Harriet gave the phone back to Warren.

'Back on the duckboards again, huh?'

'Maybe. Probably not.'

'And who's going to look after the kids? If it's a long run you can't expect Semi to cope.'

'No, especially if you ship her back to Marseilles.'

'I guess we'll have to renege on that one.'

'I'll ask Dotty if she can help. Would you mind? She might be glad to have something useful to do. I mean, I could pay her.'

'Wait till you get the part first.'

Contrary to the dictates of the Council on Alcohol Abuse, Warren's sex drive was not impaired by drink. Whether he was inspired by finishing three under par on the golf course, or the emergence of another rutting stag in the herd, he took her by surprise when she bent down to pick up her knickers. Announcing that he was going to fuck her till she fell apart, it was not long before Harriet perceived this fate to be imminent. She was humped round the bedroom to grunted cries of 'Feel that! Ah – beautiful!' that quite drowned out her own anguished cries about her slipped disc and shocking Dotty. Like the front end of a pantomime horse, she steered their coupled flesh towards the bed, but only managed the chaise-longue, where Warren succeeded in hammering thoughts of scandalizing Dotty into convulsions.

'Why don't we do that more often, Warren?'

'Phew – it takes it out of you. I'm getting old.'

'I hope it wasn't a farewell performance.'

'Me too.'

'Do you really mind if I get this job?'

'Yes and no. You're such an asset on the entertaining front. And Tiz'll feel it. She's not used to your working nights.'

'I know.'

'I'll back you up on one condition. Tiz gets the pony. You'll be able to afford it if you're in the West End.'

'Oh all right. But if Tiz gets the pony we'll really have to hang on to Semi. Someone's got to pick its hooves every day. I won't have time, and Tiz'll need help to start with.'

'By the way, you'll get to meet Avelina soon. I fixed up with her and her husband and some Danish guys to go to the opera next week.'

'Wonderful,' said Harriet. Some people, she mused, are born Avelina Vipers, some people acquire Avelina Vipers, and some have Avelina Vipers thrust upon them.

Dotty agreed to stay on and look after Tiz while Harriet went to audition.

'What's the part, then?'

'A singing matron in a hospital behind the battle lines at Ypres.'

'I wouldn't have thought she'd have much to sing about,' said Dotty.

4 ∫

The studio was near Covent Garden station, and Harriet had to walk past *Cats* to get there. It reminded her that Damian de St Croix, the young man she had met on Victoria station, was currently playing the trombone there. A mild *frission* passed through her at the thought of him, but it could not compete with the torrential *frissons* already coursing through her nerves. She feared she would bite off so much of her lower lip when she sang that she would choke on the bits.

'Harriet Dimdore?' A skinny black girl with a clipboard ticked off her name.

'That's right.' Harriet had barely got her foot in the waiting room. Besides the girl there were only a young man and an older woman, neither of whom she knew.

'With George Sherman?'

'Yes.'

'You can go in next. There's been a couple of no-shows.'

'But I—'

'The loo's down the corridor on the left,' said the girl without looking up.

'Thanks. But where's the nearest balcony? I want to throw myself off.'

'Are you OK?'

'Fine. I'll be right back.'

Furiously rearranging her short, but versatile, hairstyle in the mirror of the smelly lavatory, Harriet went over the words of her song, now 'Losing My Mind' from *Follies*. It was something of a chestnut, immortalized by the stars, but since the character was an ex-showgirl rotting in the boonies, she did not have to act. On the other hand, it was more difficult to imagine whom to address as inspiration for the cris de coeur. The singing housewife lamented an obsession with a lost love, which had seeped into the very coffee grains of her existence. But Harriet had last been infatuated on a cosmic scale as a schoolgirl, when she had had a crush on the art teacher. He had farted while giving her a lift home and that had been the end of it. Her face in the mirror, crumpled with nerves and gloom, suggested tragic loss all right – youth, ambition, memory and various bits that had been removed surgically. She sniffed back the tears. 'Perhaps I should just go home.' But Nick would be embarrassed. One did not let people down. After all, it was a show about brave lads who had to go over the top. Let them not have died in vain.

Nick smiled encouragement as Harriet entered the studio. After the waiting room, not to mention the lavatory, it seemed crowded. There were at least ten people, and a couple in leotards, chatting at one end of the room. She walked up to the table where Nick was sitting with three men and an elegant woman and was introduced. She gave the musical director a very special smile. The woman eyed her in not unfriendly fashion.

'I love that suit, Harriet. Is it Jean Muir?'

'No, Dorothy Perkins.' It was not, but it got a laugh, and suggested that she was fun to work with.

'Now, Harriet,' said the assistant producer and representative of The Amazing Truth Company, 'you know what the show is about and what your part would be, do you?'

'Yes. Nick filled me in.'

'You two have worked together before?'

'A couple of times.'

'And what's your experience in musicals?'

'Well – mainly panto, I admit. But I had intensive coaching with Lily Praed last year when I was up for *Ashes and Broomsticks*.'

'Ah. We're not looking for belters for this part, Harriet. She's a serious, mature woman caught up in a universal tragedy.'

'That's me.'

They breathed laughingly.

'You don't have any reservations about the subject matter?' said the woman. 'We have had a couple of – older people who weren't comfortable with it.'

'The Battle of Ypres? No, not at all.' She avoided Nick's eye. 'In fact I have a personal connection with it. My great uncle was wounded there. I have a memento from the battlefield. I've brought it with me for luck, if you'd like to see it.' They murmured curious assent. 'It's a rosary. I expect it belonged to one of the French soldiers. Here it is.'

Feeling like someone who would be prepared to put the Crucifixion on a chocolate box, Harriet drew from her pocket a small wooden rosary worn with use and handed it to the representative of The Amazing Truth Company.

'Good Lord,' was his apt response. He handled the rosary with reverence and passed it round. They were amazed and touched by the wooden beads, the tiny cross worn smooth elicited particular notice, giving the scene a gloss of *The Antiques Roadshow*.

'I wonder if we could work that in somewhere,' mused the musical director.

'Well thank you for that, Harriet.' The representative handed it back to her. 'When you're ready? Afterwards we'll get you to read a bit of dialogue – not much.'

Harriet took her music to the pianist and had a quick word. 'Don't drown me out on the reprise. I'll be on back-up batteries by then.'

She took up her position at a three-quarter turn from the audience. Nick called for hush. Harriet drew breath as the introduction tinkled, and fixed her mind on the dynamic hopeful from Barnes who had set out on the road that would terminate in three and a half minutes. 'The sun comes up—' In the same key as the pianist, thank God. 'I think about you—' A bit tremulous, perhaps, but that was in character. 'The coffee cup – I think about you—' It was going all right. She remembered to move downstage at the dramatic 'All afternoon doing every little chore—' As she poignantly dusted the piano, she tried to think of her innocent self, but all that came to mind was Tiz, her own dear clean spring about to flow into the polluted estuaries of experience. 'I talk to friends – I think about you—' Tiz was the next one down the tubes. Her hothearted, cuddly, ferocious Tiz. Would she ever be lonely? The thought could not be borne. A gush of terror and pity for Tiz erupted into the reprise. She was aware of the pianist upping the tempo in alarm. Instinct told her to belt it, and she yelled her way to a convincing rendition of someone about to come off their trolley.

A round of applause was the surprising response. Harriet laughed as she wiped away the tears.

'I'm so sorry. I didn't mean to get so carried away. We've just got our poll tax bill.'

Nick was concerned, but instantly saw a way to turn the situation into live theatre.

'Tell you what, Harriet, while you're in the mood, how about a spot of improvisation? I think we can scrap the reading. You'd do better on the hoof at the moment.'

Harriet studied his face for hidden meaning. He was supposed to be her friend.

The young man in the green shirt was summoned and told to lie down and act wounded.

'Now, let's say this chap is a childhood sweetheart you haven't seen for years. You're under a lot of stress, but seeing him changes you in some way. OK?'

'Is this dialogue, or do I have to sing it?'

'Whichever you're more comfortable with. Use that door for your entrance.'

Harriet went out and paced the floor. She loathed improvising. It was like playing *Just a Minute* as though one's life depended on it, which it did. How could she fake a long-lost passion shocked into life? Well there was that time when Clematis 'Hagley Hybrid' had sent out some shoots after two years playing dead. Perhaps she should just imagine Japheth brought in crippled from the football field, as it was something that she imagined all the time.

The young man was writhing in agony, even sweating. Ambitious little fart, thought Harriet. He can't get my part, anyway. After a ripple of double takes she leant over him.

'Cecil?' A good nose for period detail with 'Cecil', she felt.

'Dorothy? Aaaargh!' Harriet gasped at the coincidence, only sorry she could not rip a few tubes out. 'Excuse me for not getting up.'

'Don't, Cecil.' She knelt beside him.

'Don't what?'

'Don't hide your pain behind jokes. Everybody here does it. But not you. Not with me. My God, I never thought I'd see you here. I thought you were too—'

'Old?'

'Yes.'

'I am. Trouble is, I'm too good. They couldn't manage without me.'

Oh, bleeding nice one, ducky, thought Harriet. 'You always were – too good. The Boers didn't get you, then? You know, I've still got your last letter from Ladysmith.'

'What a relief.'

'You're doing it again, Cecil.'

'What?'

'Hiding behind jokes.'

'Sorry. Damn it – I wish I wasn't – like this – aaargh!'

'Hush. I'll fetch the doctor. Oh Cecil, I know it sounds awful, but – I'm so glad you're here. It's selfish, but – this morning I'd decided I couldn't take it any more. But now I know I must stay.'

'Cut! That's fine, Harriet,' said Nick. 'Thank you both.'

Harriet's knees were jammed and she had to be helped up by Green Shirt. She studied the faces behind the desk. Most were smiling. At what, it was impossible to say.

Back among the crowds of workaday folk waiting to cross the lights on High Holborn, anticlimax dragged at her limbs. She was numbed by the bleak despair that comes with professional suicide. She blundered down Drury Lane, swearing that if she got the part she would walk naked down Oxford Street. Instead, she found herself at the stage door of *Cats* asking for Damian de St Croix, on the off-chance that he was in there polishing his trombone.

'Kidneys!' He was clearly delighted to see her. 'Hello. Are you working, then?'

'No. I've just blown an audition. Let me buy you a drink. Make an old woman's day.'

'What – on the pavement?'

'Oh shut up. I just need a snort before I go home.'

'You're using me. Why aren't you interested in my body?'

'Actually I was earlier on. I think it was the Cornish pasty I had for lunch. I'm all right now.'

He grabbed her by the lapels. 'I'll make you forget Cornish pasties, my darling.'

Harriet squawked. 'Get your hands off me!'

Before either of them could say Citizen's Arrest, a passing Afro-American woman was beating Damian over the head with a baguette to cries of 'Lay off her, you pig,' and similar. Harriet went for the baguette, which broke in the struggle.

'Please! It's all right. He was only kidding.'

'Are you sure, honey?' The woman, whose considerable height was adorned by a plaited replica of the ziggurat of Babylon, looked disappointed.

'Certain. Thanks anyway.'

'That's OK. I'm an angel, back home, see. It's just a knee-jerk reaction.'

Damian picked bits of crust out of his hair. 'I prefer my food on a plate.'

The woman went on her way laughing.

'I have to say, Damian, I don't think we'll be seeing much of each other.'

'Why not?'

'You attract violence. You had a dust-up in the gents' loo last time.'

'Huh! Doctor heal thyself. You're the common denominator. I never have this sort of trouble normally.'

'Well let's go into a pub and see if any glasses shatter. Then you'd better keep away from me.'

Try as she might, Harriet could not raise her spirits above her ankles in the days that followed. The children, sensing her weakness, swooped in to pick her bones.

'Mum,' said Tiz, 'Dad says I can have the pony. Can I really?'

'Yes, very well.'

'Oh Mum, I love you.' Tiz crushed her rigid. 'I saw an ad in *Pony* magazine for £800. That's a steal, Mum. Can we get it at the weekend?'

'All right.'

Japheth announced he was going to join Sutton FC. 'You don't mind, do you, Mum?'

'What about your A-Levels?'

'I'll still do them.'

'Great.'

Mungo had learnt of a Sega Megadrive for sale at a mere £200. 'Where's Ipswich, Mum?'

'Suffolk.'

'That's not far. Can we go, Mum? I'll pay half the petrol.'

'All right.'

A friend called and asked her to organize the collection of jumble for the Psoriasis Society. 'I'd love to,' she said. She voted Labour in the local elections, despite the fact that the nearest Labour candidate was in Leatherhead. What energy she had went into discussing Dotty's future – in Nonsuch Crescent.

Personally, Dotty could not see what was so depressing about failing to get a bit part in a musical about carnage, but then she was the first to admit that her brow was low enough for the likes of Harriet to trample on with ease. She felt sorry for Harriet. All those bedrooms, children, money, a Daihatsu Sportrak and mullioned utility room and she still was not happy. Dotty did her best to reduce Harriet's stress quotient by crying in the spare bedroom, but she could not always restrain herself when friends called to console themselves that she was all right.

It was Dotty who took the call from George. Harriet was in the bath, preparing for her night at the opera with Avelina Viper. As it was only eleven in the morning, George thought he was being done.

'Oh no,' said Dotty. 'It's just that she's been a bit down since the audition. I expect she's hoping the waters will close over her.'

'Hold on. Are you telling me she's suicidal?'

'No, no. She sent for the plumber the other day. Now that's a long-term project. Shall I get her for you?'

'Not if she's in the bath.'

'It's all right. They've got a cordless. Hold on.'

Dotty attempted to negotiate the bathroom with her eyes shut, for modesty.

'For goodness' sake, Dotty. I'm not Medusa.'

'Sorry. Mind you don't drop it in the water. Remember *Goldfinger*.'

'That was an electric fire, Dotty.'

'Still, you don't want to curl anything accidentally.'

Dotty went downstairs and hovered. She had been in the house long enough to know that George calling Harriet was generally good news, Harriet calling George, bad. Presently Harriet came down in her towelling robe. Dotty thought she looked younger without make-up. The lapis lazuli eyes, as Harriet called them, took on an alien, trusting look.

'Dotty, I've been recalled for *Wipers*!'

'That musical thing?'

'Yes. I mustn't get too optimistic. It's probably because the director's a personal friend, but – I can't help it. I mean, Perry Saddlesmith himself will be there. They wouldn't be wasting his time if there was no chance. I'll have to practise some new numbers.'

'How about "Over the Rainbow"?'

'Dotty, don't be silly.'

'Over the Hill and—'

'Dotty—'

'Sorry.'

'Dotty—'

'Yes?'

'Are you anxious to go home?

Dotty adjusted her glasses. 'I can't say yes, because it would be impolite. And I can't say yes, because I think you want me to say no.'

Harriet put her hands on Dotty's shoulders, forcing her to look into eyes troubled, she hoped, with sincerity.

'Dotty, you can say whatever you like. You've already said it. You do want to go home.'

Dotty shifted, uncomfortable in the brace of Harriet's arms.

'I really don't know, Harriet. Of course, I would really. At least I think so. I don't know what it's going to be like on my own. It's nice of you to have me. And you know I'm very fond of the kids – especially Tiz.'

'And she of you.'

'But I'll have to get used to being by myself some time, won't I?'

'Not necessarily.'

'What do you mean?'

'Well – you're right. You have to give it a try. Why don't you go home next week for a trial period?' The final decision could be made if and when rehearsals started. 'Too much forward planning is always a mistake, Dotty. Just remember you're always welcome here. And if there's anything else I can do, you only have to say.'

'Thank you.' Harriet released her and made to go upstairs. 'There is something.'

'Oh?'

'Would you mind coming to Chapel with me on Sunday? I was talking to the woman in the paper shop—'

'The newsagent?'

'Yes. She said they've got a smashing young preacher there. It's more like a club, sort of thing. And they have a coffee morning afterwards where you can meet everyone. Only I don't like to go on my own. Not at first, anyway.'

Harriet stared at Dotty. Was she being deliberately obtuse? Was she seriously asking her – agnostic reader of the *Independent* and wife of agnostic media person – to attend some sort of evangelical thump-in presided over by the Mole Valley's answer to Elmer Gantry? Did she not realize that this sort of thing was precisely what gave give-and-take a bad name?

'Well – I—'

'It's at eleven. You could still have a lie-in.'

'Dotty, you realize I'm not a believer?'

'Oh, you won't have to get up and declare for Jesus, or anything. Only I'm a bit shy, 'cos I don't know anyone round here.'

'Well. Fine.' Harriet was appalled. If she was seen, people she had previously elbowed out of the queue at the post office might now irradiate her with knowing smiles. Paralysed by do-gooding hormones, she would end up organizing flower festivals and outings to Clacton. She put a hand to her turban, to prevent her head from splitting under the impact of being recalled for the part and the price she was going to have to pay for it. 'You'd better remind me on Saturday night. Oh blast, we're going to a dinner party in Spitalfields. Well, give me an hour to get ready in the morning. I hope Jesus won't want me for a sunbeam because I won't be in the mood.'

'He needs clouds as well,' Dotty assured her.

Harriet was not in the mood for *Il Trovatore* either, which was muzak to the main business of the evening, the long-delayed introduction to the bony novelist, Avelina Viper.

There had been a ghastly scene with Tiz, as Semi had vacuumed up the stick insects belonging to Marie Stopes' class, which she was looking after as part of her personal and social development. Tiz was hysterical with shame and fury, and accused her mother of deliberately failing to remind her not to leave the jar on the floor. Harriet had slammed out of the house, leaving Tiz rummaging through the Hoover bag. Dotty stood by with the brandy bottle. Consequently, her mind was elsewhere when Avelina asked her if she had read *Les mots et les choses.* They had scarcely sat down near the top of the grand staircase. Warren and the Danish eel magnates were at the bar.

'Er – why do you ask?'

'Your husband is trying to persuade me to put together a programme about twentieth-century philosophy for his animated puppets. What do you think?' The way she swivelled her head away from Harriet and towards the crowds coming up the staircase suggested that replies should be kept to a minimum.

'I'd like to put a torch to those puppets. They keep actors out of work.'

Avelina smiled. 'Perhaps actors should adopt more wooden working methods. Human beings are so messy. It's no wonder serious directors are turning to inanimate interpretations of their ideas.'

Harriet thought inanimate was a word she might have chosen to describe Avelina. There was a stillness about her white, bony body under the folds of purple velvet set with mirrored cloisonné, her precious features in permanent repose under swathes of spun-sugar hair. It was now no surprise that her novels were about people who did nothing, but whose interior lives were as busy as an ant-hill. 'Apart from anything else, Foucault lived in the rue du Dr Finlay. That would be a nice self-reflecting touch for a television programme, don't you think?'

'Oh. Yes.'

Afterwards they went downstairs at Bertorelli's. Harriet restricted herself to lamb's lettuce salad, as she was getting in serious shape for the recall. Avelina ordered fried Feta cheese, tagliatelle and Mississippi mud pie mousse. It was a shock to realize that she had a passion for food, and seemed incongruous when she was twittering on – to Warren, of course – about Foucault. Perhaps the food just slid down the long tubes of her body and shattered with the force of gravity. The Danes were enthralling Harriet with the problems of distribution in the poultry and wet fish trade with Eastern Europe. For one thing, they did not have enough maps. Harriet tried to say sincere things about integrated wholesale policies, while monitoring Avelina's conversation with Warren.

'The only thing is, Ulrich, I don't quite understand where all this fits in with M25TV.'

'Ah. TV production is a new venture for us. We must diversify, you know. Protein becomes unfashionable now.'

'Will you be collaborating on Avelina's series about modern philosophers? Surely there must be some Danish eggheads who need looking at again.'

Avelina's antennae were also alert. 'Are you discussing our project, Harriet? I heard you mention Poland. It reminded me that Foucault was found in bed with a man in Cracow by a lady minister from the Department of Education. That sort of incident feeds right into the plot, don't you think?'

'It would be wasted on puppets.'

'That's true, actually. It would be heavy on sex. There was that paedophile scandal at the Coral.'

'I don't like the sound of that.'

Avelina turned the sort of look on Harriet that Harriet tried to cast on Dotty – creating and simultaneously negating, in the sense that the act of creation automatically transmogrifies the potential of its opposite, a hierarchical alienation between them which subsumed Harriet's claim to the authority of her perceived *savoir*. 'Actually, it's a pity Sartre is such old hat these days.

His sufferings as a child would make wonderful television. His grandfather encouraged him to read Corneille, but completely ignored the fact that he was going blind in one eye.'

'His subconscious made the connection for him, I expect,' said Harriet.

'And we could make a link-up between the sequential isolation of the moment with the *pointillisme* that was very influential on Birtwistle, you know. Now that would take care of the background music, wouldn't it, Warren?'

'Living composers are too expensive.'

Avelina laughed and placed her hand on his arm. Harriet noted the chunky yellow diamond. Her novels did not sell that well. But then her husband was a merchant banker. Where was he, she wondered.

'Dear Warren. Ever the accountant. No, don't make a face. You know I don't mean it.'

'I hope not. It seems to be the equivalent of child molester these days.'

'Who else is in this series?' asked Ulrich.

'We're not sure. The only condition is they have to have been into sex, drugs or sadomasochism.' She's drunk, thought Harriet. 'That's why Sartre would have been so good. He was convinced he was being chased by a lobster right across Venice.'

'What a clever old poop-scoop he was,' said Harriet.

Avelina speared her with a smile. 'The English are notoriously anti-intellectual.'

Harriet was grateful to the Danes for pitching in with anecdotes about Kierkergaard's personal habits. Her brain was telling her it was Horlicks time, whereas Avelina's knew neither night nor day. It would be a relief, if she got the part, not to have to attend these excruciating entertainments. She observed the interaction between Warren and Avelina. When Dr Partridge had put the idea of their possible liaison into her head she had been horrified. But it might suit her purposes. It would make Warren feel nice and guilty, and therefore cooperative. He would not want sex, which she was beginning to think of as something that people did in the old days, like Morris dancing. If she were working he would have plenty of time to philander. The perfect opportunity to get it out of his system before their marriage went into the disposable income/Saga holiday stage.

There was an orgy of continental kissing as they made their farewells. Avelina and the Danes were still sharing a joke about *Roberte ce soir* as the taxi carried them away.

'That cat did have BSE.' Dotty spoke with triumph, as though she had done the post-mortem herself. The children and Semi, who were watching *Casualty*, ignored her. 'It's all over the *Daily Mail*.'

('Yuch.'

('Yuch.'

('Yuch.'

('Euch.'

'I'm going to become a vegetarian,' said Tiz.

'We'll see about that, young lady. I don't know that your mum will allow it.'

'What's she going to do – ram pork chops down my throat with a mallet? That's how they make foie gras in France, isn't it, Semi?'

'Que-ce que c'est – foy grass?'

'Well I never eat the stuff,' said Dotty.

'That's a non sequitur, as Mum would say,' said Japheth. 'The problem is the moral distinction between cruelty to animals for our own pleasure, and cruelty to people for their own good.' Semi, who sat next to him on the sofa despite Dotty's efforts to insert the *Radio Times* between them, smiled her approval. She tended to do this every time he opened his mouth, especially to speak.

'Talk English, will you,' said Dotty.

'Where's Mum?' said Mungo.

'They're at a leukaemia ball,' said Tiz. 'Didn't you wonder why she was in a long dress and drop earrings?'

'How did she get Dad to go? He can't stand that kind of thing.'

Dotty pulled wool from a plastic beehive. 'That Lady Herbert Whatsit's on the committee.'

'Mum likes balls.' said Tiz. 'And she only looks about forty when she's been on a diet.'

'So would you,' said Mungo.

'Shut *up*!' Tiz kicked him. Mungo punched her on the ear. Japh and Semi quickly retracted their legs onto the sofa.

Dotty put her knitting down. 'Stop it or you can both go to bed this minute.'

'Going to make me?' sneered Mungo. 'Anyway, she hit me first.'

'You wound her up,' said Dotty.

'She'd never get away with that argument in court,' said Mungo. 'But I would.'

'Well, we're not in court now, so lay off.' She swiped Mungo's head for good measure.

'Ow! I'll tell Mum you hit me. Then she'll throw you out.'

'As you like. But I don't think your mum would be best pleased to know you've been upsetting me.'

'Why not?' said Tiz.

'Well – you know. And then I've got the feeling she'll be wanting me to look after you quite a lot.'

Japheth sighed. 'Can you lot shut up. We're trying to watch the programme.'

'Did you know she's auditioning for a musical?'

'Oh Gawd,' said Mungo. 'Embarrassing. I hope she doesn't have to take her clothes off.'

'What kind of musical?' Tiz's eyes wandered back to the television screen, where the emergency team were swabbing a man with a steering column in his chest.

'About the First World War, if you please.'

'Does that mean she'd be working every night?'

'Of course. And twice on Saturdays.'

They watched in silence for a while. Then Japheth said he and Semi were going to the pub. Shortly after they left, Mungo went upstairs to play on his computer. Tiz cuddled up to Dotty on the sofa.

'Why are you so fat, Dotty?'

'I am not! Anyway, I was about to ask you the same question.'

'I hate you.'

'I hate you too.'

'Can I have an egg and cress sandwich?'

'*May* I. In a minute. I was only seven stone during the War, you know. Fin used to call me his little tadpole.'

'Yuch.'

'I was so thin I had to pin my knickers to my vest. Did I tell you about that time I left them by the road in Palestine? My knickers, that is. That was just after the War. It was that embarrassing. I was driving this American colonel. Now he was a real gent. Used to give me his issue of toilet paper. But I was terribly shy, you see. Yes, I know it's hard to credit now. Anyhow, I couldn't bring myself to tell him I needed a pee. One day we were driving along, and he must have noticed my knuckles had gone white, so he suggested we stop for a comfort station, or whatever Americans call it. Americans never say what they mean, do they? In fact I got so used to it that one time when he said he was just off into the woods to dispose of his banana skin I got *quite* the wrong impression. Anyroad, there I was squatting behind this rock, and I'd taken my knickers off so that I wouldn't – you know – pee on them. I thought I heard the door of the jeep banging. I was in such a lather that I'd keep him waiting I just jumped up and into the driver's seat and drove off. Well I must have gone a mile down the road before I noticed he wasn't there. I'd been too embarrassed to look, you see. He was very understanding about it. He could have had me court-martialled, I suppose. Now, I'll just go and make that sandwich. Brown or white?'

But Tiz had fallen asleep. Dotty sighed.

'So much for a second career on *Jackanory*,' she said.

5

Nick called to warn Harriet that the second audition was to be held in the theatre and that conditions would not be ideal. It was being completely rebuilt to allow a mounted regiment of Sikhs to trot through the audience.

Dotty's 'chapel' was a green tin hut on the Reigate Road. Harriet drew up outside it, still rigid with disbelief. There were dozens of cars outside, some of them G reg. or newer. Harriet had imagined the congregation would be bussed in from nursing homes. A notice outside said Revelation Community Church. Inside, the benches were full of chattering faithful, and billowing clouds of flora against a backdrop of fresh primrose decor. Her lungs quickly clogged up with the sweetness of tulips, the powdery bitterness of cow parsley and lilac.

'Was there a wedding here yesterday?'

'I don't think so. The reverend's not qualified to do weddings. He's a DJ on Radio Hogsback during the week.'

The harmonium struck up 'The Lord My Pasture Shall Prepare'. Harriet sang with gusto, salivating to see the vicar who could fill a tin hut on such a fine May morning. As the last verse began, a door to the right of the performance area opened and what looked like a young, clean-shaven Rasputin entered and stood at the head of the aisle. He was tall and lean, mid-thirties, and wore his dark hair shoulder length. He was dressed in a black robe and riding boots with a large Celtic cross round his neck, where it jangled against the headphones of his Walkman.

When the hymn ended he flung wide his arms. 'Good morning, sisters and brothers.'

'Good morning, Vince.'

'Let us thank God for this beautiful morning.' They bowed their heads. 'Now, who's got some good news?'

A little girl put her hand up. 'My rabbit died.'

There was laughter, but the reverend hushed it with a glance. 'Your rabbit died, did it, Croydon?'

'Yes.'

'Are you sad about your rabbit, Croydon?'

'Yes.'

'What was its name?'

'Rice Pudding.'

'OK.' The reverend took a moment to compose his features. 'Let's all be silent for a moment and pray for Rice Pudding.' Harriet ground her teeth. She should have been in bed reading the *Observer*. 'Are you happy now, Croydon?'

'Yes.'

'Wonderful. Now, today's discussion will be led by Jim Walford, and while he's coming up here let's sing "Immortal, Invisible" and raise this old tin roof!' He punched the air.

Harriet and Dotty were handed a hymn book by a woman in the row behind.

'It must be like this in Eastern Europe,' whispered Dotty.

'What – praying for rabbits?'

'No. Sharing hymn books.'

'Ah.'

A middle-aged man of homely appearance joined Reverend Vince on the platform and sat down vis-à-vis. Vince crossed his legs and flattened his crucifix.

'Now, Jim, what's the problem?'

'It's my mother, Vince.'

'Your mother. And what has your mother been up to?'

'It's rather embarrassing, Vince. She's been stealing. She has. Shoplifting.'

'U-huh. Why do you think so?'

'Well, I was round at her place the other day and while she was on the phone I nipped upstairs. To the bathroom, as she thought, but actually I wanted to look for something.'

'What was that?'

'Well, my wife and I gave her a Salton Hot Tray for Christmas one year. We thought it would be useful for sausage rolls and that, when she had her friends round for bridge.'

'Yes.'

'But we could see she never had it out, and she said she couldn't remember what she'd done with it. So my wife thought – I know this doesn't sound very nice – but she thought it wouldn't do any harm if we took it back. We've got our twenty-fifth anniversary coming up. It would be very useful.'

'Why didn't you just ask your mother if you could look for it, Jim?'

'Oh I did. She got very worked up about it. Accused me of calling her a liar and so forth. So I just dropped the subject and took my opportunity.'

'And what happened, Jim?'

'Well, Vince, when I went to look in her wardrobe, I opened the door and about two or three hundred CDs fell out.'

'Two or three *hundred*? Phew. What did your mother say about the CDs, Jim?'

'She denied all knowledge. Said they were a plant. That's the problem, you see. She won't admit it, so I don't know what to do.'

'You certainly have a problem there, Jim. Tell me, were they pop or classical?'

'All sorts. Bird song. Simply Red. Russian Orthodox Vespers.'

'Does your mother actually have a CD player?'

'No, she doesn't, Vince.'

The congregation was eager to offer advice. Most of it involved the doctor. One woman suggested that Vince should go and see Jim's mother. A young man thought she might be selling them cheap at raves to augment her pension, and asked for her phone number.

Dotty raised her hand. 'How often do you go and see your mother, Jim?'

'Every month, if I can.'

'Do you think that's enough? Perhaps it's a cry for help. If you went to see her more often, or had her to stay with you sometimes, she might stop voluntarily.'

'I hear what you're saying,' said Jim. 'But I really do go as often as I can. You see, I've got two jobs, just to pay the mortgage. I'm a prison warder – that's my main job – and I repair washing machines in my spare time.'

Harriet's hand shot up. Vince gave her a sharp look. He did not recognize her and suspected that she was a spy from *Face The Facts*. 'Do you see any connection between the fact you are a prison warder and your mother joining the crime wave? I think Dorothy's right. She's just trying to get your attention.'

'That's a very interesting suggestion,' said Vince. 'But we don't want to make Jim here feel guilty. People *are* busy today. It's one of the mega, *mega* problems of the age. But thank you, Jim. Thank you for sharing your concerns with us.' Jim was ejected from his chair. 'Now let's quietly pray for Jim and his mother and family, ourselves and our families, for the hostages in Beirut, for peace in South Africa, for the victims of inflation and injustice, for politicians and poll-tax protestors, and our national football team in the forthcoming World Cup, that they – and we – may always and everywhere reflect your glory and grace, O Lord.'

Another hymn followed, calling on the Lord to purge the realm of bitter things.

Afterwards they sat down and Vince stood thoughtfully before them. 'I've been thinking about the poll tax,' he said, 'and the divisions and distress it has caused – setting neighbour against neighbour and mother against son. I asked the Lord to guide me, and the Bible fell open at Psalm 93. This is what it says.' Harriet started to sway a little at the emphatic cadences of Vince's voice. He had a way with enjambments that was nothing short of masterful. '*Shall there be no end to the prating, the rebellious talk, the boastfulness of wrong-doers? See, Lord, how they crush Thy people, afflict the land of Thy choice, murder the widow and the stranger, slay the orphan! And they think, the Lord will never see it, the God of Israel pays no heed.*' He paused. 'Now, I don't know if there's a message there. After all, nobody's suggesting that this government is sending *tanks* to mow down women and children. Not in England anyway. We're lucky like that. We've never *been* in the position where we've had to face our brothers or sons or *best friend* down the barrel of a gun. No, we're lucky. Our brothers, or sons, or best friends are only asked to mow people down in *foreign* countries. Northern Ireland. The Falklands. Now, I know what you're thinking. You're thinking—' He wandered up the aisle and indicated individuals. '—that's not *fair*. *We* didn't start it. Or anyway, *I* didn't. Perhaps I didn't even *vote* for them. Perhaps I didn't even vote for *anybody*. And yet they do all these terrible things to us. Send our lads to be killed by *foreigners*. Close our schools. Flatten our *countryside* with horrible motorways. Charge the blind for eye tests. Let our old people *die* of cold and hunger. You'd think we would have rioted *long ago*, wouldn't you? Tyrants! Off with their heads!' Dramatic gesture. 'But no, the worm doesn't turn for any of that. The worm only turns – *when it's taxed.*'

A longish pause. Harriet had caught his drift, and found that she thoroughly approved of it.

'And we're all caught like butterflies on a *pin*, aren't we? There's no escape. Pay up, or we send the *bailiffs* in. Hobson's Choice. You know, I heard a woman talking the other day, about what it was like to have the bailiffs in. They *burst* past her old mother. They *took* the TV. Twelve years old, it was. There wasn't much else, so they took the chair she was sitting on, *feeding the baby*. And some ornaments her grandad had won at a fair. They weren't *worth* anything, but they took them anyway. And no, this *wasn't* Russia under the czars, it was Beckenham in this very year of Our Lord, 1990. So why don't we take to the streets on her behalf then? The poll tax affects all of us. We can't turn a blind *eye*, a deaf *ear*. We can't drown it in drink, or go on holiday and *forget it*. It's pressed our panic button, *good and hard*. So. What would *Jesus* do? He had a short fuse on occasions. Remember when he trashed the market in the temple, causing thousands of shekels' worth of damage? So, would He have got a return ticket to Waterloo and gone on the rampage? What do you think?' He swirled round, black skirts and hair lifting in the draught, and addressed Harriet.

'Well – er – yes, I expect He would.'

'Would He?'

'Well – as you say, He was only human.'

'That's right. He was human. But "only"? No He was not only human. He was God. And He knew it. He didn't have to ask for the right to do *anything*. He didn't abuse his power, mind. He obeyed the rules – until they stuck in his craw. Then He blew. So. Does that give us the right to do the same? "Oh, I see they're putting up prescription charges. Better get down to the town hall and dig some geraniums up."' Modest laughter. '"Oh dear, a treaty with Lithuania. Time to bomb the M25." No, we couldn't live like that, could we? We might hurt someone one day, and we'd know it could be us the next. We know that's not what Jesus wants. He said, *"Give unto Caesar the things that are Caesar's, and to God the things that are God's."* So let us kneel now and pray that this government may be moved, not by the riots and protests, but by God's spirit of justice and mercy.'

After the silence they sang a hymn, the ambiguous 'Give me Oil in my lamp, Keep me burning'.

Harriet was moved by the sermon. Not bad without notes. She could not take her eyes from Vince's face which, with eyes still closed in prayer, allowed lengthy contemplation of his features. They would look good cast in bronze, like Lorenzo de' Medici. Ah, the Medicis. Now there were real men. How sad that this young man lived, not in times of Renaissance excess, where his athletic limbs could be nipped and tucked in velvet and silk with sleeves slashed like burst sausages and jerkin jauntily open at the chest, but in an age so drab that he had to dress up as Rasputin for the bourgeoisie of Banstead for kicks.

She supposed he was gay. What a pity. Having mentally dressed him up in damask and hose, she could not but follow the process in reverse. Just then the reverend opened his eyes and looked at her. Harriet felt sure he could read her mind like a print-out and she hid her burning face in her hands.

The service continued with a game show. Members of the congregation volunteered to go onto the platform and be blindfolded, while some children gave them bits of banana and other fruits, to identify. This demonstrated the importance of the senses, for which they then gave thanks. Harriet laughed, but was not amused. She could not wait for Reverend Vince to take centre stage again. He did so briefly, to wish them all a wonderful week worshipping the Lord.

'That wasn't too bad, was it?' said Dotty.

'Not at all. I quite enjoyed it.'

'I know you said we couldn't stay for coffee.'

'Did I?'

'Have you got ten minutes, then?'

'Very well.'

'Oh *thank* you.'

The door to Rasputin's robing room was thrown open to reveal an urn and Marie biscuits. A queue formed, and Dotty joined it. Most of the congregation milled around the pews. Vince was surrounded. Harriet began to feel uncomfortable, afraid that one of these good-humoured folk would approach and ask her where she came from. She felt punished for wishing to stay and touch the reverend's flesh. Now that people were actually talking to each other, the fact of being a stranger in their midst was painful. Their not knowing her was a mark of her failure in life generally, and it had been unspeakably dumb to put herself in a position where the accident of unfamiliarity produced the effect of total humiliation. She groped for her handkerchief. When she recovered she looked up to see Dotty with the coffee cups, with the Reverend Vince just behind. He looked concerned.

'Welcome to our gathering.'

'Thank you. I'm Harriet Funkel. This is Dorothy. She asked me to come along with her as it's her first visit.'

'That's all right, Harriet. Most people are dragged along here screaming to start with. Don't worry about it.' He put a hand on her shoulder. A heatwave shot through her that would have cured rheumatism. 'You're not "one of us", right? You're cynical, secular, immune to mumbo-jumbo, right? Don't worry about it. I understand.'

'Well – no, not at all. Well – all right – yes. But I was impressed with the – sincerity of the occasion. I really mean that.' She lowered her voice, as seduction demands. A critic – no relation – had once described her voice as having the effect of warm chocolate poured straight into the bowels. She hoped the bowels of the Reverend Vince were receptive. But, like the Curé D'Ars, she had the horrible feeling he had the power to Know Sin. And a lot more besides.

'Thank you. Will you come again if I promise never to mention God?'

'Oh dear. You're not one of those atheist vicars, are you?'

'Yes. I think He's just one aspect of the space/time continuum. Only joking. But even Jesus put people first, you know. Remember the goat that fell into a pit on the Sabbath?'

'Wasn't it a cow?'

The Revd struck his forehead. 'I think you're right. Now you'll think I'm an imposter.'

'Certainly not. Anyway, that story wasn't meant as a biology lesson.'

'That one never appealed to me. After all, what woman gets to put her feet up on Sunday?' said Dotty.

'You do,' said Harriet. 'At the moment.' For once Dotty was speechless. Her chin trembled. Harriet immediately wanted to skin herself alive. She patted Dotty's arm. 'And so you should.'

The Reverend went off to mingle. He was replaced by a couple of small ladies in hats from the don't-let-them-get-away committee. Dotty was loquacious, but Harriet felt the numbing effects of alienation return and, as soon as possible, insisted that it was time to go.

The atmosphere in the car was prickly. Harriet sighed, anger mounting compassion. All right, so she should not have put Dotty down. It had been a slip of the tongue, and surely a small thing compared to Harriet's magnanimity in bringing Dotty in the first place, and quite enjoying it in the second. Of course Dotty needed compassion at the moment, but it was turning into an orgy of guilt opportunities. Irritation and fear combined into a deadly longing to cancel the audition and send Dotty home.

'If I go again,' said Dotty, 'you can just drop me off.'

'Let's discuss it when the time comes.'

'It's time I went home anyway.'

'You don't have to.'

'Tiz is getting her pony on Friday, isn't she? She'll hardly notice I've gone. Are you all right, Harriet?'

'I don't know. Why?'

'You're growling, that's all.'

'Am I? Oh, that's just a voice exercise. I was thinking about the audition.'

'I should leave the growling to the audience if I were you.'

Tiz, who had insisted on a proper English roast dinner for once, refused to eat it. 'I'm not going to eat anything until I get the pony.'

'Don't get her one, Mum,' said Mungo.

'Ape! Anyway, I'm not eating meat from now on. Do you know they put testicles in sausages? *I* don't want BSE.'

'You don't get that from testicles, Tiz.' Japh took her plate and divided the food between himself and Mungo. 'And if you don't eat you'll just start digesting yourself to stay alive. Hardly pc for a vegetarian.'

Warren flung down his fork. 'Will you cut that out! Your mum's cooked this excellent dinner and I'd like to enjoy eating it, if you don't mind.'

'Thank you, darling.'

'Ze diner is very good,' said Semi. 'But I too am going towards ze vegetables.'

'How about you, Dotty? Shall I fetch the rice cakes?'

'No thank you, Harriet. I'm enjoying my meal.'

'It's lunch.'

'Yes, I know.'

'I thought perhaps you didn't.' Dotty's habit of referring to every repast after breakfast as a meal had begun to grate.

'Well, it is half past four.'

'When one has six pounds of potatoes to peel things do get delayed.'

'I offered to help.'

'So you did. If everyone's finished I'll fetch the dessert.'

The children groaned and said they were too full.

'What is it?' said Mungo.

'Gâteau St Honoré. It only took four hours to make.'

'I might have some later.' Mungo was clearly the most sensitive of her children.

'Is there animal fat in it?' said Tiz.

'Cream and custard. Not exactly lumps of lard.'

'I told you, I'm a vegetarian. One of those fat-free ones.'

'But you didn't tell me before I made it, did you?'

'Well I've told you now. May I get down, Dad? Dotty, you've got to help me design an artificial limb.'

'Right.'

Harriet and Warren faced each other over the rubble of lunch.

'I hope Tiz isn't getting anorexic.'

'It's just a phase. I can't see Tiz going off her food for more than a couple of hours.'

'How was church?'

'Not as bad as I expected. In fact I think you ought to go along too.'

'What?'

'Don't worry. I didn't see angels on the Dorking Road, or anything. But the vicar, or whatever he is, might be of interest. He's gorgeous. Cross between Liam Neeson and Lorenzo de' Medici. And theatrical. And sincere. A charismatic, in other words. He's a DJ on Radio Hogsback during the week, so there's the showbiz element there already. I really think you should have a look at him.'

'With a view to what, exactly?'

'I thought you wanted to pioneer evangelism on M25? He might be just what you're looking for. Give him a camcorder and let him do a pilot.'

'Hey, slow down. The advertising restrictions are coming off, but we have to be careful to avoid bias.'

'Just a thought. Can you come and look at this wretched pony over next weekend?'

'Sorry. It's the spring conference in Berkshire. I'll float your idea about the reverend.'

'And the one after that?'

'Greenland. Avelina's coming. She wants to do some research into Inuit vocabulary.'

'Oh yes.'

'I know what you're thinking. It's a waste of time, sweetheart. Avelina Viper's as hot as the Elgin Marbles.'

'Don't take this the wrong way, but what does she see in you?'

'New horizons? I don't know. I guess she thinks of me as some kind of ergonomical specimen. By the way, does this reverend play golf?'

'I've no idea. Why?'

'I'm looking for a new tournament partner. Jack's having marital problems. His mind's not on the ball right now.'

Harriet was more relaxed on the way to the second audition. As relaxed as William Tell facing the crossbow, anyway. It was folly of the first water to imagine that Dotty could step into the breach at home, so it did not matter if she got the part or not. Only that morning Dotty had mixed their tights up and put the butter in the microwave. Breakfast had been a stand-up row over Libya. Dotty could not understand why President Bush did not carpet bomb Tehran if they wanted to get the hostages out.

'And it's no good saying civilians would be killed, because they were in the war, weren't they? It's a price you have to pay. Anyhow, those people wanted the bloomin' Ayatollah, didn't they? They must get what they bargained for.'

Harriet had had to leave the room before she told Dotty that one more mention of the War and she, Harriet, would bayonet Dotty herself. The War accompanied Dotty everywhere, like a chauffeur. The only good thing about the audition was that everyone there would be under forty-five.

Proceedings were delayed because Perry Saddlesmith had to deal with a crisis in the Australian production of *Noddy!* Happily she met a friend from her Greenwich Rep. days who was auditioning for the part of a repressed homosexual Hussar, so the time passed pleasantly enough between trips to the lavatory.

It was easier singing on stage. She could not see the casting panel for the lights. Perry Saddlesmith sat like God behind the sun, judging her worth.

Afterwards she had to read a short monologue in which the matron recalled her early love of bandaging. She had actually left the stage and put her coat on, when she was called back.

'The choreographer wants a go.'

'What the fuck for?'

A voice from the stalls asked her if she could waltz. 'Just the old oom-pah-pah, you know. Nigel will lead you. Just have a go, love.'

Nigel danced like the backbone of the Peggy Spencer formation team. His limbs moved with the relentless ease of a combine harvester. Pressed against his torso, a derailing marriage of muscle and Aramis talc, her legs were flung around like a string of sausages.

'Relax your shoulders,' muttered Nigel through stretched lips. 'Up on the balls – *one* and *one* and—'

'What's all this for?'

'Souls of the Dead scene. They all come back and dance with their girlfriends. They've got to get girls in it somewhere, haven't they? I'm not complaining. All the musicals these days. They're taking good dancers off the streets. Most of the girls here have only got grade three ballet. End of this phrase I'll do an underarm pirouette. Ready?'

'No—'

Nigel was not listening.

Dotty had packed and placed her suitcases in the hall.

'Probate's come through.'

'Oh good. That was quick.'

'There's not much to be sorted. Couple of life policies, that's all.'

'Don't forget to have the poll tax adjusted. Sir Hubert was very particular that I should remind you.'

'Was he? Huh.' Dotty smiled and patted her hair. She knew she should not be impressed by titles, or by those who had led action-packed lives in the international arena, but she did not often have the opportunity to practise her indifference to them.

The house in Nonsuch Crescent was suffused with the cruel softness of May sunshine, and in the overgrown garden cascades of hawthorn and the fairy breath of forget-me-nots created a magical glade. Dotty shook dead bluebottles off the mail – catalogues of polyester fashion and brochures for warden-assisted housing. A neighbour came round, releasing Harriet. She hugged a tearful Dotty.

'You've been so good, Harriet—'

'Nonsense, Dotty. It was nothing. Now remember, you can always come back if you're lonely. We've got plenty of room. Japheth will be going to Leeds in September. Did I tell you he'd got a place?'

'I worked in a munitions factory in Leeds during the war.'

'Really? What did you do in Grimsby? Penge? Frinton-on-Sea? I thought you drove a jeep in Palestine.'

'That was later.' Dotty was confused, felt the prick without seeing the pin. 'I went up there to help my auntie. Eleven kids she had. To be honest, I think that's what put me off them. Mind

you, they had an outside loo and cold water inside. Had to boil
it all on the range. Did you hear about that farmer's wife who
threw her kids in after the washing? When her husband came
home they were steaming on the lawn.'

'Dotty, please—'

'That put me off 'n' all.'

Harriet staggered down the Via Mushroom to the car, nauseous
with the image of boiled babies, seeing her own children on the
farmer's lawn. So haunted was she by the tossed-off anecdote
that the drive home, Dottyless, was not the euphoric bound she
had anticipated. And there was something about being stuck at
traffic lights with a representative selection of the British public
that also forced contemplation of the eternal verities. Something
about being a speck in a flow, in intimate but mutually suspicious proximity to the other specks, about speeding and getting
nowhere.

At least she was in the right frame of mind when she turned
on the answering machine and heard from George that she had
not got the part. They liked her enormously, but it had gone to
Perry Saddlesmith's sister-in-law. The good news, if she could
swim, was a commercial for waterproof wound paint to be made
with fifty children from the St Paul's area of Bristol. There was
another message from Warren complaining about the absence of
power showers in the hotel in Godthaab. Avelina had gone off
into the interior with a dictaphone. He urged Harriet to make his
homecoming sweet.

Japheth's A-Levels were imminent. Harriet persuaded him to
give up Sutton United until the autumn, by which time he would
be safely studying at Leeds.

'I know your game, Mother,' said Japh. He sat at his desk in
the bedroom. Semi was on the bed reading *Le Figaro*, which her
mother sent every week. Harriet had protested that she must be
a distraction. Not at all, according to Japh. Her presence soothed
him. Harriet had offered to sit on the bed, and received only
a withering look. 'You think once I'm at university I'll forget
about football. You're so narrow-minded. It's quite common for
footballers to have degrees these days.'

'Name one.'

'Well – Terry Butcher's got maths A-Level. He had a place at Trent Poly.'

'Darling, I've never heard of either of them. Besides, Terry Butcher is not my son. Look, Japh, if you were Maradona I wouldn't worry. But are you? I just don't want you to end up in the fourth division – of Life, that is. Give me a break, Japh, you know mothers are like that. Just concentrate on your education and if you're still keen on football—'

'I can teach it to the disabled?'

'Nasty.'

'OK, it was. You know what I mean. By then I'll have missed my chance. One can get an education any time.'

'Christ – All right. Compromise. Just get your A-Levels.'

'I will. Don't worry.'

Harriet put a tentative hand on his shoulder, aware that Semi was monitoring the demonstration. She boiled with resentment. 'This child came out of my inside,' she thought. 'I can touch him if I want!' But she kept smiling.

The commercial was filmed in a water palace near Swindon. Half the children had lied about their ability to swim, and only three could be persuaded to go down the White Water Experience. As Harriet stood on the platform high above the pool and peered down the plastic tunnel that curved away into potential death, she felt at one with paratroopers the world over. But at least paratroopers were not marooned in a surreal landscape of turquoise and pink engineering, a terrifying edifice of interlocking large intestines through which she would have to hurtle. She was was so petrified she forgot her line eight times. When it was time to go home she found that one of the little toads from Bristol had let her tyres down.

Warren returned with a charming granite desk set. He was worried that Tiz had reduced quite a bit.

'Isn't she eating at all?'

'Oh yes. She's trying to lose weight for the pony. How can I tell her?'

'Tell her what?'

'That she's not getting it. I didn't get the part, remember.'

'I know. I'm sorry, sweetheart. I guess you can't tell her.'

'You mean, she gets the pony anyway?'

'If she wants it so bad. With all this publicity about anorexia, you can't be too careful.'

'That's giving in to blackmail.'

'That's right.'

'Phew. I've been looking at the ads in *Pony* magazine, actually.'

They were on their way to Wembley for a performance of *Le Nozze d'Astaco*, with the megastar Paolo Totti. Four hours of distorted vibrato and a distant view of a fat diva in red satin singing things like 'The engine has stalled in third.' Needless to say it was a joint production with M25TV.

'She can't blackmail us from beyond the grave, sweetheart.'

'My thoughts exactly. But – oh God. Another live dependant. Ponies always blow up with some ghastly allergy in the middle of Christmas dinner.'

'That's OK. Christmas can get kinda boring.'

'Thanks.'

Warren gripped the wheel. He knew better than to offer banal comfort when Harriet was in her Atlas pose. He thought Harriet's complaints about the demands of dependants needing round-the-clock care were a symptom of menopause and that she probably needed hormone replacement therapy. He knew he did.

Tiziana was transported with excitement at the prospect of a pony. The boys less so. Mungo asked how much it would cost and demanded matching funds.

'It's just an excuse not to talk to me any more, isn't it, Mum? Tom's sister got a pony and he says his mum never has time for him. She can always find time to take his sister to shows, but when he wants to go to shooting club she's, like, too sodding busy.'

'Don't swear, darling.'

Japheth took a more elevated view. 'I've no objection to the child having a pony – but *now*? I'm in the middle of exams. I thought you wanted me to do well in them.'

'Darling, I do! What has Tiz's pony got to do with it?'
'Have you considered the disruption to family life?'
'What?'
'She's going to be uncontrollable. We'll all have to take turns cleaning its frigging tack, if I know you. The car will be full of hay and I'll have to go to acid house parties for a rest. This place is getting to be more like a wild life sanctuary than a civilized home, Mother. How can I study in an atmosphere like this?'
'Darling, the ghetto-blasters confused me. I had no idea you needed peace and quiet to study.'
At least a cheque for the repeat of *Not in Front of the Hamster* arrived during this difficult time.

Harriet brought up the subject of horse trading while sorting jumble for the NSPCC. She was in a spare dining room of Crumbles, an opulent gabled pile belonging to her friend, Anita. Anita was fit and tanned, and ran step-aerobics classes in the barn, after which they retired to the Eurolog swimming pool cabin. She was Harriet's best friend south of Putney. The NSPCC. attracted that strata of local society that was also up on livestock. On the whole, Harriet liked the stick-shaped Tory matrons who sallied forth from Beam End and Pineways to do their bit for the underprivileged. She left Crumbles with a list of names and telephone numbers, and useful tips for the purchaser like, Look out for low withers, and Don't forget to ask about sweet itch. Deeply grateful, Harriet was also depressed by the confirmation that a pony was more bother than a patient in intensive care. She recalled Dotty's words when the subject had first come up. 'If you can't ride two horses at once, you shouldn't be in the circus.'

6 ∫

Harriet insisted that Semi come with them to interview the pony. After all, she would have to feed it and check it for ticks when Tiz was otherwise engaged. Naturally it was couched rather differently to Semi, as an opportunity to see more of the countryside. Groans from Semi. Harriet was annoyed by Semi's lack of interest in surroundings outside a radius of three feet around Japheth.

They turned off the A25 between Bletchingley and Godstone. The roadside burgeoned with wild flowers, the hawthorns dripped bridal catkins in clotted falls of perfection that spat on contrivance. The lushness was almost rank, more Florida Everglades than rural Surrey. It stirred Deep South yearnings quite inappropriate to the expedition. She was so distracted they missed Hawk Pits Gidden Lane the first time. *En route*, she gave Semi a lecture about the etymology of place names from Anglo-Saxon times to – shortly afterwards, but failed to distract Semi from her novel. She was just gearing up to another lecture on the importance of acquiring random knowledge which might be useful later on, when Tiz screamed.

'Mum! The tractor!'

'Oh God! Sorry, I didn't see it. Everything's so overgrown.' But of course it was really Semi's fault for making her annoyed and consequently less vigilant.

They lurched down the track that led to Scragg Hill Farm. At least here the hand of Man had provided a reassuring level of tat. The house was sixties brick. The windows sported the asymmetrical ventilation flaps that made Harriet's blood boil. It was surrounded by tin barns and knocked-up stables, old cars, oil drums and cats. A short, grey-haired woman in a filthy padded jerkin and trousers came towards them and spoke to Harriet through the car window.

'Where's the loose box?'

'We're borrowing that. We thought we'd better think things over first.'

'Come on then. Which one is it for?'

'My daughter. The one in the jodhpurs.'

'Oh.'

The three of them followed the woman to the paddock, with Semi in the disgruntled rear. The pony Mrs Bloodwort pointed out looked rather fat to Harriet, but enslaved Tiz immediately. He was dark brown with knobbly knees and a lot of woolly black mane and tail and what Harriet thought were socks, or locks, round his feet. Mrs Bloodwort's lack of female charm and common politeness put Harriet off her stroke. She had a list of essential questions, but was afraid to get them out and reveal an ignorance that the woman had sensed before they got out of the car. Mrs Bloodwort had her own patter ready.

'He's fourteen years old, twelve hands. A bit flat-ribbed but quite energetic. Not cow-hocked, it's just the hair. Nice little jumper. Not head shy. Good in traffic, providing he's on the inside. He doesn't mind having his feet picked and he's never had laminitis. Shall I wrap him up?'

Harriet laughed. 'Um – where are his withers?'

'Between his shoulder blades, of course.'

'I mean – are they high or low?'

'Well, you can see that yourself. Is this your first?'

'Yes.'

'I thought so.' She whistled, and the pony ambled over.

'What's he called?' said Tiz.

'British Telecom.'

'Oh.'

'Yes. Sorry about that. My husband registered him when he was drunk – my husband, that is. That's his official name, anyway. My daughter calls him Cloud Nine, or just Cloud.'

'That's a lovely name for a pony. Cloud. Don't you think so, Semi?' said Tiz.

'Claude? Zis is for a man, ze name, no?'

'No, stupid. *Cloud*. As in sky. You know, *nuage*.'

'Ah. 'E iz dark cloud, no?' She smiled. It was her first English joke.

'What do you know about ponies! I think I'll call him Telly or we'll come to blows. Can I try him?'

'Of course.'

Tiz rammed on her hat and led Telly away to saddle up. Harriet noted the expression on her face. She had felt like that when Japheth was first put into her arms. The damage to Tiz's psyche if she did not get the pony now would be more than twice the sum of the damage if the scheme had never been mooted. It was terrifying how ideas, as casual as breath, took on monstrous solidity and, before one knew what was happening, crash-landed on the exits.

While they were waiting for Tiz, Mrs Bloodwort ran through the routine.

'All you have to do is feed him at the same time each day – after school, usually. Brush him down with the body brush. Comb his mane and tail, trim the fetlocks and clean his face and bum with a damp sponge. Pick the hooves – *away* from the frog, remember – put fly repellant on his head, clean the water trough. If he's got cracks in his hooves put petroleum jelly on them. Always check the field for ragwort and pull it up. Scoop up the droppings, check if his teeth need filing, clean the tack and the saddle – saddle soap only, of course. And make sure it's dry.'

Harriet was paralysed. It sounded like the schedule of a Victorian scullery maid. 'Is that it?'

'Well, there's his injection. And he has to be wormed every six weeks. New shoes the same. And check for lice and put powder on if necessary. And don't whatever you do let him stuff on new grass. That's very important. Are you sure you know what you're doing?'

'Possibly not. But I'm sure my daughter does. She's been on a course.'

'I daresay. But Mum has to check that she's doing it all, doesn't she? You'll be the one paying the vet.'

'True. Why are you selling him?'

'My daughter needs something bigger. She's in the house. Can't bear to watch people looking him over.'

'Oh dear.' It was spooky to know they were being spied on by a heart-broken child. Something else to look forward to.

Tiz walked the pony into the field, her eyes on stalks of delight. She put him into trot. All Harriet could think of as the two globular bottoms bumped around the field were the fifty fatalities each year that resulted from this association of man and beast. Every minute Tiz was in the saddle was a year off her own life. Motherhood. Give me anthrax any day.

'She's got a nice little seat, your daughter. But you're right. I think you had better think it over for a day or two.'

'How could I refuse now? Look at them. I could as soon drive a wedge between Marks and Spencer.'

'Just as you like. I take it you've made arrangements for a paddock?'

'Of course,' lied Harriet.

'You can't take him today, anyhow. What about Sunday morning? Then he'll have the day to acclimatize.'

'What do you think, Semi?'

'I ink I miss ze match of Cameroon now.'

'It doesn't start for at least a week, you know that, Semi. I do think you could try and look at the world from Tiz's point of view, sometimes. You do want to be a child psychologist, don't you?'

'Yes. But not 'orse *psychologiste*. Madame Funkel, since I am *chez vous* what do I do? I walk ze dogs. I feed stick insect—'

'Kill stick insect.'

'—Delivair kitten, clean fish tank, find rabbit zat 'as go onto M25 and I am keep awake all ze night by 'amstair zat come to life at 'alf past eleven! I come 'ere to look after children, no? Not *jardin zoologique*. I did not believe about you English and ze animals until now. Why don't you talk to *me* some time?'

'I thought I did.'

'Must I 'ave fur and tail, then maybe? You 'ave more to say to Gelée et Crème Anglaise zan to me.'

Mrs Bloodwort raised an eyebrow. 'Time of the month?'

'My dear Semi, I had no idea you felt neglected.' Harriet had staggered back a pace. Semi was in a passion for which she was totally unprepared. It was true that the hamster was on the razzle from bedtime until *Farming Today*, but Harriet had not realized Semi could hear it.

'I sorry,' said Semi, 'but I do not give ze fart about 'orse.'
'Right.'

Mrs Bloodwort murmured in Harriet's ear. 'Get her on Evening Primrose oil.'

Semi and Harriet were locked into separate but matching glooms on the way home. They were held up by an accident in Smallfield, hard by the Dog and Duck. Harriet watched the customers at the white plastic tables in the pub garden. Office workers mainly. Young people deep in the mating vortex, whose libido was bottled up all day at work but uncorked as soon as the bell went. The body language of the young men and women, straining towards each other across the tables, bright-eyed, verging on the hysteria that could only be relieved by sex, made Harriet gloomier than ever. It was like watching ants in coitus, unaware of the boot poised above their heads.

She was jolted as she thought she recognized Damian de St Croix. He was coming out of the pub carrying a tray of pints and macadamia nuts. It looked remarkably like him. He had said he lived in Reigate, so that would fit. But then – he would be working. Quarter to seven. Just getting off at Victoria most likely. It could not be him. The disappointment was shocking and unexpected, as if she had fallen down a pot hole in the middle of the high street.

Tiz was chattering about an incident in the playground. 'Don't you think it was unfair, Mum?'

'What?'

'Are you all right? You're sweating.'

'Am I? Yes, I'm all right. What were you saying?'

'I said, don't you think it was unfair that Gavin refused to kiss the wall?'

'What?'

'Mum, you weren't *listening*. You never *listen*.'

'I am listening, darling. I just didn't take it in.'

'I said, don't you think it was unfair? We were playing forfeits, and when it was Gavin's turn Serena said he had to kiss the wall and he wouldn't.'

'Kiss the wall? Is there something wrong with Serena?'

'No. Why?'

'Well – it seems a bit – well – lewd. For someone of her age.'

'What does that mean? Oh I know. Mrs Riddle said Matthew was lewd when he said the mop cream looked like someone had jerked off on the peaches. Honestly, Mum, we're not, like, little kids, you know.'

'Sorry. I thought you were.'

'Poor Mum. I suppose you think we should still be playing with hoops and things and drip around in Laura Ashley smocks.'

'That would be lovely.'

'Dream on, Mum. I like Matthew. He's circumcized, you know. Do you know what that means, Mum?'

'Yes. How do you know he's circumcized?'

'He showed me. I suppose you think that's awful.'

'Well – I'd be happier if I thought you could spell it.'

'What difference would that make?'

'Oh, I don't know. You always seem to be studying things you can't spell, these days. What was it last term – the Dissolution of the Monasteries? And now it's fibre optics. It's to do with putting carts before horses, darling. After all, you are only twelve.'

'Not for long. Anyway, Mozart was seven when he wrote his first cacophony. You're *always* telling me that. You can't have it both ways, Mum.'

Harriet sped out of the traffic jam, overtook a cyclist on a blind bend and almost killed them all.

'Mum! What's got into you?'

'Sorry.' Harriet bitterly knew what had got into her. The image of Damian de St Croix. Like a blood disease whose symptoms do not appear until it has taken hold. That spurt of excitement when she thought she had caught sight of him had forced the covers off her consciousness. Now she understood her odd fits and seizures. Sexual hysteria. Harriet was terrified. It was too embarrassing to confide in anyone. A sentence of solitary confinement. Condemned to go through the motions of post-modern Britain like the ghost of Madame Bovary, her body depth-charged with the exploding ferrets of lust and despair. The Devils of Dorking. Purgatives were called for. The burying of entrails at crossroads. Self-mutilation, torture and death.

'Amanda Rockwell's got a shellsuit,' said Tiz. '*Well* sad.'

* * *

'What are you doing, Mum?'

She had thought Mungo was watching the World Cup. 'Just looking for an upholsterer.'

'Why don't you use the Yellow Pages? That's just residential numbers.'

'Oh, is it?'

'Aren't you coming to watch? It's a crap game, but we'll probably be out of the competition soon.'

'Who are they playing?'

'Ireland. Huh. The Rest of the World, more like. Oh come on, Mum. The crowd's yelling "We won't pay no poll tax." It's great.'

'In a minute, darling.'

'OK.'

As soon as he was gone Harriet whipped the directory out again and continued her search under 'de'. Then she remembered the flat would be in his girlfriend's name. She flung the directory at the four-seater sofa, then tried to tear it up. Warren put his head round the door.

'Why don't you come and watch the match, sweetheart? The boys would appreciate it.'

'Yes, all right. Who's winning?'

'Ireland have scored, but it was like an own goal. See, McMahon kinda lost contact at the edge of the box. It sorta came off his foot and the Irish guy just banged it in.'

'Can't they disallow it?'

'Ho*nee*. It wasn't even off-side.'

'Oh dear.'

'Are you coming?'

'I'll just finish my drink.'

'You should watch it, sweetheart. Alcohol doesn't solve anything.'

'But I don't have a problem, Warren.'

'U-huh.'

Harriet squeezed onto the sofa between Semi/Japh. The fact that Ireland were not leading 10–0 had raised wild hopes. Even Tiz was bouncing up and down on the carpet.

Japh was in a frenzy. 'They've got to free up Barnesy. Look at him – he's so fucking hemmed in. Sorry, Mum, but it's so frustrating. They've got to play the sweeper, we'll never get anywhere like this. He might just as well be playing in a shark-proof cage. I mean – God.'

Semi stroked his hair and made cooing noises.

'I thought Lineker was meant to score the goals,' said Tiz.

'Lineker's an idle bum,' said Warren. 'He does nothing for half an hour and then misses.'

'Like Wagner,' said Harriet.

'Look, here goes Barnesy—'

A communal gasp went up as Barnes/Hermes wended the ball past three defenders with loopy grace and lammed it into the back of the net. All but Harriet leaped to their feet yelling and fell on each other's necks.

'I knew he could do it,' said Japh, flopping exhausted into Semi's arms.

'You could have fooled me,' said Harriet.

Japheth laid his head back. 'God, I wish I could do that. Just once. I'd die happy.'

'Well you've got four years to practise,' said Tiz.

At breakfast on the morning of 16 June, Japh called for prayers that Bobby Robson would use the sweeper system in the game against Holland. Harriet was indignant, even as she poured Semi her fresh Moroccan coffee. Japh and Semi joined hands and bowed heads.

'That's a bit rich, Japh. You're an atheist.'

'Not since we drew with Ireland.'

'I don't think you can get God on loan, like an umbrella from the library.'

'Ssh, Mother. Anyway, it's your fault if I'm an atheist. You should have provided me with a religious background so that I could rebel and thereby come to self-knowledge.'

'That's not fair. I always took you to the Christingle service. Until you tried to fry the marshmallow on the candle and the church had to be evacuated. Haven't you got an exam tomorrow?'

'No. The last one is next Tuesday. I thought you would never ask.'

'Sorry, I've been a bit distracted, what with British Telecom and so on.'

'Bloody nag. I swear it whinnied all night. How long is it going to stay in the garden?'

'Just until we find a paddock nearby. I didn't realize Tiz would want to get up at six to clean its teeth. I don't want her cycling alone at that time. It's bad enough her riding alone. Are you sure you wouldn't like to go with her sometimes, Semi?'

'You mean, walk behind ze 'orse?'

'Or in front. It's up to you.'

Semi drew her wonderful link sausage lips into a ball. Her eyelids drooped. 'No tank you. Unless it is a "must".'

'How long does this football thing go on, Japh?'

'It's only three weeks, Mother. Every four years. Do you think you can hold out?'

Japheth pushed away his untouched *croissant au jambon* and left the room. Semi followed.

Harriet leant over the sink, her forehead on the mixer tap. Did Damian watch football? If so, he must be very frustrated at present, having to play 'Jellicle Cats' etcetera, while his heroes toiled in the Italian sun. She could imagine that his somewhat desperate exuberance was only a step from hooliganism. Some of the worst football hooligans were solicitors from Southampton. Urbanity warped that primitive energy that she longed to be inside her – No. This had to stop. Even if it meant volunteering for the citizens advice bureau, she was Going to be Sensible.

Cries of 'Yes!!! Yes!!!' drifted up from the den as Harriet lay on her bed listening to an Icelandic saga on Radio Three. How much simpler life was then. Characters with twenty-five consonants in their names and nothing to do all day but gut fish. And they all seemed to have relations who would volunteer to go and stick a meat cleaver in the heads of people who pinched their parking space. In those days Damian would have waylaid Warren on his way to work at the Blubber Exchange, split him down the middle and come to claim her by right of conquest. If he wanted her, that is, for which she had no evidence. She sat up. How could she think of poor Warren in that way? Presumably because there was no possibility of reciprocal arrangements. Warren did not have the imagination for adultery, and was in any case one of the forty-five per cent of grown men who preferred golf to sex.

Whereas for Harriet it would not be the first lapse. The previous one was currently Minister for Overdeveloped Countries.

The Icelandic saga palled. She picked up the *Evening Standard*. Poll-tax capping endorsed by High Court. Woman found dead in house with seventy-five dogs. 'She was very quiet,' said neighbours. Link discovered between pop-up toasters and marital breakdown. On the showbiz pages an interview with *Bognor Walk* star Shirley Lamb, who is rehearsing the part of the lovelorn matron in *Wipers!* Shirley was frightfully excited at the prospect of being in a musical after a gap of fifteen years. Shirley has been taking singing lessons and was working out in the basement of her elegant home in Highgate, which she shares with biscuit manufacturer husband Bob, and their two children Apple and Silage. Apple and Silage were at a 'wonderful' boarding school in Scotland. 'The separation is Hell,' says Shirley. 'But they wanted to go. During the holidays I try to spend all my spare time with them, even if it means they have to sit and watch me sleep!'

Harriet just got to the basin in time.

England continued to progress, thrashing Egypt 1–0. Japheth sat Sport Paper 3 on the day England played Belgium. The self-lacerating pessimism that had seen England off had turned to incredulous hope, try as they all might to sandbag it with caution. The Cameroon showdown was tricky, as Semi was torn in her allegiance. Japheth and Mungo made an effort to be fair to Cameroon, praising the way they strung their passes together. Consequently Semi bore the fact that they were creamed 3–2 with fortitude. Warren was forced to withdraw remarks about Gary Lineker.

There were no more jobs for Harriet. She resigned herself to a summer following the progress of *Wipers!* from a distance, and trotting behind British Telecom for hours to liven things up.

Dotty came to tea. She was worried about some Siamese tomatoes she had bought at Tesco that, according to Dotty, had 'Chernobyl' written all over them. Harriet assured her that natural radiation was much worse than anything a tomato could emit.

'Tell that to the tomato,' said Dotty. Tomatoes apart, she

had begun to adjust to life without Fin. Neighbours took her to sequence dancing. She had enrolled on a word processing course so that she could write her memoirs of the War. A teacher had invited her to talk to nine-year-olds about her historical childhood. The children were so enthralled by the tales of middens and dripping sandwiches that she had been recommended to other schools, and was all set to build up a lecture circuit. Harriet congratulated Dotty on her resilience. Dotty sniffed.

'It's because my memories are happy ones, Harriet. At least when Fin was here he was there, if you take my meaning.'

Harriet did. Warren was in South America that time, at the invitation of a mysterious business man who claimed that vast swathes of Columbian poppy fields were owned by the Tory Party.

On the day of the semi-final against Germany everybody except Harriet had diarrhoea. Japheth was so pale and tense he could have been about to face the electric chair. Mungo burbled about Wright's ability to mark Klinsman until Japheth snapped and hit him. Harriet could hear them crashing about in the den as she did her make-up. She ignored the noise and concentrated on her face as she had another audition, for an HIV cousellor on *Casualty*. She did not expect to get it, and was not bothered, not least because she had another project uppermost in her mind.

Whether it was the ashes to glory example of the World Cup, or the obstacle-flattening gene essential to her profession, Harriet had decided to nobble Damian de St Croix. Strange how simple the operation seemed once she had made up her mind. The affair would be the no-belts-no-pins-no-pads variety, of course. Happily, these days women did not have to resort to murder or suicide to quench their lust. She did wonder if Damian was being exploited, but not for long. He would be happy to oblige, and anyway, one did not ask the calamine lotion if it wanted to soothe sunburn.

The logistics seemed straightforward. She could stay in town after the audition and, because of the semi-final, she would not be missed. She would phone to make sure Warren had arrived home, but knew that if she said she was about to throw herself off the Post Office Tower no one would bat an eyelid. It was hurtful, but some justification for the deceit.

In Boots on Victoria station for some HIV-repellant spermicide, seriously cold feet hit the pit of her stomach. She had met him here. She had been in his company for only a few hours. Was she completely mad? A repressed nymphomaniac or a New Woman with the confidence to explore her own sexuality? The trouble with modern sexual codes, she reflected as she watched the self-absorbed swill of humanity in the station, was that half the population still behaved with the petticoated purity of the 1950s, and the other half were having sex on demand as a basic human right. The trick was knowing which half one was with, or indeed, to which one belonged.

She read the counsellor's lines with shrill impatience, and afterwards circulated around John Lewis for a couple of hours, followed by another couple trying to find the way out. At quarter to seven she left a message for Damian at the theatre, asking him to meet her afterwards at a pub round the corner. Then she went into a kebab house and somehow managed to pass the time until she could decently go to The Loaded Virgin two hours early. The phone call home had gone as expected. Mungo had taken the message and cut her off.

The patrons of the Loaded Virgin were crowded round a television in the public bar. Their reactions to events on screen made Harriet think that the public had not come far since villagers had crowded round the pump to hear readings from *Pamela*, and burst into tears and rung the mourning bell when she died.

At the corner table, where she sat shredding Tetley beer mats, some punks joined her at half-time. They were analysing Waddle's shot from the thirty-five-yard line. One of them had two nose studs. Harriet wondered if snot oozed out of the holes when he had a cold.

'Wonna beer?'

'No, thank you. I'm just waiting for a friend.'

They chortled. 'If we win, 'e'll come. If we don't, 'e won't,' said Two Studs.

The second half started and they returned to the mêlée around the television set. As the half progressed the bays and howls of the drinkers crescendoed. Couples of all types stood on benches and clung to each other in terror. At one point there was a death, apparently. Women wept, and were comforted by their menfolk. Harriet looked at her watch. She repressed the image of Damian reading the note to the brass section and inviting their comments.

The crowd shifted, groaned, sagged.

'Have they lost?' said Harriet. No one took any notice. Many of them were in a state of collapse. One could have papered the walls with fuckin' 'ells. Damian was not late, but it would do no harm to check that the message had been picked up. The performance would just have ended.

The phone was in a sleazy basement corridor that reeked of old cigar smoke and the adjacent sewers. Among the graffiti someone had drawn a cross, with the message *AIDS – STOP in the NAME of LOVE*. Harriet hesitated. Did it have her name on it? She became aware that the contrast between herself, in her Wombles jacket costing £465 plus VAT, and the detritus of her surroundings, might be a fateful allegory. But the-show-must-go-on habit was too deeply ingrained.

'Hello. I just wanted to check if a message for Damian de St Croix had been collected.'

'Hold on – he's just walked out the door. I'll go and call him.'

'No! I don't want to speak to him.' But it was too late. Seconds lumbered by. Then Damian picked up the phone.

'Who is this?'

'Kidneys. I wondered if you got my note.'

'Christ. Don't you know what's going on?'

'The football, you mean?'

'Right. I'm off to a pub with a TV.'

'But there's one here.'

'I'm meeting some mates. Christ. The whole fucking future of the whole fucking country's at stake, woman.'

'Well I'm fucking sorry.'

'Drop dead.' He replaced the receiver.

Dignity, reflected Harriet on the train, is a funny old thing. Like a chain, it is as strong as its weakest link. But she knew she had not been crying because her dignity had been spattered all over

Southern Region. If the scheme had gone through she would have been crying too. As Dotty put it when Tiz burst into tears on first seeing British Telecom in his new tack, 'She's not crying. She's leaking.'

7

The mutual whinnies of Tiz and British Telecom woke the household early. Warren brought Harriet some coffee.

'See you on Saturday, sweetheart.'

'What? Where are you going now?'

'Hong Kong. Didn't I tell you? They want to make a propaganda feature about the boat people.'

'But I've got tickets for *The Saucepan, Its Lid, the Lid's Knob and An Episode of The Victorian Kitchen* tonight.'

'Sorry. Take Anita. I have to go. We lost, by the way. Japh's real cut up about it. Try and distract him if you can.'

'That's Semi's job now, surely.'

'Hon*ee*—'

Harriet was not even sure if Japh was at home. Once dressed she tiptoed to his room and listened at the door. Her heart beat high with rage as she heard Semi's low voice answer his, but all she could make out was 'Waddle' and 'suicide'. To burst in and catch them in the act of discussing penalty shoot-outs would seriously undermine her authority, so she knocked first.

An hour later Semi wandered down and pushed the Hoover round for a bit. Then Japh appeared and said they were going to the Water Palace.

'Semi doesn't have to walk Tiz tonight, does she, Mum? It's so expensive to get in, it's not worth it if we have to rush back.'

'All right. But I do think she should do it at least once before she leaves. I mean, if she's going to have children herself.'

'What's that supposed to mean?'

'Nothing.'

'She wouldn't be daft enough to let her kids ride, anyway.'

'That's an insult. Just go, will you.'

'What's the matter with you?'

'Nothing. It must be the curse.'

Harriet had never told the children she had been gutted after the birth of Tiziana. It was useful to be able to retire to bed with a hot water bottle occasionally for no particular reason.

After they had left, she went to the phone and made an honest attempt to find a partner for *The Saucepan* etc., but none of her friends was free. After the rejection of the night before this seemed like a plot to isolate her from human contact. She sought her friend the sherry bottle and, tormented by the thought that the whole of London would by now have heard of the failed seduction and that the whole of London included Warren, she got through several tumblers of the stuff, but failed to come up with an explanation as to why she had not thought of that in the first place.

The doorbell rang. She was expecting a delivery of Snow Goose table mats from the cancer catalogue.

It was Damian. At least she thought it was. Despite the season he was obscured by crash helmet, white scarf and floor-length leathers.

'Hi.'

'Good morning. What are you doing here?'

'Dunno really. Come the dawn I felt a bit bad about last night. I mean, you do choose your moment, don't you.'

'The wrong one, obviously.'

'What did you want to see me about?'

'What?'

'You wanted to see me. You left a note, remember? What are you on – aluminium pills?'

'Sorry. I didn't sleep very well.' Harriet tried to look grim, to hide her relief that he had not guessed her purpose. Well why should he? It had not been on the news, only in her head. She brightened up, tossed her hair about. 'It wasn't important. I happened to be in town for an audition and I ran into this rap musician I thought you'd like to meet. Come in, now you're here. You can have the grand tour after all.'

'No thanks. Just the bedrooms.'

'Oh, for Heaven's sake!'

'You've no sense of humour, you.'

He followed her into the kitchen and she poured him a glass of water while he removed his gear. She was glad he had come. His actual presence, in her own house, was so prosaic it restored her vision of normality, revealed the scaffolding behind the film set of illusion.

'We woz robbed, of course.'

'What do you mean?'

'That wanker of an umpire shouldn't have given Platt off-side for the second goal – and Braehme should have been sent off.'

'This off-side thing seems to be a bit Erewhon-ish, doesn't it?'

'Eh?'

'Well I don't see how you can blame the strikers if they're not properly covered.'

'No, no. You don't understand.' He took some apples from the bowl and demonstrated. 'You see, unless he's in his own half, it depends whether he's nearer the enemy's goal-line than the ball – unless there are two defenders nearer to it – unless of course he's got it from a goal-kick or a throw-in or—'

'Yes, I see. Would you like to see the pony?'

They strolled down the garden to what Harriet referred to as the Wilderness, where British Telecom was temporarily fenced in. Damian was surprisingly up on horticulture, and had some advice on lily beetle.

'Kill the bastards. At the beginning of the season just pick them and squeeze their heads off with your thumbnail.'

'Yuch.'

'It's a buzz! If you're too prudish you can drown them in petrol.'

'How come you know so much?'

'My dad's a market gardener. It's in the genes.'

'What a rich brew they must be.'

He chuckled and looked at her, his eyes doing a slalom between the flags of her body language. 'What was that rap guy's name?

'What?'

'You know – that guy you were with last night.'

'Oh – him.' Harriet turned rapidly up the garden path. 'Paul something. He never told me his other name.' She was now bolting for the safety of the utility room. Once inside she began to toss clothes into the machine.

Damian watched her from the door. 'You don't put black jeans in with white nylon. Don't you know anything?'

'How dare you. There isn't a stitch of nylon in this house.'

'A fibre snob. I might have known.' He strolled over to the basket and picked up a black bra. 'Whose is this?'

'Tiziana's.' Harriet stood with her back to him, one hand on the Bold-All-in-One, the other sweating freely. She was paralysed by a high-speed jet of pheromones from his warm, hesitant body, stunned like a calf before the slaughter.

'It looks more like your size to me, Kidneys.'

'I wish you wouldn't call me that. I was drunk that night.'

'You call yourself that!'

'Well the joke's over.' She turned round to snatch the bra from his hand, and was clamped into his arms, nay, halfway down his throat, all thoughts of his unsuitability and the lightness of rectitude burned up in phosphorescent coils of lust. Glued together by the teeth, somehow jeans, knickers and T-shirts joined the pile of dirty washing as he kneaded her breasts and buttocks with the practised ease of a TV chef. But the moment approached where pulling bits off each other no longer sufficed. He pressed her hard against the washing machine, so that the programme jumped from 'Pre-wash' to 'Rinse'. Harriet straddled over the porthole, her bare bottom comfortably jammed on top of the programme selector buttons. 'Now—' she muttered. 'Now!'

'Hang on!'

'What? Oh fuck—'

'Yeah, hang on. Where are the bloody things—' He rummaged through his jeans on the floor.

Harriet's teeth were clenched. 'Come *on*—'

Damian sat back on his heels to put the rubber on. 'Come down here on the washing. It's comfy.'

'No. Someone might come to the door.'

'You'd better put your clothes back on if that's what you're worried about.'

'Are you going to rabbit on all day? We could break for lunch, if you like.'

'All right, Mrs!' He grabbed her by the hips. 'Uurgh. What's that?'

'What?'

'Is that a scar?' He prodded among her pubic hair to get a better look.

'It's where I had a Caesarian.'

'Yuch. I've never seen one. It's gross. How do they get a baby through that? It's too small.'

'Well I suppose it's shrunk. The skin stretches when you're pregnant.'

'Did you have stitches or clamps?'

Harriet grabbed hold of his head. 'Take a closer look.'

Harriet knew the affair could not last once the younger children had broken up for the summer holidays. She decided to make the most of it. Its inevitably short duration enabled her not to think very much about those aspects that disturbed her – like his white socks, and the thought of Tiziana's reaction were she to find out. Tiz would have no hesitation in hitching them both to British Telecom and dragging them round the M25. This frisson of danger was supposed to be one of the perks, but Harriet felt it showed her age that deceit now filled her with more dread than delight.

It was amazing that the arrangements for meeting were no less fraught than before the sexual revolution. She could not bring herself to perform in her own house again, not least because Japheth and Semi were liable to interrupt them when they were not at it themselves. They parked in a spot overlooking Ranmore Common once, but were interrupted by a policeman warning them not to leave their handbags in the car because of a spate of thefts. Hotels were out. She might be recognized from *Not in Front of the Hamster*.

That only left his flat, when the girlfriend was away serving in-flight dinners for the nation. Fortunately, this was quite often, but it was not a comfortable choice either. The girl's intimate possessions were everywhere, and while Harriet took some comfort from her dubious taste – the flat had more floral borders than the gardens of Great Dixter – there was the nagging sense that she was letting the side down, gazumping another woman when she was publicly committed to solidarity.

On the other hand, the ambience of Reigate, its hills covered with snaking streets of Edwardian houses redolent of parlour palms and Dr Crippen, seemed eminently suitable. Although the thick lace of yore was replaced by Austrian blinds, those bay windows were undoubtedly meant to conceal dark deeds.

There was surprisingly little evidence of musicianly clobber, just a keyboard, some CDs and a bust of Leonard Bernstein.

'I hope you change the sheets,' said Harriet as they lay sated on the low-slung pine bed. Its stumpy finials and cloud-covered duvet made Harriet feel she was laid out in a shopping catalogue.

The midday sun irradiated her from without, the heat of swollen flesh warmed from within. Her muscles still throbbed deeply, ebbing through her body like an anaesthetic. She wondered which bits still did that in view of the operation.

Damian sighed. 'You can't let go, can you.'

'What do you mean? I practically split open.'

'I don't mean that. I mean what are you thinking about? Your imagination's in a vice of trivia. It doesn't matter how turned on you are from the neck down, you're thinking about something else.'

'Oh God. Don't, Damian. You're going to say something like *Why aren't you there for me*? aren't you. What did you expect – Elvira Madigan? That's all male fantasy crap. My life is in a vice of trivia. Everybody's is. Oh go on, say it. *I want something more—*'

'Supposing I did? You couldn't even say the word.'

'Damian, please. I know what you're thinking – I'm emotionally repressed or something. You wonder if I've ever really been in love. You don't know anything. You don't understand anything.'

She assumed the foetal position and sank her teeth into her knees

Damian was remorseful. He tried to hold her. 'Just tell me about it.'

'Oh shut up.' Reduced to oblivion she might be, but the grate of a cliché still got through. 'It's just – when you're young you think – huh – it's always going to be like this and – then you realize it never is and – you see your own k-kids g-going over the same cliff and – you wish they d-didn't have to and – you d-don't know why you're alive any m-more—' The tears broke through.

'Hey, that's crap, Harriet. I mean – you're here. *We're* here. We have brilliant sex. Things do still happen. It's just crap, that.' She sobbed into the pillow. He caressed her hip. 'Listen, I think you're just depressed because you didn't get that part. Don't worry, there'll be others. You know what it's like – if you hang on long enough everybody else drops dead.'

Harriet gurgled with despair as this missile sailed into the void. Damian snuggled up behind her. She could feel his penis harden between her buttocks. He gently moved her leg and slipped inside her.

After this mould-breaking scene the relationship entered its elegiac phase. Harriet dropped her resistance to Real Feelings. And because the passion was more sincere its life expectancy was foreshortened. Harriet began to chafe at the restrictions imposed by sincerity. Damian got fed up with changing the sheets. The school holidays promised a timely termination.

The day before Tiz broke up they took a ride on the Docklands Light Railway. They discussed their travel plans almost as though they would meet again. Damian was off to the Seychelles, Harriet to Bude.

'Warren travels so much he'd just as soon stay at home really.'

'This Warren person doesn't exactly look after you, does he.'

'He does his best. Do you intend to look after your wife when you have one?'

'Yeah. I do, actually. I know I screw around now, but when I've got a missus and kids, that's it. They'll be what I live for. Otherwise, what's the point?'

Harriet half laughed, half choked.

'I'm not going to Bude, Mum. Semi's invited me to stay with her family. So I'll be spending the summer in St Honoré Les Sables. It's in Brittany, if you're interested.'

'Japh of course I'm interested.' Harriet was also cut to the quick. 'Couldn't you have broken it more gently? I mean, I know at your age you don't want to come with the family, but – why do you have to make everything such a face-off? Does Dad know?'

'I'd tell him if he were ever at home.'

'Don't exaggerate, Japh. That's just an excuse.'

'He wouldn't say anything if I did tell him. That's just experience.'

'Are you sure you're expected? Wouldn't Semi's mother have got in touch with me?'

'I'm over eighteen, Mum. I don't actually need your permission.'

'You'll be out of the country when your A-Level results come out.'

'Yes, but not out of the known world, Mum. Mungo can get them for me. And Mum—'

'What?'

'My A-Level results don't matter. I've been given a try-out for Tattenham Drovers and I'm pretty sure I'll get in.'

There was a long silence. 'Japh, could you wait until I'm off the lavatory before we discuss this?'

Warren was at a financial conference at a five-star hotel in Braemar.

'Listen, sweetheart, don't panic. I'm sure we can defer his place for a year. He might have come to his senses by then. If not – well, frankly, there's not a lot we can do. At least he'll have a job. Footballers these days get paid a fortune.'

'For endorsing Y-fronts.'

'Why not? How do you think *TV* is financed, for God's sake? Listen, I have to go. Relax, sweetheart, he may not make it. Most of the kids who get to the top have been in training centres for years.'

'I suppose you realize we've booked a ten-berth former alms-house.'

'It's only one less. OK, two. Hell, we should have asked him before we booked. It's only natural he'd want to go off on his own at his age.'

'Not like this. He's supposed to hitch-hike to Guam with a group of chums.'

'Why don't you ask Dotty? I guess she won't have any plans for a vacation this year.'

'Well—'

'Think about it. She could help out. It would be more of a rest for you.'

'Only from the neck down.'

Dotty was delighted in principle. But after the Iraqi tanks had flattened Kuwait she was not so sure.

'It's like the invasion of Poland all over again,' she moaned. 'I think I should stay here and keep my head down.'

'But Dotty, I don't think Saddam Hussein has got his eye on Cornwall.'

'How do you know? There's going to be a war, I can feel it in my bones. We were at Broadstairs when the last one started. I remember Fin had just gone to lie down. He'd eaten some rotten welks. The landlady was a real oddball. She'd only eat fat off the meat. Gave the lean to the Pekinese. It was hot weather – just like now. You felt like they'd announced the end of the world. You young people can't imagine what it was like.'

'It's not for want of telling, Dotty dear. If you're that scared you had better come away. London is a much more likely target than Bude.'

'That's true. It's so hot, I could do with a sea breeze. And Fin always said summer wasn't summer without a dip in the sea.'

'You mean – you swim?'

'Of course. Don't you?'

'Yes – but – Look, think it over. It's a very long drive, you know. By the time you get back the benefits of sea-bathing have generally worn off, I find.'

'Then why do you go?'

'Why indeed. So you won't?'

'What?'

'Come.'

'I didn't say that. Tiz would like me to, I expect. We can sag off for a sausage in batter while you're struggling with your aubergines.'

Harriet paled. 'Dotty, promise me you're joking.'

The sight of British troops, some younger than Japh, landing in Saudi Arabia, together with the prospect of Dotty eating sausages in her bathers, put Harriet off the whole idea of going on holiday.

'We won't be able to relax with our minds in the Gulf, Warren. It seems so frivolous with our lads out there.'

'Sweetheart, don't be naive. They aren't our lads, fortunately. And we've paid in advance.'

So Bude it was. Or rather, Trewithers Lodge, which was scattered, along with several other tasteful conversions, around the mouth of an inlet several miles up the coast. The ten-hour journey was characterized by tense discussions about Dotty's cache of Werthers Original, which ended, to Harriet's satisfaction, when they had to stop for Tiz to be sick. Mungo was in a mood because Japh was not there. Japh's absence brooded on them all. As Confucius might have said, when a corner is removed from a triangle, the wind of change is the first thing through the gap.

'Is there a hosepipe ban?' Harriet glared at the trickle of water.

'That's a shower, honey.'

'I know. It just makes you wonder how bad things are down here.'

'Maybe there's an airlock. Here, let me try.' Warren fiddled masterfully with the taps. The trickle became a drip. 'I guess they haven't turned the water on yet. I'll go see the caretaker. Jesus, this country. How do you think they manage in Las Vegas? It's in the middle of the fucking desert.'

'Ssh. Dotty will hear.'

'So? I don't have to creep around watching my language because Dotty's here, do I?'

'It was your idea to invite her.'

'Why didn't you refuse? You know I sometimes say these things before I've had time to think about it. Jesus. What are we going to do? I can't live without a shower.'

'Hire a desalination plant? Look, I'm hot, tired, I've got to unpack and cook dinner. Just shut up and go and get the bloody caretaker.'

'We'll eat out tonight.'

'Oh no, I can't go to a restaurant. I must smell like a kipper.'

'Then what do you suggest, sweetheart?'

'A picnic? In the car. This is a British holiday.'

'Don't I know it. I'm going to demand a rebate. The infrastructure of this country is like some fucking African republic.'

'Ssh! This place must be full of *Guardian* readers. You'd lose your job.'

'Yeah. And you'd lose yours.' Warren's face, red and glistening under the damp curls, was unlovely. Harriet caught the flicker of guilt in his eyes before he turned away and slammed out. She chucked the lavatory dolly after him.

'What do you mean by that! Warren! Oh, no—'

The door had rebounded in its own draught and the dolly had gone straight through to hit a print of eighteenth-century Trewithers, which crashed to the floor. The glass had broken into a spider's web over the image of fishwives suckling their sprogs at the cottage door. She picked it up and took it through to The Room. Dotty stepped gingerly down the stairs. She had changed into cycling shorts, a Breton T-shirt and flip-flops.

'Everything all right, Harriet?'

'Does it look like it?' She waved the print at her. 'Oh – I'm sorry, Dotty. I just had a row with Warren about the water and suddenly he's accusing me of – well – sponging off him! The nerve. And it's he who doesn't like me working. Oh God.' She sank onto the sofa. 'Holidays. They're worse than bloody Christmas.'

'Well, Harriet, as mother used to say, the stall be clean when the ox be gone.'

'What?'

'I think she meant people are messy, love. You can't have one without the other.'

'Suppose not.'

'You're both tired after the journey. Where are the kids?'

'The children? They went to the beach.'

'Will Tiz be all right? It was always Japh kept an eye on her, wasn't it?'

'Don't worry. The sea's very calm at the moment. No Atlantic breakers. Pity, really. I love the terrifying noise they make.'

Dotty sucked her lips. 'These flagstones are dead slippery. There should be fitted carpet. Now look, Harriet, I'll go home, if you like. Perhaps it's not such a good idea having a—'

'Witness? No. Do stay, Dotty. I feel it might be quite useful to have an ally.'

'Right. I won't mention it again. But if you change your mind—'

'I won't. You don't feel like putting the kettle on, do you? There's only a trickle of water, you may have to wait a while.'

'No matter. I've got flat shoes.'

Dotty pottered off to the kitchen. Flat shoes. Harriet could remember saying something about flat shoes to Damian, but not when or where. Her eyes rested on the armchair beside the huge blackened fireplace. If only he were sitting in it. If only they could vacuum seal that part of their lives, or their dependants would go on a world cruise for a year or two. Her knickers began to zing at the remembered shafts of pleasure. She slowly unzipped her jeans. Dotty had put the radio on. 'Are you all right? she called from the kitchen.

'Yes, fine. Thanks, Dotty.'

'The Yanks have landed in Saudi Arabia.'

'Oh dear.'

'Bet it's not as hot as here.'

'No.'

'Eee, I'd like to get my hands on that Saddam whatsisname. Mind you, I'll bet he drinks Carling Black Label.'

Harriet sighed and shuddered as the ripples broke on her shores.

The beach was too hot for Warren's freckled skin type. Nor did he respond well to sand in the Camembert. On day two he suggested to Mungo over breakfast that he might like to come to the golf course. Mungo, on his fourth bowl of Frosties, looked alarmed.

'I don't play, Dad.'

'You could learn. There's nothing to it. I'd be happy to teach you.'

'Why didn't you teach him at home, then?' said Tiz, noting that her bemused brother was lost for words.

'Yeah,' said Mungo. 'That's a good point.'

'There's no time at home. You guys are always doing your own thing. That's what vacations are for, isn't it? They're supposed to give us time to do things together.'

'Yes,' said Tiz. 'You're supposed to do things together with *us*.'

'Oh great. Some vacation for me. I'm the one who needs a vacation, for God's sake. I work. Your whole lives are a vacation.

'No they're not. We work much harder than you because we

have homework. You won't let the boys get jobs in case they're too tired for school.'

'OK, OK.' Warren got up violently. 'Sorry I asked.'

Mungo squirmed. 'It's not that I don't want to, Dad.'

'Then what?'

'Well—'

'Forget it. I'll see you guys later.'

Mungo pushed his Frosties away. His face was contorted with the effort of understanding the strange wave of – thingies that swept over him.

Tiz regarded him with lofty pity. 'I don't blame you for not wanting to go. A – golf is the stupidest game in the world. B – Dad only picked on you because you're the only male in the family now. If Japh had been here he'd have picked on him.'

'That's right. It's not fair. Now I feel rotten that I didn't want to go and it's not my fault at all. I hate Dad. He spoils everything.'

'Mum ought to go with him. It's her job to keep him sedated.'

'Yeah.'

Harriet and Dotty had been shopping in Bude in the so-called cool of the morning. Mungo could not rest until he had Harriet's stamp of approval on his attitude. He helped her carry the shopping in from the car.

'It's not fair, Mum. Dad wants to ruin my holiday. I don't want to play golf. He's only picking on me because Japh isn't here. He thinks we ought to have some buddy thing together because he's my dad, but we *don't*, do we! It's embarrassing, Mum. Anyway, there's this girl I met on the beach. I promised I'd be down there today. *Please*, Mum.'

'All right, darling. But – well, it wouldn't hurt you to spend one day with Dad, would it? We are here for three weeks.'

'But Dad never wants to spend time with me normally.'

'Darling, he never has time. Perhaps he's trying to put that right.'

'But it would be so *embarrassing*, Mum. All those old men in baseball caps. *Please*, Mum. Look, why can't we go sailing instead? That's fair enough, isn't it? That way he'll know it's not because I don't want to do anything with him. Well it is, but there's no need to tell him. I wouldn't mind taking some sort of boat out. At least no one could see us.'

'The bay isn't safe for sailing, here. You'd have to go to the Tamar Lakes.'

'Even better.'

'I'll see what I can do.'

Mungo ran off to get his bathers. Dotty, putting the tins away with feeling, avoided Harriet's eye. Her rear view, however, was eloquent. It said, That Mungo is the most Spoilt, Unfeeling, Ungrateful Brat I have Ever Encountered. Thank God I have been Spared.

Harriet's gorge rose. What did Dotty know of the bloodsucking manoeuvres of familial dynamic? Of course Mungo loved Warren, really. He was just punishing his father for making such a public exposure of Warren's recent failure to cultivate a relationship with Mungo. Mungo, because of the temporary failure of the relationship, did not feel close enough to Warren to express his sense of rejection personally, but chose to channel it through Harriet in the hope that it would be referred to Warren in an acceptable package. The atmosphere would be fraught for a while, and both parties would look out for an opportunity, signposted by Harriet, to heal the breach – such as Warren suggesting a Coke at a pub with a Family Policy. They would all come home high on *esprit de corps*, Mungo would offer to play golf, Warren would graciously let him off, and they would all go to bed feeling warm and wanted and glad they had each other after all. It made Harriet feel like Henry Kissinger at times, but what mother did not? She was certainly not going to bother explaining all this to Dotty, whose smug satisfaction at her own childlessness resulted in an obtuseness about real life akin to Marie Antoinette's. Someone who damp-dusted with Anti-Bax every day was hardly qualified to comment on the problems of those at the cutting edge of Life on Earth.

'When I've finished this, would you like me to Hoover the fireplace?' said Dotty.

'No I wouldn't!' Dotty was so startled she dropped the kidney beans. 'I'm sorry, Dotty, but I haven't come on holiday to Hoover fireplaces.'

'Right. Well, would you mind if I sat down and read the paper?'

'For God's sake, you don't have to ask me if you want to sit down.'

'Right.'

The phone rang. Dotty moved, stopped, her eyes darting wildly, in a panic as to what was expected of her.

Harriet went to answer it. It was Avelina Viper, asking for Warren. Harriet explained that he was playing golf and offered to take a message.

'Actually, I'm rather glad to have caught you – my dear. It's just, well, Warren invited us to join you in Cornwall and at the time it wasn't possible to fit it in, but the thing is we were going to Eilat for two weeks, but because of the Gulf situation, it's now considered too dangerous, so I was wondering if we could come down for a day or two after all. If it's too much trouble – in all this heat—'

'No—'

'No? You mean it is too much trouble.'

'No, of course not.'

'You're sure?'

'Yes, of course.'

'Good. Piers will be delighted. He adores Cornwall. I wouldn't have asked, but he gets frightfully depressed by London in the summer. Will Thursday be all right?'

'Yes.'

'About teatime. *Bis Donnerstag* then.' She put the phone down.

'Dotty!'

Dotty precipitated herself over the sofa in answer to the call. 'What is it? What's wrong?'

'Do you know what Warren's done? Not content with – I mean, he's invited his bloody bony novelist and her husband – they're arriving on Thursday.'

'But Harriet, why didn't you say it wasn't convenient?'

Harriet fell backwards onto the sofa. 'I don't know. Because I'm an idiot. I was in shock. Well I couldn't, could I? If Warren's working with her on some project. It could sour relations.'

'Ring back and invent some excuse – say you'd forgotten that someone else was coming – like your mother.'

'From Australia?'

'How's she to know?'

'She might find out from Warren that it wasn't true.'

'You could always say you got the dates wrong.'

'All right. Why not. Her number will be in Warren's filofax. Mind you, I'm still going to chop his tongue out.'

'I'll hold him down. Fancy his asking people on your holiday!'

Harriet ground her teeth, but said nothing. They found the number, but Avelina had already put the answering machine on. Harriet did not like to leave a bald message.

'Ring back tomorrow,' said Dotty. 'I'll do it if you like. I know. I'll say you've been taken poorly, then she won't think you've delegated the servants to deal with her.'

'Dotty, don't talk like that. You're a brick. I don't know what I'd do without you.'

'Well you won't have to, will you?'

Try as Dotty might, it proved impossible to get past Avelina's answering machine. Dotty left ten messages anyway. To avoid unpleasantness, Dotty had persuaded Harriet not to mention the matter to Warren. But when it proved impossible to be sure that Avelina was not coming, Harriet began to regret the concealment.

On the Wednesday Warren and Mungo went to the Tamar Lakes, which allowed Harriet and Dotty to talk freely under the beach umbrella, while Tiz played with a ghastly family from Market Drayton.

'We'd better get the beds ready, just in case,' said Harriet. 'I'm not sure you should have mentioned typhoid fever, though. It's a notifiable disease. She could check it out.'

'Why should she? We've given her the finger, so to speak. That's hardly going to encourage her to come, now is it?'

'It would serve Warren right if she did come. He's probably forgotten all about it. Honestly, why should I feel guilty about hurting the wretched woman's feelings? She hasn't got any.'

'Why is the sky blue?' sighed Dotty.

8 ∫

Thursday dawned at the usual time, and Harriet was awake to hear every twitter. Her nightie was soaked. As the sun rose over the Cornish yardarm she could swear it had an evil grin on its face. Surely no one in their right mind would drive so far in this weather. She crept out of bed and went down to enjoy a solitary cup of tea and a read in the cool quiet of The Room. No sooner had she curled up on the sofa than Mungo came down. She tried to look pleased.

'What on earth are you doing up at this hour, darling?'

'Well, touché, Mum. I couldn't sleep. It's too hot. Can I have a Tab?'

'No.'

'Why not?'

'They're to take to the beach.'

'I'll pay for it.'

'Oh all right.'

It was not only out of habit that Harriet gave in. Mungo, naked apart from his *Star Wars* boxer shorts, puff-eyed and truculent, appeared to her as startling as a famine ad. in Harpers and Queen. His thin limbs and armpits were sprouting dark down, his body at the peak of awkward conformations, neither the charming compactness of the child nor the golden equation of the man. It was a moving sight, and Harriet felt she would like to give him one last cuddle before he grew up. The fact that it was dawn lent poignancy to the nascence of his young life. He went to fetch the Tab and sat by her feet.

'Are you crying, Mum?'

'No, of course not.'

'Mum.'

'What?'

'Can we go to Tintagel today? I mean, we've got to go some time. You love history.'

'You don't.'

'I like King Arthur and all that crap. And Tanya's family are going, so from my point of view it would be the best day to go.'

'Ah.'

'You'd like them, Mum. Tanya's mum's a laugh. She's a special constable. She had her arm broken at the Cup Final.'

'Hardly a basis for friendship, darling.'

'It's only for the day, Mum. Why do you have to be standoffish? I thought actors were supposed to be interested in people?'

'We are, darling. But I'm on holiday, and frankly, forcing adults to play together doesn't always work.'

'Thanks a lot. You don't actually have to *do* anything with them, you know. Just have a cup of tea, or something. But oh no, that's too much trouble. Nobody does anything for me in this family. I'm just the piggy in the middle, like Dotty says.'

'Dotty called you a pig?'

'No. You see, there you go again – thinking the worst of people. She says families of three never work. One always gets left out.'

'What the hell does she know about it?'

'Just because she doesn't have children herself, doesn't mean she can't have opinions about them, does it?'

'But, darling, it's not true. If anyone gets left out it's Tiz because she's the girl.'

'Oh. Right. And what does she get as compensation?' His lip trembled. 'A bloody pony. She gets a bloody pony and I can't even go to Tintagel for the day.'

'Mungo – don't. Oh all right, if you're going to make a test case out of it, I'll see if I can persuade Dad.'

'He won't mind. He'll be pleased that I've initiated a family outing.'

'But it's so hot. And there's washing to do.'

'Get Dotty to do it. She won't mind. You know she likes to be useful.'

'That's exploitation, though.'
'Then she can come with us.'

Warren's reaction was as Mungo had predicted. He regarded the plan as proof that his efforts to 'get close' to Mungo were bearing fruit. Mungo could do no wrong for the moment. Tiz picked up the interference on her antennae and protested that she had promised to spend the day with the tenants of Trewithers End, whose daughter was also pony mad, and therefore an ideal friend. Harriet thought she might be allowed to go, but Warren was afraid this would be a detrimental blow to Mungo's experiment in family engineering. A row ensued, which ended with Tiz locking herself in her room in tears. Harriet only managed to lure her out with the promise of a new martingale for British Telecom, a day's hack with her new friend and a trip to the sheepdog trials at Kilkhampton. Harriet conveyed to Dotty that it would be a good idea if she stayed at home in case 'anyone' turned up. Dotty was delighted at the prospect of a day on her own, even though it meant preparing squid salad for supper.

They met Tanya and co. outside The King Arthur Experience.
'Can we go in later, Mum?' said Mungo, determined to be pleased by everything.
'All right.'
Tanya's parents, Jo and Jim, smiled a lot, and depressed Harriet immensely. Jim wore a Millwall T-shirt. He had a faraway gleam in his eye that was ignited only by collections of early plastic toys. The couple made a living from toy fairs. They had barely fought their way through the crowds of German courting couples to the XVIth Century Shoppe before Harriet herself was able accurately to price a 1951 Corgi tip-up truck. Jo, whose tan had acquired the crackle-glaze of age and whose boobs bobbled beneath a bright green tank top, walked ahead with Warren. By the time they came to the end of the village street, where the path descended to the castle site, the children had fallen behind. Harriet fanned herself with a copy of Cornwall's Archeological Heritage, stunned by the heat, the plastic replicas of Camelot, the crowds, the Merlin masks and the prospect of spending the rest of the day with Jo and Jim.

'Actually, I think I'd rather go to The Olde Post Office,' she said.

'Oh, that's a shame,' said Jo, lighting a Marlboro.

'What's The Olde Post Office?' said Warren.

'Well – it's an old post office.'

'You mean, you don't want to see the castle after we've come all this way?'

'It's the crowds, Warren. The promontory will sink.'

'I don't think there's any guarantee that The Olde Post Office will lack for custom, sweetheart. Mungo will be kinda disappointed if you don't see the castle.'

'Why did you give him such a funny name?' said Jo.

'It's Scottish,' said Harriet. 'We don't like fancy foreign names.' She forgot about Tiziana and Japheth for the moment.

'Just fancy foreign husbands,' laughed Jo, but her eyes glinted with the message – *I may wear white nail-varnish and use a sunbed but I am not stupid, so watch it.*

'Look,' said Harriet, 'I'll wait for the kids. Why don't you all go on down? You can take your time.' Pilgrims from the site were groaning up the steep path like extras from *The Bridge on the River Kwai.*

'OK. But you will come with them, sweetheart?'

'Yes, all right.'

Jim, relieved, led the way. Harriet could hear Warren speculating to Jo about a possible feature on forenames on the M25 arts programme, *The Junction with the M3 Show.*

Mungo, Tiz and Tanya dawdled up, licking Mr Softees.

'Where on earth have you been?'

'There was a queue for the ice-cream. Don't shout at Tanya, Mum. It's rude.'

'I'm sorry, Tanya. It's not personal.'

'That's OK, Mrs Funkel.' Tanya's magically sweat-free face was a model of vacant perfection. The long brown hair hung in a graceful slick down a narrow back. She wore a pink bikini and Doc Martens. Harriet felt a maternal urge to throw a towel over her.

'Come along. Dad will be stranded with – I mean, just hurry up.'

'I can't,' said Tiz. 'It's too hot.'

'Would you rather see The Olde Post Office?'

'Yuch.'

'Come on, then. Hold my hand.'

Jo and Jim volunteered to stay in the queue for tickets at the tourist hut while the children joined the queue for drinks at the café. Warren sat beside Harriet on an uncomfortable knoll from where they contemplated the steep ascent to the castle.

'You know,' he said, 'they say Arthur never even lived here.'

'Considering he probably never existed that's hardly surprising. Why would anyone want to live here? Imagine getting a piano up those steps.'

'It is romantic, though. I wonder if there's a Cornish independence movement, like there is in Wales and Scotland.'

'Do you feel a programme coming on, Warren? What will you do when you retire, and life doesn't present itself in televisual packages, but just sort of goes on and on?'

'Oh, there's lots of things in my life that just go on and on already, Harriet.'

'What do you mean by that?'

'Nothing.'

'Nothing' being the marriage, of course. Harriet felt a chill. Two remarks did not amount to a dossier, but could they be coincidence? It was true that their marriage had perhaps become one of those lukewarm things that the Almighty chooses to spit out. Perhaps the strain of pretending to enjoy himself was beginning to tell. He had been making such an effort, eagerly seizing every opportunity to create the kind of atmosphere that would justify the expense of the holiday. There was a crack in his voice which touched her.

'Why don't we go out by ourselves tonight, Warren? The squid salad. Bugger. Well, we could go to the cinema. Or tomorrow night. We could take a picnic to a moonlit cove.'

'Are you kidding? That's not your style, sweetheart.'

'Does that mean "no"?'

'I don't go for picnics. Not in this country.'

'It doesn't matter.'

Perhaps he was getting homesick for America at last. There was no accounting for taste. They sat in silence until the expedition re-formed and they set off up the path to the castle.

Harriet lolled against a crumbled column and squinted down at the crawling, glinting sheet of green sea that broke in lethargic splutters against the black rocks. There was a light breeze up here that cooled her sodden cleavage. The brief exchange with Warren had opened up a pit of depression that dragged at her limbs, mind, future, all possibilities and purposes of existence. Distractions like Damian apart, their life together was all that was on offer in practical terms. Happiness was relative: they had grown together, like the jacaranda that wove itself into the lace curtains. Warren had never given any indication that he was not happy. It was as if they were in a cable car over a deep ravine, and Warren had opened the door.

She closed her eyes. Strong hands were clapped over them. She screamed and tore them away.

'Scared you, did I?'

It was Damian.

'What the fuck are you doing here?'

'That's nice. I followed you.'

'What? All the way from London?'

'No, no. Only today. I knew you were near Bude, so I went to the tourist office and asked where *Guardian* readers were likely to rent a cottage and they suggested Trewithers. At least, they did when I explained what the *Guardian* was. I only followed you this morning. I'm camping at Wappa. It's just near you. I'm a regular gumshoe, aren't I?'

'Are you mad? Warren's just over there. In the blue shorts. Photographing the children.'

'Nice.'

'I thought you were going to the Seychelles?'

'We were. But Pansy's been called up because of this Gulf business. She's in the Territorials. I didn't want to go on my own.'

'You're joking. And that woman with the green boobs is a special constable. All these women in uniform. It makes my secret life seem so dull.'

'Thanks.'

'Here comes Warren. You won't say anything, will you?'

'Course not.'

Warren stepped up his pace when he saw Damian with Harriet. The void that had opened up between them was quickly filled with a tip-up truck load of possessive anxieties. What would Damian think of Warren's sunburnt tulip-trowel nose, his skinny legs furred with reddish fuzz, the T-shirt with its fluorescent traffic cones? Surges of protective tenderness for Warren tangled with the dread and guilt that his meeting Damian entailed. She introduced them, saying only that Damian was he who had shared the taxi from Victoria. Warren looked relieved, and shook Damian's hand with warmth.

'Hi. You down here on your own?'

'Yes. My girlfriend's been called up.'

'Is that so? Are you the one who plays the trombone in *Cats*?'

'That's right. What a memory.'

Indeed. Harriet flushed cold. 'Damian's camping, darling.'

'That's too bad. Do you play golf?'

'Yes, I do a bit.'

'What's your handicap?'

'Oh about ninety-five I should think.'

Warren laughed. 'Let's hope you're a good liar.'

('What?'

('What?'

'I mean you have to have a max. of around eighty for the clubs round here.'

'Ah. Right.'

'Listen, the kids are hungry. Why don't we all go and get some lunch?'

'With Jo and Jim? Where are they?'

'They turned back. I guess they'll be waiting for us in the café.'

'Great.'

'Sweetheart, please. Mungo's having a really great time.'

'Yes. He seems to be bungie jumping off a plinth, too.'

'What? Oh no—'

Warren ran off to save him.

'You'll like Jo and Jim,' said Harriet. 'They're the twin valleys of civilization.' She watched Warren's distant antics with irritation. It was, of course, a good thing that Warren had taken to

Damian. What annoyed her was Warren's patent relief at the arrival of another bloke on the scene, a fellow chap, furnishing a mini-caucus of chaps which somehow seemed necessary to validate his activities. How fervent now was the regret that she had not followed the instinct that pointed to The Olde Post Office.

Mungo sulked on the way home. He had been invited to stay with Tanya's family in their mobile home. Harriet felt obscurely hurt by the request. Why did children always want something more? Give them an inch and they take the circumference of the earth. This trip was supposed to be a family solidarity exercise, not a device for driving Mungo out of it altogether. She refused. Mungo was almost in tears of outrage. He accused Harriet of vicious snobbery and an overall plan to humiliate him in front of his friends at every opportunity. He kicked the seat and thumped the car door in a frenzy, making strangulated animal noises. Harriet soon felt like Ivan the Terrible. Even Tiz took Mungo's side.

'They couldn't have sex,' she thoughtfully pointed out. 'Not in a mobile home with the parents next door.'

'The fact that they are both under age should be an even greater deterrent.'

But there was the rub. She had not yet recovered from the affair of Japheth and Semi, and she was indeed worried about the consequences of throwing Mungo and Tanya together overnight in a small space. But to say so would be to invite a stoning with moral outrage from the entire family. Why did the day have to end like this, with her speared like a wild pig as usual? Her own voice was unsteady.

'Mungo, you wanted to go to Tintagel. We went. You wanted me to be nice to Jo and Jim. I was. Why can't that be enough?'

Tiz signalled a hint to Mungo to back down, but he ignored her.

'So? It's not like I want to go clubbing in Penzance, Mum. I bet if Tiz wanted to spend the night with that girl in the compound, you'd let her.'

'Tonight? No, I wouldn't.'

'Why not, Mum?' Tiz was not prepared to suffer actual inconvenience to support Mungo.

Warren sighed. 'Do we have to discuss this? Tiz hasn't been asked to stay with her friend, so let's drop the subject.'

'As a matter of fact, I have. I wasn't going to mention it until we got home and you'd had a couple of gins. I thought it was the least you could do after making me spend the day with Mungo's boring friend.'

'Not tonight, darling. Surely you can see that it wouldn't be fair?'

'Too right it's not. So I have to suffer because you're afraid Mungo would have sex with Tanya?'

'Of course not. It's nothing to do with that.'

'What is it, then? Not "our sort of people", is it? I bet if they were film producers who lived in a converted lighthouse you'd let him go like a shot.'

Warren laughed. 'She's got you there, sweetheart.'

Harriet thumped the glove box. 'For God's sake, Tiz, why do you think Mungo's interested in that girl? For her conversation?'

'I thought you said it had nothing to do with sex?'

Mungo glared at her through narrowed eyelids. 'That's the pits, Mum. You've really done it now. Don't expect me to have any respect for your opinions from now on.'

Mungo and Tiz folded their arms and turned their hostile gaze on the passing countryside. They said nothing further, and when they got home shot out of the car and into the house. There was a white Mercedes parked alongside the boundary hedge. They had come.

'It's Avelina Viper and – Mr Viper, Warren. I forgot to tell you. She called earlier in the week.'

'Hey, that's great. The more the merrier.'

'No, it is not great. I can't stand this, Warren. Why do you always invite people without asking me?'

'Well she told me they couldn't come, sweetheart.'

'They're *your* friends – you look after them.'

'Sweetheart, if you're gonna be hostile—'

'I am *not!*'

'OK, OK.' He stopped halfway out of the car. 'In view of the foregoing, I guess I should tell you I said Damian could come pitch his tent in the yard. It can't be much fun camping on your own. He won't get in the way, though. Are you OK?'

Harriet had leant back and closed her eyes. 'Yes. Just leave me alone for a few minutes, will you?'

'Sure.'

Warren went inside. Harriet could hear his high octane greetings. How relieved Avelina must be to see him, having encountered only Dotty and a re-enactment of the War in the Desert. Presently Tiz came out with her Care Bears duvet, and marched defiantly towards Trewithers End. She glanced round and caught Harriet's eye, muttered an evil spell and strode on again. Harriet was too shattered to be angry. Her only thought was reluctant admiration for Tiz's bottle. Was twelve too young to join the army? Shortly afterwards Dotty emerged, doing a pantomime stalk on tiptoe.

'What are you doing out here, Harriet? For pity's sake come in. Ma Viper's rabbiting on about crucks and ridge trees, whatever they are. And her old man's got diarrhoea. I thought I'd warn you.'

'Oh no. In a water shortage. We'll have to bring sea water up in buckets. We should have told Warren, Dotty. How did it go with the squid salad? Will there be enough?'

'Well, *he* won't be eating anything, will he? And Tiz has gone to her friend over there.'

'I know.'

'Mungo's in a paddy. He says he's going to walk back to London.'

'I think I'll go with him.'

'Don't you dare. By the way, have you read any of her books?'

'They're called novels, Dotty. Yes, I've read one or two. They're brilliant. All about the interior life of psychopathic architects and such.'

'She should pay more attention to the interior life of Mr Viper.'

'Don't. Come on. Over the top.'

'You've got a bit of lettuce in your teeth.'

'Have I? Thanks.'

Harriet removed the vegetation and followed Dotty into the house.

Avelina and Piers, whose real surname was Caldicott, were seated on the sofa with large gins. Piers was even taller and thinner than his wife. Warren slouched at ease in the chair, a proprietorial coup softening his normally tense expression. Piers, thought Harriet, must once have been suavely handsome. He had a rakish, newshoundish face and spaniel eyes, currently whirlpools of mortification. Harriet remarked on how cool they both looked after the journey. Avelina was elegant in white trousers and navy blouson.

'The Merc has air-conditioning,' she explained. 'It's heaven, but I did wonder in some of the traffic jams if we would suffer the fate of the President of the Congo's Rolls. Do you remember? The funeral procession was constantly held up because the air-conditioning kept overheating. It was the Congo, wasn't it? I remember thinking at the time what a tragic symbol it was for the influence of the West on African culture.'

Dotty appeared with the Punjabi Twirls, and put them down rather tartly on the coffee table. 'They're not complaining, are they? They've got lager factories, and the civil service we left them. All their bloomin' chiefs are corrupt, everybody knows that's what's wrong with Africa. What did they want with a Rolls? If they're so proud of their culture they should have had an ox cart.'

Piers raised his head. 'The African temperament lends itself to display.' He had a sensuous, bedroom voice. One longed to hear more.

Warren saw that Harriet was trying to disappear under the floorboards and tried to lighten the atmosphere. 'Dotty is unconvinced that the world was better off before the Brits discovered it.'

'I wish you wouldn't use that expression, Warren,' said Dotty. 'It's so nasty and brutish. Do the Welsh call themselves British, by the way? Or the Scots? Then why do we have to?'

Avelina heard Dotty's outburst with glacial amusement, as though the fire dog had uttered an opinion about the origins of matter. 'I fear you are steeped in ambiguities, my dear. You appear to condemn the African for failing to adopt Anglo-Saxon attitudes, and praise the Welsh for the same thing.'

'As a matter of fact I can't stand the Welsh either.'

'Excuse me—' Piers made a hasty exit to the bathroom, from where the repeat rifle explosions of crap could be clearly heard. Harriet was frantic with embarrassment for Avelina, raising her voice and rattling the ice cubes to create a diversion. Quite unnecessarily, as Avelina calmly searched Dotty's face for signs of Creutzfeldt-Jakob disease. Piers' unsuccessful attempts to get the lav to flush seemed interminable. Other noises suggested he was trying to sluice it down with tumblerfuls of water from the tap. Warren led the conversation into the calmer waters of the invasion of Kuwait.

The Vipers were adamant that they would impinge on family arrangements as little as possible, and spend daylight hours visiting iron-age hut circles.

'Let's hope they have loos,' muttered Dotty, as the Merc drew away after breakfast. It was almost lunchtime, as Avelina had kept them talking about cultural philosophy and its impact on didactic revisionism. Or it might have been didactic philosophy's impact on cultural revisionism. Secretly she was as glad to see the back of the Vipers as Dotty was, although she was still angered by Dotty's Luddite attitude to the realms of higher thought.

'I think we've milked Piers' bowel movements of their potential for humour, Dotty.'

'Pardon me. What are you going to do with the rest of the day? What's left of it.'

Mungo came in from the beach with the same question.

'Are you going to hang around here all day, Mum? What's for lunch?'

'Can't you see we haven't cleared away breakfast yet? Surely you can amuse yourselves here for one day.'

Dotty tiptoed into the kitchen.

'It's boring here. There's nobody I know here today. Can we go to Padstow?'

'If you're so bored *you* clear away breakfast and *I'll* go and be bored on the beach.'

'Why should I? They're not my things. I only had some toast.'

'Fourteen slices. You ate a whole loaf.'

'Oh, begrudge me my food now, do you? As well as everything else.'

'What "everything else"?'

'Forget it. I hate this fucking place.'

'Mungo!' He ran out of the house, slamming the blackened door with its jangle of latches and fairytale castle keys. Harriet made to follow him, but Damian was coming through the wicket gate. Harriet muttered a curse. Damian dumped some swag bags and tent pegs on the lawn.

'You've gone off me in a big way, haven't you?'

'Ssh! Don't you dare say anything. What did you expect? How would you like it if I moved in with Whatsername? And with the kids around! They have instincts like sniffer dogs.'

'I only wanted to see you. This wasn't my idea.' He drew her into his arms.

'Stop it! Don't touch me. Warren's upstairs, for God's sake. If you breathe a word to him I'll kill you. I mean it.'

'I told you I won't. I don't want the almighty wrath of M25TV on my head, do I?'

'There's no need to mock the afflicted.'

'Well, can I have some water for my kettle?'

'I suppose so. Come in.'

Harriet shut the door and led him into the kitchen. As she did so she heard Dotty's flip-flops retreating to the sink.

Dotty became ominously silent after the arrival of Damian. She took to lowering her eyes as she scuttled past Harriet, and answering queries in monosyllables. Harriet half expected to wake up one morning with a scarlet 'A' nailed to her chest. On the other hand, Avelina was greatly perked by his arrival. She revealed in her exchanges with him an unexpected enthusiasm for bebop and Italian league football.

At first Damian continued to cook for himself on the Primus, but Warren soon invited him to join the family for meals, for a modest sum. His value as a distraction for Tiz and Mungo, and as a golfing partner for Warren, was inestimable, even Harriet admitted, although it still irritated her that Warren joined them more often now that a bloke was involved. The trade-off was not without its clause of Sod's Law. Harriet found herself without anyone to play with, moving around the periphery of the party on auto-pilot, in the same orbit, in effect, as Dotty.

They would find themselves stranded in hostile unease under the beach umbrella while Damian organized cricket or taught Mungo and Tiz to surf. Yoked together as outcasts, Harriet's objections to Dotty became pathological – her well-oiled pink legs and cracked toenails, the phoney-humble cooperation with Harriet's requirements, the *Daily Mail* and Werthers Originals, the daily Lincoln Creams, every breath she took. The suspicion that Dotty knew about the affair with Damian shortened her temper still further.

Warren sensed her tension once his own had been released by the arrival of their guests. They seemed always to be passing each other up and down the mood scale. Fortunately for Harriet it was too hot for sex, never mind the exhaustion brought on by cooking for eight every night. Warren suggested it might be fun to masturbate him instead. He was convinced that giving him a thrill was just the fillip that Harriet's mood required. Harriet grimly obliged. She did not want to add Warren's resentment to the atmosphere.

Piers was a minor consolation. She found herself alone with him one evening. Dotty had retired early, and Warren, Avelina and Damian had taken Mungo and Tiz to see *Back to the Future III*. Harriet was amazed that Avelina had agreed to go. Her attitude to the children was inspired by the emperors of China. But, as she confided to Harriet in a rare moment of womanly confidence, Damian was the real attraction. His energy amounted to a kind of innocence that dissolved the cynicism of the effete in a magnetic undertow. Avelina had been drawn to Warren's energy field also. With any luck the two of them would form a particle accelerator that would pulverize her to smithereens. Harriet bashed the hell out of the ice cubes with her swizel stick.

'What was that, my dear?' said Piers. He looked at her with melting compassion. She liked Piers. From a woman's point of view he seemed as trustworthy as a gay vicar. 'I thought I heard you say "I wonder how long she'd last in a microwave." Perhaps I was mistaken.'

'Did I? How strange. I – I was thinking about tomorrow's dinner.'

'I can't help feeling there are quite a few people round here who would be candidates for extinction in your eyes at the moment. You look stressed.'

'No, I'm not. Well, all right, I am. It's nothing serious.'

'Nonetheless, I think we've imposed on you long enough. I'll make an excuse to Avelina. We can leave tomorrow.'

'Please don't. As I told you, I've already planned tomorrow's dinner.'

'Tuesday, then.'

'I'm sorry if I've given the wrong impression. It's not you and Avelina, really.' She lowered her voice. 'It's Dotty. She's getting on my nerves. It was a mistake to bring her. We did it as a favour. Well, I don't regret that but – You know what it's like when you're living at close quarters with someone whose habits annoy you. They're quite innocent – you like them, really – but you start hearing them chew and breathe and – I don't know – even the way they crack their eggs makes you want to attack them with a machete. And then you start anticipating whatever it is that annoys you – or anything. In the morning you wake up tense, just screwed up to be set off by the least thing. I disgust myself like this, actually. It's like being some sort of sadist on the lookout to punish his victim. But you can't say anything, because they haven't done anything. You have no case against them. I mean – look, I'm shaking. It's ridiculous.'

'Umm. When I was in the army in Cyprus there was a case of a young corporal who was court-martialled for murdering a chap he shared a room with. There was no motive, other than the fact he couln't stand the way the chap wiggled his ears. It made a little clicking sound, apparently. Went on all night. He just cracked and strangled him in his sleep. Whenever he had to describe what happened and he got to the bit where he was lying awake listening to this chap's ears wiggle, he'd go berserk all over again. He bit himself on the arm to relieve the tension.'

'I know how he felt. But surely, if he was that stressed someone in charge should have picked it up?'

'Should have done, yes. They were all under stress at that time. I suppose you're too young to remember EOKA.'

'It rings a bell. Like the Mau Mau.'

'Yes. Those organizations are always cited as evidence that terrorism works. But of course it only works in a just cause

– in this case, independence. It seems absurd now, doesn't it, annexing whole continents.'

'Dotty would say they were grateful.'

'I like Dotty. She's so amusing.'

'You don't think I should plant a small bomb in her sponge bag, then?'

'No, I don't. What I advise at the moment of tension is to let it out in some way. Do the yoga pant – or sing a song.'

'Eh? Piers, do you speak from experience? I had thought you were as laid back as a floorboard.'

He smiled and sat up as if shifting his body to take the impact of revelations. 'Well, now—'

'Mum! Mum!' Tiziana crashed through the door. 'Mum, guess what? Dad hit a man in the cinema! He sat on Damian's lap and Dad thought he was a gay trying to get fresh and they had an argument and Dad hit him! He's had to go to hospital!'

'What are you talking about, Tiz?' Harriet had long feared that Tiz's consumption of additives in junk food would lead to some kind of derangement of which this might be the first sign.

'I've just *told* you. It's true, isn't it, Mungo?'

'Yes, it is, Mum. I've never seen Dad like that. He wasn't even drunk. It was fantastic.'

'Where is Dad?'

'He's at the police station. Can we go back and see the rest of the film tomorrow? We had to miss the second half.'

Avelina and Damian came in. Their forced smiles increased Harriet's anxiety.

Damian was subdued. 'It all happened so fast. This bloke got up – to go to the bog, I presume – and when he came back he was, you know, looking at the screen instead of where he was going. Happens all the time. Then he sits down on my lap, and Warren told him to, like, watch it, and when he heard the accent he started calling Warren a fucking baby killer and stuff like that. Warren just slugged him right in the face. Broke his nose, I think.'

Harriet felt sick. 'This isn't happening. The awful thing is, I wish it had been the other way round.'

'No, Mum,' said Tiz. 'The awful thing is, this man was *blind.*'

'Partially sighted,' corrected Avelina.

'All right, partially sighted. So it wasn't his fault, you see. Dad hit a *blind* man. Isn't that dreadful?'

'He didn't say he was partially sighted,' said Damian. 'He just started in screaming at Warren.'

'Sadly, there is no evidence that disability improves the temper,' said Avelina.

'If he was partially sighted,' said Piers, 'why was he at the cinema?'

'He was being fully integrated into society, Piers,' said Avelina. 'The deaf go to concerts these days. And you wouldn't believe the things they get up to in wheelchairs.'

'Do they do the high jump?' said Tiz.

'I'm sure it's only a matter of time. A seige engine could be adapted.'

Tiz giggled guiltily. 'Avelina, you are awful.'

Avelina looked at her for perhaps the first time. 'So I am. Do you know what it is? Violence. It makes me feel quite liberated.'

Harriet was incensed and alarmed by the small explosion of chemistry between Tiz and Avelina. 'Talking of liberation, when is Warren getting out? Shouldn't I go down there?'

'They're waiting for cover to take him to St Austell,' said Damian. 'He's been charged under Section 5 of the Public Order Act, apparently. But he specifically said you weren't to go to him. He's embarrassed, I suppose.'

'There's no need for him to be,' glowed Avelina. 'Warren was absolutely magnificent. I very much doubt if there will be a prosecution. Any decent lawyer could prove that he was the victim of an unprovoked racial attack.'

'I hope you're right,' said Harriet. 'Think of the impact on his career if it got into court.'

'Sod his career,' said Damian, 'what about his self-confidence?'

'Don't worry,' said Avelina. 'The police were clearly more concerned about the reputation of Bude as a family resort.'

In the morning Harriet counselled everyone to behave normally when Warren came down. He had been brought home by the police at 2 o'clock, drunk half a bottle of whisky and passed out.

'You'd better stop shaking in that case, Mum.'

'Yes. Look, why don't you and Mungo go out? We don't all want to be sitting round like vultures.'

'That's not fair. I want to make sure he's all right.'

'Yeah,' said Mungo. 'He needs our support, Mum. If we go out he'll think we're rejecting him.'

Dotty came in with more toast. 'They're right, you know, Harriet. It's like getting back on a horse when you've been thrown, isn't it, Tiz? Those first moments are very important, or you could lose your confidence for ever.'

'When were you last on a horse, Dotty?'

'Well – never. But as Dr Johnson said, you don't have to be a carpenter to know if a table wobbles.'

'Yeah, Mum,' said Mungo. 'You're always criticizing Mrs Thatcher, but you've never been prime minister.'

'All right, all right. Just don't say anything about it.'

'Honestly, Mum, as if we would.'

'All *right*.'

A door opened upstairs and they fell silent, listening to Warren's footfall. Presently he flopped down the stairs.

'Hello, Dad,' said Tiz. 'How are you?'

'Did they beat you up in the police station?'

'Are you going to lose your job?'

'Will they drum you out of the golf club?'

'Do you think the chap's friends will come and get you?'

'Will we have to take time off school to be witnesses?'

'For God's sake, you two!' Harriet rounded on them. 'What did I just say?'

'It's OK, sweetheart. It's just natural curiosity. Is there any fresh orange juice, Dotty?'

'I'll go and squeeze some.'

'Tell me what happened, Dad,' said Mungo as he tucked into spaghetti shapes. 'Why did they keep you so long?'

'Only as a precaution. To see what kind of shape the guy was in. But he wasn't kept in the hospital overnight, so they let me go. I have to go back tomorrow. Today.'

'You shouldn't have hit a blind man, Dad,' said Tiz.

'Partially sighted,' spat Harriet.

'I know I shouldn't, sweetheart. But he said some pretty mean things, too.'

'Were you trying to impress Avelina? Because you certainly succeeded.'

'No, I was not. In fact I'm sorry she was there. I hope I can trust her to keep her mouth shut.'

'Piers is a freemason,' mused Harriet. 'Perhaps you should get him to go down to the police station and give them the old thumbless handshake.'

'That's a myth, sweetheart. And then he'd probably be arrested for trying to pervert the course of justice.'

'It's worth a try.'

'Are they still in bed?'

'Yes. But they're going tomorrow.'

'Good. What say we go down to Padstow and hire a boat and cruise the coast for a change?'

'Wow!'

'*Yes*!' Mungo and Tiz went as far as to hug each other.

'Shall we give Damian a hint to be off, too?' said Harriet. 'And just be the four – I mean, five – of us, as we planned?'

'Sure. But not, like, right away, or he might think we blamed him for the incident.'

'Well you can put me on the coach in the morning,' said Dotty. 'No, don't say anything. I've had a lovely time, but I think you ought to be on your own for a bit. To be honest I can't wait to get back to my own bed. That horsehair's killing my back.'

'Oh, don't go, Dotty,' said Tiz.

'Tiz, don't be selfish,' said Harriet. 'It's Dotty's decision.'

'Right,' said Dotty. 'I'll collect my things together after breakfast.'

Dotty could not quite disguise her disappointment that Harriet had not begged her to stay, despite genuinely wishing to go. Warren undertook to speak to Damian, and to enquire about sea-going vessels, after he had been to the police station.

As an earnest of good spirits, Mungo agreed to be the horse while Tiz and her friend from Trewithers End schooled him in dressage. They went off to the beach with a picnic and coils of washing line.

Piers volunteered to go with Warren and Damian to the police station. Warren promised to have a word with Damian before they got back.

Harriet settled herself on a deckchair on the lawn in a state of relative bliss. She thought it discreet to be out of the house while Dotty packed. The phone rang, and Dotty called from an upstairs window.

'I think it's that agent chappie, Harriet.'

'Oh. Damn.' She got up reluctantly and groped her way to the phone in the Jacobean gloom. She had almost forgotten who George was.

'Hello. What's up?'

'Sorry to disturb you, Harriet, but I thought you'd kill me if I didn't.'

'What is it, George?'

'It's Shirley Lamb. She's joined the Children of God and gone to California. I'd call that a nervous breakdown, personally. Can you take over? Are you still interested?'

'What are you talking about?'

'*Wipers!*, love. You know, the lovelorn matron. I have to know if you can come back to town and take over.'

'Er – God – I don't know. It's such a shock. I'm standing here in my bathers—'

'Don't torment me, Harriet. Is it yes or no? I have to know by tonight.'

'Can I ring you later?'

'Very well. Don't forget. You can ring me at home.'

Harriet put the phone down and fell into a chair. She listened to the sounds of Dotty padding between the bed and the chest of drawers. The equivalent of the last train revving up to pull out of the station. Harriet ran up the stairs to Dotty's bedroom. Dotty started.

'Is anything wrong, Harriet?'

'No. Something's come up, Dotty.'

Dotty smoothed the creases in the pink pyjamas she was holding and drew her mouth into a meaningful rosette. 'Not your breakfast, I presume.'

'No.' Harriet sat on the bed, trying to keep her eyes off the fascinating contents of Dotty's suitcase. So many matching Aertex knickers she had never seen. Hard also not to wonder how many rat points she deserved for literally lowering herself before Dotty, so that she would appear vulnerable to Dotty's superior height and, she hoped, beneficence.

'I suppose you've got the chance of a part, have you?' Dotty packed on – callously, Harriet thought – but at a slower pace.

'That's right. It's that musical about the Battle of Ypres. You remember? I auditioned for it about the time Fin died. The thing is, Dotty, it's such a rare opportunity. Well, people do go sick and have to pull out, but not often in a new show that's bound to be a hit. You'd be surprised how healthy people stay in the circumstances. And – let's face it – how often is this likely to happen to me at my age?'

'It's not right, making musicals about that sort of thing.'

'What sort of thing?'

'War, and that. Suffering. Life in the trenches. Mown down like grass, they were. Like it says in the Bible, Man that is born of a woman, he cometh forth and is cut down like a flower. How would you like it if one of the boys was killed and some poncy producer proposed to make a musical about it?'

'Not very much. But it was a long time ago.'

'What's wrong with romance? *Seven Brides for Seven Brothers* – now that's my idea of a musical. Not all this death and drugs and whathaveyou. What will it be next, *Aids*, the Musical?'

'Yes – I mean, let's hope not.' There was no encouragement in Dotty's words. Harriet just wanted to crawl away and have a cry by herself. 'So – you don't feel able to—'

'Able to what, Harriet?' She shut the lid of the suitcase. 'You haven't asked me to do anything yet. A lesser person might think they were being taken for granted.'

Harriet blushed and stood up. It was just as well. In no time Dotty would be rolling over her in a Chieftain tank. 'That wasn't my intention, Dotty. And if I do seem to take you for granted it's only because you're so much part of the family now. I *was* hoping you would stay on so that I could do it, but it doesn't matter. You obviously disapprove of the whole venture. In a way I agree with you.'

'Well – it's not as if it's grand opera, is it? You get cabinet ministers going to the opera. There's maybe some point to getting heavy about war and things. But a musical's supposed to be a laugh.'

'Indeed. No, you're right. Of course, my not being in it won't actually stop it going ahead. I just hope that whoever gets the part has the same sense of responsibility about it that I would have had.'

'What do you mean?'

'Oh, nothing. It's just that I would have tried to bring as much dignity to the proceedings as they deserve. Sometimes actors are awfully irreverant, you know, and their irreverance tends to flatten values, so that in the end nothing is sacred.'

'I'm sure you would be very good in the part. You're cut out to play the martyr.'

'Thanks. Well—' Harriet moved towards the door.

'Couldn't Warren look after the kids?'

'He isn't around enough. And you know men, Dotty. They mean well, but they don't have that knack for anticipating danger. And Semi's all right for short hauls, but I wouldn't expect an au pair to take my place for a long run. I wouldn't be easy in my mind unless there was a responsible woman in charge. Never mind. It doesn't matter.'

'It's a shame there aren't more women who think like you, Harriet. These days they just bung the kids in the childminder's and pick them up again like dry cleaning.'

'Not my style, Dotty.'

'Have you told Warren? Does he mind?'

'I thought I'd ask you first. Otherwise there's no point.'

Dotty opened the case and rearranged the top layer of Jonelle jumpers. 'I must admit, I was looking forward to going home, Harriet.'

'I know.'

'I expect Tiz would be pleased if I stayed.'

'Oh she would. She thinks of you as her nan.'

'All right, then.'

'You mean—'

'I'll stay – for now. But it won't be for ever, Harriet. I have my own life to lead, you know.'

Harriet smiled, but remained calm. 'Thank you, Dotty. Thank you so much. I promise I'll start making alternative arrangements as soon as possible. Well, as soon as it's clear the show's going to run. Perhaps my mother would be willing to help. She's been talking of coming home. Well, we'll see. I'll go and find Warren and talk to him right away.'

'He's at the police station.'

'Bugger. So he is. Still, I'm sure he won't mind. He's been a lot more relaxed since he's had someone to play golf with.'

'Huh. Damian de St Howsyafather, you mean? Did you see *The Omen* by the way?'

'No. Why?'

'Just joking. Funny that, isn't it? I thought Damian was *your* friend.' Dotty avoided Harriet's eye. 'Quite a good friend, seeing as he followed you down here.'

'No he didn't. We met by coincidence. Whatever gave you that idea?'

'The way he looks at you, Harriet, that's what.'

'I can't help the way he looks at me.' Harriet paced about. 'All right, Dotty. You're right. He did follow me down here. It's so embarrassing. He developed a bit of a crush on me, if you must know. After we met again in London by chance. I hardly know him, really. It's true his girlfriend has been called up, but it wasn't coincidence.'

'I thought not.' Dotty patted the jumpers with satisfaction.

'You can imagine how I felt when Warren asked him to camp in the garden. But since Warren's kept him so busy on the links it's been easier. I'm sure he's cured now, anyway. There's nothing like living with a person for putting you off them. I mean—'

Dotty chuckled. 'I'll remind you.'

'But what a sleuth you are, Dotty. Perhaps you should track down Yoevil and Kean.'

'Huh. I daresay they arranged it themselves to get publicity for *War and Peace on Ice*.'

Harriet was suddenly melted with gratitude to Dotty, and joy in her misguided, but droll, opinions. She put her arms round

Dotty and hugged her. 'I'm so glad we've come into each other's lives, Dotty. It seems the most natural thing in the world.'

Dotty returned the hug. But when Harriet had gone she muttered, 'As the spider said to the fly.'

9

The Vipers took Harriet home and came in for a cup of tea, before continuing to Hampstead. Avelina provided her own Bamboo Pekoe, which Harriet made up under instruction.

The silent house basked in its emptiness, like a sensate creature. Triffid-like nasturtiums had grown up over the front door and spiders webs between the candles. Despite the drought the wisteria, honeysuckle, roses, campsis, clematis, fremontodendrons, cotoneasters, ivies and actinidias that clothed the walls had flourished, their leaves clotted out the light. The still, suffering trees around the house cast a deeper shade, turning it into a verdant cavern under layers of organic matter.

'Do you know, I've never been alone in this house at night,' said Harriet, more to herself than the Vipers. 'Perhaps I should pick up the dogs tonight.'

'Are you frightened?' said Avelina. 'Surely not.'

'No. But it makes you think, doesn't it?'

'I don't have any problems in that department, my dear.'

'Harriet was probably referring to the absence of the family,' said Piers.

'Yes, that's right. I shall probably wander round the house asking an imaginary audience Who am I? Or even, Am I?'

Avelina bristled. 'Tom Stoppard has a lot to answer for. If I were you I would walk around naked with a gin and tonic practising scales.'

'Would you?' said Piers.

'We had better be on our way. Good grief, what's that?'

A roar of motorbike had been quickly followed by an urgent ring at the door. Harriet went to answer it.

'Harriet Dimdore?' The courier was a touching sight in shorts, vest and helmet announcing Heaven Sent Deliveries.

'Sign here, please.'

Harriet could see it was the script of *Wipers!* Adrenalin gushed into her veins. Salome must have felt much the same when presented with the head of John the Baptist – yes, she asked for it, but . . .

Avelina was impressed. 'So it's true, then.'

'Did you doubt it?'

'No. It just seemed so improbable. Well, I wish you luck, Harriet. I would come and see it, but musicals aren't my thing, I'm afraid.'

'I'll come,' said Piers. 'Don't worry, you'll be marvellous.'

'Thanks.'

As soon as they had gone Harriet anxiously flipped through the vocal score to assess its difficulty and count her songs. Fortunately most of them were quartets with homesick patients, one solo and a duet with the legless captain. This took place on the night before the captain, in defiance of the authorities, was due to resume command of his men in the trenches and, if possible, crawl over the top with them. Harriet mopped the sweat from her brow. Would the critics understand?

> *One last kiss*
> *Before the candle sputters –*
> *One last kiss*
> *Before you go*
> *To where the pennant flutters.*
>
> *Love knows if*
> *Or when we'll meet again.*
> *Love is true*
> *When life betrays*
> *And turns our dreams to mayhem.*
>
> *Don't go, don't leave me now*
> *We've found each other after all these years.*
> *Give up this crazy plan to lead your men*
> *And I'll give up my stupid nursing school.*
> *Live like a hero, don't die like a fool.*

Reprise: *One last kiss etc.*

After this the script could only be a disappointment. Harriet read it three times, until the moon rose over the M25. The phone rang. It was Tiz, wanting to know why Harriet had not called.

'This isn't a very good sign, Mum. You've forgotten about us already.'

'Of course I haven't, darling. I'm missing you like mad.'

'Enough to go and check up on Telly?'

'I'm sorry, darling, but I have to start rehearsals in the morning.'

'But Mum, I have to know he's all right. I bet he's got mud fever. That girl never brushes him down properly.'

'Not in this weather, darling. The nearest mud is in the Arctic Circle.'

'I see. Well I hope you enjoy yourself, even if I can't.'

'But you can still go on that hack, can't you?'

'I don't think I'll bother. It will only remind me of Telly and make me sad.'

'It's only another week.'

'Only! I expect Telly will have forgotten me as well by that time.'

The Moldavian Culture Centre in Kentish Town had been made as aesthetically uplifting as possible. No expense had been spared on whitewash and potted plants. Harriet took that in while peering through the porthole into the main hall. She was drenched with sweat and shivering. The hall reeked of sunshine and well-meant attempts to put the occupants at their ease and took her right back to A-Levels. She would not have been a bit surprised to be told to sit at a desk and write for three hours on the origins of the French Revolution. As she was an hour early there were few people in the hall. A pianist improvised half-heartedly. Harriet went in. Nobody noticed, so she approached a couple of girls lolling against a list of Moldavia's war dead. One of them was the female lead, Melanie Pace, best known for her role as an Argentinian spy in *Sink the Belgrano!*

'You don't know how glad we are to see you,' said Melanie. 'Poor Shirley. Marvellous voice, but talk about picky – she wanted to rehearse with maggoty biscuits. Just as well she cracked up when she did.'

'I'll say,' said the other girl. 'I have this scene with her where she comes into my *auberge*, right, after the boyfriend's died and everyone's, like, drinking and having a good time, and she flips and wrecks the joint and—'

'I know. I wanted to talk to Nick about that. It seems a bit out of character for a virginal matron in her forties.'

'But that's the *point*, Harriet. It shows what war does to The Women They Love. And it's a good excuse for a soupy chorus of repentant boozers. I think that scene's going to be great, actually. This little bugler boy picks her up and asks her to dance and they all waltz to The Cloth Hall Blues.'

'I dread having to dance in that stingray headgear.'

'By the way,' said Melanie, 'did I hear you say "Nick"?'

'Yes. Why?'

'Haven't you heard? He's been replaced.'

'Why? What happened?'

'Well – we're not sure. Usual crap about artistic differences. He objected to the mounted Sikhs on grounds of taste, or rather, smell. Saddlesmith decided he wanted him to do a revival of *Careless Rapture*, and he wouldn't volunteer to go, so they made out he was temperamentally unsuited to *Wipers!* He did make a few jokes about the bonking wounded, and stuff like that.'

'So who's taken over?'

'See that squirt in glasses – looks about nineteen? Straight from Cambridge. All he's ever done is a gay version of *Little Women* as far as I know. Still, let's face it, in a thing like this it's the choreographer and the computer that do the real work. You'd better go and introduce yourself, Harriet. We'll be doing warm-ups in a minute.'

'What does he do for warm-ups – bayonet practice?'

'No, we're soldiers regressing to the womb. We've got to about three and a half.'

'Do you think I could get out of it on grounds of age?'

'Now, now, Harriet. You know you're dying to get in touch with yourself. Go on, he's looking at you. His name's Andreas Figg.'

The hall was filling up. When she apprached Andreas Figg he took her hand in both of his. 'Thank you for joining us, Harriet.

I'm sure you have a lot to teach us. We're working on attitudes to death, but I'll talk to you later. Welcome.'

Harriet fell in as near the back as possible. After the choruses the choreographer took over. Before the knees-up she reminded the girls that if they had had periods they would have been using boiled rags. As the tempo speeded up Harriet's heart, which had not been asked to do much more than walk upstairs for some time, went berserk and tried to escape. She went bright red all over and, when they were finally allowed to lie down, noticed she was covered with a rash, and had a mirage of her deckchair on the lawn of Trewithers Lodge.

Andreas divided them into groups – playgroups – in which they re-enacted the Battle of the Somme from a child's point of view, and then were encouraged to assume the stillness of death. Harriet lay stuck to the dirty parquet with sweat, the sun broiling her remains. Half the cast fell asleep. Andreas tiptoed among the bodies, encouraging them to see lights at the end of tunnels, to fill their beings with peace, relief, remorse. Harriet thought he was several screws short of a tool kit, but at the same time tears seeped from her eyelids. It was Japheth she was, his warm face sucked into the cold mud, steel stuck through his guts just by the belly button where he had once been joined to her body.

At the break, Andreas introduced her to the company. Afterwards she was taken off to a small room by the assistant musical director to go through the numbers. He was a bright-eyed, gnomic young man called Christopher, permanently filled with wonder at her potential, skilled at making arpeggios seem fun. Harriet felt confidence flood her being. 'Wonderful!' said Christopher. 'Now do it again, but imagine you've got a fountain in your stomach.'

Harriet prayed that she would not have to rehearse on Saturday morning, as the Cornwall party was returning in the afternoon, but it was not to be. Her evenings consisted of walking from the front door to the bathroom, learning lines in the bath, gin and bed. On the Friday she was up till midnight changing sheets. With luck she would be free by one o'clock and could shop at Asda on the way down the A3. This meant taking the car into town, for which she should allow two and a half hours' journey time, but there was no help for it. If the family returned to an empty fridge and no Wotsits she would be on the run.

The Saturday rehearsal was with the legless captain, Peter Makeweight, an actor of the just-get-on-with-it school, whose tortured inner life was entirely digestive. Apart from a few elderly generals and the Archduke Ferdinand the cast was a sea of youth. Peter Makeweight appeared as something of a life raft. This was reinforced by the fact that he was one of only two heterosexual males in the cast. Andreas was not the other one, but he was determined to show that his experience of love, loss and epic sacrifice was transferable. He put his arms round both of them and spoke in a low voice, as a technician humped furniture in the background.

'You two have a very, very special place in the show. You give it – gravitas. Your relationship counterpoints the whole tragedy of lost youth thing. Without you two, it could be just a glorious cliché, but I'm relying on you to give the theme resonance. Are you with me on that?'

'Oh yes,' said Harriet.

'Absolutely,' said Peter.

'Now, I'm going to leave you alone for a few moments, and I want you to kiss each other. That's all.'

'Right.'

'I trust you.'

'No problem.'

Andreas cleared the room and left. Peter stood demurely with his hands clasped in front of him, facing Harriet. She could see the laughter in his eyes. 'I wish I hadn't had that peperoni sandwich now. How do you want it – French, straight, or the full *plat du jour*?'

'Imagine I'm Greta Garbo.'

'She's dead.'

'I thought you'd enjoy the challenge. Let's get on with it. I've got to go to Asda this afternoon.'

It was two-thirty by the time Harriet got away, and she was still in the queue at the check-out at six. At quarter to seven she resigned herself to the fact that she would not be at her post when the family arrived. There was a further delay of forty minutes on the Ewell bypass, during which the butter and ice-cream melted.

Warren and a disgruntled Mungo were unpacking the car in the driveway. The hall looked like a refugee centre. Warren smiled thinly as she kissed him on the cheek.

'Sorry I'm late, darling. I had to rehearse this morning and then I got held up in the traffic.'

'How's it going?'

'All right. Tiring.'

'We're all tired, sweetheart.'

'Yes. I'm not claiming to be tireder than you, Warren. Where's Tiz?'

'She went straight off to see Telly. Dotty's making some tea.'

'I forgot about Dotty. You didn't bring Damian home with you, I hope.'

'Why do you say that? I thought you liked him.'

'I do. It's just having strangers in the house. Certain strangers, anyhow.'

'Damian was great with the kids. They had a wonderful time after you left.'

'You mean they didn't before?'

'No, sweetheart. I just meant that if we'd been on our own it would have been kinda dull for them.'

'Perhaps we should hire him by the hour then.'

'Sweetheart, I'm tired.'

'So you said.' And of course Harriet could not be tired because the cause thereof was her own doing. She took the shopping into the kitchen. Dotty was listening to Radio 2 as she wiped down the surfaces.

'Hello, Dotty. You don't have to spring clean today. Everything's in such a mess.'

'I can't abide a dirty kitchen. God knows what mine looks like by now. Could you run me over there tomorrow, Harriet? It's been empty that long.'

Harriet knew despair. She had counted on spending Sunday in deep communion with the sun lounger and the psychology of virginal matrons. 'Don't you want to relax for a bit? I don't want you to get overtired.'

'Well, I'd suggest Monday, but I suppose you're rehearsing.'

'Yes.'

'It's right awkward not knowing how long I'm going to be away from the place. I wonder if I shouldn't rent it.'

'Oh I should, Dotty. After all, even if the show folds you can always stay here until the tenants' contract is up. But I'm sure it will run for at least a year.'

Dotty sniffed and resumed scrubbing. Harriet was depressed at the shift she sensed in Dotty's manner – less Nana Darling, more Mrs Danvers. Suppressed doubts surfaced. When Semi returned the kitchen would reek of couscous *and* Jimmy Young, and if Dotty went power mad into the bargain it would take Ken Russell to do justice to the scene.

'Dotty, if you're not sure about this arrangement—'

'No, no, Harriet. I didn't mean to imply that. You can't let everybody down now.' So she had changed her mind. 'It's just that I've never been away from home for so long. And – and it's hard – not being where Fin was—' Her mouth trembled.

'I'm sorry, Dotty. I hadn't given enough thought to your missing him. You must think me terribly selfish. Well, I expect I am. Here—' She took the sponge from Dotty's hand and gave her a hug.

Dotty wept a little. 'I expect there's a bus I can take.'

'No, don't think about it, Dotty. It's no trouble, really.'

Mungo crashed through the door. 'Hi, Mum. What's for dinner?'

Harriet was annoyed at being caught in a compromising situation with Dotty. 'Darling, is that your way of saying how pleased you are to see me?'

Mungo crossed his arms and cocked his head. 'What's your way of saying it, Mum? You've been home half an hour and you haven't even asked where I was. Of course you asked where Tiz bloody was, didn't you?'

'Darling, I saw you when I arrived. I knew where you were.'

'Great. That puts me somewhere between the dogs and the gin bottle in your estimation then. I'm going out.'

'Mungo—'

But he was already crunching over the gravel on his bike.

'I don't know why you let him speak to you like that, Harriet,' said Dotty.

'If I knew he was going to I wouldn't.'

'You should punish him. Then he wouldn't do it again.'

'Dotty, give me a break. He's only saying what he thinks. Anyway, he's nearly fifteen. What am I supposed to do – stop him watching *Blue Peter*?'

Dotty pulled a face. Warren popped his head round the door. 'How's that tea coming?'

'It's ready.'

'Great. I'm starved, sweetheart. If you could rustle up some dinner I'll get going on the laundry.'

When he had gone, Harriet said, 'Warren seems remarkably cheerful. Considering he's just come back from holiday. In my experience it brings on suicidal depression in most people.'

Dotty turned away. 'Perhaps Warren isn't like most people.'

The radio news bulletin's upbeat, life-affirming tones spoke of British families escaping to Syria across the desert, guided by Bedouin. Harriet thought how much easier it would be to keep the children amused in such circumstances than in the arid wastes of the school holidays.

Dotty was riveted. 'We're not the only ones with sand in our knickers then,' she reflected.

Dotty insisted that she could find her own way back from Nonsuch Crescent. 'Although I suppose I should take driving lessons at this rate.'

'We'll pay,' promised Harriet. In Dotty's absence she got Tiz to test her lines when she finally hit the sun lounger at four o'clock. Tiz sat at her feet in a spotted swimsuit, sucking a lolly.

'*Nurse, I can't stand this dreadful pain/The morphine, please/I won't ask you again,*' she droned.

'*My son, your journey's at an—*'

'Mum, how can you sing this crap?'

'For God's sake, don't keep interrupting, Tiz. I'm trying to concentrate. Anyway, it only sounds crap because of the way you say it. I'm sure it will be very moving.'

'Yes, the audience will be shitting themselves.'

'Will you stop talking in that vulgar way! This is hopeless.

If you aren't going to help me I'd be better off listening to the tape.'

'All right, all right. Where were we – *The morphine, please/I won't ask you again.*'

'*My son, your journey's at an end, I fear*/Er – *Hold my hand, by morning/The supply train will be here.*'

'*What is that dreadful light beyond the hill?/They're coming for me, my hands are frozen to the gun/Is this what politicians mean by/A place in the sun?*'

'*I'll fetch the padre/Are these your letters home?*'

'Mum?'

'*What?*'

'When's Japh coming home?'

'Next weekend. He's only on holiday, darling, he's not in the trenches.'

'I know. But suppose he were? It would be awful, wouldn't it? I suppose he's not that bad. At least he doesn't hit me all the time like Mung does. I'd be dead chuffed if Mung was dying in the trenches.'

'No you wouldn't. Tiz, can we please get on?'

'Do I have to? It's so boring.'

'Oh, give it to me.'

'I've got to ride Telly now, anyway. It's been too hot. I'll do some more later. What's for dinner?'

'Dad's doing a barbecue.'

'Ugh. I don't know how you can eat meat when you're studying that stuff about maggots in wounds and amputations and stuff. Charred flesh is the last thing I'd want for dinner. What am I having?'

'I got you a trout.'

'Mum! I told you I don't eat fish either. Neither fish nor fowl. You never *listen*.' She rattled the sun lounger in passing.

Japheth phoned to ask if Harriet could meet him at Victoria the following Sunday.

'Could you possibly come down to Sutton, darling? It's just that I have to go to Victoria six days a week at the moment.'

'That's not my fault, is it?'

'Of course not. But we're going to go into the theatre the following day, and I really must be word perfect.'

'Well, can Dad pick me up? I've got so much stuff.'

'He'll be on a day trip to Calais with the marketing staff, unfortunately. You might pass him in the Channel.'

'Man, can't he leave me alone? What about Dotty?'

'She doesn't drive – yet.'

'Fine. I'll walk.'

By the time Harriet got to Victoria she was in a panic. The tape of the score, which she had taken with her for some last-minute infused learning, had stuck and broken the cassette player. She had been hoping to finally master the scene where she went berserk in the *auberge*. Andreas had assured her that when the orchestra was there she would get her note from the didgeridoo – the noble captain had become an Australian in the course of rewrites. With the whole cast looking on, the scene had become a test of nerve of Scheherazade-type proportions. It made the customary advice to relax and allow the voice to emerge like backed-up piss somewhat redundant.

The conservatory for trains swilled with blue jeans, brown legs, backpacks and the twitter of foreign twangs. The crowds of young, questing spirits who could go for six months on three pairs of knickers intimidated Harriet, reproached her need for a schedule and hot showers. Even when young the idea of sacrificing convenience for adventure had struck her as something that should be left to the SAS, and she would have been hard put to it to bivouac her way across the living room.

She took up her position opposite the platform as the train disgorged its backpackers. None of the knackered faces was Japheth's. The crowd thinned out. She strained harder to examine the few remaining. It was now half an hour since the train arrived. Obviously he had been arrested for drug smuggling. Or got drunk and fallen onto the propeller. Or had an argument with a French sheep farmer and been burnt as an unwanted British import. A bearded young man approached and asked for a light.

'Get lost.'

'Mum!'

'Oh Japh – I didn't recognize you.' She flung her arms round him and he patted her regally.

'Don't you like it?' He stroked the designer stubble.

'Well – it does make you look older. Quite a man, in fact.'

'It had to happen, Mum.'

'Let's go. Congratulations on your A-Levels, by the way. You'd better get on to Leeds first thing in the morning.'

'We'll discuss it in the car.'

Japheth prattled on about St Honoré Les Sables until they were well past Putney – the sand buggies, the sailing, the midnight beach parties, the glut of galettes. His encomiums on Semi's family – their openness and yet togetherness, their traditionalism and yet their modernism, their English as well as their French – left Harriet strangely silent. Japheth eventually noticed and fell silent too. After a few minutes he said, 'Mum, I'm definitely not going to Leeds.'

'Aren't you, darling? Where are you going then?'

'To Tattenham Drovers. I mean it. I'm sorry.'

Harriet barked. 'You don't know what you're talking about. It's just a phase. You can't make a career out of football. What do they end up doing? Well?'

'Mum, I'm too young to worry about ending up. Anyway, the good ones do all right. They become TV commentators or something. Or managers of England.'

'One of them does. And the rest end up coaching Winnipeg Wanderers or running laundrettes. I've looked into it, Japh. I know.'

Japheth looked out of the window and drummed his fingers on his knee, a knee that seemed a lot hairier than Harriet remembered. 'I'm going to do it, Mum. You know, some people would be very proud that their son had been accepted by Tattenham Drovers.'

'There are a lot of funny people about.'

'I hate you, Mum.' There were tears in his voice.

'Japh – O God—'

They completed the journey in silence. When they got home Japheth was surly with Tiz and Mungo, who had made a real effort to repress their excitement at his homecoming. His rejection of their welcome then obliged them to repress their hurt feelings under spades of insults, and demands to know to what extent the holiday, which had produced nothing but facial hair and bad temper, had been subsidized by their parents.

'Why did he have to come home?' demanded Mungo. 'He's eighteen now. He should have left home. Can I have his room?'

'He will be leaving if he has his way,' said Harriet. 'He says he's going to play for Tattenham Drovers.'

'What! I don't believe it. He's crap, Mum. He thinks he's a striker, but he couldn't hit a ball into a circus tent.'

'He's not that bad,' said Tiz. 'Shut up, Mung. If Japh works for Tattenham Drovers Dad won't have to pay for him to go to university and there'll be more money for us.'

'Oh *yeah*. We won't see any of it.'

The set – a complicated affair of revolving cafés, hospital wards, gun emplacements, a floating War Office and an apron that opened up on a network of trenches – was not, of course, finished. Rehearsals were continually interrupted while Andreas, in headphones, communicated with computer control. The main problems were with the apron, or rather, making sure everyone was off it before it rose to reveal the trenches. An 'acceptable level' of casualties occurred before this was sorted. The hospital beds, which were on grooves, came to life and ram-raided the back of the set. The *Evening Standard* reported the incident under the title 'Killer Beds Spook War Show', although there were no fatalities. Perry Saddlesmith and the backers were delighted. The heavy advance bookings were boosted by ghouls hoping to witness a pile-up. When not needed, Harriet went for costume fittings in Barking, and continued to practise with Christopher.

Semi was to return on the Friday, and Japheth went up to Victoria with Harriet in the morning to meet her. The hostage Brian Keenan had just been released in Beirut, so they had plenty to talk about.

'Honestly, Mum, how can you ponce about in a musical about war when there are things like that still going on? I mean, just because that sort of thing never happens in Europe, doesn't mean war is dead, you know. Don't you think it trivializes the whole thing rather?'

'It's just a job, darling. I was lucky to get it. Anyway it's going to be very moving. Ordinary people relate to musicals. Your attitude is very elitist.'

'Ordinary people can't afford to go to the theatre.'

'I don't think that can be true. More people go to the theatre than to football matches.'

'Do they? I don't believe it.'

Japheth tossed his hair, defiant, but could not quite hide the pain from Harriet's statistical hit. Harriet bit her lip, having sworn to keep off the subject of footie at least until after opening night. But thinking of feet reminded her of the scene with Tiziana the night before when her daughter had learned that it would be Dotty who went with her – on the bus! – to Sutton to buy her new school shoes. Tiz had cried for three hours.

Abutilon
4th September 1990

Darling Mummy,

We were all pretty devastated by your news. My one consolation for your being Down Under was the thought that you and Melvyn were so happy together. Well, the irony is that you were. I can quite understand that feeling that you were living with a stranger when you found out. Thanks for the newspaper clip, by the way. Is he going to prison? Will you be able to divorce him for unacceptable behaviour? I wonder if your friends are supportive, or whether they instinctively tar you with the same brush. I'm not surprised you thought he was having an affair. Poor Mummy – what a horrible shock. I dread telling Tiz, she is such an animal lover – even snakes. You should have heard the fuss when the au pair Hoovered the stick insects. I haven't heard such a racket since Mungo got a revolving space ship stuck in his hair.

Dearest Mummy, I wish I were there to give you a hug – lots of them. However well-meaning friends are, there is no substitute for family at times like this. I suppose it is too soon to start thinking about your future, but do think about coming to see us. It would do you good to get away, and perhaps give you a chance to decide if you want to come back here permanently. You know you can stay as long as you like. Dotty is still with us, but I am not sure for how long.

After many delays the first night is scheduled for two week's time, with a week of previews. I am so sick with nerves it is impossible to think about anything else. I miss your support so much. Warren is as helpful as he can be considering he is so busy, but his presence doesn't lower the blood pressure as a mother's does. It seems absurd at my age to say that I still need your approval, but I don't think children ever grow out of that. But I mustn't rabbit on about my own needs. I just wish there was something I could do to help. I presume you have told Peter. He will probably get some satisfaction from the fulfilment of his predictions about Melvyn. But not even Peter could have predicted that he was capable of such disgusting acts. It's just horrible. It's funny, all the Australians I have met here have been charming, gentle people. You have had appalling luck. Do take care of yourself, darling Mummy. I *know* you are strong enough to put this behind you. We'll be thinking of you every minute, and *do* come and see us soon.

All my love,
Harriet.

She posted the letter while shopping for first-night presents. For the captain, an Edwardian cigarette case, a witty comment on the scene in which he is reprimanded by a British officer for smoking straight from the packet. Zip lighters for the other chaps and smelling salts for the ladies.

On the home front the shopping expedition had also been successful. The fashion for orthopaedic clodhoppers was well under way, and Dotty had been pleasantly surprised by Tiz's choice of hideous black lace-ups. Dotty took Harriet aside and reminded her of her intention to take driving lessons. Harriet paled.

'I didn't think you were serious. You said you couldn't adapt to traffic after the desert, Dotty.'

'Yes, I know. But I'd be much more use to you if I was independent. I feel rotten about getting you up to take me to chapel on Sundays.'

'Ah yes. How is the Reverend Vince?'

'Fine. He's organized a trip to a Center Parc in Nottingham. You know – one of them theme bubble places.'

'Has he, indeed. Tell Warren. It sounds like one of his fly-on-the-wall documentaries.'

'Reverend Vince is not a publicity seeker, Harriet. It's just a junket for the congregation.'

'Dotty, I don't wish to be unkind, but I think your faith in the Reverend Vince is misplaced. Most people would stop at nothing to get on television.'

Dotty drew herself up. 'Very well, I'll ask him. You'll see.'

Harriet immediately saw her tactical error, but her gorge rose to meet her regrets. 'You're probably right. Look, about the driving lessons – why don't you find out about – er – age restrictions and so forth, and if there's no problem I haven't forgotten I promised to pay for them.'

'It doesn't matter. I can still ride a bike.'

'Oh don't be such a dog in the manger, Dotty. I'm sorry I said that about the Reverend Vince, but the two things are utterly unrelated!' Harriet picked up a Balinese duck from the console table and bashed it down again.

Dotty's face was momentarily frozen, and then molten with understanding. 'You're all nerves at present, aren't you, Harriet? Stupid me. I tell you what, you go to bed and I'll bring you up a Choc-O-Mint. It's a big day tomorrow.'

'Yes. I may not get home until very late. In fact I meant to ask you if you could make shepherd's pie or something. Tiz is having a friend round. Keep Semi out of the kitchen anyhow.'

Dotty's eyes lit up. 'Can I rig up a booby-trap?'

10

The day of the first preview was also Japheth's first day at Tattenham Drovers. When she saw him in his new 501s and Global Hypercolour T-shirt the fact finally sank in. She had woken up at five-thirty after a night on Death Row, squelching with dread. Not just of performing, but of possible mishaps. At the dress rehearsal the War Office, which was suspended over the stage on a kind of JCB, had failed to retract, and wobbled over the delicate scene where the captain's lifeless body is brought back to the ward. At the moment where he sang his dying words – *In other fields we'll gather flowers, you'll see/Till then, be happy/Do not weep, but live, for me* – the JCB had jerked into life. The furniture was screwed down, but Harriet was hit on the head by a spitoon and a map of the fortifications around Antwerp. Then there were the horses. The regiment of mounted Sikhs had been reduced to a symbolic pair of greys on loan from the Lifeguards. Their entry through the auditorium on a specially built ramp, pulling the young hero's coffin on a gun carriage, was the climax of the finale – when the horses agreed to come in forwards. Under the sceptical eye of an officer from the RSPCA and a representative of Animalwatch the pair had been trained separately and only introduced at the dress rehearsal. Any more signs of stress, like trying to jump the first three rows of the stalls or head-butt the conductor, and Westminster Council would be called upon to bar them from the show.

Japheth toyed with his Cheerios, keeping his eyes downcast. 'How are you getting there? It's near Crouch End, isn't it?'

'Dad's taking me. He'll drop me off at a tube station.'

'And how long will that take?'

'Quite a long time. I'll have to live closer to the ground if they keep me on.'

'Japh, please don't do this. Is it because I've been so distracted lately? Please don't ruin your life to punish me.'

Japheth threw down his spoon. 'You've been distracted all my life, Mum.'

'That's possible.'

'I mean – bloody hell – look at the facts, Mother. I scored ten goals in my first term at Chortleberry Lodge, played for the under 15s at Cordwainers when I was eleven, I was top scorer in Mole Valley juniors for three years running, and now I'm a trainee with a team five places from the top of the first division, and you think it's all to attract your *attention*? I mean, if I'd wanted to attract your attention I would have given up football and become a ballet dancer, or set fire to myself, or something.'

'Is it because of Tiz, darling? I know you and Mungo always say I favour her, but I don't really, you know, it's just that perhaps you don't realize how little girls feel when they have high-achieving older brothers.'

'You mean, am I joining Tattenham Drovers because I'm jealous of Jellyroll Désirée Polly?'

'Darling, I think catty remarks like that betray more than you intend. For one thing, she isn't a jellyroll any more.'

'For God's sake, Mum, will you stuff this pseudo-psycho crap. I love fucking football – that's all there is to it.'

'Japheth, there's no need to – Oh, Semi. What are you doing up at this hour?' Semi was not only up, but stunned the senses in dazzling white jeans on her five foot legs, and moist red lipstick, so that her mouth reminded Harriet of close-ups in TV operations. 'Are you going somewhere?'

'If you don't care. I go wiz Jat today.'

'But it's not your day off, Semi. You know it's your turn to walk with Tiz and Telly.'

Semi raised her fig-coloured eyes to the ceiling and let out a slight whistle. Japheth was incensed.

'Mum, it's only one day. Semi wants to give me moral support. You know what that is?'

'All right, all right, you've made your point. But you can tell Tiz that she can't ride tonight.'

'Why should I? Why can't she ride alone for once?'

'Do you want it on your conscience if anything happens to her?'

'It won't be on *my* conscience, Mother. You bought her the pony, you should be the one walking behind it.'

Harriet thumped the table. 'You're so sanctimonious I could *kill* you.'

Japheth smiled as he rose from the table. 'Well, I'd really have your attention then, wouldn't I? If you'll excuse me I'll go and see if Dad's ready. I'm so lucky he's not off selling programmes about gay policemen to the Eskimaux. Perhaps it's Dad's attention I'm after.' He put a mock questioning finger in his mouth. 'Did you think of that?'

Warren put his head round the door. 'Tiz has no clean socks, sweetheart. Can't you hear her screaming?'

'Not when the dishwasher's on.'

'By the way, what's it like round the station at night? Security wise.'

'It's quite safe. There are always one or two people about.'

'Perhaps you should go from Dorking instead. The parking lot is well lit over there.'

'But that's much further out.'

'What about Damian? Couldn't you come home with him?'

'Damian? Oh, *Cats* comes down before us, I think. But it may be after, eventually. They're still cutting.' Bugger Damian. Warren seemed to have accepted him as a family pet. He was supposed to be a ship that passed in the night, not a regular ferry service.

'Oh. Well, good luck.'

'Thanks.'

Harriet watched them drive off. Only Semi spared her a backward glance. She could see that Warren was bolstering Japheth with meaningless chatter. Japheth was probably nervous. She should have wished him good luck, too – and given him an invoice for five years at Chortleberry Lodge and seven at Cordwainers Hospital. Warren's complacence on the subject was inexplicable. But he had been somewhat semidetached since she started work. She had expected low-level tolerance, sarcasm, a notched stick of domestic tasks inadequately completed. He had grumbled when obliged to go the American Ambassador's birthday party on his own, but compensated by cancelling Glyndebourne and the Austerlitz Ball. An obscure unease, that he was behaving as if there were some advantage to himself in the upheaval, waited to be considered when she had settled into the run. In the meantime she went to see if Tiziana's socks had fallen down behind the cistern in the airing cupboard.

The previews went well. The machinery worked, nobody dried, the horses appeared to have been doped and could hardly make it up the ramp.

'They'll have to adjust the dose,' said Pamela/Archduchess Ferdinand/Left-wing nurse/Landlady of the *auberge*, with whom Harriet shared a dressing-room. She was standing on her head.

'Do you really think they're doped?'

'Of course. They don't just do it to race horses, you know. You go to an auction. All the nags are strolling round saying 'Peace, man.' But you get them home and the first thing they do is dismantle the stable. My sister was caught like that. She bought this pony for her son, and he seemed really docile in the ring. Then when he got on, the pony not only bolted, he bucked the kid off and then turned round and tossed him back up again before he landed.'

Harriet felt sick. She had just reluctantly agreed to let Tiz ride alone, providing she was equipped with a mobile phone, pepper spray and personal alarm, none of which would be any use if she was unconscious.

'Aren't you going to do your exercises?' said Pam.

'I don't feel like singing now.'

The thought of Tiziana's likely mortality, and a report in the *Evening Standard* about a little boy who had bravely failed to survive four liver transplants, chastened Harriet. When she got home she left a note on Japheth's door. *Darling Japh, I hope you had a good day. I know I'm being a bit obtuse about your problem, but try to understand that from my point of view it's as if you were convinced you were a Ming vase. I don't know where to start trying to comprehend how you can do this. But I will try. Love, Mum.* After all, what did money matter? Japheth's education had enabled him to play five sports to county level and, thanks to the Duke of Edinburgh's Award Scheme, survive for two nights in the wild. Besides, it would be very awkward if Japheth still had the hump on the first night and refused to go.

The stage door entrance was jammed with flowers, including a five-foot pyramid of orchids. A distressing number of Harriet's own floral tributes bore messages urging her to 'go over the top' in style. That was exactly what it felt like – a life expectancy of fifteen minutes. The reference made Harriet uneasy, as she imagined Dotty's comments. She detached all the messages and put them in a drawer.

The mood in the bunkers was a cross between New Year's Eve and the night before Agincourt. Perry Saddlesmith, the Irish composers and some sick-looking backers came round to wish them good luck and dispense gifts. Pam actually did throw up, which was a welcome distraction. Their dresser, a former policewoman known as Boxer, was indignant. While Pam had her microphone fitted, she dabbed at Pam's costume with a damp sponge. 'There's vomit on these pearls. Get them off, I'll have to wash them.'

'There isn't time!'

'Yes there is. They'll stink otherwise and put everyone off.'

Over the tannoy came the sounds of the audience, the twitter of birds on a wire turning to the rolling boom of a hippo convention, punctuated by laughter and the ominous shimmer of violins. 'I want to go home,' thought Harriet. But home was silent and empty now. The family had all turned out, plus Dotty, Semi, Harriet's brother and his family, assorted close friends and the chairman of M25TV.

Harriet's partner in the Waltz of the Ghosts popped in with a last-minute gift – a thermometer wrapped in cat gut and loo paper.

'It's lovely. I was dreading another bedpan.'

Pam crossed herself. 'Come with me, Harriet. We, who are about to—'

'No, don't say that.'

With Boxer holding the Archduchessly train they hurried down to the stage.

Harriet's party was waiting in the crowded foyer. Japh and Tiz were arguing, but stopped when they saw her. She thought they smiled with the sincerity of an MP at a constituency barbecue, but their congratulations were effusive. Indeed Dotty looked as if she had been crying. Warren hugged and kissed her.

'Well done, sweetheart. It was terrific, wasn't it, kids?'

'Did you really enjoy it? What about you, Dotty?'

Dotty, who had risen to the occasion in a Thatcher blue dress and jacket from Bentalls, raised her eyebrows. 'I can honestly say I've never seen a better musical, Harriet. Now I mean it. It was very moving – just as you said.'

Harriet kissed her warmly. 'I'm so relieved you approve.' This was not straight irony, more a recognition that against all judgement, it was Dotty's opinion she most dreaded and prized.

The children's praise was more muted. 'Was that chap meant to get a bayonet in his foot, Mum?' said Mungo. 'It was dead realistic.'

'No he wasn't. He's all right, though. There are bound to be teething troubles.'

'I liked the horses best,' said Tiz. 'How did they get him to eat that lady's Cornetto?'

'That wasn't in the script either. It was her fault, she shouldn't have been eating in the auditorium.' The only other tense moment had been when the sound system became briefly linked with the control room of a taxi company, and the action was overlayed with loud requests to pick up a fare in Tower Hamlets.

Harriet was punch drunk with relief and glory. Everything was working out exactly as she had hoped, especially now she knew Dotty would not be tut-tutting in her soul. 'Well, let's go then. Warren, do you think you could get a taxi?'

'Actually, Mum, Semi and I are going to a club,' said Japh. 'You don't mind, do you?'

'Oh. No, of course not. How are you going to get home?'

'We'll probably stay the night with a mate of mine from work.'

'I see.'

'And I think I'll take Tiz home, if you don't mind,' said Dotty. 'It's been a lovely evening, Harriet, but I'm very tired, and Tiz has got school in the morning.'

'I'm not a bit tired,' yawned Tiz.

'That means I'll have to go to the stupid party on my own,' said Mungo.

'We'll be there, darling.'

'You know what I mean, Mum.'

'Then you'd better go home too.'

'Will we be missing anyone famous?' said Tiz.

'Like who?'

'Jason Donovon?'

'Well, if he's there I'll get his autograph.'

They put Dotty, Mungo and Tiz into a taxi, and watched, mute, as Japheth and Semi disappeared into the hard-faced shifting crowds of night owls in the Strand.

Perry Saddlesmith had hired the penthouse suite of a converted munitions factory for the party. The decor was all yellow brick and blue pipes. By the time they got there the cabaret had started. Warren made for the sales director of Channel 4. Christopher, the voice coach, was beside himself with praise. He enthused about her B flats for a while and then said, 'You seem a bit sad, Harriet. Or is it just general *tristesse*?'

'Yes. No. Don't tell anyone I said this, but now I've done it, I feel like going home and putting my feet up – like, permanently.'

'Oh, no, not a pub in the country.'

'No, not that. It's just that it's so long since I've been locked in to eight shows a week. I hope I've still got the energy.'

'You'll find it when you're settled in. Thank goodness we don't have to stay up for the papers these days.'

'I don't suppose I'll rate a mention anyway.'

'God was pleased with your performance. He told me so himself. You should go and have a word with him.'

'Was he? He's so much younger than I am. I always feel I'm talking to the infant Dalai Lama.'

'Did you hear that story about him and the tile-cutter from Plymouth?'

Christopher whispered in her ear. Harriet was immediately restored to *joie de vivre*.

Warren came to take her away at one-thirty. 'I know it's kinda early, but you mustn't overdo it.'

They started the long kissathon that eventually led to the exit. A chauffeur-driven Lagonda with gardenias banked on the back seat awaited them. Warren smiled coyly.

'Warren – you angel!' She flung her arms round him. Nose to nose she said, 'This is the best of all, darling. Thank you.'

'Don't expect this every night, now.'

They drove off. In the rear view mirror the chauffeur saw a young man in evening dress rush out of the building and wave frantically at the speeding car. The chauffeur stepped on the accelerator.

Warren woke her up as they turned into the drive.

'That's funny,' said Warren, 'the lights are on.'

'And that's a police car.'

Warren dismissed the driver. They stood looking at the house, suddenly cold and dizzy with foreboding. Harriet's first thought was that Dotty, Mungo and Tiz had surprised a burglar, and a pile of bloody corpses awaited them. Warren took Harriet's hand, trying to negotiate the interface between the balm of the evening's triumph and the swirling chaos of unknown horrors. The gardenias Harriet was holding made her feel like a Hammer Horror bride as they crossed the threshold.

The console table in the hall had been overturned, the Balinese duck, vase of asters and collection of Mother-of-Pearl visiting card holders were strewn across the floor. The reproduction tapestry of The Triumph of Galatea had been ripped from the wall. The glass on the prints of La Rochelle was smashed. Through the open doors of the other rooms they could see the rubble of destruction. Jelly and Custard slunk out of the kitchen, morbid with guilt. Jelly tweaked his tail in the doomed hope that they would be instantly exonerated, but seeing the case was a non-starter they slunk back into the kitchen.

A policeman came to the door of the sitting room.

'Mr and Mrs Funkel?'

'Yes.'

'Come in, please.'

Dotty sat on the sofa crying into a handkerchief, with the children huddled on either side. Tiz ran up to Harriet, wrenched the gardenias from her arms and flung them to the floor.

'They've – huh – smashed the televisions, Mum – huh – the *pigs* – I – huh – hate them I – huh – wish they were – huh – *dead*.'

'If we hadn't gone to the show this would never have happened,' said Mungo.

'Oh – my – God—' wailed Dotty.

'What's happened here?' said Warren to the policeman, a moustachioed heavyweight who looked extremely bored.

'As you can see, sir, the place has been done over. Your parties here aren't able to say if anything has been stolen. But it looks like a piece of deliberate vandalism to me.'

'Where did they get in?'

'Through the kitchen door. Smashed the glass.'

'Didn't the burglar alarm go off?'

At this, Dotty's legs shot straight out in a convulsion and she howled afresh. 'It's all my fault! I forgot to put it on. I'm not used to them things – all the excitement—'

Harriet stared at her. 'I meant to call and remind you. It's my fault, too.'

'It's true, I'm afraid, sir. This will adversely affect your insurance claim I should think. They don't accept collective amnesia as an excuse.' He evidently thought this was quite amusing.

'Can we get another TV tomorrow?' said Mungo.

'For God's sake, Mung. You can use the one in Japheth's room for the moment.'

'He never lets us.'

'Well he'll have to. For Christ's sake – our whole home is trashed and all you can think about is the fucking TV.'

Mungo jumped up, tears breaking through. 'You're the one who keeps reminding us the TV pays the bills, Dad.'

'OK, but—' Mungo ran upstairs. 'I'm sorry, Officer. We're kinda shocked here.'

'That's perfectly natural, sir.'

'What's the procedure?'

'My colleague's checking the other rooms at the moment, sir. And we'll try and get forensics round in the morning, so don't touch anything. In the meantime, if you could establish if anything is missing we'll be back to go over the case in detail.'

'Tomorrow?'

'Oh no. I should think it would be about three weeks. There's always a backlog when the hoods come back from their holidays.'

'Terrific. You mean, we can't touch anything for three weeks?'

'No, you can clear up after forensics have been.'

'Great.'

Harriet put a hand on Warren's arm. 'I think I'm going to faint.'

Dotty vacated the sofa and Harriet was laid out on it.

'I'll go and get some water,' said Dotty.

Warren kicked aside the pile of broken-backed books and anxiously fanned Harriet with a first edition of *Tarka the Otter*. 'This is too much for my wife right now. She's just opened in a show in the West End. She's exhausted already.'

'Ah yes,' said the officer. 'That new musical. Your kids were telling me about it. Quite a few Thespian folk round here. And Laurence Olivier was born in Dorking. You wouldn't think it, would you?'

'They certainly don't advertise the fact.'

'Perhaps your wife wouldn't mind signing my notebook when she comes round. I took my wife to the theatre last year. *42nd Street*. Fabulous. We don't normally go, to be honest, but we'd won a trip round the London sewers at a Rotary Club do, so we thought we'd make a day of it.'

'I see.'

Harriet raised herself on one elbow. 'Officer, forgive me for interrupting, but something has occurred to me about this.'

'Oh yes, madam? What's that?' He opened his notebook.

'It must have been someone who knew about the first night – someone who knew we'd all be out. The house is never empty normally – unless we're on holiday.'

'There must be lots of people round here who know you're in that show, madam. How about the milkman, for instance?'

'Yes, I suppose he does. I believe I did mention it.'

'Why would the milkman want to wreck the house?' said Tiz.

'He wouldn't, darling. The officer just means that far more people would know about it than we realize.'

'Talking of which, can you think of anyone who might bear a grudge against any of you?'

They thought, but shook their heads. Dotty came in with the glass of water.

'Semi might have,' said Tiz, 'but she was at the show.'

'What about you, Dotty?' said Harriet. 'Have you upset anyone enough to make them do this?'

Something about Harriet's phraseology made Dotty feel fingered. 'No, I haven't been here long enough.'

'Well, it's probably just aggravated burglary,' said the officer. 'A lot of the kids who do this sort of thing are high on drugs.'

Warren was horrified. 'God, I hope so. I'd hate to think we'd been deliberately targeted.'

'Darling, this couldn't be Channel 4's doing, could it?'

Warren laughed. 'Oh yeah. That would be the good news.'

But good news was not on the face of the officer's colleague, who came in with Mungo.

'I'm afraid the upstairs is a bit of a mess, Mrs Funkel. They didn't touch the children's rooms, but they left a message in the bathroom. Perhaps you'd better come and have a look.'

They all hurried upstairs. Written in nail varnish on Harriet's bathroom mirror were the words 'Fuck the arseholes.' Harriet and Dotty started crying.

'Umm,' said the first officer. 'Still, it's not conclusive. As to motive, I mean. However, it's very neatly executed. Not the sort of thing you would expect from someone in mid-rampage, as it were.'

Tiz clung to Harriet. 'Mum!'

'What, darling?'

'British Telecom! Do you think they've hurt him?'

'No, I'm sure they haven't.'

'What's that, madam?'

'It's her pony. But he's in a field down the road.'

Tiz grabbed the officer's arm. 'Come on. You must take me down there to see if he's all right.'

'No, darling, it's too late.'

'But Mum, I couldn't sleep if I didn't know.'

'I'll go with them,' said Dotty, roused for a moment from calculating how long it would take her to pay off the bill for damages from her pension. Harriet gave way. The trauma still left room for the zephyr of a thought that, despite appropriating a share of Dotty's guilt, the residue would provide a useful counterbalance to Dotty's moral one-upmanship.

The remaining officer kept them talking while the horsewatch party carried out its mission. They seemed to take hours, but it was only because, as Dotty said, the dratted thing was hiding and they had to tramp round the field with a flashlight. He was unharmed. This fact lifted their spirits to relative heights. The officers left amid good cheer on all sides, as though after a successful dinner party.

Tiz begged Harriet to stay with her until she went to sleep, but it was Harriet who nodded off first, slumped over Tiz's ankles.

They were all still in bed when forensics arrived. Mungo and Tiz woke up too late to go to school. The excitement of the investigation restored their morale. Tiz felt well enough to go for a ride after lunch. A reporter and photographer from the *Mole Valley Advertiser* arrived, followed in the afternoon by several more from London. Harriet was too stunned to object.

The phone rang all day, mainly Harriet's friends gushing congratulations into the answering machine. Warren had gone to work at lunchtime, but he called later to see if she was up to the evening performance.

'No, I'm not. But I have to. Pam's my understudy. She's had to learn four parts already. I can't put this on her so soon.'

'I'm sure she wouldn't mind. Have you seen the reviews?'

'No, of course not. Dotty didn't even go for the *Daily Mail*.'

'I've got one from the *Independent* here. Do you want me to read it?'

'OK.'

'Listen to this. "*Wipers!*, with its poignant counterpointing of elegiac grandeur and gut-wrenching realism, sets a new standard for the popular art form best able to interpret contemporary history at a level which reaches both beyond intellectual examination and deep into the heart of the collective unconscious. Andreas Figg's direction is sensitive to the tragic theme, as well as uncannily sure-footed in garnering the life-enhancing quality of a generation still wedded to heroic altruism." How about that?'

'Goodness. Is there anything about the performances?'

'Sure. They're mainly about Melanie. There's something in the *Mirror*. Wait a sec. Here. "Melanie Pace as the gutsy girl who follows her lover to the front, has a voice that could launch a rocket. Tender and tough by turn, she never allows the vocal fireworks to dominate a heartrending and committed performance. She is—" wait for it "—well-supported by Harriet Dimdore as the frustrated matron, and Peter Makeweight as the matron's amputee sweetheart." You see, you did get a mention.'

'Well supported. Hmm. The elastic stocking prize.'

'Oh, come on, honey, you know they don't go into detail. I'll bring them home. Shit, I've got a meeting at the ICA tonight. How about I meet you after the show?'

'I'd almost forgotten about the show, Warren.'

'I know. In a way it's maybe a good thing you have to do it. It might take your mind of the break-in.'

'It's not my mind I'm worried about.'

'Can't you get some rest?'

'Hardly. The house is full of reporters.'

'What? How come? Why did you let them in?'

'I can't remember. I feel so gob-smacked I don't know what I'm doing, I suppose.'

'I wish you hadn't done that, Harriet. I really do.'

'But you know what they're like. They'd only climb drainpipes and take shots through the windows.'

'Still, I really wish you hadn't done that.'

Dotty was appalled that Harriet had not cancelled the performance. 'You'll make yourself ill.'

'If I get ill it won't be the show's fault,' said Harriet, with a look. 'The show must go on. Ballerinas dance with broken toes, you know.'

'Huh. If grown women prance around pretending to be fairies, what do you expect?'

'Dotty, do you understand the expression "non sequitur"?' Dotty grinned. 'Dead meat?'

11

When Harriet arrived at the theatre she found a bouquet, from Perry Saddlesmith, of ismene, agapanthus and galtonia, the flowers outnumbered two to one by fronds of gunnera in its infancy, and fresh figs.

Word of the break-in had spread, and sympathetic visitors trooped in and out of the dressing room. Andreas came in to give her some concentration coaching, which involved imagining she was a seed developing into a full-size marrow. It was not too much, she reflected, to hope that the positive spin-off from the break-in might outweigh the negative. Afterwards, everyone said that her performance was better than ever.

At Victoria, she kept an eye out for Damian. Cats did, in fact, come down at approximately the same time as *Wipers!*. But if he came she did not see him. Instead she was kept company by two middle-aged couples who had just been to *This Is Your Life – Former Prime Minister*. They were engaged in a lively discussion about whether to allow twelve-year-old girls to shave their legs, a topic on which Harriet had much to say.

It had been decided, with much sadness, by the British Ice Dancing Federation, to declare the throne empty. The trail on Yoevil and Kean had gone cold. It was rumoured that MI6 knew perfectly well that they were being held by a terrorist group in the Kurdish part of Turkey, but that the government did not want to offend a member of NATO by interfering in its internal affairs.

'I thought they were Armenians?' said Tiz.

'All terrorists work together these days, darling. Like the Red Cross.'

'It's all that Saddam Hussein's fault,' said Dotty. 'If it wasn't for this Kuwait business, Mrs Thatcher would have more time to worry about them.'

'My guess is she'll find time just before the next election. You know, I bet they did arrange it themselves. Don't you think it odd that no one has claimed responsibility?'

Dotty looked at Harriet as though she had suggested that Princess Diana had had a sex change operation. 'May you be forgiven for having such evil thoughts, Harriet. This isn't America, you know. We fought for this country so that Yoevil and Kean could get where they are today.'

'Perhaps it's time to re-enlist,' spat Harriet as she slammed out of the room.

Could it be that the vandals had a Dotty at home, or that she had previously been lent out to some innocent family now crazy for revenge?

She retreated to the bath to cool off. It had become a redoubt to which she increasingly resorted, where she fought with memories of *The Servant*, and the conflicting imperatives of compassion for Dotty's situation and the necessity of hanging on to her until a suitable replacement could be found. She was tempted to risk going it without Dotty, were it not that Semi's term was nearly up, and her commitment to the household had reduced itself to care and control of Japheth. In the morning Semi waved him off and mooned around the house all day moving the occasional ornament, until it was time to set off to meet him after training.

Dotty had gradually taken over the day-to-day household management, one advantage of which was that Harriet could stay in bed while Dotty gave Mungo and Tiz their breakfast. Tiz seemed to be losing weight too fast under the scheme, in a way that could not be accounted for by veganism alone. Harriet tackled Dotty on the subject as Dotty sat with her Maxwell House, Lincoln Creams and *Daily Mail* after the morning's chores. The regularity of Dotty's habits was like a dripping tap. If only she would go mad and have Jaffa Cakes instead.

Dotty scanned the racing results with arched brows. 'I really don't understand you sometimes, Harriet. One minute you think I'm stuffing the child with cholesterol, and the next I'm starving her to death.'

'Children do lurch from one extreme to the other. Anorexia is such a problem these days. I'm not accusing you of anything, Dotty. It's just that you're in a much better position to observe her eating habits than I am at the moment.'

Dotty returned to the front page. 'Aren't you deluding yourself a bit, Harriet? Anorexia is a symptom, not a disease.'

'Of what, in this case?'

'That's not for me to say.' She sniffed. 'I see Germany's been reunited. Heigh-ho. Why did we bother?' Harriet made for the door. 'Oh, by the way, Harriet, I took your advice and rented out my house. I heard from the estate agents yesterday.'

'Did I advise that?'

'Why, yes. Several times, actually. Especially after the break-in. Why, do you think I'd be better off selling?'

'No. Renting is much more flexible. How long for?'

'Six months to start with. Maybe a year for the right tenant.'

'A year.' Harriet sat down again.

'That is what you wanted, isn't it?'

'Yes, it is. It's nothing personal, Dotty, it's just that I haven't got used to the idea of doing eight shows a week for that long. And I haven't got over the break-in, either.'

At this reference Dotty put away the paper and sat up. 'Can you not sleep either? I know what you mean. It's the thought of those scum being out there like wolves in the night, waiting to pounce, isn't it? You could just – ooh, I don't know. The birch is too good for them. They should be exterminated. Why should tax payers support scum like that? They're bound to be on social security.'

'Dotty, please don't let's get into that argument again.'

'Huh. I bet they don't get this sort of thing in Iran.'

'It was the bloomin' ayatollahs you wanted to string up last week.'

'Yes. Well. They do have some good ideas, I suppose.'

'Dotty, those kinds of punishments don't even work once the novelty has worn off. You know, there was a soldier in Wellington's day they calculated got four thousand lashes in the course of his career. If it worked as a deterrent you'd think the first two thousand would have been enough. The bystanders fainted. They were spattered with bits of flesh.' Dotty turned slightly green. 'Anyway, I'm not so much worried that it will happen again. It's the thought that we were picked out. None of the neighbours have been done over like that. And the odd thing is, the only thing that's missing is Warren's razor.'

Dotty gripped the edge of the sofa. 'Cut-throat?'

'No, Philishave.'

'Did you tell the police?'

'Yes. But they think he might have left it in a hotel. He didn't, though.'

'That's a clue.'

'Why?'

'At least it means they're old enough to shave.'

Japheth was still not speaking to Harriet. He only got the opportunity on Sundays, but made the most of it. *Wipers!* was running smoothly, and Harriet began to enjoy herself.

One Monday evening she was called to the stage door to claim two men in suits. The taller one proffered a box of After Eight, so she presumed they were not detectives. The one with sandy hair, crinkled like the beach at low tide, shook her hand.

'Mrs Funkel? My name's Harry Parker, and this is my colleague, Derek Shingle.'

'How do you do? What can I do for you?' Harriet's mind darted, tadpole-like, among possible identities for the duo. The most obvious was that they represented the yobs who had wrecked the house and had come to reveal their ultimate purpose. 'Did you enjoy the show?'

'Ah. Well we haven't actually seen the show. We've been at The Ra-Ra and we were just passing so we thought we'd pop in for a chat. I should explain, we're on the coaching team at Tattenham Drovers. Work with your lad Japheth.'

'Oh, I *see*. In that case – I'm delighted to meet you.'

'Fancy a kebab?'

'Pardon?'

'Or something stronger? We'd like to have a word about your lad, Mrs Funkel.'

'I see. I have to say, I'm very tired. But, perhaps a quick coffee?'

Harriet led them into the nearest hotel. She chatted of wigs and window boxes, while her mind grappled with the novelty of the situation. Harry and Derek sat on the edge of their seats, stirring ounces of multicoloured crystals into the coffee. Harriet tried to look imperious, but relaxed.

'We're very pleased with your lad, Mrs Funkel,' said Harry. 'There's a lot of potential there. Of course, he's missed out on the training side. He didn't go to a Centre of Excellence, I gather.'

'We rather thought the school covered that.'

'Private school, wasn't it? Private schools don't give their lads much leeway in what they do outside. It makes me weep to think of the talent that goes to waste in the upper classes.'

'I'd never thought of that. Certainly, a career in football was not what we had in mind.'

'That's right. You wanted him to go to the university, I understand.'

'Leeds,' added Derek, unsmiling.

'Thank you. I hadn't forgotten. To be honest, Mr Parker, I'm still hoping he will. My husband was in favour of letting him work this football thing out of his system. He is eighteen. There's nothing I can really do to stop him. And I must point out that Japheth was very keen to go to university himself – before the World Cup, that is. It all blew up after that. Like people rushing out and buying tennis racquets straight after Wimbledon. I'm sure a lot of chaff is blown before such a wind, but it settles down eventually.'

'Have you said as much to the lad?'

'He knows my views. What are you getting at, Mr Parker?'

'Well, like I said, your lad's got a lot of talent. He wants to play striker because that's, like, at the sharp end, but we're trying to persuade him he can be more use mid-field. He's got a well slide-rule pass.'

'He's the type of player who'll help us nail the lie we're all zone-oriented over here,' chortled Derek.

'So what's the problem?'

Harry shuffled. 'It's the inner man we're more concerned about, Mrs Funkel. You see, if he's going to make it, he's got to have two hundred percent commitment. We've talked to him a lot, and our psychos have as well, and we're agreed he's not entirely happy with his decision. He's even talked about going to the university and taking up football again afterwards. Of course, it's not impossible, but it won't be with us. He's got to make up his mind, or he's wasting everyone's time, not least his own.'

Harriet was chuffed to know that Japheth was not completely lost. 'What you're trying to say is, that his lack of commitment is all my fault, and if I could "get behind him", or whatever the phrase is, then everything would be all right.' Her heart beat high with resentment at the idea that trying to save Japh from a life of knee injuries, yob culture and advertising ball bearings on his shirt made her a bad mother.

'Something like that, yes. Look, don't get the wrong idea, Mrs Funkel. We all understand you're worried about the lad's future.'

'His present, too, actually.'

'Well, all right. But, with respect, I don't think you have much idea what the game's like today, at the very top level. Believe me, I wouldn't be here if I didn't think your lad had got what it takes. Why, one of our star centre forwards has just bought a chain of garages. Why don't you come down to the club, talk to people, let the lad show you round. It would mean a lot to him.'

'I shall certainly do that when I have more time. But you must also understand that I haven't stood in his way. I've tried to be sympathetic. If you ask me, it's Japheth himself who is having doubts, and he's transferring them by blaming me.'

Harry and Derek exchanged a puzzled look at this piece of Byzantine reasoning. 'At least come and watch him play. We might be trying him out against Bognor in about six weeks' time.'

'I have a matinée on Saturdays, I'm afraid. Otherwise I would. I appreciate that you take a holistic view of his development. But don't forget that Japheth is still an adolescent. You shouldn't discount the element of childish rebellion in his choices.'

'Don't worry. I've got kids of my own.'

'And how would you like it if they wanted to go on the stage?'

'Same way your parents did, I daresay.'

'Well. There you are then. I'd probably agree with you. Most actors want their children to become accountants.'

'Swings and roundabouts, eh? Or did you get married at eighteen as well?'

'No. As well as what?'

'Your lad.'

'What?'

Harry and Derek drew breath sharply. 'Oh. Perhaps we're mistaken. We thought he was married to that French girl he's always with.'

'Of course not. Did he tell you that? That's absolutely absurd. He wouldn't get married without telling us. It's quite preposterous.'

'Yes. Well. We'd better be going. Thank you for talking to us, Mrs Funkel. Are you OK?'

'Perfectly. I'll stay here for a moment.'

'As you wish.' He picked up the bill for coffee. 'I'll get this.'

'Thank you. And could you ask them to bring me a scotch and water?'

Harriet crept along the corridor to Semi's room and put her ear to the keyhole. Foreign murmurings came from within. Holding her breath and deafened by her own heartbeat, she turned the doorknob and went in.

Semi was alone, lying on her back in a Tattenham Drovers strip, her long legs splayed over the duvet like a deck chair frame. She was talking in her sleep. Harriet thought she made out the words *pistache de terre*. She tiptoed in and stood by the bed, peering to see if the light from the landing glinted off a wedding band. Semi's hands were ringless, but Harriet had an idea that Continentals were wayward in these matters. Her eyelids flickered over rolled-up eyeballs. The eyelashes were as thick as the brushes in a car wash. 'Put out the light,' muttered Harriet, 'And then, put out the light.' How easy it would be to take the spare pillow and place it over Semi's face. Harriet burned and trembled, seared to the spot. An unseen force seemed to move her hand to the pillow, but as she drew it away Semi opened her eyes and briefly stared, blindly, then closed them and rolled over on her side. Released from the spell, Harriet ran from the room.

Warren was snoring. Harriet went into their bathroom and stood over the sink, trying, and failing, to be sick. She shook with terror at what she had done, or nearly done, or thought of doing. Not just at the urge to smother Semi, but at the memory of that momentary thrall to a force beyond her control, a demon she would not even wish on a herd of swine. She looked at her sweating, grey-green face in the mirror, and thought of the consequences if she had not been stopped by Semi opening her eyes – the trial, Japheth's hatred for life, Mungo and Tiz left motherless, the publicity, shame before the world, the grief of Semi's parents. An image of those flaming haunches of British lamb rose before her – lambs to the slaughter. She slid onto the floor.

Harriet woke at six in a panic. She had had a nightmare in which she had accidentally murdered Tiz by sending her sleeping bag to the cleaners without first checking whether she was in it or not. Without thinking, or remembering why, she got up and went to Semi's room and went straight in. Semi sat up, shocked.

'How are you feeling, Semi?'

'*Pourquoi?*'

'I thought I heard you cry out.'

'*Non*. I am good.'

'Right. Sorry. You can go back to sleep for half an hour. Sorry.'

Back in her room, Harriet crawled back into bed, soggy with relief. 'I must have dreamt it. It can't have happened. It must have been a nightmare – the stress of finding out they—'

She sat up again. 'Warren, wake up. I tried to murder Semi last night. Warren!'

'What? What did you say?'

'I tried to murder Semi last night. I nearly smothered her.'

Warren sat up, his face contorted with – yes – laughter. 'You did what?' Harriet repeated what had happened. Warren became more serious. 'You must be mistaken, sweetheart. Why would you want to kill Semi? She hasn't been near the kitchen for quite a while.'

'I didn't. Of course I didn't. I'm sure I didn't really. It's just that last night I had a visit from two minders from Tattenham Drovers. They implied that Japheth and Semi had got married.'

'You're kidding. Now *that's* weird. Do you believe it?'

'Of course not. Should we confront them?'

'Not again, for Chrissakes. If Japh doesn't want us to know I guess he has his reasons.'

'Perhaps they'll get divorced without telling us, too.'

Warren took her hand. 'Listen, sweetheart, don't take this the wrong way, but – you haven't got a – thing – about Japh, have you? Like – you know—'

'Incest? Sicko! I won't even deign to deny it. What a disgusting suggestion.'

He laughed. 'Well you did just confess to attempted murder.'

'Murder's nothing compared to that.'

'I'm sorry.'

'Do you really think I could lust after my own son?'

'Hey, I don't know. I guess folks who go in for that kind of thing are in denial anyway.'

'Huh. I can see someone being in denial about their real motives if they're doing, say, a PhD. on the influence of pornography on the genitals, but you couldn't fool yourself about incest.'

'I'm not suggesting you'd do anything about it.'

'Thanks!'

'OK. Forget it. I'm sorry. You're under a lot of stress right now. I guess that's it. Maybe you should go see the doctor.'

'What's the point? I can't take tranquillizers at the moment. So what should we do about this putative marriage? Wait for him to speak? Sit around like Quakers at a meeting?'

'I guess so. Maybe it has something to do with her residence permit. Maybe they do plan to get divorced after a while and hush the whole thing up.'

'That can't be right. I thought EU citizens were allowed to work here now anyway.'

'Oh well—' Warren got out of bed. 'I have to shift. I'm meeting Damian at the club at eight-thirty.'

'Oh yes? Why him? Isn't there anyone else to play with at the club?'

'It was his idea. Any reason he shouldn't?'

'No. I never see him at the station.'

'He's living in Epsom now. The girlfriend left him for another cabin attendant.'

'Really? Male or female?'

'What do you mean?'

'I mean, did she leave him for a man or a woman?'

'Hell, I don't know. It never occurred to me to ask. Why don't you go back to sleep?'

He went into the bathroom, and the roar of the Super Niagara Power Shower began. The family had complained in vain that the noise of this torrent woke them up. This morning Harriet found it rather comforting, as the noise of massed brass bands will temporarily subdue pain. She threw an arm over her face and groaned. Japheth. Semi. The show. The break-in. Dotty. Warren and Damian. Of course she was under stress. The chances of Warren finding out at least one of the reasons if he and Damian played golf on a regular basis were shortening. Supposing he did? To judge by Warren's suggestion that she might be bonking Japheth, perhaps he would not be unduly disturbed.

Harriet decided that the incident in Semi's bedroom, although it had not happened, was a stroke of Fate. She acknowledged that she had neglected Semi, and that it was time to make overtures. Semi was at first suspicious when Harriet began smiling at her, and asking her the French for proportional representation and pancake batter. But Harriet persisted, and Semi cast off her fear that Harriet's behaviour heralded a request to spring clean the cupboards, or take a course in stable management before she was allowed to leave.

Harriet took Semi to lunch at Harvey Nicks. Once Semi's reservations were set aside she opened up with what seemed like gratitude, deepening Harriet's guilt. Semi talked – about her family, her ambition to be a child psychologist, the wickedness of Britain's attitude to French agricultural policy, the superiority of French literature, the awfulness of English bread, the cleanliness of the Paris subway. Harriet was amused by her frankness, wondering if there was a pun there. She was encouraged that Semi did not sound like someone who intended to spend her life in the British Isles.

Afterwards Harriet took her to the theatre and showed her round backstage. Semi was obviously bored stiff and did not even manage a polite smile. Perhaps by way of compensation she kissed Harriet on both cheeks when they parted. Harriet disliked the practice, always afraid of getting her nose jammed in manoeuvres, but was pleased by the gesture. The event had not worked as a forum for confession, but had revealed enough insights into Semi's thinking to make Harriet almost sure she was not married. She could of course check every registry office within a ten-mile radius of Tattenham Drovers. But that would carry the risk of finding out it was true.

Next morning Harriet told Dotty of the new *entente cordiale* that had been established with Semi, despite the failure of the backstage tour. Dotty rattled her *Daily Mail*. 'Perhaps you should take someone who appreciates it next time.'

Harriet cursed. Putting Foreigners First was just the thing to give Dotty the hump, which she could not afford to do.

Harriet received a generous cheque for the recording of *Wipers!*, which she put into a special fund for redecorating after the break-in. They hoped that this would help obliterate the sense of violation. The police had offered family counselling, an alternative to detection at which Dotty, particularly, scoffed.

'Just because it wasn't a proper burglary they're not interested,' she complained. 'They couldn't find a hamster in a pet shop, that lot.'

'If you think you can do any better, why don't you?' said Tiz.

'I might just, at that. I have my theories.'

'Really?' said Harriet. 'Who?'

'That would be saying.'

'I hope you're not serious,' said Warren. 'You can't interfere in an official investigation.'

'What investigation? All they did was hide behind the rhododendrons for a night or two to see if it happened again.'

'What more could you do?' said Warren, testily. 'Suss out your underworld contacts?'

'Not underworld, perhaps. But I do have contacts as it happens.'

'She means the Reverend Vince,' said Harriet. 'Don't you, Dotty?'

But Dotty refused to be drawn. The next day, on the pretext of going to the chiropodist, she took the bus to Banstead police station.

Warren was away, as guest speaker at the Cornish Celtic Arts Festival. Harriet had been looking forward to a lie-in undisturbed by the Super Niagara. For the previous two weeks she had been at the theatre all day as well as all evening. Perry Saddlesmith had called for changes to the first act hospital scenes to get a better balance with the battles. The musical director had complained that she was losing pitch, which meant more sessions with Christopher. The understudies had to be rehearsed, as did the new members of cast who had taken over due to illness. In fact, Harriet was so tired she could not sleep, but tossed and turned all night between dreams in which she walked naked off the stage and sat in the lap of the Lord Mayor of Huddersfield.

She was woken up by Mungo jumping up and down on her feet yelling that Tiz had stolen his hot water bottle for the fucking horse.

'It's got horse poo on it. Look.' He held the Donald Duck aloft. 'You must punish her, Mum. You never do.'

Tiz came in, still in her nightie. 'It's not poo. It's just a bit of mud.'

'So you did take it, darling?'

'So what? He's always borrowing my Game Boy without asking.'

'I'm entitled to borrow your Game Boy, you cow, because you broke mine. Aren't I, Mum?'

'Yes, but not without asking, darling.'

'But she didn't ask if she could borrow my hot water bottle. You'll have to buy me a new one. I'm not using anything that's come into contact with that nag's bum hole.'

'I couldn't ask him, Mum,' wailed Tiz. 'He was at a basketball match and it was an emergency. I thought Telly had colic and I wanted to make him better so that you wouldn't have to spend money on the vet.'

'Then why didn't you use your own hot water bottle?'

'I couldn't find it. I think Semi's stolen it.'

'Oh *yeah*. That's rich, isn't it, Mum – accusing Semi of theft when everyone knows her room is such a shit-hole she can't even find the bed.'

'I was only trying to save Mum money, you pig!' Tiz hit Mungo on the arm. He thumped her in the stomach and they were immediately locked in mortal combat on Harriet's legs.

She leapt out of bed and tried to drag Tiz out of the room. 'How dare you behave like this! Stop it!'

Mungo had Tiz in an arm lock and was kicking her. Harriet grabbed her dressing gown and threw it over his head and pulled it tight until he released his grip. She was gasping for breath. Tiz rolled onto the floor and Mungo threw the dressing gown across the room. 'Go to your room, Mungo – and I don't want to see you again until you apologize.'

'Why should I? She started it.'

'And you could have killed her!'

'I wish I had!'

He ran out, pushing Dotty aside as she looked on from the doorway open-mouthed.

Tiz was crying. 'I hate him, Mum. Why can't you get him adopted?'

Harriet fell rigid onto the bed. 'You shouldn't have taken the hot water bottle, Tiz.'

'But Mum—'

'Go and get dressed.'

'No. Mum, I'm reciting a poem at Harvest assembly tomorrow. Can you come?'

'What time?'

'One o'clock.'

'I'm sorry, darling. I've got to rehearse again.' Harriet had to admire her reflexes. It was the perfect moment to give the guilt winch a good heave.

'Why? Can't you get someone else to do it?'

'That would be like getting someone else to have your operation, darling. I'm sorry. I'd love to come. Why don't you say it for me now?'

'It's not the same. I'm not going to school unless you say you're coming.'

'Don't blackmail me! I've said I'm sorry, now go and get dressed. Now!'

Tiz ran out crying. After a few minutes' deep breathing Harriet went along to Mungo's room. At first he refused to open the door. When he did so, Harriet could see why. He had torn down all his Guns 'n' Roses posters. 'Darling, you musn't fall into that trap all the time. She provokes you verbally, and you use it as an excuse to really hurt her. You must learn to control yourself.'

'In other words, she can do as she likes and I can't do anything.'

'But darling, surely you can see that fighting only makes things worse.'

'Tell her that!'

'I *do*. Oh Mung, come here and give us a hug. I know it's hard, but please try. Next time she does something just tell me and let me deal with it, all right?'

'OK.' He stood like an unplugged dalek as she put her arms around him. 'Mum, can I go to Alton Towers with Philip for my birthday?'

'By yourselves?'

'I'm fifteen, Mum.'

'But still – I'll ask Dad. In the meantime I'll lend Tiz the money to buy you a new Game Boy. How's that?'

'Actually, I'd rather have some new games for my Megadrive.'

Harriet tried going back to bed but could not sleep. She lay in the bath with a wet flannel over her face. On the *Today* programme, pundits were arguing the merits of Mr Heath's plan to negotiate with Saddam Hussein for the release of British hostages. She wondered if Saddam would let her take their place.

Dotty requested Fortnum and Mason for her tea. Unlike Semi, she was less forthcoming than at home. Harriet offered the olive branch of compliments to Mr Heath on his triumphant return from Iraq, but Dotty could not forgive him for taking Britain into Europe, and thought he should defect to the Liberals.

'Fin was a Liberal when he was young,' she sighed. 'Like Churchill. But then he had changed, so Fin did too. He thought the great man must know best.'

'I can't agree with you there. Churchill's feet of clay are only too apparent in hindsight.'

Dotty attacked her millefeuille with a bun fork. 'And what good does that do? It makes me so mad when these nobodies in the universities try and destroy the reputation of men like Churchill who can't answer back. If it wasn't for Churchill—'

'They wouldn't have the freedom, bla, bla, bla. Look, Dotty, we don't often have the opportunity to talk. You seem a bit down. Do you ever wonder if you've made the right decision to come to us?'

'That's funny, I was going to ask you the same thing. I won't deny it was a shock living with the kids at first – I was fond of my eardrums. But I've always loved kids, Harriet, despite what you may think.'

'Did you ever consider adopting?'

'Yes. But we decided against it. Fin was afraid they'd be bad blood.'

'Oh Dotty, human beings are so much more complicated than that.'

'Your lot certainly are.'

'Perhaps we'd better get going.'

Dotty perked up during the backstage tour. She was thrilled to meet a group of chorines relaxing in an upstairs junk room, and broke into a dance routine she had last performed at a VE Day party in Camberwell. Harriet dragged her out before they got hiccoughs from laughing. She left Dotty talking to Boxer the dresser, whose former life in the police force immediately established a bond, and used the telephone in the corridor to phone home and make sure Semi had remembered to fetch Tiz from school and give Custard his antibiotics. When she returned to her dressing room, Dotty was reading the telegrams and cards.

'Oh – Harriet. I hope you don't mind me looking at these. The drawer was open.'

'No. You're welcome.'

'You didn't get any funny ones, did you?'

'Not really. There was one which urged me to 'wipe' the floor with the critics, which I think was meant to be droll.'

'Not that kind of funny. I mean, not very nice ones. Like from someone who didn't approve of the show.'

'Oh dear. Dotty the great detective. Are you seriously trying to solve the break-in?'

'It's just a thought.'

'But if someone had a grudge against the show they would

have attacked it directly. Anyway, I didn't. Though there were a couple of unsigned ones.'

'Where? Can I see?'

'For God's sake, Dotty. It isn't that unusual. Anonymous fans—'

'Not in your case, surely.'

'Thanks a lot. Here they are.'

Dotty read them out. One was a postcard of the tomb of the Unknown Warrior in Westminster Abbey which said, *We shall remember them.* 'That's a bit threatening, isn't it? Could be.'

'Could be quite the opposite. That they're glad the memory is being kept alive.'

'Can't read the post mark.' The other one was on a sheet of lime-green airmail paper and read, *The stars look down. The rats look up.* 'Huh. That's not very nice.'

'No, now I come to think of it, it isn't.' Harriet took the note and frowned. 'At the time I just took it as a vague reference to the setting – you know – mortality, the rats in the trenches – that sort of thing. But there's no reference to me personally.'

'No. You're not a star.'

'Or a rat?'

'Where was it posted?'

'God knows. I threw the envelope away.'

'That's unfortunate. You didn't show them to the police, then?'

'Of course not. There's no reason to think the attack was aimed at me. Look, Pam will be here in a minute. I'm afraid you'll have to go.'

'That's all right. Do you mind if I take these?'

'Yes, I do. Warren was right. Leave it to the police, Dotty. What would you do with them – DNA testing?'

Dotty shrugged. 'As you wish. But I don't know how you can sleep in your bed until they find out who did it. Or rather, why.'

'I'll have even more trouble sleeping if I have to worry about you tracking down vicious thugs.'

'It certainly isn't easy on public transport. My instructor's booked the driving test for January 13th.'

'Good. Then you can volunteer for meals on wheels. That should keep you out of trouble.'

*   *   *

At the beginning of November the nominations were announced for the Society of West End Car Parks awards. *Wipers!* was nominated in five categories including Show Most Convenient for Commuters.

Harriet had been surprised to learn that Avelina Viper was one of the judges, knowing her views on musicals. It also meant that Avelina had seen the show without making herself known to Harriet. Perhaps she had been so disgusted that she could not look Harriet in the face afterwards.

On the other hand, the competition for Best New Musical was encouraging – *Gardeners' World*, a green musical that had transferred from Glasgow's Poll Tax Theatre, *Doll!*, an adaptation of *Hedda Gabler* and a football musical *LIV-ER-POOL!* that had been designed to coincide with the World Cup. Harriet was suffused with pride as Melanie sang her number, Save Your Big Guns For Me. Melanie looked a knock-out with her head in bandages. For some reason the snooker champion Jamie McDougall had been chosen to present the award. He was too nervous to say anything, fumbled with the envelope and muttered *Wipers!* with relief into the microphone. Harriet clapped until her hands hurt. Warren leaped to his feet. Even Peter Makeweight, who was at their table trying to look bored, could not keep his grin under control. He had just bought a laser dinghy on credit.

As the following week was half term Harriet hoped to spend some time with Mungo and Tiz, and suggested the Museum of the Moving Image. Unfortunately, the only day they had not already booked up with their friends was her matinée day. On the Tuesday Tiz went hacking with one of the Amandas, and Mungo was in Sutton shopping with some friends. Dotty was at a primary school demonstrating how to make semolina pudding. Harriet decided to make the most of it with a quiet read. She fell asleep after ten minutes.

The phone rang. It was W H Smith in Sutton. Mungo had been arrested for shoplifting and would she please come immediately. Harriet put the phone down and stared at it for a moment, then burst into tears. Still crying, she ran out, grabbed her handbag and jumped into the car. She was shaking so much she could hardly get the key into the ignition. Pits of shame and terror opened before her. She could not imagine feeling more grieved and humiliated if she were on her way to see Mungo publicly hanged.

As she roared up the A217 Harriet tried to think of mitigating circumstances – first offence, all kids did it. On the other hand she would buy the shop, if necessary, to prevent a prosecution. What was this the Chinese year of – testosterone? The Gulf situation could still end in a world war, and it seemed only last week that Warren had come to the attention of the Cornish police, with a trial still a possibility.

Harriet parked behind Tesco and sat for a while, gripping the steering wheel. There was only one thing for it. Lie. Militant feminists might puke, but she had to face the fact that this might be Mungo's protest against perceived neglect since she had been in the show. Or perhaps her so-called favouritism towards Tiz. Or Warren's frequent absences. Or being half-American and unable to cope with dual identity. Or being the piggy in the middle. Or not being as good at sport as Japheth. Perhaps he was worried about the Gulf. Or unemployment. Or AIDS. The ozone layer. BSE. The lump in Custard's back. When you thought about it, it was surprising the poor child could even get out of bed in the morning. She had brought him into the world; it was only equitable that she use her talents to help him.

She had been directed to go upstairs. A large security man stood outside a door marked 'Private'.

'Mrs Funkel?'

'Yes.'

'This way, please.'

He directed her into an office. Mungo was sitting on a hard chair opposite the desk. He had been crying, although he tried to look cool.

'Mungo, darling, what is all this?' She sat beside him and put a hand on his arm, but he shrugged it off.

The security man pushed a small pile of cassettes towards her across the desk. 'I'm afraid we caught your son trying to leave the store with these, madam. They're empty, as it happens, but that's beside the point. He had tried to conceal them in his underpants.'

'Oh Mungo – how disgusting!'

'I'm perfectly clean,' he protested.

'He tells me he was with two other boys. It seems they dumped their loot and got away.'

'It's true. He was with two friends. Mungo, why on earth did you do it?'

'Dunno.'

'He's fifteen. Is that right?'

'Yes. What will happen? Will you call the police?'

'This store has a strict policy on shoplifting, Mrs Funkel, which includes making an example of those old enough to prosecute. Now, I can tell your son comes from a good home and that you're very upset about it.'

'I certainly am.'

'Can I get you a glass of water?'

'No, thank you.' Contrary to what Harriet had been expecting – that is, a sadist with attitude – this man was positively humane, resigned rather than vengeful. Her plan began to wobble. It's success, however, was more likely.

The man addressed Mungo. 'Aren't you ashamed to upset your mum like this?'

Mungo shrugged. 'Yeah. 'Spose. I didn't mean to. I didn't think.'

'Is there anything you want to tell me, Mrs Funkel? Problems at home, that sort of thing?'

Harriet gasped, and looked down. 'Could I have a word with you alone?'

'Sure. Come outside.'

They stood in a quiet corner by the greetings cards. Harriet trembled and tears came to her eyes. 'I don't know if there's anything in this – I'm not trying to make excuses for him – oh dear—'

'Take your time.'

Oh, what a nice man! I am a worm, a beetle. 'You see, I was told last week that I had – have – cancer. Breast cancer.'

'I see. I'm sorry.'

'I told the children – I have three. They'd been expecting it, but – I thought at the time that Mungo didn't really react – didn't get upset like the others. But – I don't know – perhaps this is his way of – I don't know. He's the middle one, you see. They're often the

most problematic, aren't they? Poor Mungo. He's not very bright
– and his brother's just got into Oxford – Oh dear, I'm sorry—'
She fumbled for a tissue in her handbag. 'Am I wrong? I know
it's no excuse—'

'No, no. That's probably got a lot to do with it. I really am very
sorry. Is it—?'

'Terminal? One never knows. Naturally, I try to be optimistic.'

'And he didn't react, you say.'

'That's right. But he's always been such an easy child at home.
Very quiet. Too quiet, as they say.'

'Perhaps he needs counselling to come to terms with it. Have
you got a Macmillan nurse? They're excellent at helping the
families.'

'No. No it hasn't got that far yet. I've just had the diagnosis.'

'If you like I can give you the number of the family counselling
service. The sooner the better, I would say.'

'You're so kind—'

'Well – in view of what you've told me, I'll let him off, this time.
But he's got to understand that this really isn't the way to cope
with stress. For one thing it's bad for you – in your condition.'

'Yes.'

'Mindless little buggers. Don't worry, I'll destroy the record and
pretend it never happened. That's the least I can do for you.'

'Oh my God—'

'There, there. Dry your eyes. Here.'

'Thank you.' She blew her nose and pulled herself together.
'Please don't say anything to him about it now. He would hate
to break down in front of you. I'll talk to him at home.'

'Of course. I'm really sorry. I hope you pull through.'

'You've been so understanding.' She managed a melancholy
smile.

Mungo looked distinctly worried when they went back into
the room.

'Go along with your mum now, young man. And mind you
look after her.'

'Eh?'

'Come along, darling. We'll go to McDonalds and have a
good chat.'

'What? You hate McDonalds, Mum.'

'Just – come along, darling.' She took a firm hold on his arm and steered him downstairs. They shook hands with the security man, Harriet all grateful radiance, and she placed an arm lovingly around Mungo's waist as they walked through the shop.

'Can I get a magazine, Mum?'

'No!' spat Harriet. 'Let's just get out of here.'

'But Mum—'

Outside, Harriet raised her eyes to the heavens and muttered, 'Sorry!'

Mungo munched a pensive chicken nugget on the back seat as they drove home. Harriet had not trusted herself to discuss the incident until they were alone. Despite theoretical sympathy with Mungo's many problems, anger – fuelled by guilt at having to deceive that nice man – was now pushing all other considerations glacier-like before it. Mungo read the back of her head accurately and slouched behind his paper bag.

'Well, *darling*, what have you got to say for yourself?'

'Dunno.'

'*Dunno*? How *dare* you? I *humiliated* myself to get you off the hook, and all you can say is *dunno*? What the f –, hell do you think you were doing? Why? You've never done anything like this before.'

'Everybody does it, Mum. I'm a late developer.'

'Don't you dare take that tone with me, Mungo. What's the matter with you?'

'Nothing. It was Darren's idea anyway.'

'And then they cleared off and left you to it. Some friends they are.' Mungo shrugged. 'Anyway, I can't believe this is the first time you've been with kids who do that sort of thing. Why did you weaken this time?'

'It's no big deal, Mum. I'm probably the only kid in the school who hasn't done it.'

'So if they were all having their eyeballs pierced, you'd do that too, would you? Don't you realize it's exactly that craven caving in to group pressure that allowed the Nazis to flourish?

'For God's sake, Mum, don't be stupid.'

'And don't kid yourself you're liberating the stuff from bloated capitalists, or whatever, you're just putting the price up for poor people who are honest enough to pay.'

'Yes, Mum.'

'Urrrrrrgh.' Harriet bounced up and down and rattled the steering wheel.

'Watch it, Mum. You nearly hit that cyclist.'

'Well if I did, it would be your fault.'

They stopped at traffic lights. Harriet sagged. 'Darling, if you can't appreciate what you did is wrong, at least think of the consequences for yourself. If the school found out, you might be expelled.'

'Great.'

'Mungo, don't be foolish. Are you sure there isn't something behind all this?'

'Like what?'

'I don't know. Are you upset about Japh and Semi?'

'Eh? What about them?'

'Or is it my working so much lately? You can tell me, you know. I won't be upset.'

'Mum, that's bullshit. That's ape, Mum. It's got nothing to do with that.'

'Perhaps you don't realize it, though.'

'I don't. I never think about you at all, usually.'

'I see. So you wouldn't be pleased if I gave it up when my contract ran out?'

'What? No, don't, Mum. I'm glad you got the part. I'm very proud of you, actually. For Chrissakes don't give it up because of me. That would make me feel really great, wouldn't it? Besides, you're no spring chicken. You won't get many more opportunities.'

'Thanks. But promise me you won't do anything like this again, Mungo. I really will get sick.'

'Sorry. You won't tell anyone will you?'

'I'll have to tell Dad.'

'All right. But not Tiz. If you tell Tiz I'll – I'll kill myself.'

'Not this week, darling, please.'

12 ∫

There was much talk in the dressing-rooms of the imminent downfall of Mrs Thatcher. According to one of the boys, who claimed to have had trade with a junior minister, the pillow talk in Sloane Square confirmed the conspiracy to see her routed in the leadership election. The Kim Il Sung of Finchley was doomed.

'I can just see Ma Thatcher pacing the floor in the small hours comparing the dispatch box to a yawning grave,' said Harriet, as Boxer stabbed pins into the stingray headdress. 'Do you think she'll have visions of the men who went down in the *Belgrano – Tomorrow in the Commons – think on me!*'

'Now, now,' said Boxer, 'that's no way to talk of the dead. She may have made mistakes, but if there was a war on, who would you rather have in charge, Mrs T or some drip like John Major?'

'Don't be daft, Boxer. They'd never elect a nonentity like him.'

Tiz had taken to pouring organic apple juice on her oatmeal. She still had a stone or so to go before hallucinations set in, but Harriet could not help worrying. She did not want to say anything for fear of aggravating the problem. Instead she sat opposite Tiz while she ate, with an expression similar to Munch's *The Scream*.

Tiz sighed. 'Mum, I'm not trying to kill myself. But there's a cross country coming up in December and I don't want to be a burden on Telly. Don't worry.'

'Oh darling, that's like telling a river not to flow.'

Harriet got up and put her arms round Tiz and pulled her against her stomach.

'Mum, I can't breathe.'

'Sorry.' Harriet released her. Tiz continued to eat individual oat flakes.

Harriet was moved by the strangeness of Tiz, her metamorphosis foreshadowing the subtler process of her withdrawal into the outside world. Tiz had developed a silence, an internal night safe to which Harriet did not have access. It made Harriet leaden with a sense of helplessness.

And every time the phone rang, Harriet expected it to be the police informing her that Mungo had mugged an old lady, or dropped a paving slab onto the M25. To vary the diet of anxiety, she engaged Semi in talks about her prospects, as she was due to leave them in a matter of days. Semi hedged, said she was going to stay with friends in Kent. How did she come to have friends in Kent? Harriet was too busy fretting to notice that Dotty was keeping her under surveillance also, and that some of Dotty's supposed visits to enlighten the next generation about chummies and egg-free cakes were an excuse to visit the Reverend Vince and pour out her fears that Harriet was cracking up.

Harriet's osteopath had rooms around the corner from George. After a taxing session with her leg round the back of her neck being jumped on to the fart of popping tendons, she decided to call on him.

George's whiskery faced showed alarm, quickly smothered in smiles.

'It's all right, George, I haven't come about money. I was just passing. I see you've moved my photo.'

'Only right and proper, Harriet. I had my doubts, I know, but you put them to shame. How's it going?'

'Very well. Usually does with a young company, don't you think? Lovely girls, especially the boys. They often come to me with their problems. I have surgery hours now. That keeps the numbers down.'

'Good, good. Voice bearing up?'

'Just about. George—'

'What?'

'Apparently the Beeb are casting for a series about women murderers. I was wondering if I should try for it.'

'Well now – could you manage it? Have you got a second at the moment?'

'No, but they're looking for some.'

'Are you sure you could take on a day job? You look tired, love.'

'It was just a thought. We look set for a long run, but you never know.'

'Well, you don't need the bread, fortunately. It's a bit early to panic. Was there anything else? I don't want to hurry you, but I've got a South African kid coming at three.'

'No. I'm meeting my son in half an hour. I was just killing time really.'

'Flatterer.'

Japheth was sitting on a bench opposite the Odeon in Leicester Square. His arms were looped over the back of the bench and his left foot lolled on his right knee. The trainer at the end of his thin, black-jeaned leg looked like a large wheel clamp. He surveyed the youths playing frisbee in the pale sun with a lordly air.

'Hello, darling. Have you been here long?'

'Ten minutes.'

'Shall we go for a drink? Cup of tea?'

'Can we just sit here for a bit? Are you cold?'

'No.' She drew her coat around her. 'What did you want to talk to me about? I think I know. You and Semi, right?'

'Partly.'

'What's the other part?'

'Mum, I did warn you. The thing is, it's just not practical to live at home any more. The fact is I've taken a flat in Muswell Hill. And Semi's going to move in with me.'

'The little liar—'

'Why do you say that? You've always had it in for her.'

'No I haven't. Let's face it, Japh, ever since she's been here she's behaved as if it were a penal colony. I've made a real effort, if you must know.'

'She was homesick. You never took any account of that. What

did you make her do on day one? Make Christmas pudding. Very
tactful.'

'I was under the impression that the French could cook. I
thought it would take her mind off things. Anyway, she told
me she was going to stay with friends in Kent after she left us.
That was a bare-faced lie.'

'Only because I told her not to say anything. I wanted to tell
you myself.'

'You left it rather late, didn't you? Aaagrh!' A frisbee came
flying towards them. Harriet jumped up and caught it and threw
it back. Japh was reluctantly impressed.

'That was good, Mum. Perhaps I get my sporting talent from
you after all.'

'That wasn't talent. That was six weeks training as a circus
artiste for *Annie Get Your Gun*. So, I suppose you've moved in
already. Fathered any children you want to tell me about while
we're at it?'

'Mum—'

'Well why do you have to spring *faits accomplis* on me all the
time? Don't you trust me?'

Japh's profile, whipped by silken swatches of hair, was immobile. 'It's not a question of trust, Mum. I trust you in the sense
that I can anticipate your reaction to any given development. If
I know there will be a negative response I prefer to trust myself,
that's all.'

'You seem to be addressing me from the utmost branches of
the Tree of Knowledge, Japh. It's a painful fall.'

He looked at her directly. 'Fuck off, Mum.' He got up and
walked quickly towards Charing Cross Road.

Harriet ran after him, panting to keep up. 'Japh, do stop. If
you walk away you lose the argument.'

'I'm not arguing, Mum. And I'm not talking to you if you're
going to be so fucking sarcastic.'

'All right, I was. But that's what I fucking well thought. I'm
past editing my thoughts for the up-to-nine watershed for you,
Japh. And if you're so fucking sure you know how I'll react to
everything, why can't you handle it?'

Japheth stopped and looked at her curiously. 'You said "fuck".
Twice. I can't say I was prepared for that.'

'It's something we can do together.'

They stood on the pavement saying 'fuck' in unison, until a concerned member of the public from Singapore started asking passers-by where he could find a policeman.

'Oh, no, not the Fuzz again. Quick.' She grabbed his arm and ran down Orange Street and kept going until they found a Mah Jong shop. They looked at the price of incense balls for a while, then Harriet decided it was safe to go out.

'You know, I do want you to treat me like a child, Mum. That's because I thought proper parents were supposed to encourage their children to be independent. I have fantasies of you showing me how to make a casserole for under £2, and do amazing things with pillow ticking.'

'I will, I will. We haven't mentioned Dad. He'll miss you so much. When you were little he couldn't take his eyes off you. He even wanted to take you to work.'

'It's some time since that was the case.'

'So, when will you go?'

'I'm not sure. I'll take my things a few at a time, so you'll hardly notice.'

'Oh Japh—'

'Mum, you're not going to cry in the street, for God's sake—'

'No. I'm all right. It's the thought of those bare patches on the wall when pictures are taken down. So melancholy.'

'Then I'll leave them. It's ironic our talking like this finally. You know I'm not leaving because of sex, or even Semi, really. It's just that for the last year or so I've felt like one of the homeless in a bed and breakfast establishment. Do you know what I mean?'

Harriet nodded, but could not reply.

The next morning Harriet switched on the radio to hear that the tyrant had fallen. Mrs Thatcher had made her last exit from Downing Street. In the afternoon she watched the Prime Minister's magisterial performance in the Commons – all the brio of the partial drunk, the dignity of a martyr on the scaffold. Harriet, who had looked forward to this moment as to the news that the Queen had changed her hairstyle, was moved to tears of cosmic loss.

Dotty was riven between grief for the fate of her leader, and joy unbound at the departure of Semi. Mungo and Tiz managed to hide their own distress at Japheth's going behind requests for his room, mountain bike, and for his pocket money to be shared between them. Harriet found their brutality in the matter hurtful, but supposed it was better than having to cope with their pain as well as her own.

Japheth removed their clothes and effects over a two-week period, and, on the day the French chairman of Le Chunnel gave his British counterpart a green furry frog to mark the breakthrough under La Manche, Warren drove Japheth and Semi to Muswell Hill with the last of their things. Harriet promised they would all come to lunch as soon as possible, despite cries of 'I'm not going' and 'There's nothing to do in Muswell Hill' from Mungo and Tiz. As it was a Saturday and Harriet had a matinée, she was spared the actual moment of departure.

Dotty brought Harriet breakfast in bed on the Monday morning, although Harriet could not stand crumbs down her cleavage.

'Are you going to get a replacement for Semi, or do you think we could manage?'

'You'll have to have some help, Dotty. Perhaps a cleaner.'

'Do you know what they charge? £5 an hour!'

'That's not unreasonable. *I* wouldn't get out of bed for £5 an hour.'

'No, you wouldn't. Harriet, I don't want to press you, but I did say I'd stay for six months. If you don't have anyone living in by then, I'd feel obliged to stay on.'

'Oh – yes. I really must get moving on that. The trouble is, I don't have the energy to interview au pair agents at the moment.'

'Tell you what, why don't I do that for you?'

'Would you? Thanks, Dotty. I'll speak to the agency, transferring power of attorney, or whatever. But don't you have enough to do? How's the investigation of the break-in going?'

Dotty fiddled with the bedclothes. 'I've got a shrewd idea who it was. What's that phrase you're always using – shareshay la fum. I can't prove anything. Not without a search warrant.'

'*La femme*? You think there was a woman involved? The police said it bore all the hallmarks of contract thugs.'

'Perhaps they were.'

'A-hah. How fascinating. What woman would have such a grudge against us? Bring me my address book, I'll go down the list.'

'There's no need to be sarcastic. Personally, I'd have thought it was better to know it was someone with a motive, providing they've got it off their chest.'

'Cold comfort I'd call it.'

When Dotty had gone Harriet fed the toast to Jelly and Custard and ruminated over the coffee. Dotty's idea was clearly ridiculous, unless some unknown rival for her part had been depending on it to feed fourteen children and become crazed with jealousy. There were other kinds of jealousy. Perhaps the relationship between Warren and Avelina Viper was serious. But the thought of Avelina going down to South London and hiring hoodlums for a rumble was utterly laughable, not least because it was Warren's home as much as Harriet's. Not that Harriet was laughing. Perhaps it was Piers.

The weather had turned bitterly cold. Harriet swore Dotty to secrecy and turned the central heating on for a couple of hours in the middle of the day, when she took her gloves off to write Christmas cards. The prospect of Christmas without Japheth was hard to bear. They would of course be invited, but she could not imagine Semi volunteering. The room was dark. Freezing gravel hit the windows. She put her hands over her face and heaved with sobs that occasionally erupted in shuddering snorts. Unnoticed, Dotty came to the door and shook her head, adopting a resolute expression.

Two days later the Reverend Vince came to call. Harriet was about to go to Guildford for Christmas shopping, which she lost no time in telling him. She assumed he had come to see his *soi-disant* parishioner, Dotty.

'Mrs Outwood isn't here, I'm afraid.'

'It doesn't matter. I can see her on Sunday. Listen, I've got to go in to Radio Hogsback for a few hours. I'll give you a lift if you like.'

'Well—'

'I've got the old hearse. It's cold, but healthy.'

'Is that why you're dressed like the Red Baron?'

'The who?'

'Never mind. Did Dotty ask you to come?'

'Yes. She thought you needed someone to talk to.'

'What? I've got loads of people to talk to, starting with my husband. Why can't she mind her own business?'

'Look, she asked me to come. I have. That's the end of it if you like. But I do have to go into Guildford. And I've got my own parking space.'

'How could I resist?'

Close to, the bulging outlines of the hearse seemed almost obscene. By contrast, the front seats were small and hard, presumambly to encourage respectful posture. They were almost on a level with the cabins of more conventional HGVs. In the space where the coffins had rested was a mattress, and cabins had been put in along the sides. The mattress gave Harriet food for thought. Was Dotty's recommendation enough to assure her that he was not a psychopath who would take her up to Ranmore Common and give her a good seeing to? Ah well, into each life a little rain must fall.

'I suppose driving around in a death wagon is no sweat for a vicar.'

'I'm not a vicar. That's a sideline.'

'You know what I mean. Where are the seat belts?'

'There aren't any. Don't worry, it only does thirty-five miles an hour. Does religion embarrass you?'

'No. Yes.'

'Then we won't talk about it.'

'It's politics or the weather, then.'

'Take your pick.'

Harriet laughed. She could feel a panic attack coming on.

'You're not one of those divines who can see into people's souls, are you?'

'Have you got one?'

'Watch it. Just because I'm a woman—'

Harriet felt self-conscious driving into Dorking in the front seat of a hearse. Better than in the back, at least. 'I know someone who couldn't decide whether to move to Dorking or Australia. He chose Dorking, after much thought.'

'Cough it up, Harriet.'

She did: her impatience with Dotty, Tiz's eating problem, Japh and Semi, the break-in, the anonymous letter, her worries about Warren and Avelina, Mungo's shoplifting and her desire to get out of the show and sleep for a year or two. She omitted the fling with Damian. It might give him ideas, and anyway she had to save something for the return journey. They were in Merrow by the time she had finished.

'Are you still awake? I suppose it must all sound very trivial.'

'It's true your problems aren't epic, but they're generously spread. Is there an area of your life that isn't giving you grief?'

'We don't have financial worries. That's something.'

'Then why did George Sanders commit suicide?'

'Eh? That's a bit tangential isn't it?'

'I mean, you bring out this crumb of comfort like a child who boasts of being top of the failures. If you think money can be used as aspirin, why don't you buy some gold taps while you're in Guildford?'

'It's not very Christian to sneer at people who buy gold taps. It's only a small step in the pursuit of happiness. The trivial pursuit of happiness, I suppose you would say.'

'No, I wouldn't. It's a sacred pursuit, whatever form it takes. It's what distinguishes us from the animals.'

'Actually I thought it was Art that distinguishes us from the animals. And universities. And religion. And laughter. And Queen of puddings. And public transport and – perhaps I'm being too prosaic.'

'Too something or other. Yes, you are.'

'And you are being too ambiguous. You sneer at people who buy gold taps and then refuse to condemn them.' She was beginning to sound like Avelina. 'Look, I just don't want to get emotional. I don't know you well enough. It's my hormones. Besides, I feel guilty about getting emotional. The show reminds me every night that I don't have problems at all.'

'Is that why you want to get out of it?'

'Don't be ridiculous.'

'You're afraid that if you admit you're unhappy, you'll crack up?'

'I am not unhappy! Don't say things like that. It makes me feel so – violent – I could do something really stupid. Oh God, I haven't told you about—' About the near smothering of Semi. 'It's just boring old stress. Everything's come at the wrong time.'

'When would be the right time?'

'If you come up with any more pop-up aphorisms I'll jump out.'

Harriet had forgotten how hilly Guildford was in comparison to Oxford Street. She pounded up and down the high street, decided on a book and a Portuguese jug at the top of the hill, thought there might be something nicer in Debenhams, trotted down there, decided the jug at the top of the hill was nicer, and when she got back there, realized she should have bought cycling gloves for Mungo in Debenhams. She caught sight of her haggard face in the window of River Island. 'God I hate Christmas. Why don't I have the guts to reduce it to a chestnut soufflé and a few carols?' The window did not reply.

The Reverend Vince had been pondering Harriet's dilemmas. 'I'll only make a general point, Harriet. As far as the kids are concerned, you musn't think your working has set them off on suicidal tendencies, or forced Japheth to leave home. I do a phone-in, and I get loads of middle-class parents tearing their hair out because their little goody-goodies have suddenly turned into drug addicts, or vandals, or sex fiends. They talk as if the kids were computers that had got a virus. Kids today are subject to so many outside influences and you have no control over them. It's not your fault.'

'That was lovely. More tea, Vicar?'

'Jesus! I'm glad you're not my mother.'

'How old are you?'

'Thirty-six.'

'No chance.'

He did not stop in the drive, but further down the road. 'I

suppose I should say that if you do ever want to talk, I'll listen.
But I can see I'd be wasting my breath.'

'Are you angry?'

'Yes.'

'No doubt you know a million ways to deal with it.' She looked
at him. There did seem to be something strangely back-lit about
his hazel eyes. 'Are you sure you don't have special powers?'

'There are no special powers, Harriet. Only perceived ones.'

'You have an answer for everything. No – don't say it.'

Dotty was watching *Ill Met by Moonlight*, with a mug of tea and
her feet up on a pouffe. She had thoughtfully placed the *Radio
Times* on it first.

'Have you been shopping?'

'Yes.'

'Can I see?'

'There's nothing interesting. Travel sewing kits, narrative nut-
crackers – you know the sort of thing. Dotty, why did you ask
the Reverend Vince to come and sort me out? It's so insulting.
Do you mind turning that thing off?'

Dotty zapped the television and clasped her mug closer. Her
glasses steamed up. 'Well, you won't go to the doctor—'

'I don't need a doctor. Anyhow, the doctor cannot alter the
human condition,' realizing too late that she sounded like the
Reverend Vince now, 'and neither can the Reverend Vince.
Please don't do that again. I realize you were only trying to
help, but please don't.'

'Very well. I don't know any other vicars, any road. Not
round here.'

'Good. But if you come across any aura cleansers or Hay dieters
kindly keep them to yourself.'

'As you wish. By the way, I think we've got a new au pair.'

'Really? What nationality?'

'Spanish. Her name's Carmen, believe it or not. The agency's
going to ring you in the morning.'

'Goodbye couscous, hello paella. Let's hope she can't cook.'

Harriet collected Carmen from her previous residence in Regent's
Park on the following Sunday. She could not help laughing.

Carmen was an uncanny clone of Dotty herself – small, sturdy, bespectacled, a constant prattler and exuded optimistic energy. Her English was excellent, with an accent that sauced every utterance.

The contrast with Semi was marked. They all got a horrible shock when Carmen rose at six-thirty on Monday and tossed her mattress out of the window to air, and proposed following suit with all the other mattresses. Harriet gently informed her that the English climate did not lend itself to putting the bedding outside in mid-winter, and besides, the neighbours would assume they had bed bugs.

'What ith bed bugth?' she demanded, and made a note of the explanation in a pocket book she carried on her at all times. Undeterred, she set about taking down the curtains and washing the windows on both sides, for which she required an extension ladder. After lunch she retired to her room to study adverbial clauses.

'Hell,' thought Harriet, 'she'll be asking me the difference between synecdoche and metonymy before long.' She did wonder briefly if the household could withstand the impact of Carmen. They would certainly try. She inspired the utmost trust and confidence. After she settled down, she would be a suitable replacement for Dotty, as she had a driver's licence, slobbered at the thought of mucking out stables and was willing to talk to Tiz for hours about trotting techniques and equestrian shampoos. She called everyone 'my dahling'.

All told, an atmosphere of surrender to superior forces settled over the house. Harriet was hurt that nobody but her appeared to miss Japheth, or even notice he was not there. The others were more than compensated by the increased efficiency levels and the special glow that comes from having one's knickers ironed.

Carmen watched television to improve her English, which ruined *Strike It Lucky* but was a small price to pay for the many benefits. And the chances of her forming a liaison with Mungo were, to say the least, remote. Carmen was in love with her cousin, Jaime Maria, and gave side-splitting imitations of Jaime Maria's characteristics. Jaime Maria was a very serious young man with a Vespa with no brakes. Jaime Maria was of god-like appearance, the mere sight of him would cure warts. Jaime Maria played the cello and kept exotic fish and was double jointed. He was a journalist, hence Carmen's obsession with the News. Jaime Maria was going to the Gulf for his newspaper. They all took to going around sighing 'Ah, Jaime Maria, vine of my heart—' Harriet was chilled at the propects for Jaime Maria. Iraq was on full alert, the Saudi desert crawling with allied troops. Dotty had responded to the call to write letters to British soldiers. 'That's all they need,' thought Harriet.

Harriet was in a bunker writing party invitations but she could not concentrate because the Germans were playing 'Putting On My Top Hat' on trumpet to keep the enemy awake. Then she woke up and realized it was the doorbell. She got up and went to the window, expecting to see a police car. There was a strange car in the drive, but she could not see who was at the door. Noises within the house suggested that someone had got up. She put on her dressing gown and hurried downstairs.

Carmen, bundled up in a replica of Napoleon's greatcoat, was talking to a tall woman in a headscarf, Avelina Viper. Avelina was crying. Carmen was adamant, repulsing Avelina's attempts to cross the threshold.

'Avelina! Whatever's the matter? What are you doing here?'

'Harriet – my dear – I am in need of consolation.'

'What is contholation?' said Carmen.

'Sympathy. Probably the same in Spanish. What's happened Avelina? Come in. It's all right, Carmen. This is a friend of ours.'

'Shall I prepare some refreshment?'

'No, thank you. You go back to bed. I think Dotty's up, too. Tell her not to worry.'

'Very well.'

Harriet turned to show Avelina into the den, but she had already found her way.

'May I help myself to a drink, Harriet?'

'Of course. I'll light the fire.' The ball of flame soon brought the faux Coalite to a glow.

'Can't the chimney be reopened?' said Avelina between sniffs.

'Hardly. I've just had this put in. Tiz was giving me a hard time about pollution.'

'Piers always used to – Oh Harriet—' She dissolved into tears.

Harriet sat beside her. 'Avelina, is Piers dead?'

Avelina shook her head. 'Unfortunately not. He's left me, Harriet. Just like that. I came back from a conference – *Deconstructing Thomas Peacock* – and he'd – gone. Taken all his clothes.'

'I don't believe it.'

'It's true. He left me a note! Can you imagine? It wasn't on the kitchen table but— Oh, how could he insult me with such clichés! He – hic – said he – hic – didn't know me any more. What does that mean?'

'Goodness, I don't know. You're the novelist. When did this happen?'

'Tonight. I got in about ten. I was so shocked, Harriet. Piers has always been so – loyal. Not much else, perhaps, it's true. He was so supportive when I didn't get the Booker. He said winning it was a confirmation of second-rate talent. That's true, don't you think?'

'I'm afraid I don't follow these things. But yes, Piers always seemed devoted. You were like Yoevil and Kean, apple and pie – this is incredible. Is Piers in trouble? He doesn't know Asil Nadir, does he?'

'We had him to dinner once. But what possible trouble could Piers be in?'

'Share rigging? Insider dealing?'

Avelina stopped crying. Even blotched and swollen, her face retained its Nordic elegance. Harriet thought Piers had run off with a bar maid. 'You're so practical, Harriet. I knew you wouldn't fuck around with phoney sentiment. That's why I had to see you, rather than my real friends. And Warren means a lot to me. We're an odd couple, Warren and I. He understands women so well, doesn't he? I used him in *Parturition*, did you notice? The man who has an affair with his sister while writing a thesis on the legend of Geb and Nut.'

'That's some creative crucible you've got there, Avelina.'

Avelina sobbed. 'I shall never write again, Harriet. I only started when I married Piers. When I found out I couldn't have – hic – children. He thought it would be a good idea. He was right. I could never have done it without him. What shall I do?'

'Avelina, this is going to sound like Dear Marje on a bad day, but did Piers know you felt like this about him? Perhaps, however hard he tried, he was a little bit jealous of your success. Perhaps he felt neglected. You know men, they feel neglected if you don't cut their bread and butter into soldiers, however nice they are.'

'Surely not Piers. He was as selfless as a nun.'

'You didn't give him any other cause for jealousy, did you? Is it possible he may have misconstrued your relationship with – Warren, for instance?'

'Oh no. If I had had sex with Warren I would have told Piers. We never placed bureaucratic restrictions on one another.'

'I see.' Well, it was the bar maid, then. 'Be creative about this, Avelina. If you were a character in one of your novels, what would you make her do?'

Avelina laughed dismissively, but a light came on in her head. 'Who was that funny little foreigner in a blanket who opened the door?'

'That's Carmen, our new au pair.'

'Well, I might have someone like her as my character's house-keeper. She responds to the woman's despair and pursuades her that they should disappear together – to the Arctic Circle, perhaps. The icy tundras of unknowing. It's a metaphor.'

'Ah.'

'They crash land into a time-warped community of mind-stretching exotics on the run from Fate. A Samurai warrior who cannot die although the sword is still stuck in his belly. Lord Lucan – he would have been horribly disfigured in a fire. A black white witch from Senegal whose parents abandoned her on the edge of a volcano. Paracelsus. I suppose Piers – that is, the husband – would eventually give up the illusory reality of the world for the spiritual peace of her parallel universe. Funny little foreigner person would reveal that she was in love with the wife. There would be a terrible dénouement inside the glacified carcass of a doodlebug.'

'That sounds terrific.'

'The ice novel cometh, you know. South America's cold potatoes already. I think it has to do with the millennium. The poles symbolize the extremities of the century.'

'How interesting. The Booker's as good as yours.'

'Hardly, my dear. I'm more likely to get the OBE nowadays.'

'Whatever. But you see, you're still a positive geyser of invention. In fact this experience could imbue your work with a new passion.'

'We'll see. He might come home tomorrow. He always cooks Sunday lunch. Oh dear—'

'Don't cry, Avelina. Here, let me pour that. I don't think you'd better drive back tonight. You can have Japheth's room.' She yawned.

'How kind you are, Harriet. How I envy Warren.' She put an arm around Harriet and placed quivering kisses on her forehead, cheeks and nose. Harriet went rigid, not just at the idea of Avelina's artistic largesse extending to bisexuality, but 'envy Warren'? Enough to trash the house? Could Dotty have got it right? It would explain why Avelina chose to come to this house, rather than any other. Criminals were always drawn back to the scene of the crime.

Harriet untangled herself. 'Let me show you your room. I'm afraid I'm rather tired. I had two shows today.'

'How appalling for you. Why don't you do something at the National? You might only have to go on twice a week.'

'I've never been asked.'

'Serge is a friend of mine. I'll have a word with him, if you like.'

'Oh. Thanks.'

Harriet showed Avelina to Japheth's room, found her a nightdress and toothbrush. When she got back into bed she lay awake for some time. It was distinctly odd having Avelina in the house. It had not seemed so in Cornwall. One visited people with seaside cottages on much flimsier excuses than friendly acquaintance. If one discounted the criminal motive, there must still be something quite special about the friendship between Avelina and Warren that she did not understand at all. It was therefore strange that her great friend Warren had rolled over and gone back to sleep in Avelina's hour of need.

The following morning Harriet closely observed Warren's reaction to Avelina. There was little to go on. Avelina was tearful in explanation, Warren correct, but neutral, in sympathy. Their exchanges were necessarily brief as, with the exception of Carmen, they were all going to lunch with Japheth and Semi in Muswell Hill.

It was, in Harriet's opinion, torture.

Mungo and Tiz watched television. Warren read the *Sunday Telegraph*. Harriet and Dotty were left to talk to Japh while Semi prepared an Indonesian meal for a change, with peanuts and soy sauce in every dish, which made Dotty feel sick. Harriet was almost sick with pity for Japh, so proud, in the face of his siblings' scorn, of his curtainless flat, the white walls enlivened by Semi's Moroccan prayer mat and a gouache of the Manchester United air crash. Mungo and Tiz were rude about the food. Semi retired in tears to the bedroom. Japh laid into his siblings for upsetting her and they had a screaming match which at least had the comfort of continuity. Dotty discreetly did the dishes. Warren fell asleep. Mungo insisted on going home. Harriet berated him for hurting Japh's feelings. Japh said, not to worry, he didn't have any feelings after eighteen years in this family. Warren woke up and suggested that Japh might like to go for a pint. Japh said he would only if Semi came with them. It took three quarters of an hour to pursuade her, including forced apologies from Mungo and Tiz. After they had gone, Mungo and Tiz passed out in front of the television. Dotty was in agonies of indigestion.

When Warren, Japh and Semi came back they brought the flushed bonhomie of the public bar with them, which fell on the graveyard-of-aspirations mood in the flat like a jumbo jet. But by then they could politely leave. Harriet hugged Japheth and Semi and said they had had a lovely day. Japheth was drunk enough to suspend disbelief for the nonce. He came down to wave them off looking quite cheerful. Harriet tried to put a positive gloss on the event, praising the closeness of the flat to the tube station.

'You can say what you like, Mum,' said Mungo, 'we're not going there again. It's boring.'

'You probably won't be asked.'

'Good.'

They stopped at a Burger King on the way home.

The phone was ringing when they got in. It was her mother from Australia. She sounded excited. Harriet told her about

Japh and Semi. Then her mother asked if she could come for Christmas. A friend who worked for Qantas had been able to get tickets at the last minute. Harriet was ecstatic.

'Of course you can come, Mummy. Stay as long as you like.'

'Thanks, darling. I've got a surprise for you.'

'You can't be pregnant—'

Her mother laughed. 'It's much better than that.'

Harriet relayed this intriguing remark to Dotty. 'What on earth can it be?'

'At her time of life? A bladder transplant most likely.'

13

Warren bestrode the Christmas festivities. A Trafalgar Square size blue spruce again dominated the hall, despite Tiz's protest that killing trees was murder. Fairy lights were strung roung the house until it resembled a motorway pub, and interior decorators were commissioned to bind evergreens around the banisters, the front door and the major mantlepieces – this year fashionably decorated with vanilla pods and bleached moss. As Harriet was working, the hospitality programme had to be curtailed, in effect to an At Home on the Sunday before Christmas. Deprived of his annual chance to seat the county at his board, Warren did mutter.

'It's just as well with Mummy here,' said Harriet, as they drove to Heathrow at dawn. 'It would be a strain for her. There are enough oddballs in the house as it is.'

'Carmen isn't an oddball.' Carmen folded Warren's socks together so that they could be separated and put on in two easy movements.

'Can we keep Carmen for ever?' said Tiz.

'Don't be stupid,' said Mungo.

'Mum, he called me stupid. Can I hit him?'

'No. Just apologize, Mungo.'

'Why should I? She knows perfectly well Carmen's only here for a year. It makes me sick when she puts on her dumb little girl act.'

'Will you two shut up and stop upsetting your mum,' said Warren. 'It's a big day for her.'

'Only for me?' thought Harriet. Warren's choice of words summed up the explosion of indifference that had greeted the announcement of her mother's arrival.

'And mind you two don't ruin the visit rowing all the time. Your grandma's paid a lot of money for this trip.'

'It was her idea,' said Tiz. 'Why do we always have wrinklies around at Christmas?'

'Would it make it any better if I invited Damian?' said Warren. 'He's on his own right now and he can't get back to his family.'

'Oh yes!' squealed Tiz. 'Please say yes, Mum. Damian's fun.'

Harriet was flummoxed. This buddy thing with Warren had gone far enough. She did not understand why they could not indulge their passion for whacking balls round hummocks on their own. At this rate she would have to pay her debt to the community for the rest of her life. 'Why us? Where has he spent Christmas up to now?'

'With his girlfriend's folks, I guess. But she's not in the frame any more.'

'But what about his friends in the business? He must have loads of mates.'

'Honey, I don't know. I asked him. He said he'd be alone. Maybe he's embarrassed to admit it to them.'

'But not to you?'

'Look, sweetheart, if it's such a big deal, forget it. But you know what the suicide rate's like at this time.'

'Suicide!' said Tiz. 'Oh Mum, if Damian killed himself because you wouldn't let him come, it's as good as murdering him. We could never celebrate Christmas again.'

'For goodness sake. I haven't said he couldn't come.'

'Thanks, Mum. Now we have something to look forward to.'

Harriet ground her teeth. From her point of view Damian's suicide would not be without its perks.

Despite the hour, Terminal 3 swilled with the humanity of all nations. Glass-eyed with exhaustion, they lumbered around like gaggles of oil-slicked ducks.

'Is that a real machine gun?' said Mungo in awe, as a couple of security guards walked past them.

'No, it's a dummy, dummy.'

'Don't start!' said Warren.

Harriet was nervous. She had not seen her mother for seven

years, ever since she had followed the snake torturer Melvyn Proud down under. Of course, they had only known him as an ophthalmic surgeon on exchange in those days. Harriet's mother had worked as a volunteer hospital visitor, a particularly welcome service to those with their eyes bandaged. Harriet's brother Peter had been cynical about the relationship from the start, citing the medallion, the fact that Melvyn was already thrice divorced, ten years younger than their mother and apparently bathed in Versace's L'Homme. Out of habit Harriet disagreed with him, although she was devastated, and convinced her mother would never stand the climate. But Melvyn was on paper quite a catch for an unemployed widow. It had been a harrowing farewell in this same building.

Mungo and Tiz soon got bored and went off to look for game machines. Warren sat reading the paper as Harriet paced the floor. Who knows what seven years of scorching heat and lamingtons might do to a person. Every time a trolley appeared with a small woman behind it Harriet started and smiled. But when a chic figure with glistening caramel-coloured hair in a bright green leisure suit approached her with open arms she was unprepared.

'Mummy – Oh—' They hugged and kissed.

'Darling, Harriet – let me look at you. Are you all right? You look tired, my darling.'

'We had to get up so early. I'm fine.'

'Is the family here?'

'Most of them. Warren's over there. I'll go and get the others.'

'Okeedoke.'

Harriet laughed, slightly hysterical, and ran off to round up Mungo and Tiz. Warren was still clasped to the green polyester bosom when they came back. Mungo and Tiz stared at their grandmother, whom they remembered as a rather withdrawn woman in Eastex suits with a pure white Mia Farrow haircut. They remained rigid in her embrace.

'You're looking good, Pauline,' said Warren, 'considering what you've been through and all.'

'We won't talk about that, Warren dear. I'm in great shape. And this is why. Harriet – everyone – this is Frazer, my fiancé.'

Pauline put out a hand to bring forward a short man in a navy blue raincoat who was standing behind her. Harriet had assumed he was someone to whom her mother had been heroically friendly on the flight and was hanging around in the hope of a lift. Frazer had the air of a wealthy OAP. The white hair was expensively coiffed, possibly permed. He wore a diamond signet ring and a fashionable turtle neck. His hard, close-set blue eyes were set off by the tanned wrinkles like marbles in a crumbly cheese. They were about as expressive as he shook hands all round.

Harriet was speechless. Mungo and Tiz exchanged Oh-my-God-not-another-dodo looks. Warren filled the breach.

'Hi there. Welcome to England.' He smiled, with the insouciance of one for whom the extra laundry would not be his problem. 'Is this your first trip?'

'That's right.'

Pauline's smile was frantic. She clung to Frazer's arm. 'I told you I had a wonderful surprise for you, Harriet. Isn't he a pet?' Harriet now noticed that her mother wore an engagement ring, three diamonds the size of chick peas. 'You don't mind, do you darling? We'll – you know – share a room, and you were always such a good sport about that sort of thing.'

'No. That's fine. You've just taken my breath away for the moment.'

'Tell me about it! Listen, you don't have to worry that we'll be a burden on you for long. We thought as soon as Christmas is over we'll go to London and then tour the country a bit. Frazer has relatives in Lincolnshire, don't you sweet-heart?'

'That's right.'

'But – I thought—' Warren put his arm round Harriet, sensing that she was about to collapse with disappointment. All the long, intimate talks she had envisaged with her mother after the children went back to school, the walks she had planned on the Downs and Headley Heath, places she could not be bothered to explore alone. Having her mother at table on Sundays, at her side in the car – Not to mention the reserve fantasy where her mother decided to come home and live with them, Dotty went back to Nonsuch Crescent, Carmen became a

British citizen and they all lived together in mutual support in a perfectly clean house.

'I'm very happy for you, Mummy.'

'Thank you, darling.'

'How many husbands will that be, Gran?' said Tiz.

'Only three, my darling. Well – no – four. There was poor Jim, wasn't there.'

'The one who was killed in the war?'

'Yes, dear. We were only married ten days.' Pauline lowered her voice, embarrassed to discuss her serial monogamy in front of Frazer.

'You'll get on like a house on fire with Dotty.'

'Oh, I know Dotty of old.'

'Is this your luggage?' said Warren, somewhat superfluously Harriet thought. 'We'd better get going. I'm afraid I have to go to the office this afternoon.'

The drive home was strained. Tiz had to sit on Mungo's knee and he complained that he would have gangrene by the time they got to the house. Tiz said she could not get comfortable because his knobbly bit was sticking in her leg.

'Tiz, please! What will Gran think of such a conversation?'

Her mother laughed. 'It's all right, darling. I think it's great the way kids today are so open about everything. Do you know, Tizzy, on my wedding night in 1940 I didn't even know what sex was. My mother couldn't bring herself to tell me.'

'Urrrgh. What a revolting shock. I think sex sounds absolutely disgusting, actually.'

'Yeah, me too,' grinned Mungo.

'Mungo masturbates, Gran. He gets these porn magazines from the caretaker at school and—'

Mungo shot her up to the roof of the car. 'Shut up, you hag.'

'Does he now.' Pauline looked at Mungo with mock wonder. 'We'll have to have a special talk, Mungo my darling. But you give him a break now, Tizzy. He's quite capable of telling me all his wicked ways himself.'

Tiz decided she hated grandmothers. Liver spots were just about the most disgusting thing she had ever seen. Mungo, on the other hand, saw that his grandmother understood blokes much better than his mother did, and quite looked forward to airing his grievances about Harriet's bias in the war against Tiz.

Harriet felt obliged to recover her initial faltering welcome to Frazer by addressing him exclusively. It was a thankless task.

'So, you're a judge, Frazer?'

'That's right.'

'Were you born in Australia?'

'Yes.'

'Do you have children?'

'Yes.'

'I expect you're a cricket fan.'

'That's right.'

Harriet nobly resisted the urge to ask him if he liked dressing up in corsets and having his penis tickled with a feather duster.

'When are we there?' said Tiz. 'I've got to buy Telly's Christmas present this afternoon.'

Harriet was upset to see that her mother now smoked.

'I started lighting Frazer's. But at my age, what does it matter?'

'But surely, you have "everything to live for", as they say.'

'Do they? You seem to absent yourself from that sentiment, my darling. You do like Frazer, don't you? I know he's a bit quiet, but so considerate. You've no idea.'

'Aren't you going to take your coat off? You've got marmalade on the sleeve.'

'I think I'll keep it on for a bit.'

Harriet set the heating on twenty-four hours.

As Tiz had predicted, Pauline and Dotty got on like Noddy and Big Ears. Dotty found the radiant, coloured Pauline much more chatty than the pensive, grey one, and the sympathy of an experienced widow was especially welcome. Dotty even got Frazer to say 'I don't like biscuits.' The three of them formed a unit within the household, Pauline and Dotty usually talking across Frazer's upright, chain-smoking body.

Harriet had got permission for her understudy to stand in for her on the Saturday before the At Home, so that she could direct preparations. She had forgotten how less tiring it was to do two shows a day than prepare whole salmon, aioli, spiced beef, ten different salads, garlic bread, salsa sauce, dips, cheese straws, Amaretto chocolate torte, macedoine of winter fruit and syllabub for sixty people. Pauline and Dotty sat at the kitchen table preparing vegetables, managing one celeriac an hour as they reminisced about doodlebugs and gadgets for turning marge and milk into cream. Fortunately, Carmen knew what was required. Harriet reflected that she was the only au pair they had had who took the string off celery. Why could Japheth not have waited for this paragon?

Japh and Semi arrived in good time. Pauline was bowled over by her man-child grandson, and almost as enthusiastic about Semi.

'What's the matter, Harriet?' she said, catching her alone in the kitchen. 'You don't like that girl, do you? Why not?'

'I don't dislike her, Mummy. But they've both been very deceitful. And they're far too young to settle down as a couple.'

'Are you sure you aren't just jealous, my darling? She loves him, you know. I could tell straight off, she's the kind of woman who'll always put her man before her kids, and knowing what men are like, it's the only way to keep them.'

'I don't care how much she loves him. It's preposterous to expect Japh to be faithful to the first person he sleeps with.'

'Perhaps he won't be. But I bet you anything you like they'll stick it out.'

'Do you guys have drinks?' Warren came in and handed Harriet a glass of red wine. 'Knock that back, sweetheart, and get smiling.'

Harriet did as she was bid and went out to greet the first guests, the chairman of M25TV, and his wife, who cut a striking figure in layered hessian from Pour Les Autres. Warren took them over. Quickly the house filled up. Frazer sat immobile among the huddles discussing the Duchess of York's weight and Shevardnadze's resignation, indifferent to the bits of lollo rosso and garlic bread that fell on him from the plates of those juggling crockery and challenging concepts with their mouths full. Harriet began to feel ill. Her stomach hurt, and pulses of nausea bubbled in her throat. Bravely she pressed on with the mingling, and urging of herring pâté on her guests. But she could not get her mind off her insides, which were churning mincemeat, throbbing pain that threatened to implode and spatter her guests with intestines. She staggered out of the room just as Avelina Viper arrived with a neighbour who made squeegees for the textile industry, ran to the bathroom and threw up with a force last seen in *The Exorcist*. For a while she lay on the floor panting, then gingerly sat up and remained still to make sure her head was not still revolving. She dragged herself to the bedroom door, watching the stairs. After some time Japheth ran up them.

'Mum! There you are. What's the matter? Are you ill?'

'Ssh. Get me to a hospital, Japh. I'm dying.'

'Are you serious? You always exaggerate, Mum. You've probably had too much to drink. Look, Dr Peach is here. Why don't I ask him to come up?'

Harriet clawed his arm. 'No! I'm not breaking up the party after peeling forty-five peppers. Help me up – hospital—'

Japh was convinced by the ochre flush that flooded her face as she grasped his hand and heaved. 'I'll get Dad.'

'No, not Dad. He's got to hold the fort. They haven't started the desserts yet – urgggghhhh—'

'Mum!'

'Go and tell Grandma. Ask her to cover for me – aargh – Go on. Hurry.'

He ran downstairs and came back with Pauline, who wanted to go with Harriet to hospital. Harriet persuaded her she would be more use at home fending off enquiries as to her whereabouts. Her mother stood *cave* as Japh helped Harriet downstairs and out the back door.

He took her to the Accident and Emergency department at Epsom Hospital. The initial diagnosis was food poisoning, at which Harriet fainted, thinking of the carnage that might already have struck her guests.

Japh waited until she came round and then hurried back to check.

But when he arrived home everyone seemed riotously well. They disposed of the dessert selection like industrial vacuum cleaners at the same time as Harriet's stomach was pumped out. It was only when people began to leave that her absence was noted. Japh explained discreetly to Warren what had happened, and as soon as the more eminent guests had gone he slipped away to phone the hospital. Harriet was asleep, but he could visit her in an hour or so. Tiz was frantic.

'Is Mum dying?'

'Sweetheart, you're obsessed with death. Mum's going to be fine. It's just something she ate.'

'What?'

'How should I know?'

'Why are you so ratty, Dad? It's not Mum's fault.'

'Did I say that?'

'Can I come with you?'

'No. Mum will be real tired. You stay here and help Carmen clear up.'

'Not unless Mungo does too.'

'Christ, you're not going to start quibbling about that with your mum—'

'I thought you said she wasn't dying?'

'You go, Mr Funkel,' said Carmen. 'Tithiana is beside herthelf, I think.'

Harriet was hooked up to a drip. 'Happy Christmas,' she whispered and started to cry. 'I'm sorry I spoiled the party.'

'Don't upset yourself, sweetheart. Nobody noticed. It was OK. It was great.'

'Did anyone else get ill?'

'Not that I noticed. What did you have for breakfast?'

'An apple. I got it off a witch that came round selling them.'

'Very funny.'

'Don't let them wash the dishes. If lots of people die they'll have to get forensics in to take samples.'

'That's crazy, honey. You must be delirious. Nobody's going to die.'

'Can you ask Dotty to stuff the turkey tomorrow? No – tell her not to stuff the turkey. You get salmonella these days if you stuff the turkey on Christmas Eve. I don't know why. You never did before Delia Smith was invented.'

Warren anxiously felt her brow, and called a nurse before leaving.

*   *   *

Harriet felt well enough to go home the next morning. She was installed on the sofa. Pauline and Dotty took over the Christmas dinner campaign. Tiz provided her mother with paper, scissors and felt tips, and instructions to produce a dozen napkin rings with Christmas puddings on.

In the evening they gathered round the fire for the distribution of gifts. Tiz was postman. Mungo complained that she kept missing his turn and a fight started. Pauline separated them and kept Mungo at her side thereafter. The cries of flabbergasted delight nearly lifted the roof, but Tiz and Warren, whose hoards fell into generic patterns, were genuinely pleased. Tiz got a bottle of horsefly spray, a purple silk, a green and white silk, a pink silk with white stars on it, a whip with a rubber hand on the end, a set of jumping bandages, a dressage jacket and a year's supply of hoof oil. Warren was blessed with a travel caddy, a jumbo driver, a Miracle Knee Support, an ArcRite swing tester and a set of Spalding Top Flite SDs. He was at first disconcerted when he opened Harriet's gift – an etching-and-splodge art work entitled *Man Running Away From His Feelings*.

'What the hell's that supposed to mean?'

'It's a joke, darling.'

'Oh. That's OK then.'

Dotty caught Harriet's gloomy eye as they shovelled the glistening rubble of wrappings into a plastic sack. She shrugged. 'It keeps people employed.'

The weather brought more employment opportunities overnight. They woke to the boom of the wind, trees strained into yogic backbends, milk bottles on the move, whole branches skidded along the street, cars wobbled, tiles crashed onto the drive. Warren and Mungo spent the morning in the attic with plastic sheeting and buckets. The wind whistled right through the double glazing, carrying the smell of sprout water, roast turkey and the washing day whiff of pudding steam into the furthest reaches of the house. There was a power cut. Dotty panicked, afraid the turkey would putrefy while it waited. Harriet lost her temper.

'Don't be such a wimp, Dotty! We won't eat it until it's properly cooked, however long it takes.'

'Huh. I'm surprised you're not bothered after what you've just been through.'

'That wasn't food poisoning. Nobody else got it.'

'I hope Damian gets here all right,' said Tiz. 'That 2CV of his could take off in this weather.'

'Damian? Oh no, I'd forgotten he was coming. I haven't got him a present.'

'Mungo and I have. We got him a Gameboy so that he'll have something to do in the boring bits when he's working. He's quite childish in his way, isn't he?'

Damian arrived at quarter to two with presents for them all, wrapped in the *Daily Telegraph* and string.

'You shouldn't have,' said Harriet sincerely as she opened her packet. It was a china model of a washing machine. She felt slightly queasy. Did this reference to the past point a finger at the future?

'That's a funny present,' said Warren.

'Well what do you give to a woman who has everything?'

'Silver grape scissors,' said Dotty.

'Don't throw the paper away,' said Damian. 'Read it.'

'What – all of it?' Harriet flattened the sheet. It was the page which contained the favourable review of *Wipers!* 'Ah – that's sweet, Damian. You kept it all this time.' She half rose, her left cheek forward for a kiss. Instead, Damian put his hands on her shoulders and kissed her lightly on the lips. He smelt of orchids and cinnamon. His wind-ruffled black hair tickled her nose. Memories stirred in her knickers.

'I'm bored,' said Mungo. 'When's dinner?'

'Damian has to play a game with us,' said Tiz, 'as Japh isn't here. Can I get the old Totopoly out?'

'We don't play games before lunch.'

'But when will that be?'

'Oh all right.'

'I hate Totopoly,' said Mungo. 'Why do we always have to do what she wants?'

'I've got a much better idea,' said Damian. 'Hide and Seek.'

'Yeah. Great.' They ran off. Damian sat down.

'Aren't you going to look for them?'

'In a mo. I need a drink first.'

'Good idea. Perhaps we can leave them until after lunch. You're a born parent.'

'No thanks. I had the aversion therapy that week in Cornwall.'

They eventually sat down at five-thirty. Harriet had been sick again and could not eat. Carmen was subdued. Mungo was in a mood because he was missing a film on television. Frazer, who had downed half a bottle of Glenlivet while waiting, did not seem to know where he was and kept going to the lavatory, possibly to consult a map. Tiz refused turkey, and even stuffing, because it had bacon in it. Pauline, who was also squiffy, got cross and accused her of ingratitude after Harriet had gone to so much trouble. She considered that vegetarians were no better than moral cowards and think of all those poor boys in the Gulf – how could they be expected to kill people if they couldn't even face a pork chop? Tiz said that they only had to kill bad people, but animals were good, and anyway the Minister of Defence was a vegetarian and she would be sick if she had to watch that poor bird being hacked to pieces any longer and could she eat her dinner in the kitchen. Harriet refused, because if she was going to be a vegetarian she had to be one in the real world. Dotty tried to lighten the atmosphere by recalling that Fin had had a bullet removed from his behind on Christmas Day 1943. Warren and Damian discussed Ian Woosnam's chances in the US Masters. Damian asked Frazer if he was sorry he was not at home for the test series.

'Yes,' said Frazer.

'How do you think they'll manage without Thompson and Lillee?'

'They're gay,' said Mungo.

'No they're not, dear,' said Pauline. 'I don't think there's much of that in Australia.'

'I was wondering about those two myself,' said Damian. 'After all *Caught Thompson, Balled Lillee—*'

'*Bowled*! *Bowled*!' shrieked Frazer. 'Look, if you want fairies, what about that David Gower then, eh? Did you see the test last year? He wouldn't know a leg trap if his dick was caught in it!' Gasps from the ladies. 'Wafting his bat round the place like a bloody wand. You pitch a ball at his stump and he'll toss it straight into backward square leg, mate. Oh yes, England's glory days are over, mate. All right, you get Russell and Smith in there, they get 170 for 2 and then you're all out for 171. And your *bowlers* – well – They're all over the place, mate. Make a flash in the pan look like an all-night rave up.'

They stared at his purple face in silence. If Jelly and Custard had now sung the duet from *The Pearl Fishers* Harriet would not have been a bit surprised. Frazer crushed a walnut, which had been scattered artily by his plate, with his bare hand. This man is a judge, thought Harriet. Thank goodness he was not available in the event the England cricket team were arrested for disorderly behaviour.

Pauline laughed nervously. 'You touched a raw nerve there, Damian dear. Of course, he doesn't really think David Gower is homosexual, do you Frazer?'

'Yes.'

'Oh darling, of course he isn't! You see, Frazer's never got over that test when Botham took five wickets in twenty-eight balls. He talks about it in his sleep, you know.'

'Why don't you hit him, Dad?' said Mungo. 'Like you did that blind man in the cinema.'

'Shut up, Mungo. Frazer's our guest. I guess he's entitled to his opinion.'

'You said we weren't to tell people to shut up. Perhaps you'd like me to go to my room as well. After all, it's only Christmas.'

'Go any damn place you like.'

'Fine!' Mungo threw down his National Trust napkin and ran upstairs.

'Why can he leave the table and I can't?' said Tiz. 'It's not fair.'

'That was a bit harsh, Warren dear,' said Pauline. 'Mungo was just trying to make conversation.'

'Pauline, what's with you? He wanted me to hit your fiancé.'

'Not literally, dear.'

'Well,' said Dotty, '*somebody's* got to bring the pudding in. Come on, Carmen. This is the high water mark of family life in Britain.'

The pudding was brought in to half-hearted applause. The

holly caught fire, fell off and burnt a hole in the tablecloth. Only Pauline and Dotty toyed with a portion. Frazer went upstairs. Warren and Damian offered to do the dishes.

Tiz snuggled up to Harriet on the sofa. 'It's been a horrid Christmas, Mum. It's all Damian's fault. He started it with that stupid joke. I wish he'd never come.'

Dotty had been granted permission to spend New Year's Eve with her neighbours in Nonsuch Crescent. Pauline and Frazer had left for their tour of the distant relations. Mungo was staying at a friend's house, leaving Tiz alone with Carmen to throw lonely streamers round the empty house. Harriet wanted to go home after the show and be with them, but Warren was making something of a test case out of the arrangements. They were invited by the chairman of M25TV, and as he had graced their festivities, Warren felt they were obliged to return the compliment. Harriet rather thought that Warren was in fact spreading his corporate tail feathers, and wanted to prove to his boss that he could produce his woman when the occasion demanded. He promised to bribe Tiz with The Horse of the Year Show in compensation.

Consequently, Harriet was in no mood to party as she left the theatre and made her way to Aldwych station. After this latest Christmas, the obligation to celebrate traditional festivals was like having to eat dinner with a stiff on the plate. She could not decide which was the greater waste of human endeavour – pretending to be a singing matron in the theatre, or playing a real walk-on role in the universe. London no longer exhilarated her. Its density and diversity now forced daily contemplation of multifarious insignificance. She was just penning a mental letter to Ingmar Bergman to offer her services for nothing, when she noticed a little girl lolling against a street lamp. The child was stick thin, and stood feigning nonchalance with her hands in the pockets of a white plastic bomber jacket with acrylic collar. The narrow, rabbity face was yellow under the lamplight.

'Are you lost, dear? Are you waiting for someone?'

'Piss off.'

'There's no need for that. Don't be frightened. I just thought you looked a bit young to be hanging around on your own at this time of night.'

'I'm with me mum.'

'That's all right, then. Where is she?'

'In that pub.'

Harriet was indignant. She had clearly stumbled upon a sprog of the fabled underclass, of no doubt single parents who nightly left their offspring on the pavement outside a boozer, or locked them in flats to be burned alive. 'How long have you been here?'

''Bout an hour. Dunno.'

'Would you like to go in and look for her? Perhaps she doesn't realize how long you've been here.'

The child shrugged. 'I expect she'll be out in a bit. She was going to meet some bloke.'

'Bloke' put the tin hat on it. The girl's mother might already be lying in a pool of her own blood among the dustbins behind the pub.

'We'd better go in and see. You never know, she might have become unwell or something.'

'How d'ya mean?'

'Well – she might have fainted in the crush. Come on.'

Now alarmed, the girl let Harriet take her hand and lead her into the pub. The smoke choked like a damp bonfire. Bodies were so tightly packed Harriet had to yank the child along as though through stiffly folding doors. Her mother was not in either of the rooms downstairs. They went up to the Ladies, a hell hole painted elephant pink with a stained loo and high flush tank with a broken chain. Nothing. Harriet struggled back to the bar. When she stated her business, the barman became abusive. It was half past eleven. Warren would soon start to worry if she did not turn up at the party. She took the child back outside.

'Are you sure this is the right pub?'

'Yeah. Course.' She started to cry.

'Listen, what's your name?'

'Madonna.'

'Well – Madonna – where do you live? Do you know the phone number?' She shook her head. 'The thing is, I have to go now, but I can't leave you here. Why don't I take you to the nearest police station? They'll look after you, and it will be the obvious place for your mum to enquire for you.'

'No! I'm not going to no fucking police station. They'll do my mum for not looking after me proper, and put her in prison.'

Harriet was impressed by her legal knowledge, but she said, 'Of course they won't. Children get lost all the time in London. They'll give you cup of tea and a biscuit and let you play with their walkie-talkies and your mum will find you in no time.'

'No! I'm staying here where she told me.'

'But it's not safe. Someone could stop and bundle you into a car and you'd never see your mum again.' The child started to howl. Passers-by glanced at them. 'You really must come with me now, Madonna. If anything happened to you it would be on my conscience.'

'Fuck your conscience.'

'Right. That's it. Come.' She grasped the child's arm and pulled her along the street. Madonna squealed and tried to prise herself free. Their way was blocked by a couple in matching anoraks. The man said, 'Is that your child, madam?'

'No. As a matter of fact—'

He produced an ID. 'Police.'

'Oh, thank goodness. I was just bringing her to the station. She's lost her mum. She was hanging around outside The Poet and Grapes. Perhaps you could take her? I'm supposed to be at a party.'

The woman bent down to look Madonna in the eyes. 'Is this true, love? Has this woman been trying to help you?'

'No!' Free of Harriet's grip, the child rubbed her arm and looked at Harriet with venomous pleasure. 'She dragged me away. My mum only went in to use the phone. Can I go back now? She'll be well worried.'

'You said you'd been there an hour!'

'I never.'

'It's true! I took her into the pub to look for her mother. Ask the barman.'

'Oh yes?' They looked at Harriet as though she had just confessed to throwing a dog off a high-rise tower block. 'Would you mind returning to the pub in question, madam, so that we can verify your story?'

'Yes I would. I'm supposed to be meeting my husband.'

'This is somewhat more important than festive high jinks, madam.'

Harriet could see she had no choice. Tears of frustration threatened. By the time the police were satisfied, even taxis would be unobtainable, and she would be the one to end up behind a dustbin with her throat slit. Her mind again leapt forward to her funeral, a vision that presented itself so frequently these days she had even chosen the hymns. The woman walked in front with Madonna, and the man steered Harriet by the arm.

'Wait a minute.'

'What is it, madam?'

'Nothing. I thought I saw someone I knew.' She peered across the road, twisting her head to follow the unmistakably tall figure of Avelina Viper – and what looked like the curly head of Damian de St Croix at her side. 'I don't believe it – not those two! It's a joke—'

'Not your husband, was it, madam?'

'No. But – that couple – we sort of introduced them but I never thought – She's this novelist, you see, and she's so much older than him, but she's got this thing about energy, but it never occurred to me she'd plug into him – I mean—'

'Yes, madam.'

Harriet was still in a daze when they reached The Poet and Grapes. For a moment she did not grasp the fact that Madonna had run up to, and grasped the knees of, a blonde woman in leggings and leopard skin raincoat who had been pacing up and down the pavement. The police persons exchanged a grim look and simultaneously produced their notebooks.

'See!' said Madonna in triumph. 'I told you she'd be out in a bit.'

The mother cried with relief. 'I was worried sick,' she sobbed. 'I only popped in to use the phone. Ten minutes tops.'

'Excuse me,' said Harriet, 'that can't be true. I was with the child myself for nearly half an hour. I assumed she was abandoned.'

'Abandoned! Like shit. Who the hell are you, anyway?'

'Did you at any time give this lady permission to assume custody of your daughter, madam?'

'Like shit!'

'How could she if she wasn't there?' said Harriet.

'In that case, I'm afraid I must ask you to come to the station and answer a few questions.'

'What? Look, I'd love to, but I really don't have time.'

'Come along, madam. You don't want the bracelets, do you?'

14 ∫

Harriet was taken to Bow Street police station and left alone in a stifling windowless room. After some time, two women detectives came in. One of them sat at the desk in front of Harriet and shuffled forms. She was about twenty-two. The other woman, who sat beside her, had the air of a training supervisor. Harriet was asked for lengthy personal details, including height, and what she was doing in London. When *Wipers!* was mentioned, the girl looked up, surprised, at her colleague, but was nodded on.

'May I ring my husband? He'll have got the police out himself by now.'

The older woman got up. 'I'll do it. Have you got the number?'

'Yes. I brought it with me in case I couldn't find the place.'

In the absence of her supervisor, the younger woman relaxed. She asked Harriet about her home life, and whether she had enjoyed Christmas. Harriet knew that her best chance was to co-operate cheerfully, and painted a picture of family fun that Dickens would have died for. It had been especially wonderful to have her mother there – it had made the traditional routines so very precious.

The young woman's eyes flickered like a bird's. 'Your mother, you say. Do you get on with her?'

'Goodness, yes. We're like Morecambe and Wise. We're very close. Not geographically, of course, since she's been in Australia.'

'Why did she go there?'

'She married a surgeon. They're divorced now.'

'Will she come back here to live?'

'No. No, she's going to marry again, unfortunately.'

'You don't approve?'

'Well – whatever makes her happy is fine by me, but – to be honest, we don't like her fiancé very much.'

'You've met him, then?'

'Oh yes. He came with her for Christmas.'

'I see. So you didn't get as much of your mother's attention as you would have liked?'

Harriet paused and looked at her interrogator with serious condescension. 'That's right. I started wetting the bed and refusing my Weetabix.' The young woman suppressed a giggle. 'I think I've tumbled your tune.'

'Pardon?'

'You are hypothesizing that I was so jealous of my mother's new boyfriend that I went out and abducted that lying toadette to get more attention for myself?'

'That's your suggestion, Mrs Funkel, not mine.'

'Please – can't we finish this farce? I think you're doing a terrific job, and I'm really, really glad you chaps are so hot off the mark to protect young children, but if you think I would want any more, either in this world or the next, I can only conclude that you have none of your own. Am I right?'

'That's irrelevant, Mrs Funkel.' But she had blushed. 'Many women have a completely irrational desire for children.'

'Huh. For being pregnant, perhaps. For some fantasy emotional soup where they can forget the outside world. But not for looking after brats like Madonna.'

'Have you had a hysterectomy?'

'No. That is, yes, but—'

'Don't you know?'

'Of course. Actually, I have, but I never told the children. I thought it might upset them.'

'That could be construed as denial, Mrs Funkel. Perhaps you can't accept your infertility.'

'Oh for God's sake. I paid a fortune for it.'

Colleague returned and summoned the young woman outside. When she came back, she told Harriet she was free to go. 'I probably shouldn't tell you this, but it seems the mother has several convictions for soliciting, so that makes you the more credible witness.'

'Thank you. I appreciate that.'

She accompanied Harriet to the exit.

'So,' said Harriet, 'next time I see an abandoned child I should walk by on the other side, should I?'

'Perhaps you should compromise and fetch a police officer.'

'That's rather difficult when they're all disguised as hobos.'

'Happy New Year, Mrs Funkel.'

In the taxi to Camden, Harriet slumped in despair. How could she now deny the influence of the planets? They must be drunk. The case against Warren for hitting the blind man in Cornwall was still pending, their home had been wrecked by vandals, Mungo had started a life of crime and she had narrowly escaped doing porridge for kidnapping. Tyrants had fallen, drought burnt the land, the Third World War was about to break out in the Gulf. Perhaps God had just come out of a coma. Not the goody-goody God of the New Testament, of course, but the one who detonated whole cities if they got lippy. Time to pack the family on a life raft and head off to – where? The Pacific? Too many nuclear tests. The poles? Too many holes in the ozone layer. South America? Too many generals. They were trapped.

The taxi driver, a Jamaican, regarded her quizzically in the rear view mirror. 'You OK, Miss? You sure look like you could use a party.'

'Huh. What have you got to be so cheerful about?'

'Me? Aw – I from the Islands, Miss. I always cheerful.'

It was after one o'clock when Harriet arrived in Camden. Voices dropped as she entered the house. Mr and Mrs Chairman of M25TV welcomed her with lush effusion and brought her a plate of stuffed courgette flowers. Warren's solicitude fooled all but Harriet, who saw beneath it a boiling pit of resentment. On the drive home he listened to her version of events in silence. His failure to express anything, let alone outrage, gave her an insight into the trials of rape victims in Islamic societies.

'Warren, why don't you say something? You know what it's like to be done over by the police. Perhaps you think I really was trying to abduct her.'

'You have been acting kinda strange, lately, sweetheart. And you did try and smother Semi—'

'No I didn't.'

'OK, OK. But why did you have to get involved?'

'How can you be so callous? Supposing it had been Tiz?'

'Tiz would never be in a situation like that. If these people let their kids hang out like that, they're beyond help. Who do you think you are – Elizabeth fucking Fry? I was totally humiliated. You're right. We should have stayed home.'

The following day Harriet's resentment levels had risen to meet Warren's own, and she decided not to tell him about Avelina and Damian as punishment. The atmosphere between them was atom-splitting. Tiz sided with Warren, Dotty with Harriet. Mungo and Carmen gave neither toss nor fig and oozed an indifference the consistency of non-drip paint, which made Harriet snappier than ever.

They all went in silence to an Open House at The Carlton, home of a bathroom fittings magnate whom Warren knew from the golf club.

Dotty surveyed the chicken tikka, goujons and physalis mousse with curled lip. 'Do you think I could ask for a sandwich?'

'Don't you think they've gone to enough trouble already?'

'Only joking. Harriet, before you start circulating, there's something I want to ask you.'

'Is it something too delicate to ask at home?'

'Perhaps. Let's get out of the way.'

They took their provisions into the deserted music room and put their plates on the piano. Dotty took a fortifying swig of Soave Classico.

'The thing is, while Pauline was here we got talking.'

'Yes, I noticed.'

'To cut a long story short, she wants to buy my house.'

Harriet spluttered. 'What? What do you mean?'

'She wants to buy my house. As an investment. And rent it out. Then she can always come back and live in it if Frazer croaks.'

'But – but she was hardly here a week.'

'I know. Still, you know your mother. She doesn't beat about the bush. We went over to see it while you were at your matinée.'

Harriet was stunned. The subterfuge. The deceit. How could her mother plan to buy any house over here without telling her, let alone Dotty's.

'The thing is, it all depends on you. Because I'd, like, have to stay put while you need me. But I could invest the money, and then when you don't need me any more I could buy a little flat.'

'I thought you couldn't wait to get home, Dotty.'

'That was before I got the estimate for the rewiring. It'll be hard to leave, but I know it makes sense.'

'Why did Mummy never mention it to me?'

'I had to think it over first, and I promised Pauline I'd sound you out. I don't suppose you know how long you're likely to be in the show?'

'Not indefinitely. I'm so tired.'

'So it could all work out quite nicely.'

'Only if Carmen stays. I'll think about it.' That is, try to divine the immense, but at present indecipherable, question mark that hung over the scheme.

Two days later a girl called Ariel Scott-Filibert from *Woman's Hour* phoned to ask Harriet if she would take part in a discussion about Having a Go. Someone had informed her of Harrriet's false arrest, but she claimed not to remember who it was. Harriet fumed. Her suspicions fell on Mrs Chairman of M25TV, who was a failed actress.

'I'm sorry. I couldn't do anything that might be bad publicity for the show.'

'How could it be if you were totally innocent? Do reconsider, Miss Dimdore. Your action raises huge questions about the safety of children in public places, doesn't it?'

'Yes, but there must be others—'

'Of course. But your – shall we say – minor celebrity is a huge plus for the angle. I mean, your being an actor. People think of actors as being tremendously right-thinking – always supporting the Labour Party and speaking out for prisoners of conscience and things. They'd be terribly shocked that someone like you could get involved in an incident like this.'

Harriet wondered how they would react if they knew she had

tried to smother the au pair. 'I'd still have to clear it with the management.'

'Would you mind? asap, if you would. We'd like to do it while the sales are still on.'

Dotty was anxious for a verdict about the house. Pauline and Frazer were to return to Abutilon for two days before going home. Harriet could not decide before discussing the matter with her mother. They arrived while Harriet was recording the item for *Woman's Hour*, and she greeted Pauline coolly when she came home.

'Dotty tells me you want to buy her house, Mummy.'

'We did discuss it, yes. It's just an idea at the moment.'

'Oh. I thought perhaps you'd already had a survey done.'

'No, darling. Are you mad at me? Do come and sit down.'

'I'm not mad at you, Mummy, but why couldn't you have told me first? Discussing it with Dotty behind my back – it makes me feel like – well – like a child.'

'I didn't mean to hurt you, darling. I guess I'm just so used to making my own decisions.'

'After all, I'm the "me" with whom Dotty will be abiding until she finds another place. I mean, I know we have au pair girls, but we're not a refugee camp.'

'Of course. Don't you get on with Dotty?'

'Yes, well enough. That's because I'm out a lot. Oh, I like Dotty tremendously. But living with her is something else. It would probably be the same with anyone who didn't exactly fit. Their presence looms exponentially. It sort of grows like a mutant plant until its tentacles fill the house.'

'The big Little House of Horrors, eh? Poor Dotty. Still, I don't see any problem. You'd be able to give her notice when you're coming out of the show, wouldn't you?'

'There's no need to wait till then. Carmen's such a treasure, we could manage without Dotty. Japh isn't here now. Mungo and Tiz will soon be outnumbered by minders.'

'You miss Japh, don't you? Mungo and Tiz feel that you do.'

'Can't say I'd noticed. They behave more like the mob that invaded the Tuileries and tried on Marie Antoinette's wigs.'

'That's just their way of coping.'

'Are you suggesting I don't understand my own children?'

'No, darling. Don't be so sensitive. But you must admit Mungo at least is not very happy at the moment. Japh always held the limelight. Now he's gone and Mungo doesn't really know how to step into it. I tell you what. Why don't you send him over to us in the summer? We could find him a little job, maybe. It would do wonders for his self-esteem.'

'Have you booked the ticket already?'

'Of course not, darling. Don't be mean.'

'He'd have to really want to. It's so far. Still, the land of *Neighbours*—'

'Exactly. He'd have so much to tell his mates when he got back.'

'And if we were down to Tiz, we could dispense with Dotty sooner rather than later.'

'I won't say anything to him now. I'll write when we get home. That way he won't feel pressured.'

Nor did Harriet. But somehow she had tacitly agreed to the sale of Dotty's home.

It reminded Harriet of *The War of the Worlds*. Bombing down the A217 from Sutton, she switched on the radio to hear an American voice give a running commentary on the explosion of cruise missiles and smart bombs from his vantage point under a table in a Baghdad hotel. Having missed the introduction Harriet thought at first it was one of those satirical news programmes the BBC did so well – *Up the Bulletin* or *Thank God There Isn't One*. But it went on too long, even for a BBC joke.

At home everyone was in bed, except for Warren who was in Upper Volta. She put on the TV in the den, and sat watching it in her coat. The American voice, wobbly with fear, created a convincing sound portrait of imminent extinction to accompany the fire-streaked sky and wheeze-thud impaction. Harriet started to shake until she rattled. Conditioned to think that the Middle East was the fuse that would ignite the world, the terror was numbing. Engulfing. In the circumstances. This sort of thing did not happen nowadays. It was a tale told by Dotties. Suppose Japheth had succumbed to the lure of formation skiing and rescuing babies from rubble and joined the army? She might now be a witness to his immolation. Or worse. The unknown terror of captivity and torture. This was no little local difficulty. It could be Armageddon. She could not drag herself away from the spectacle, plugged into even deeper gloom by the shared vocabulary of real and imagined drama and its laughable attempts to squeeze the substance of real pain. Hypnotized by explosions, she fell asleep, awakened at three-thirty by the pain of having her head in her armpit.

As the war in the Gulf hotted up, the weather in Blighty became so cold that by the middle of February Mungo was spending Saturday afternoons digging pensioners out of ice floes in their own bedrooms. Every night when Harriet came home from the theatre she watch the end of *Newsnight* with Carmen, whose revered cousin Jaime Maria was covering the war for a Galician newspaper. From the moment Carmen heard that Jaime Maria had volunteered she shut down like a submarine, performed her duties in silence, spent hours on the phone to Spain, the cost of which she worked out to the last penny and left by the phone, from where Mungo and Tiz would often remove it for safe keeping. Harriet offered to release her if she wished to go home, but she declined.

'I can't do nothing there,' she shrugged. Her syntax suffered from lack of use.

The sale of Dotty's house to Pauline was completed, amid general observations of its timeliness in view of the bad weather, burst pipes and so on. She promised to take them all out to dinner on the proceeds but, out of respect for Carmen, not until the war was safely over.

Houses for *Wipers!* were thin. The cold and the snow-stymied trains kept people away. '*We* turn up,' grumbled Pam, 'why can't the audience?' Morale suffered. Perry Saddlesmith came to see the show unannounced, sacked half the cast and ordered regeneration workshops for the rest. Peter Makeweight went sick and was replaced, which involved more rehearsals. Harriet began to regret that she had not become something straightforward and boring – like a sleeping policeman.

Warren, too, became withdrawn. The station's advertising

revenue was in decline. They rarely made love, and when they did it bore all the hallmarks of a worming operation.

Tiz lost another half stone and threw away all the insect repellants.

One evening Harriet came home early because of a power cut in the theatre, and found Dotty watching *Come Dancing*. She poured herself a whisky. The flat-voiced lady commentator reached peaks of spontaneous eloquence.

'Pia is from Denmark,' she said brightly. 'She's a very glamorous girl who is coming on strongly in the legs and feet department.

'Gill and Tony have improved a great deal since Brighton. Unfortunately, Gill's shoulder line is too high. This leaves something to be desired in the balance area.

'Phil and Sharon are very quick. Except in the knees. Sharon takes too long straightening her knees. Consequently she appears less comfortable with the rhythm. Too many loose ends there I'm afraid, Brian.'

'I am going mad,' thought Harriet.

Dotty fell out with the Reverend Vince over the Gulf War. He took an anti-Western Imperialism line, which emptied his tin hut of all but a few elderly Liberal Democrats. He had wanted to take a coach-load to protest to Parliament about atrocities committed against retreating Iraqi soldiers. In the event he could not even fill the hearse.

Harriet now woke on Sunday mornings to the strains of radio worship and the smell of fried tomatoes. She began to scour the property pages for one-bed maisonettes.

Carmen gradually regained her poise when the war ended. Tiz let her have a go on British Telecom, as a reward for the patient months Carmen had spent trudging behind them in all weathers. British Telecom did not know what had hit him. Carmen had him galloping forwards and backwards, trotting sideways, jumping five-barred gates and high-stepping to 'When the Saints Go Marching In'. Carmen modestly admitted that she had been riding for fifteen years. Afterwards she asked Harriet if she might be permitted to rent a pony for the summer so that she could accompany Tiz aloft, at her own expense.

'Well of course you can. Why didn't you say anything before, Carmen?'

'Ah. I watch. I wait. I choose the right moment. I do not want Tithiana to be intimidated by my expertithe, you know.'

'You are perfectly amazing.'

This revelation doomed Dotty's tenure as chief care assistant, if doom were needed. Dotty was mindful to stay in the area, what with her new friends acquired chez Reverend Vince, to whom she was trickling back, and the full programme of Dotty in Wartime talks that she visited on local primary schools.

They found a delightful one-bedroomed, cottage-style home in a new development of tile-hung hutches near Reigate, called Maidens Walk. It would be full with a table and chair, but it did have a Zanussi hob, waste disposal, optional chair lift, Indian Ivory bath suite, electronic entry phone and a level walk to the shops. Solicitors were engaged and a survey commissioned. Harriet had every hope of installing Dotty in 2A Maidens Walk by Easter.

To celebrate the death of the poll tax, Harriet's new legless captain was to hold a champagne celebration with cabaret. Harriet was cast as Margaret Thatcher in an extract from a little-known opera of the same name by Mussorgsky. She was rummaging through her wardrobe for fur hats, and when she found one went to ask Carmen for her opinion.

Harriet found her on the phone in the den. She stood up as Harriet came in, a habit that had proved incurable. Almost immediately she fell back, and the phone dropped from her hand.

'Carmen! Whatever's the matter?'

Instead of replying, Carmen hurtled herself at Harriet, almost knocking her over. She burst into tears on Harriet's bosom, which she just reached. Harriet led her back to the sofa, the one on which Avelina Viper had disgorged her grief over Piers. She felt like the Statue of Liberty – Bring Me Your Tired, Your etc.'

Carmen was jabbering in Spanish. Harriet stroked her head

and held her tight. She extracted the words Jaime Maria from the flow.

'Carmen, has something happened to Jaime Maria?' Carmen howled, confirming the worst. 'Wait a minute, I'll get you a brandy.'

Carmen's teeth rattled against the glass. 'My mudder telephone. Jaime Maria – Jaime Maria—' She broke down again.

Harriet, sickened by the loss of this paragon she had come to know and love, could not help her mind leaping forward to the consequences of the tragedy. Carmen would want to go home, leaving Harriet dependent on Dotty and necessitating the postponement of her move to 2A Maidens Walk.

'What happened, Carmen? Can you talk about it?'

She nodded. 'Jaime Maria – he take my brudda and sister to the skating—'

'Rink?'

'Yes.'

Harriet experienced a screwing up of dread at what was to come. Had Jaime Maria been decapitated after falling from a triple salchow meant to impress the cousins?

'Jaime Maria – he crash – wid another – so – head to head—'

'He was head-butted?'

'Yes. And then – huh – another go over his hand – it come away—'

'My God, no—'

'Yes. When he come to the hospital—' She collapsed again.

'Was it shock? Did he die of shock?'

Carmen nodded. 'Why? I don't know why – my mudder think maybe his nerves got bad – in the war – I don't know—' She curled into a heaving bundle on Harriet's lap.

Harriet had no trouble believing in the power of shock to kill. The thought of Jaime Maria's accident brought her near to fainting, the cold cells of her body gyrated like lottery balls as her mind careered through conflicting emotions – the imagined agony of Jaime Maria's parents, relief that it was not her own child shifting into panic that at any moment it might be. Exasperation that her domestic arrangements were once again on the fire. Regret that she had not accepted Semi's offer of her younger sister as a replacement melting into shame that she could pretend for a moment that she had not welcomed Carmen as a gift from the gods.

One effect of the tragedy was to drive Dotty seriously back into the arms of the Reverend Vince. As the only one in the household with access to the spiritual life, she took it upon herself to ask him to call with what comfort he could. She also suspended the morning fry-ups.

When the Reverend arrived, Carmen was preoccupied with arrangements for her departure. She accepted his condolences with dignity and retired to her room. Dotty and Harriet were left alone with him. He seemed uneasy out of his milieu, perched on the edge of the sofa between two pillars of society. Harriet suspected that he was trying to disguise feelings of self-righteousness about the death of Jaime Maria, as if it vindicated his stand on the war, and the suspicion made her hostile.

'Would you like me to say a prayer?' His large hands indicated its possible dimensions.

'Thank you,' said Harriet, 'but I prefer to pray in private.'

'Poor Harriet. What a year this has been for you. What else can happen, I wonder.'

'The pony could get out and drown in the neighbour's swimming pool. Sorry, that was trite in the circumstances. I can only think how grateful I am it wasn't my own son. I feel a bit – disorientated – I don't know—'

'She's a nervous wreck, Vince. Taken on too much.'

'I'm under contract, Dotty. There's nothing I can do about it.'

'And how are you going to manage without Carmen or me? I've found a lovely little house, Vince. I'm moving in a couple of weeks. Then there'll be no one here when the kids get home from school. Warren's away most of the time, and Harriet often isn't here during the day, what with extra rehearsals and whatnot. I'm surprised those kids aren't on drugs, frankly.'

'Oh, I expect they soon will be.' Dotty's portrait of neglected children and absentee parents infuriated Harriet. It was the usual obtuse travesty of the mysterious bonds within the family.

'I suppose she'll have to get another au pair,' Dotty went on. 'Lucky girl. Probably can't speak the language and she'll be stuck in this dead-and-alive rhododendron plantation on her own most of the time.'

'Aren't the children old enough to look after themselves?'

'They can operate the microwave, if that's what you mean. But would you leave kids alone in this barn of a place night after night?'

Harriet snapped. 'If you put it like that I'll obviously have to break my own leg, won't I? Go back to full-time housework and the occasional bit part in *Crimewatch UK*. That's what you'ld like, isn't it, Dotty?'

'Now, please—' The Reverend feared a punch-up, in which he would get hurt. 'I don't think a slanging match is appropriate just now, do you?'

'I don't care what you think,' said Harriet.

'Harriet! How could you be so rude?'

'It's all right, Dotty. Just leave it. Harriet's under a lot of stress.'

'*She's* under stress? What about me? What do you think it's been like for me all this time, mourning Fin in my heart, and living with this lot who never think about him from one minute to the next with their acting and their riding and their useless television programmes—' She was flushed and tearful.

'I'm sorry, Dotty.'

'Yes, you always say that. But you just don't notice the way I feel. There's a lot you don't notice. You don't know the half of what's going on in your own family.'

'Like what?'

Dotty blew her nose. 'It's not for me to say, is it? I'm not qualified to understand these things.'

'Well,' said the Reverend Vince, 'when you're in your own place I'm sure you'll communicate much better.'

'That won't be for some time, unfortunately,' sniffed Dotty. They looked at her, puzzled. 'Well, I can't leave them in the lurch, can I?'

'But Dotty, you just said—'

'I know. I was waiting for you to ask me. I couldn't believe you didn't ask me—' She started crying again.

Harriet was pole-axed. Mungo was going to Australia. Herself,

Dotty and Tiz. High Noon at Abutilon. Who would be the first to crack – or fire?

'What about Maidens Walk? I thought you were so keen.'

Dotty sighed and wiped her eyes. 'It's all right if you like surfaces resistant to two thousand degrees centigrade. You can't move for sheltered housing round here. There'll be others.'

Carmen's farewell should, Harriet thought, have been set to music by Puccini. Tiz, Dotty and Harriet went with her to Gatwick. Tiz was hysterical, and cried on Dotty's shoulder as Carmen was swept past Passport Control and into the bowels of the departure lounge.

'Will she really come back in the autumn, Mum?'

'I hope so, darling.'

They returned to Abutilon in gloomy silence, taunted by the heartless beauty of the unfolding spring. In what season was it, Harriet wondered, that Hamlet found all the uses of this world flat, stale and unprofitable? Spring propelled one into the light, the open, the contemplation of Nature's ability to renew itself, and the failure of the human body to do the same.

Warren returned from a creative conference in Milton Keynes a worried man. Apart from falling revenues, the ITC was mumbling about the balance of programmes. Harriet reminded him about the Reverend Vince.

'After all, he has one foot in the media and one in heaven already. And he is quite charismatic.'

'Would he appeal to the youth market?'

'Very much so. I'm sure he could slither over into environmental issues with no sweat. The Creation, and all that. Why don't you go and have a look at him? Mind you, I can't really make him out. When he's in preacher mode he's lit up, awesome. But off stage he shuts down, as if it embarrasses him.'

'Is he ready for a career move?'

'Probably. Radio Hogsback is a summit only in name.'

'Maybe I'll take Damian along. He's my reference point on youth culture.'

'Whose youth? He must be thirty at least. You'd be better off taking Mungo.'

But Warren only laughed. He kissed her on the cheek, which was as far down as he ever got these days. 'Thanks, sweetheart. I'll look into it.'

Several weeks later the back row of the hut was filled with grim-faced marketing executives from M25TV, Warren, Damian and the Assistant Head of Programmes. After initial hesitation, the Reverend Vince returned with verve to the task of persuading the congregation to vote for the Green Party. At the end of May he received a letter asking him to go to Orbital House for consultations.

At the beginning of June an accident occurred in the theatre. There were those, namely Dotty, who said it was the result of auto-suggestion. A rogue chip in the circuit that controlled the scenery caused the ward to revolve in the middle of the amputation scene. The patient, who was straight out of drama school, panicked, sat up and head-butted Harriet, who was arranging his pillows. She reeled off the revolve into the trench, fell on a pit prop and broke her collar bone.

'It's just not your year, is it?' said the company manager as she was loaded into the ambulance.

Dotty was deeply satisfied, and put forward the theory that the rogue chip had been triggered by Harriet's stress levels.

'Don't talk crap, Dotty,' said Harriet. She lay in bed with the curtains drawn.

'But don't you think it's odd that you were in a head-to-head collision, just like Jamie whatsit?'

'Do you think I made that happen too?'

'No, of course not. But it's a bit of a coincidence, isn't it? It must have been on your mind.'

'The fucking Gulf War was on my mind, but I didn't start it.'

'Language!'

Although Harriet had longed for the opportunity to sleep all day, she had not anticipated it in quite this form. To start with she was in too much pain to sleep. Flowers arrived in flotillas. Sam and other friends came to see her – once. George phoned. The P45 was never mentioned, it just hovered over the conversation. The long-term implications flitted through her mind, but found no resting place. She did wonder why Warren was not more gratified at the prospect of her unemployment. Mungo and Tiz shared Dotty's view that Harriet had unconsciously brought the accident upon herself. On the whole they would rather have had a mother working than one wrapped in bandages hogging the television channels. Tiz was slightly mollified by the fact that Harriet would be able to witness her triumphs in Chase-me-Charlie. The abrupt change in routine, and her invalidity, created a sense of living in an air-lock. The rain slewed incessantly out of graphite skies, so that the house became an actual air-lock as well as a metaphor for a vacuum-sealed unit in the torrents of Life.

Harriet watched Wimbledon from the first shots on the sodden courts until light stopped play, if there was any. She also watched *Today at Wimbledon* in the evenings for an explantion. In the second week the weather cleared up, and the final was played in temperatures of over one hundred degrees Farenheit. She watched until the sun went down over the Mixed Doubles, and on Monday morning woke to an empty and meaningless world.

Dotty brought her a pile of murder stories from the library.

'Are you sure this is a good idea?' she said, examining the titles. *Death of a Relative. The Axeman of New Malden. The Kitchen Sink Murders. Death Caught Her Napping.*

'I thought you might try your hand at one after you've read them. It can't be that difficult.'

'You write one then. I'm useless at writing. I haven't the patience.'

'Pity. It's something you could do from home.'

'Dotty, I could make patchwork quilts from home. I could play the stockmarket from home. I could run a mail-order sex aids business from home. I don't *want* to. I want to get *out* occasionally.'

'All right, all right. Don't get your knickers in a twist.'

Being at close quarters with Dotty all day was worse than the pain. The day was charted with Dotty's inflammatory habits – the ritual Lincoln Creams, the squeak of her crêpe soles, her contempt for Jelly and Custard and yet her admiration for John

Major, her insistence on replacing the tea towels every two days, and yet her inability to replace the bath mat sideways on the edge of the bath instead of at right angles. Harriet did not understand how anyone could live with such a chaos principle. Whenever Dotty was out she rang her friends to complain about her. They feared that Harriet's centre was not holding.

It was no surprise when Andreas telephoned inviting her, in other words, to give up any thought of returning to the show. She had been replaced by an actress recently made redundant from *Eastenders*. Afterwards Harriet went into the garden. Yes, the relief and release were there. The release of someone from a treadmill, only to wander the salt plains of perpetual night.

Mungo began weight training and experimenting with hair gels in preparation for his trip to Australia. Tiz went pony trekking in Scotland. The Serbs, the Croats and the Bosnian Moslems unleashed their pent-up animosities in a medieval bloodbath with which, after her experience with Dotty, Harriet was in total sympathy.

Dotty resumed house-hunting and Harriet found it therapeutic to go with her. They looked at Hottlesham Hall, a mental hospital whose residents had been ejected into the community to make way for luxury maisonettes. Dotty was quite taken with the communal barbecue facilities, but could not overcome a fear that the place was haunted by the insanitary insane.

'Dotty, your attitude is barbaric. Mental illness is – well – it's physical actually. It has to do with junction boxes in the brain breaking down. It happens to normal people.'

'That's what they'd like you to think, so as not to alarm the population. But they never get better, do they? No, I could never get a wink of sleep here, Harriet. Supposing they kept coming back because they forgot where they lived?'

'That's what the electronic gates are for I expect.'

'And that's another thing. The way those gates open and close like magic. It's weird. I'd feel like Count Dracula.'

They concentrated on bungalows. In a village near Dorking was a chalet/bung. that quite took Dotty's fancy. It was white, with bulbous mullioned bosoms, yellow shutters with heart-shaped cut-outs, stable doors, a breakfast bar and coved Artex ceilings. The carpets were covered with plastic sheeting and the window sills with porcelain nymphs and souvenirs of Ibiza. It was in a deserted street of regular chalet/bungs. and the odd sixties detached, with roof pitched at an Alpine angle. All of which gave the impression that a part of Worcester Park had been dumped in a field. The lady who owned Terra Firma had taken the morning off from her job as manager of an optician's in Dorking in order to show them round. She was nonplussed by Harriet's barks of laughter as each vista of plastic sheeting was revealed. The demonstration of the dimmer switches sent Harriet off into paroxysms of mirth. Dotty and the lady quickly established a rapport of mutual concern. While Harriet inspected the well-stocked borders, Dotty explained that her cousin was recovering from heroin addiction.

'At her age!'

'Yes. Well. She got in with a rather fast set in Guildford.'

'Oh I see.'

'I'm sorry, Dotty,' said Harriet as they drove home. 'It was the Louis Quatorze video cabinet that set me off.'

'Excuse me if I don't see the joke. It's not like you to be so ill mannered. Now for goodness sake, don't start again. Do you want me to drive?'

'No! No, I'm all right. Did you like it then?'

'Very much. Yes, I think I could be happy there.' She consulted the details. 'I see part of the garden is *devoted to the cultivation of vegetables*. Do you think the person who did this used to write obituaries?'

For some reason the idea had Harriet once again in hysterics.

Warren was keen that Harriet should sue The Amazing Truth Company for damages. Harriet was lethargic.

'George can take care of it.'

'You would be entitled to serious money.'

'We don't need the money. At least, that was always your line. Are you worried about your job, Warren?'

'No, not really. But with the new franchise arrangements

we're all more vulnerable. By the way, I've booked a cottage
in Bamburgh for the last two weeks in August.'

'Bamburgh? You mean the one in Northumberland?'

'That's correct.'

'Well, I don't give a shit. You couldn't get much further from
the Cornish police. Was that the idea?'

'No. Though it looks like they've decided not to prosecute,
which is good. No, I thought it would be interesting. There's lots
of Roman forts and stuff in that area. Mungo will like that.'

'He won't be there. He's leaving in two days.'

'Shit, so he is. I'd forgotten. Shit, I'll be the only male in a hen
house. Would you mind if I asked Damian? We could play golf,
and you'd have some peace and quiet.'

'Do as you like. I've told you, I don't give a monkey's.'

'Sweetheart, don't you think you should see the doctor?
There's this new drug in the States called Prozac—'

Harriet did not say a word on the way back from seeing Mungo
off to Australia. She went upstairs early with the whisky bottle
and got in the bath and then dozed on the bed. Some time later
she heard screams coming through her headache. She heard
Tiz running downstairs, and got up reluctantly. Perhaps Dotty
had hanged herself because she had been having an affair with
Mungo.

Instead, Dotty was sitting on the bottom stair, shaking with
wild sobs. Warren stood over her, and when he saw Harriet,
made a gesture of helplessness.

'I don't know what's wrong with her, sweetheart. Some item
on the *Ten o'clock News* set her off. I didn't see it.'

To Harriet's knowledge Dotty had no other relations so dear
to her that their exit in a plane crash, or similar, would set
off such grief. She sat beside Dotty and put an arm round the
quivering body.

'Ssh, ssh, Dotty. It's all right. Has something happened to Mrs
Thatcher?'

Dotty shook her head.

'What is it, then?'

'I – I – c-c-can't t-tell you—'

'Dotty, you must tell me. If nobody's died it can't be that bad.'

'It-t-t is.'

Tiz had joined them. 'Gazza's going to play in Italy,' she suggested, helpfully.

'Shut up, Tiz. Come on, Dotty, what is it?'

'You'll k-k-k-kill m-me.'

'What? Don't talk nonsense.'

'Are Jelly and Custard all right?' said Tiz. 'I'll just go and check.'

'Come on, Dotty. Spill the beans.'

Apparently this was the wrong thing to say, as Dotty succumbed to convulsions for a while longer.

Eventually she said, 'It's my m-m-m-m-money.'

'Your money. The money from the sale of your house?' Harriet, who was not thinking very fast, was relieved.

'I i-i-invested it.'

'Good. In what?'

'Well – I w-was in S-Sainsbury's – that s-super store on the A25.'

'And?'

'They had this – I d-don't know what you call it – this s-stand thingy – in the forecourt—'

'Who did?' Harriet could only think of promotions for Toasticles and Continental sausage.

'This f-finance c-company. Matterhorn International it's c-called.'

'Go on, Dotty.' Harriet had begun to freeze over.

'There was this v-very nice lady in g-glasses. Very smart. Sh-she said I could m-make a lot of m-m-money if I invested in their With Profits Shorthold F-Fund.'

'Were they members of LAUTRO?' asked Harriet coldly.

'Eh? I d-don't know. She was so nice, H-Harriet. Not a young g-girl or anything. Forty at least. And it was S-Sainsbury's. I th-thought it would be all right—'

'Full marks for brand recongnition,' said Warren.

'But they probably had nothing to do with Sainsbury's! Did you sign something there and then?'

'Oh no. I went to their offices in Croydon. Th-that was another thing. It was huge. All m-marble, and Mozart in the loos – you know—' Even now, Dotty took comfort from this edifice. 'They asked me lots of questions about m-my life p-plan strategy. Then th-there was a c-cooling off period, she c-called it, and after that I w-went back to sign the contract. It was all p-properly done.'

'Except the company has collapsed anyway.' Harriet now realized why Dotty feared her reaction. No money, no Terra Firma. Dotty was destitute.

'Yes.' Dotty broke down. 'The d-directors have d-done a moonlight—'

'How much was it?' said Warren.

'A h-hundred and th-thirty thousand p-pounds. I kept ten th-thousand in the current account.'

'We'll still get birthday presents, then?' said Tiz.

'A hundred and thirty thousand pounds,' said Harriet.

'I'm s-so s-s-s-s-sorry, Harriet,' said Dotty. 'It w-won't happen again.'

15

Dotty no longer had any entitlement to housing in her tribal homeland of Twickenham. Harriet offered to leave her in a basket on the doorstep of Reigate and Banstead Town Hall. Warren declined, but then he had always had a tough time understanding Harriet's problem with Dotty. He was away a lot, and anyway he found Dotty's pithy Twickenham humour refreshing, and was indifferent to the fact that the bath mat was not facing Mecca.

No one was more aware than Dotty of the skids under her feet. While privately feeling that she had as much cause for grief as anyone, possibly more, she saw that her position was not unlike that of the Little Princess, banished to the attic on a flying freehold. She redoubled her efforts to cheer Harriet up. While relaxing in Bamburgh she showed Harriet an advertisement for cleaning fluid that had removed President Gorbachev's port wine stain. Ex-President Gorbachev. She tried to rouse Harriet's indignation that the only nice man ever to rule the Soviet Union had been deposed. And him on holiday too.

Harriet's eyes barely flickered as Dotty waved the newspaper in her face. Another flagstone floor. Another downstairs bathroom with no shower attachment. There was always the North Sea to liven things up, delivering a kill-or-cure massage of ice-cold water that left Harriet paralysed from the waist down.

Tiz found a nearby riding centre, and Warren and Damian dropped her off there before going to the golf course. After a day or so, Harriet could not face the beach, alone with Dotty behind a plastic wind break, staring out to sea, while all around colonies of natives chattered in their downhill slalom accent.

Warren urged her to go on a day trip to Housesteads. She pleaded exhaustion, and Dotty went in her place. Despite this, Warren and Damian were laughing and in expeditionary mood. Harriet watched their departure from behind the fibre glass curtains. It was true that Warren had been more cheerful, boyish even, since Damian, as if he had found someone to play with. It seemed a harmless enough from of mid-life crisis. And yet Harriet could not shake off the dream-like menace that their presence together produced – as in dreams in which the babysitter turns out to be Vlad the Impaler in disguise.

Damian avoided her whenever possible. In front of the others he treated her with flippant familiarity. Harriet became engorged with resentment. He had to go.

One evening when Warren suggested they walk along the beach to Seahouses for dinner, Harriet agreed. Warren was delighted. He thought the holiday must be doing her good.

Tiz ran in and out of the water, skimming stones. Dotty laboured in the sucking sand. Warren offered her his arm. Harriet attached herself to Damian. He tried to pull away, but she kept up with him, so that the others were left far behind.

Harriet panted. 'Wait a minute. We'll lose them.'

'I don't see how. The beach is in a straight line.' But he did stop.

They looked back to where Tiz gambolled in the shallows, and Warren and Dotty plodged arm in arm against the backdrop of the medieval Sizewell.

'Well. How are you, Damian?'

'Eh? Fine.'

'I'm so glad you could get away.'

'You're so bitter, Harriet. I know it must have been tough coming out of the show, but there's lots of musicals being cast in the autumn. Now you've made your mark, I expect you'll be snapped up.'

'No. As you say, I've made my mark – proved my point. I'm too old and too tired for that kind of commitment. It's telly or nothing now. Maybe the odd stint at The Almeida.' Damian smiled. He looked relieved to be having a normal conversation. 'No, my problems are closer to home.'

'Oh yeah?'

'I miss you, Damian.'

He laughed, and did a knees-up on the spot in lieu of bolting. 'What do you mean by that?'

'Isn't it obvious? I associate you with fucking, and when you're around I want it. It's a learned response.'

'Shit.' He ruffled his hair. 'I thought you'd cooled off.'

'So did I. I was mistaken. Don't misunderstand me. It's all right when you're not around.'

'You mean, you want me to piss off? How are you going to explain that to Warren?'

'If you don't, I shall have to tell him everything. I don't know how else I can convince him that this *Jules et Jim* thing doesn't work.'

'No, please don't do that. Look, I'm leaving on Saturday anyway. Can't you hold out till then?'

'We'll see.' They watched the approaching party. Tiz had taken Warren's other arm, so they formed a balanced triptych.

'Why did you split up with your girlfriend, Damian?'

'What?' He shrugged. 'She went off with a cabin attendant.'

'But you've been on your own ever since. Why?'

'No special reason. What's it to you, anyway?'

'I'm not sure.'

'It's funny, I thought it was Dotty that was bugging you, not me.'

'She is. Look, you don't get a thrill from snuff movies, do you? Do say yes. You might be just the person I'm looking for.'

'Eh? What's got into you – sicko.'

'You could murder Dotty for me.'

'What the fuck are you talking about?'

'Have you any idea how long the waiting list is for council flats? Especially as Dotty is so comfortably housed at present. Don't you think that would hot things up between us? Did you see that French film where Romy Schneider went down on Michel Piccoli on the stairs, slithering about in buckets of half-dissolved bodies? It was widely acclaimed.'

'What was?'

'The film.'

'Maybe, but it wasn't a training video, was it?'

'No. I couldn't stand anything gory. Just a gentle push off a battlement or something.'

'You'd never get Dotty up all those stairs.'

'You'll do it, then?'

'Of course not! If it's that bad, why don't you just tell her to shove off?'

'Where to – bed and breakfast?'

'She might prefer it to being pushed off a battlement.'

'Warren wouldn't hear of it. He feels responsible for Dotty because she's helped us out. And him, when he first came to England.'

'And you don't.'

'Yes I do. But I'd still like to murder her. Lots of old people get beaten up by their carers. I can understand it. Just imagine if Dotty was incontinent, as well as calling for the return of corporal punishment all day.'

'But she isn't.'

'No. All I'm saying is, I can understand how things get out of hand when you're trapped with someone who drives you nuts.'

'Why don't you just campaign for more day care centres?'

'Murderers aren't usually up to organizing their own therapy. They do stupid things – like throwing the weapon into the nearest hedge.'

'Harriet, seriously, this is a deeply wacky conversation. Why don't you tell Warren you feel like this? I'm sure he'd see the sense in letting Dotty go.'

'But Damian, I don't want to share my thoughts with Warren. Only with you. I only get a kick out of talking like this with you.'

Damian's face was grey and glistening. 'You scare me, Harriet. You never went on about snuff movies and stuff – before.'

'We never had time to get acquainted – before.' Tiz had broken away from Warren and was running towards them. Harriet punched Damian's arm. She laughed. 'Only kidding. It just shows what you think me capable of, doesn't it? Don't worry, I'm a very ordinary person.'

Damian looked strangely unconvinced. When Tiz reached them, he offered to race her along the sands.

After they had been restored with scampi and chips, in what Warren called an ethnic diner, Tiz requested a stroll round the harbour. Damian, who had failed to settle, offered to walk back and fetch the car. Tiz and Warren, heady with the romance of fishing clobber, set off hand in hand.

The small, chunky boats got Dotty going on Dunkirk. One of her cousins had been rescued on a vessel called the *Daisy Beacon*. Subsequently he ran off with the harbour master's wife – the very Daisy Beacon after whom the boat was named. Dotty and her family had cut him out there and then. He was ungrateful and unpatriotic. Anyway, Daisy Beacon was an upwardly mobile tart who was only using him to establish a base in the metropolis. Dotty was chuffed no end when she left him for a tree surgeon from Birmingham after eighteen months.

Harriet gazed at the oil-slicked water slopping between the harbour wall and the creaking boats, tormented by fantasies of Dotty vanishing beneath it.

Tiz came and dragged Harriet by the arm. 'Come on, Mum. They do trips to the Farne Islands. Dad says we can go.' She stood Harriet in front of three large boards advertising excursions.

'I couldn't possibly, darling. I get seasick.'

'It doesn't matter. They're open boats. You can throw up over the side. Oh do come, Mum. We never do anything together. You'll enjoy it. We might see baby seals. And they have roseate terns nesting there.'

'Goodness. All right.'

They decided to make the trip the very next day.

When Damian was informed, he was none too keen. 'I hate birds. All they do is peck and shit.'

'Don't come, then,' said Harriet.

'I think I'd better. Someone should keep an eye on you.'

Away from the coast, the silent swells of the sea kept Harriet subdued. The fumes from the engine mingled with the vapours of poached egg that she had foolishly had for breakfast. She could

not even be amused by the sight of Damian sitting beside Dotty
with her arm clasped firmly to his side.

'Where are the loos?' said Dotty as she cast an initial eye round
the black rocks.

'Maybe you'll have to squat behind the lighthouse,' said Tiz.

'Have you ever been up a lighthouse, Dotty?' said Harriet.
'Lovely views.'

'Of what?' demanded Damian.

Dotty, standing between them, looked from Harriet's smiling
to Damian's frowning face bemused. It reminded her of an
incident in a Chinese restaurant when two waiters had argued
in Cantonese over her won tons.

'Heights aren't my thing. Just park me on a rock and pick me
up later.'

'What a waste, Dotty,' said Harriet. 'Don't you even want to
see the chapel? Come, take my arm.' Warren and Tiz had gone
ahead, happily bonding in their proximity to marine life. 'Why
don't you catch them up, Damian? We'll just take it slowly.'

Damian looked unhappily after Warren and Tiz. Harriet was
almost moved by the sight of his lonely figure stranded on a
nugget of birdlovers' paradise. Stripped of its social context, his
presence in their midst was graphically intrusive.

He shrugged. 'OK.'

Harriet suspected he would spend the day mooching about on
his own. She did not think she would be troubled by Damian for
much longer.

Dotty was scathing about St Cuthbert. 'What did he have to
go and cut himself off in a place like this for? Call yourself a
Christian, and then go and abandon your fellow man for a life
of total self-indulgence.'

'Self-indulgence? Look at the place. He wasn't exactly lying
under a palm tree listening to his favourite records.'

'Huh. The St Cuthberts of this world are nothing but self-
promoting masochists. They may fool God, but they don't fool
me.'

'Well, one day soon you can remove the scales from God's
eyes personally, Dotty.'

'Can we go back now? I don't like this place. The moon must be like this.'

'No birds on the moon.'

'The birds make it worse.'

Harriet agreed that they did make the isolation more sinister. Hitchcock apart, she disliked the way their eyes swivelled, silent and judgemental. At least garden birds were always busy. This lot just stood around in drifts looking bored, occasionally taking off for pointless spins over their terrain.

'Oh look – a guillemot,' said Dotty.

'How do you know that?'

'Evening classes. Birds of the British Isles. We also did Leather-work 1 and 2, Anglo-Saxon Surrey, Make Your Own Coldframe, Esperanto. French Polishing, Egg Painting, Prepare Your Car For Winter, Get By In Croatian, Piano Tuning – I forget the rest. Oh – and I did Cake Decorating For The Blind. That was when my mother was still alive. That was to help her, really. She made her own sugared violets at one time.'

Harriet looked around her, although it could hardly be avoided. This lump of rock set in a turd-infested sea, a pin-point of planet on which people like Dotty did Leatherwork 2 and Esperanto. She started to laugh.

'Are you all right, Harriet? You're not having one of your turns?'

'I have to fart.'

'Where are you going, Harriet? Wait for me.'

Dotty hurried carefully in Harriet's wake as she walked towards the shore line. Dotty caught up with her on a promontory spattered with bird droppings. Harriet sat down and hugged her knees, her laughter turned to gulps of frantic misery. Dotty, puffed and perplexed, put a hand on her shoulder.

'Have you considered HRT, Harriet? You can't go on like this.'

Harriet started to laugh again, in ripples like the trills of a harp.

'Can you walk?' said Dotty. 'We'll miss the boat.'

'In a minute.' Harriet stared at Dotty's floral plimsolls. Just to the right of them was a large gully in the rock, at the bottom of which lickspits of sea groped, tongue-like, into fissures. How easy it would be, with a sudden flash of her leg, to topple Dotty down the gap. The tide would come in, Dotty would go out. Harriet was gripped by the same sweating torpor as when she had stood over Semi.

Dotty held out her hand. Harriet took it and heaved herself up. Dotty lost her balance and slipped backwards. Harriet grabbed her arms. Dotty shrieked. From the windy middle distance came an answering cry. It was Damian, leaping over the rocks towards them. He pulled Dotty away.

'I've been looking for you everywhere. What's going on? Did she try to push you over?' Harriet thought how unsuited his ageing boy's face was to serious questions.

'Of course not. Harriet had one of her turns, and I was helping her up, that's all.'

'Are you sure?'

'Don't be daft. Why on earth would—'

'Really, Damian,' said Harriet, 'fancy frightening Dotty with such rubbish.'

'Yes,' said Dotty, easing into the slippers of reassurance, 'downright wicked, I'd call it. I would remind you that Harriet is your hostess, young man.'

Harriet picked up her holdall and began to walk away from them. She spoke in high camp tones. 'Anyway, would I try anything in a place like this where there's no hope of escape? I'd have to be crazy.'

'Menopause,' said Dotty. 'Men-O-pause. Funny that.'

Harriet refused further expeditions, turning down Hadrian's Wall and the kipper factory with equal firmness. Her eyes lit up briefly over a brochure of Hermitage Castle, the bleak trysting place of Mary, Queen of Scots and her lover Bothwell. The walls were so precipitate. She tore it up.

Damian went home at the weekend. His absence left an uneasy tension. Dotty steered so clear of Harriet that she wondered if Damian had told her about the supposed threat to her life. It was not that funny that Damian had not recognized the spiel as a load of porkies. Perhaps it was no bad thing. If Dotty took it seriously too, she might also get itchy feet.

*　　*　　*

They were rallied by an unexpected visit from Japheth. Semi was with her family at St Honoré Les Sables. Japheth was tanned from his bonding binge with Tattenham Drovers in the Bahamas, and had been lonely in the flat. He was now treated by the family as an honoured guest. But without the magnet of Mungo's sibling rivalry there was no epicentre for him. Harriet suppressed tears as the full weight of anticlimax settled over the initial euphoria. Warren talked manfully with Japh about Tatters' chances in the Twiglets Cup. Tiz told him about an outbreak of strangles in a stable near Caistor and then drifted off. Dotty cooked him full English breakfast. He helped Harriet with the washing up.

'It's not the same without Mungo, is it, Mum? He's a right bell end, but it's well boring without him.'

'Yes, well, family holidays do need families to put flesh on the bones.'

'Now we're all leaving home I suppose you'll start shoplifting and calling people up at three o'clock in the morning.'

'Don't flatter yourself. This is the time of life when Dad and I are scheduled to build a conservatory and go on Saga tours.'

'It would be more to the point if you took up golf.'

'Dad already has a golf partner.'

'Has he been down here?'

'Just left.'

'How flattering. As soon as I leave, Dad has to find a replacement. I wouldn't have thought he noticed me enough to miss me.' His voice had a challenging edge, which turned the statement into a request for reassurance.

'Do you think that's what it is? I wondered that myself. If Dad suddenly feels the need to surround himself with Youth.'

'Damian's hardly that. He's just a sidekick, isn't he? Americans always need sidekicks. They can't function by themselves.'

'You don't think it's a subversive protest about my working?'

'Who knows?' Having failed to elicit reassurance, Japheth was not going to offer Harriet any. 'I hope you do get another job, Mum. It will keep your mind occupied.'

'My mind is occupied. In fact it feels like the West Bank at times.'

'There you go. You turn away every well-meant suggestion, like you were defending an outcrop or something.'

Harriet laughed. 'Do I? Oh I do miss you, Japh. Nobody else talks to me like you do.'

'Then it's just as well you're getting used to me being away in stages.'

'Why – what's the next one?'

'Well – I didn't want to mention this yet but – well, Semi doesn't want to stay in England for ever. There are some very good clubs in France.'

'I see.'

'Be grateful I'm not a tennis pro.'

'Oh I am.'

'Er – look, Mum, I think I'll go back this afternoon. The season's started already – I got special leave. But I think I'd like to paint the bedroom before Semi gets back. You don't mind, do you? I don't want to spoil your holiday.'

'Does a bucket of water spoil the rain?'

Harriet returned to Abutilon at the same time as President Gorbachev was restored to the Kremlin, and with similar feelings, no doubt, that the holiday could have been more relaxing.

Warren invented tasks for Harriet to perform, like getting the photographs of their Victorian ancestors enlarged into soft-focus heritage portraits. Dotty resumed the eggless cake circuit. Harriet made enquiries about retraining as a speech therapist, accompanied Warren to dinner parties and the opera, and had the sofa recovered in toile de Jouy costing £102 a metre.

But no jollification could throw off the dread of Dotty, with which she struggled as a canary on whom a waterbed had fallen.

Mungo broke his leg skate-boarding the day before he was due to come home. Harriet spoke to him shortly after the operation. Harriet worried about his missing school.

'Can't I go to school here, Mum? Gran wants me to stay. Think of all the money you'd save.'

'We've already paid for this term, darling.'

'Don't you have Loss of Fees insurance? I'm ill.'

'The money's not the point, Mungo. Of course you must come home.'

'Why?'

'Well – we miss you.'

'So I have to come home to keep you happy? What about love is letting go, and all that?'

'Darling, don't you think you have an obligation—'

'Oh God. You'll be throwing Queen and Country at me next.'

'Have you become a republican?'

'As a matter of fact, yes. Look, can I stay or not? It'll only be for a couple of years. You can't really stop me.'

'Darling, you've become so abrasive. I don't like it. If you feel you want to punish us for something, that's all the more reason why you should come home and sort out why you feel like that.'

'What are you talking about, Mum? Ask Dad. I bet he won't mind. The doctor's here. I've got to go.'

Plans were well under way for *High Spirits*, the new youth-oriented Sunday morning show that the Reverend Vince was to present. Dotty disapproved. The first show was to come from the tree house chapel of a small Taoist community on the Orinoco, with a sideline about the evils of the petrochemical industry. It unsettled Dotty's belief that the Reverend was publicity shy, and she resented his desertion of the tin hut.

'Though I dare say he's acting from the highest motives,' she told Harriet.

'Yes. Money.'

'I'm glad I'm not as cynical as you, Harriet. I think it would poison my liver.'

'If only,' thought Harriet.

16

As the Reverend Vince was soon to set off for the Orinoco, Harriet began listening to Radio Hogsback, as the opportunity to hear him strut his stuff would soon be gone. She enjoyed the phone-in best. A typical caller was the mother of a young man, a drug addict, who had escaped from police custody, broken into her home, killed the dog with an onyx table lamp, left the bath running so that the ceiling collapsed, and threatened his mother with a broken beer bottle if she did not give him her pin number. She wanted to know if she should go on paying for his mobile phone.

It was not long before Harriet wanted to join in. Her voice disguised in the dolorous cheese-grater tones of Scottish arts presenters, she rang the station and explained that she had an old aunt living with her who got on her nerves, but she could not turn her out because she was homeless.

'And why does she get on your nerves – Elspeth?'

'Ah don't rightly know, Vince. I canna explain it. Ah could gi' ye a list of crap that don't add up to a hill o' nail clippins, but it's kina like the ghost in *Macbeth* like – I think, sod it, I canna live wi' this. And then ah feel guilty as weeell.'

'Have you explained all this to the housing department – Elspeth?'

'Aw, come off it, Vince. Ah canna tell the Housin' Department to get her off my back or I'll stick a wee dirk in her. They'd have me arrested.'

'Tell me, Elspeth, is your house overcrowded? You might have a case if it were.'

Harriet paused. Was he on to her? 'Not exactly, no. The thing is, Vince, I wonder if there's somthin' wrong wi' me. Like, some days I think o' those poor bastards in South Africa an' that, an' I think, hell, it's not much to put up with, an' the next minute I'll think, hell, she's drivin' me soddin' barmy, d'ye ken?'

'You've raised a very real dilemma there, Elspeth. Don't forget, if you think you can help the number is 485980. We'll be right back.'

There followed a commercial for Ladas. Harriet was giggling as she put the phone down. Then, with the speed of a nappy down a shute, her mood changed. What did she think she was doing? The gin had worn off. The phone rang.

'It was you, wasn't it?' The Reverend Vince spoke. He sounded angry. Harriet started to shiver. It was thrilling, in a masochistic way.

'Was what me?'

'Don't fuck around with me, Harriet. If it wasn't you, you'd be a lot more surprised to hear from me. Why did you do it?'

'All right. I confess. What's the problem? I wasn't abusing your programme or anything. It's a genuine case.'

'Then why the hoots mon crap? Unless you wanted to make a complete arsehole out of me.'

'It never entered my head. I didn't know you'd be so upset. Why are you so upset?'

'I've got to go.'

Harriet switched the radio on again. He was talking to a woman in Byfleet whose husband could only make love in a boiler suit. She left a message for him to ring her back.

'Vince, I don't want to leave things like that. I think I do want to talk to you, that's why I did it. I didn't have the guts to put it directly. I'm sorry.'

'That's OK. I'm sorry too. I have Friday mornings free.'

'Where shall we meet then? Better be somewhere public, I've had enough of – oh never mind. I know. The RHS gardens at Wisley. Say ten-thirty?'

Harriet woke early. She did not want to talk to the Reverend Vince at all. She had only said that to alchemize his anger into sympathy. The truth was he gave her the creeps. They had been acquainted, on and off, for some time, and yet she knew nothing more about him than she had at the beginning, like why he had no partner of either sex, why he was a Christian. Sexy Christians in black leather who rode around in hearses gave out a disturbing fusion of signals. And why did he devote his Sundays to the spiritual comfort of middle-aged proles such as herself? There was no point in talking about Dotty. The situation was intractable. She and Dotty would end up like the protagonists in *Ethan Frome*, gridlocked in the bitterness of guilt and gloat.

It was a perfect September morning. Harriet was repulsed by the gaudy autumnal profusion. She found the slow decay of nature a cruel torment, and would have much preferred it if the leaves all fell off overnight and borders were rotovated at their peak. She had said as much to Dotty.

'Well I'm glad I wasn't. Rotovated at my peak, that is.'

The Reverend was waiting by the turnstiles. This time the leather trousers were topped by a porridge-coloured trench coat over a white turtle neck. He had already acquired media chic. It suited him. Brought him into focus. Bodied forth the easily digested packaging of canned experience. Both sensed they had arrived at a party that was already over. They argued about who should pay. Harriet won. They went through, and followed the path to the sunken garden. Harriet feigned fascination. The Reverend, unlike Damian, revealed no hidden horticultural depths. Stopping only to raise an eyebrow at the fruit cages, they ploughed on through the shrubbery walks and the Alpine house and up onto the wide greensward that rose gently between the perennial borders, England's lasting gift to the world.

Harriet coaxed him into talking about *High Spirits*, to stop him getting round to Dotty. She was guarded in her reaction to some of the projected programmes, such as the vegetarian mass from Findhorn. Vince was enthusiastic – almost. There was still that enigmatic vein of restraint that had characterized his vicaring.

They reached the top of perennial hill, beyond which the formal gardens merged into a field. A half-acre or so of giant dahlias lay in the middle of it, like soft porn relegated to the top shelf so that visitors of a sensitive disposition would not be disturbed by their vulgarity. Indeed, few had ventured so far.

Harriet was tired, so they sat on a grassy bank overlooking the lurid patchwork.

'How do you get on with Warren?'

'I haven't seen much of him since the series was set up. It's run by the Human Aspirations Department.'

'Vince, I must come clean. It was my idea.'

'I guessed. Are you having second thoughts?'

'No, *I'm* not. It's just – can I be frank?'

'If you must.'

'There is something about you that bothers me. You seem to be like someone serving a sentence. You're very effective. I'm probably the only one who's noticed. Perhaps I'm completely wrong, but – there's a warp of lassitude to your woof that just doesn't go with the job. Tell me to shut up, if you like.'

'Take it as read.'

'All right.'

They sat in silence, staring at the wadge of surreal blooms. Harriet thought about dahlias, how, with careful husbandry, they could be preserved, divided, intensively cultivated to flower for generation after generation without death. It would only be a matter of time before a plant welfare group organized violent resistance to this exploitation. The Reverned plucked the grass.

'I'm not a real priest. I have no qualifications for it.'

'Yes, everybody knows that. I just wondered if you'd been inspired by Billy Graham and then woken up with a headache.'

'There's something in that.'

Harriet kept very still, afraid to scare the rabbit back into its hole.

'My motives were too subjective, I've been aware of that for some time.'

'Whose aren't?'

'Then I would say to myself that, anyway, pure altruism was a kind of spiritual arrogance, so—'

'You forgave yourself.'

'Not exactly. I rearranged my complexes to suit the prevailing wind.'

'And which wind was that?'

'We came here to talk about you.'

'So we did. Don't worry, nobody talks about women. Go on.'

A small elderly couple emerged from the dahlias dishevelled and brushing petals off their clothes. They tottered towards the restaurant open-mouthed, as though they had just seen the Queen Mother.

'I saw Him, you see.'

'Who?'

'Jesus. The Lord.'

'Goodness.' Harriet's eyes revolved. What a difference a word makes. She had thought the Reverend's enigma concealed sceptical rationlism, not paranoid schizophrenia. She stared at the retreating backs of the old couple, imploring them to turn round. 'What were you on?' she laughed.

'Banana skins.'

'Come again?'

'Banana skins. It turned out I was allergic to them. Some people are. They contain hallucinogens in certain stages of decomposition.'

'Why were you eating banana skins?'

'I wasn't. The bananas were contaminated.'

'When was this?'

'About ten years ago. I was working for a magazine called *Pus*. I don't suppose you've heard of it – typical rock/anarchist/obscene publication.'

'That was before your conversion, I presume.'

'Yes. It was in Sheffield.' He paused. 'I was married then.'

This was more of a shock than the visions. To her surprise, Harriet experienced a flush of jealousy. The Reverend had been unclaimed all the time she had known him. The idea of his being in love, in bed, with a woman, which should have added a dimension of comfortable normality to his image, had the reverse effect. 'What was she like, your wife?'

'Passionate. She was an animal rights campaigner. I met her at a demo to free oysters in Whitstable that I was covering for the paper. She wasn't a classic beauty or anything, but she had a face that made beauty seem boring, and thick wavy hair down to her waist, the colour of shantung.'

A nostalgic description. Harriet had last heard of shantung in 1969.

'We loved each other very much. We did. But you know, being

hard up and both of us working – she was working undercover as a cashier in a butcher's shop – and we did the clubs every night, so we were always tired. Anyhow, we had rows sometimes. You know, when you're young you sometimes almost start rows on purpose to create energy, so the sex is better afterwards.'

Harriet got prickly heat. This was hurtling towards the centre of the earth stuff. She was not quite ready for it. 'I don't remember that far back.'

The Reverend was in distress. He rubbed his face. 'One night we had an argument. Jesus, it was so trivial – I can hardly bear to think about it—'

'Nothing is trivial in marriage, Vince. Or anywhere else really. Think of the peace negotiations that have failed because they couldn't agree on the seating arrangements.'

'True. But this was worse. The light bulb had gone in the bathroom. She'd gone in there to – you know – fix her diaphragm. The irony is, she thought the pill was dangerous. We were both a bit drunk. She started complaining because I hadn't fixed the light. It was a fluorescent strip, she claimed she didn't know how to take off. I said it was time she started doing things like that for herself. Feminism wasn't much cop in Sheffield at that time. Men still openly expressed doubts. She was so useless technically, she'd call an electrician to change a Hoover bag.' He spoke now with fond pride. 'Anyhow, we had a flaming demarcation dispute – you know how it goes. Well – I got her into bed. It was fantastic – for me. Because I was so angry, I suppose. But not for her. She lay there like a sandbag, and turned away as soon as she could. Jesus, this is so difficult.'

'I know.'

'Well, I said something about that too. She said if she got pregnant it would be my fault because she thought she might have put toothpaste on the diaphragm. So I said – I said – she'd better not be, because – because I had two kids by my real wife in Scarborough and that she – Jackie – and I weren't really married at all.'

'God. Why did you say that?'

'Just to hurt her. God forgive me. Just to hurt her. I would have told her it wasn't true, but it was too late. She got up, went to the bathroom – threw up – and died. Just like that. Weak heart. I didn't know. Her mother said afterwards, she couldn't bring herself to tell me in case she – she lost me. It was wrong – but how could I blame her?' The Reverend covered his face with his hands and shook with sobs.

'That wasn't your fault. It really wasn't. But how terrible—'

He pulled himself together. 'You see, Jackie was a Catholic. A rather mixed-up one. She'd demonstrate for the right of women to have abortions, but the idea of committing adultery with a man who had children – well, it was just too much for her. I knew she was like that. She still went to confession. I wanted to shock her, and I knew how to do it.'

'It was the heart condition that killed her, not you.'

'So everyone said. But I never told them the whole story. You can imagine how I felt, getting so much sympathy when I felt like a murderer. Do you mind if we walk?'

'Whatever you like.' Harriet was sobered by the tragedy, but still keen to know the connection with Jesus and the banana skins. She put her arm around him, and he her, and they limped off towards the dahlias. There were narrow strips of grass between the elephantine plants, some of which rose even over the Reverend Vince.

'After she died, I couldn't stay in Sheffield, but I didn't know what to do. I was suppurating with guilt – I wanted to punish myself. I felt unfit to live. So I made myself do everything I hated doing. Everything. It was psychotic, really. Some of it was so stupid you'd think I was having a mental breakdown. Which I was, in a way. I'd start the day with a cigarette before breakfast. I hate smoking. I sold my car and went everywhere by bus. I went to church – Baptist chapel to start with. I forced myself to eat parsnips – and bananas. That was when it started. I'd always hated bananas. Coincidence, or what. That was when the Lord appeared to me, or so I thought.'

'So that was why you had never had hallucinations before?'

'Yes. But pretty soon I started seeing all sorts of people – Lenin, Geronimo, traffic wardens—'

'Didn't that make you wonder if you'd made a mistake about the Jesus one?'

'I wanted to believe it. All right, it was a message mixed up with others, but that didn't mean it wasn't genuine. You cannot imagine what a relief it was to find a purpose in life after Jackie died.'

'So how did you end up on Radio Hogsback?'

'One of the punishments I gave myself was to come to the home counties. You know, we'd always thought of this area as the place where you sold your soul for a Bovis Home, that it's inhabited by robotic middle managers and brain dead Tories, and women with accounts at Harvey Nichols.'

Harriet flushed. 'That's pretty accurate.'

'When I got here I worked for a pop star in Weybridge. Dave Fudge. He was a guitarist with The Erections. He died, as you know, inhaled Vim when he was drunk. Just at that time I saw the ad for the job at Radio Hogsback. It was sick, but I think the association with Dave gave me a phoney kudos. His death was big in the pop world.'

'And the church?'

'At the beginning I went C of E. I tried the Catholics, for Jackie's sake, but they were too sexy. I wanted something paralytically boring. Much to my surprise, there were some quite decent, ordinary people in the congregation. But they hated their vicar. He made them sing from the New English Hymnal. You know, like in 'Abide With Me' it says, *Oh God, you'll never change*, like He was an inveterate gambler, or something. At the same time, the vicar ran the place like a prison ship. The youth club wanted to do *Noye's Fludde* for the flower festival, but he wouldn't hear of it because Britten was gay. Well, that was the last straw for some of them. It split the parish down the middle. For a while it was like Belfast at the height of the Troubles. In the end, a group of them asked me to arrange something informal, because I was in show business, as they put it. The chapel used to be a scout hut, but they can't get people to run the scouts any more. Sad, isn't it? I don't know a reef knot from a day at the races, or I'd have done it myself.'

'You must have felt that their need was sent to save you.'

'That's right. Even as I – changed – the bond with them got deeper.' He stopped, making Harriet stumble. 'By the time you and Dotty came, I felt a complete fraud. But neither did I want to let them down.'

'Don't blame yourself. You might have been right in the first place – that it was meant to happen as it did. They say God moves in mysterious ways.'

'He's gone off the edge of a cliff as far as I'm concerned.'

'And now you don't know whether you should do the programmes. I mean, there are many forms of deprivation, and I'm sure the housewives of Byfleet are a much neglected group, but to go public—Yes, I do see the problem.'

'You do think I should pull out then?'

'No. Well – no. Look at it this way. Supposing the Pope changed his mind – decided the Jews had got it right after all – do you think he'd admit it? Of course not. Not because of the tiara and the free travel, but because of the mental suffering it would cause to millions of people. It would be a much harder road than that of faith, but – well – nobler, in a way. Sorry, I must sound like *Thought for the Day*. Perhaps I should take over your phone-in. Damn – what's that?'

Unnoticed, clouds had rolled in over the dahlias, and the first rods of rain hammered onto them. There was a loud whack of water on trench coat.

The Reverend stopped again. Harriet pulled her jacket over her head. Her eyelashes were clotted with raindrops, but she did not like to wipe them in case her mascara smudged. She peered up at his face, which was transfigured. With what, she was not sure, but whatever it was, the veil had been torn away. He looked down at her, as if about to say something, then changed his mind and drew her into a deep, famished kiss. Harriet's brain was stunned, but her body ignited like a blow torch as the Reverend's hands found her buttocks.

'Wait! Please—'

He drew back, and looked up and down the floral corridor. They stood by a particularly angry variety of blood red, shading to burgundy and puce, arrested in a spiked explosion around a livid yellow eye. He took her hand and pressed in among the plants. The stems squeaked as they snapped. He took off his coat and felled a patch of plants with his foot, trampled them, and laid the coat on top and pulled her down onto the corrugated bed. 'Fucking dahlias,' sighed Harriet, as he parted her thighs.

George had left a message asking if she wanted a part on *Crime*

Daily. She turned it down, partly because it sounded like a description of her lifestyle. She had emerged from the dahlias delirious, but disoriented, and terrified of prosecution by the Royal Horticultural Society for criminal damage. They had fled the gardens and stopped in a lay-by in a back road near Ripley. The Reverend got into her car and put an arm around her. She could not look at him.

'Are you sure no one saw us? I don't want to get in the papers again. What if it did? What would the kids think? Can zoom lenses see round corners?'

'I'm sorry you've regretted it so soon. I'm sorry, it was my fault. I was just so grateful that I'd finally been able to talk about things. Gratitude is a kind of love, you know.'

'You could have given me a bunch of flowers. We were in the right place.'

'You do regret it, then.'

'No. No, not at all. I've always been attracted to you. I shouldn't have come if – Oh dear, that makes me sound like a bitch on heat. How repulsive.'

'Don't.' He stroked her arm and looked at his watch.

'You'd better go. You'll be late.'

'Yes.'

'There's just one thing.'

'What?'

'That wasn't part of your punishment programme, was it?'

He laughed. 'No. But it sounds as if it was part of yours.'

'Well, I am a woman.'

'Crap. You've got to deal with that.'

'Very likely. And no, I don't want to talk about it.'

'I'll say goodbye then.' He kissed her hand.

Harriet watched him nose his car into the road and was suddenly thunderstruck, jumped out and flapped her arms at him to stop.

'What is it?'

'HIV. I just remembered. Have you had a test?'

'Oh, that. Don't worry. You're the first since Jackie.'

'What!'

'Truly. You don't have to worry. Take care.'

Harriet gawped after him. Was she expected to believe that he had been faithful to his wife's memory for ten years? Who did he think he was – Peter Abelard? In her estimation the vacuum that nature most abhorred was the vacancy in a man's bed, and however much he mourned his departed, it filled up with the regularity of a rock pool at high tide. More incredible still was the fact that he had ended his fast with her. Of course, it had been spontaneous. There was no reason to think he had deliberately chosen an old banger in which to become acclimatized to the return of his licence.

She went back to the car and slumped behind the wheel. Her knickers were sticky. She had to go home and have a shower. That would get Dotty's radar dish revolving. All considerations shrank before the prospect of Dotty waiting at home for her. Could any Fagin, Rasputin, Svengali, Big Brother, L. Ron Hubbard or Captain Hook inspire the same mesmerizing dread as Dotty? She leaned her head on the steering wheel and the tears fell through it onto her gently steaming lap.

Even Warren now sensed that changes had to be made. He reminded Harriet that they had agreed after the break-in that they would sell the house as soon as things settled down.

'You always wanted to move back to town, sweetheart. Now's your chance. Maybe we could get a place with a granny annexe for Dotty, or there might even be enough to get her a place of her own.'

'If we moved to Hampstead, you mean? You're joking. It's more expensive than here. Besides, I couldn't move Tiz to another school until she's done her GCSEs.'

'Honey, kids are adaptable. You're obviously not. I'm like, opening a door, and you're refusing to go through it.'

'I'm not. It's circumstances. It wouldn't be fair on Tiz. Besides, there's a recession coming. We might be lumbered with an overpriced property we couldn't get rid of.'

'Who forecast this recession – Michael Fish?'

'Just leave me alone, Warren.'

What Harriet could not bring herself to tell Warren was that the stripped pine groves of North London had lost their charm. Her career had troughed. What was the point of proximity to high-flying media folk endlessly engaged in the proliferation of short-lived phenomena? One was enough. Perhaps she had been influenced by the Reverend Vince. It was time to turn her mind to higher things.

Warren did not bring up the subject again for several weeks. There was a dug-in air about him that made Harriet wonder if he was selling the house behind her back. She checked the mortgage agreement, to make sure that he could not do so without her consent. Warren was out more than ever, busy with paperwork for the franchise renewal. Tiz virtually boarded at the home of her horsey friend Appalachia, and when Appalachia was at their house the two girls stayed in Tiz's bedroom, alternately drawing up specifications for dream horses and love letters to boys they met at roller disco.

M25's bid was accepted. Buoyed up by confirmation of his scheduling skills, Warren became bold and decisive. One evening he tossed a letter on the table in front of Harriet. It was from their neighbours, Golden Vistas, possibly the finest rest home in the southeast. The owners, Mr and Mrs Piscopo, had heard a rumour that Abutilon was to come onto the market. They begged to be allowed first refusal, as it had long been their wish to expand operations with a caring terminal wing to which their expiring residents could transfer with as little disruption as possible.

Harriet trembled. 'Did you put them up to this? How else could they have known?'

'No I did not. Maybe Dotty mentioned it. Or Tiz. Who knows? Anyhow, I couldn't make them want to buy it, could I?'

'A terminal wing! What do they call it? *A personalized hospice facility*. Do you realize that means people will come here to *die*. How could you?'

'Honey, I'm surprised at your attitude. It's a great service to people. They have to die some place. We will too some day.'

'I know all that – but – can't you understand how I can't hand over this house to be a sort of extermination camp? Not when we've had the children here – brought them home from the hospital. Can't you see that? I couldn't do it.'

'I know what you mean, sweetheart, but isn't that, like,

hanging on? Our kids are OK – they're great. They're *alive*. Does it really matter what the building's used for?'

'So it's just a building now, is it?'

'Look, we'll never get another offer like this. Did you read the bottom line? £850,000. On the nail. With that kind of money we could buy you a house in your precious Hampstead, take care of Dotty and have enough left over for livery stables for Tiz. Everything we need to do.'

'Not in my house. It's sick.'

'Sweetheart, you're wrong. I understand you're emotional about it right now, but think about it. Like I said, it's a great service they give these people. You just can't see it right now.'

'I know what these private homes are like. They'll probably bump them off to keep up the turnover. Boiling them in the bath – bedsores – people strapped to the loos – in my house!'

'Cut that out, will you! They have very high standards over there. There's a waiting list.'

'Those old people can still talk. If they're terminal, no one will ever know what happens to them.'

'This isn't like you, Harriet – the opportunity to do something fine like this.'

'Come to think of it, even if we sold it to someone else, they might sell it on to Golden Vistas. I'd rather not move at all.'

'Is that final?'

'Yes.'

'OK.' Warren spoke quietly. Far too quietly.

Harriet spent Sunday at a Pony Club show watching Tiz and Telly. Shows brought out the worst in both of them. Telly scattered poles to the four winds and Tiz was reprimanded for bad language. She refused to give up until he had gone clear. Torn between mortification and pride, Harriet trudged to and from the hamburger stand for change to finance the struggle. Hairnetted young riders waiting to compete exchanged mocking smiles. Harriet wanted to break their ponies' legs and shove the owners up their arses. All right, so Telly was a lemon, but Tiz was a hero, and one day Harriet would see to it that she got the bestest pony in the whole wide world.

Most of the trailers had left the field and the sun was going

down when Telly, desperate to go home, finally went clear. The
old man who took the money had long since given up charging
Tiz for a go, and fallen asleep in his deckchair. Tiz was indifferent
to the loneliness of her victory. The look of triumph on her face
illuminated the gloaming of the abandoned field. 'Persepolis,'
thought Harriet, 'you ain't seen nothing like this.'

Warren was eating ice-cream from the carton. Tiz babbled on
about the tears and triumphs of the afternoon. Warren made
gratified noises.

'You should have been there, Dad.'

'I'm sorry, sweetheart. I have too much work right now. Next
time, I promise.'

Tiz went off to repeat the tale to Dotty.

'I thought she spent Sunday night with Appalachia,' said
Warren.

'Usually. But she's too tired after the show. Are you feeling
all right?'

'Sure. Why?'

'I see from the bin that you've eaten two quarts of ice cream.'

'There was no lunch today. I'm hungry.'

'Dotty was supposed to get you something.'

'She did. About ten hours ago. What are you doing now?'

'Bath, I think. I'm cold.'

'You will come down afterwards?'

'If you like. Why, have you timed a bomb to go off?'

Warren snorted into the ice-cream. 'No. I guess I'll go watch
TV for a while.'

'It's the first episode of *Inside the Rubber Boot* tonight, isn't it?
I'll be down in time for that.'

Harriet presumed that Warren's curiosity about her movements was his way of hinting that she should watch *Inside the
Rubber Boot* with him. It was a series that he had so far been
unable to sell, even in Malaysia.

Inside the Rubber Boot started at eight forty-five and had just
begun when Harriet joined Warren in the den. He was hunched
on the edge of the sofa, force feeding himself Doritos.

'Where's Dotty?' asked Harriet.

'Watching something in her room. Should I call her?'

'No – No. Tiz in bed?'

'On the way.'

'Do you reckon she misses Mungo?'

'No.'

'Good.'

Harriet struggled to keep her eyes open as the programme previewed the series – *The Rubber Barons*, *Rubber and Colonization*, *Death and the Rubber Workers*, *Can Rubber Really Cure Cancer*? The animations had started when the doorbell rang.

'I'll get it.' Warren bolted out of the room.

Male voices, sotto voce. Harriet pulled her kimono into more modest coverage, glad that she had not yet removed her make-up.

Warren led the Reverend Vince and Damian into the room. Harriet's temperature dropped. Their leather jackets and unsmiling faces raised ghosts of assassins in Jacobean tragedy. She almost cried out not to be sent from this world unshriven.

They murmured her name and sat down.

'What on earth are you two doing here? I didn't think you knew each other.'

'I asked them to come, sweetheart. We have to talk.'

'What about? Why in front of them?'

'Let's get everyone a drink first.'

While Warren poured, Harriet glared at the two assassins. Vince was the most uncomfortable. He mentioned that England had beaten Scotland at Murrayfield. This went down like a lead Zeppelin and he did not elaborate. Damian sat hunched in the chair, hands in pockets, eyes on the floor.

Harriet sat immobile, willing her brain not to work. She had an idea of what was to come. Vlad the Impaler was about to throw off his mask.

A bouncy jingle announced the end of *Inside the Rubber Boot*. Warren turned it off and sat beside Harriet.

'Honey, I asked Vince to come along because I thought – I thought you might need some support.' He paused, hoping she would say something, but she kept her eyes on the wall above Damian's head, slowly stroking her chin. 'Well – it was kinda difficult to know how to do this the best way. That is – I could have talked to you eyeball to eyeball of course, but – well – this

isn't really a private matter. There are two people involved here.
Well – three, including you. No, I guess there are more than that.
Jeez, how many of us are there?' His large hands shook. 'OK.
The thing is, sweetheart, things happen that you don't plan on.
This is what we're dealing with here. I know what you're going
to say – I don't know what I'm doing – Maybe you're right.
Maybe this is all happening in a parallel universe. You won't
believe this, but I've tried everything to pretend that nothing's
happened. I don't want to hurt you, Harriet, truly I don't. I still
love you, sweetheart, really I do. And if it's any consolation –
well, I guess it won't be – if things had turned out different, that
is, if they hadn't turned out at all—'

Damian emitted a croaking sigh, leaned his head back and
closed his eyes.

'What I mean is, I wasn't looking for out. Now that's the
truth. But now that it's happened – well— Remember that old
Cal. Tech. motto, The Truth Shall Set You Free? And you said,
that should be Money, not The Truth? Well – in a way both
things are in play here. What I mean is – the truth is different
now. And I have to acknowledge that. As for the money thing
– You see, I don't want you to be short, honey. That's why I was
pressing you about the offer for the house. Maybe we couldn't
run to two places in Hampstead, but there are other areas. Some
guy in the office was telling me Parsons Green is very nice. Right
on the subway there. And, like character Victorian – the sort of
thing you like – you know – chequered footpaths and stuff.'

'Before I am installed in a semi with original bootscraper in
Parsons Green, are you going to tell me what you're talking
about, or don't you have the guts to put it into words?'

'Guts? Whoa. I thought we might get round to that. If you
think it doesn't take guts to do this, sweetheart—'

Damian sat up and looked Harriet in the eye. 'We're in love.
That's what he's trying to say.'

The Reverend Vince's hand moved to a cushion, which he half
offered to Harriet in case she needed a throwupticle.

'Damian, do you have to shove it down her throat?' said
Warren. 'Sorry. I guess I should have put that another way.'

Harriet put her hands to her face to hide the silent gags
of laughter. 'I'm sorry. I'm not being very politically correct,

am I? In love. Oh my God—' She keeled over, clutching her stomach.

'Told you,' said Damian. He got up and paced the floor.

'She's in shock,' said the Reverend.

'Thank you. That's very helpful.' Warren was nonplussed. He had been prepared for high drama, a noble medium commensurate with the serious agonies through which he had passed to reach this moment. Harriet's hysteria degraded the scene, as when someone farts at a funeral. It certainly reminds those present of the diverse planes of human existence, but loosens their grip on the plane which they are trying to inhabit at the time. Warren had laboriously overcome each doubt, each small conversion a building block with which to construct a vision of life-enhancing beauty and magnitude. Harriet's reaction to the first public viewing presented a very different perspective. Was it all just – silly? And phoney. Or both. He sagged.

Damian leaned forward. 'Is that it? Aren't you going to say anything else?'

Warren looked at him. Damian's eyes worked with furious eagerness, the competing expressions of pleading, anger, hope and panic banked like TV monitors. Warren saw what he had to lose, and the vision rose again.

'It's not that I don't want to talk about it, honey,' he said quietly. 'I guess I just know there's no way I can make you believe it. I had a hard time believing it myself.' Harriet had calmed down, and gone back to stroking her chin. 'Hell, I'm not – gay. Neither is Damian. You know that. It's the weirdest thing. I mean – I always liked Damian. I made no secret of that. And then there's the golf thing – but that had nothing to do with it, really, except it meant we got to spend a lot of time together. And that was it – we fell in love. I wish you could be as happy as I am, Harriet, truly.'

Harriet's eye fell on a photograph of Tiz giving Telly his birthday cake. Boiling tears rolled down her cheeks.

'I was in denial for the longest time about it, honey. I guess we both were. Then the point came when I had to face it. It was when we were on vacation that last time. Damian told me you didn't want him around any more. That made me realize I couldn't face that. That I was with him all the time – in my head. And not with you. I'm sorry. It didn't seem right to go on that way.'

Harriet's voice was a dark whisper. 'Apart from in your head, where else were you with him?'

'How d'you mean?'

'Did you meet somewhere to fuck?'

'Honey, please, this isn't about sex. It really isn't. That's what I'd like for you to understand.'

'But did you – meet him anywhere?'

'One or two times at Avelina's place. That's all.'

After she had given the bitch full board and lodging, consolation and respect for her intelligence.

'What about the children?'

'Ah. Now I've given a lot of thought to that. See, if we go through with this deal with Golden Vistas, we could each buy a place. Say you were in Parsons Green, and we were in—'

'Will you shut the fuck up about Parsons Green!'

'OK, OK.'

'This isn't the moment to discuss the property market,' said Vince. 'What Harriet needs to know is that you're not deserting her.'

'Absolutely. That's why I want us to live real close, sweetheart. When Mungo comes home he can choose who he wants to live with. And Tiz – well, I thought we could share her, like she could go to the one school, but kinda live with both of us.'

'I wouldn't let her within a hundred miles.'

'Now, sweetheart, that's childish—'

'Don't you know he fucked me first? Perhaps he's hoping to work his way through the entire family?'

Damian laughed, stupefied.

'Yeah, he told me about that. I was pretty shaken at first, but then, when I saw the attraction—'

Dotty put her head round the door. 'Would anyone like a sandwich? Ham and tomato? I was just making myself one.' They all declined. 'Oh well, I'll make them anyway. You'll probably change your minds when you see them, if I know men.'

This observed phenomenon summed up for Harriet exactly what Warren had experienced with Damian, and reminded her of the futility of standing between a man and the object of his desire. Dotty's manner in offering refreshments was remarkably cool in the circumstances. She must have heard raised voices, and she was intimate with the Reverend Vince.

'Does Dotty know?'

'Dotty?' Warren looked as though he had never heard of her. 'I've no idea. I haven't told her.'

'I bet she does,' fumed Harriet. 'I bet she's known all along, the sly old bag. She was always saying I didn't know the half of what was going on in this family.' She addressed Vince. 'Did she discuss it with her confessor, I wonder? Is that why she sent you round to hold my hand? Well, you might as well tell Warren about D-Day in the dahlias now, mightn't you? It will fill in the time until I get back.'

Harriet charged across the hall towards the kitchen, where Dotty was slicing tomatoes to strains of the Warsaw Concerto. She wrenched the knife out of Dotty's hand.

'They don't want fucking sandwiches.'

'Oh. Very well. Perhaps Tiz would like one.'

'She's cleaned her teeth.'

'Oh.'

'Look at me when I'm talking to you! You knew, didn't you, about Warren and Damian?'

'There's no need to take that tone with me, Harriet. It's not my fault.'

'But you did know? How?'

Dotty took Harriet's hand. 'Look, love, we're all victims in our different ways. Let's stick together. Wait here. There's something I want to show you.' She took off her apron and went upstairs.

The front doorbell rang several times. Harriet moved quickly to answer it. It was a Nottingham Knocker.

'Good evening, madam. Before you shut the door, I just want to say how sorry I am for disturbing you on a Sunday night, but I'm saving up for my fare back to Manchester, you see. I can't stand this sodding job, to be honest, so I won't take up much of your time – oh, are those your dogs?' Jelly and Custard had loped out to welcome him. The young man, who was a corker, with soft brown eyes and an enchanting northern burr, crouched down on the doorstep to fondle the dogs. Harriet was confused. Guileless young men like him had died out in the home counties. This one should be spending his life tending sheep on his native moors, a lamb sticking permanently out of his rough-hewn jerkin, not hawking fluff removers in an alien land. 'I've got a dog. His name's Barker. I really miss him. Think I'll go back on the catering course, but I couldn't get housing benefit, see. Talking of catering, I see you were in the middle of something, were you?' He indicated the knife in her hand. 'Perhaps you were cutting up chicken? I've got just the thing. See these scissors? They're more like shears, really. Guaranteed for twenty years. I've tried them. They go right through chicken bones like they was sausages – tin cans, anything. Or perhaps you need a de-mister for the car with the winter coming on? Say goodbye to spit and a hankie – one wipe with this and your windscreen'll sparkle like the Milky Way. That's a special offer – £1.99, and the Magic Crunchers are £6.99. Would you be interested at all?'

'No. I'll give you some money. Then just go away, all right?'

'Sure.'

'Wait a minute.' She left him playing with the dogs and went back into the kitchen to get some money out of the Amaretti tin. Dotty came in holding a small dark object.

'What's that?'

'Warren's shaver that was taken in the break-in.'

'What?'

'I told you I suspected a woman's hand. They didn't touch the children's rooms, you see. And first thing I thought when I saw the damage was, Hell hath no fury like a woman scorned. Then when I heard that Damian had broken up with his girlfriend, I put two and two together. To be honest, I thought it was your having it off with him that got her going, but then – well, I went to see her. I think her real name's Rhiannon, not Pansy. Something like a chain of cinemas, anyroad. She gave me this. Wanted me to put it back. Modesty prevents me from saying where it's been, if you follow me. She wanted to have a laugh thinking of Warren using it, not knowing the sights it had seen. Love! I don't know.' Dotty sighed. 'Anyhow, this Rhiannon told me all about it, because Damian had told her. By that time she'd met someone else, so she'd got over it. This shaver's the only proof. She hadn't dared get rid of it – didn't fancy midnight trips to the river and all that. I promised her I'd dump it, in due course.'

'And what about me? Did you promise for me, too?' Harriet shouted. She had a pain in her chest.

'Promise what, love? Oh, you mean you'd like to take her to court yourself? Well, you could try, but she's married a South American chap she met on a plane – naturally – and gone out there to live. Columbia, I think she said.'

Dotty got out another knife and went back to slicing tomatoes. 'To tell you the truth, I was frightened I'd be had up for interfering with the course of justice, or whatever. And then, she was really sorry, and what was the point? As for Warren and Damian – I thought he might get over it and no harm done. You couldn't be more disgusted than I am, Harriet. I never did like that Damian. He never sits up straight, have you noticed? Backbone like an S-bend. But there you are – there was a lot of it in the war.'

'The war's been over fifty years.'

'Don't I know it. But – I'm sorry, Harriet, but this family – I know it must be a terrible blow for you, but let's face it, this family's days are over, aren't they? The boys have talked with their feet, and Tiz is trying to starve herself to death. I thought when I came here, my word, how does she put up with it. Talk about the experiment that failed, I never—'

They were Dotty's last words, on this occasion. Harriet raised the knife that was still in her hand and plunged it into Dotty's chest.

17

The Nottingham knocker went to hospital in the same ambulance as Dotty, as he was suffering from shock. Dotty had not recovered consciousness. In falling onto the quarry tiles she had staggered against the counter top, clutched at the Cappuccino machine for support, and brought it down on her head. Tiz, also looking to cancel her order for sandwiches, had gone into the kitchen to find Harriet sitting at the table staring at the autumn crocus, and Jelly and Custard licking the blood from Dotty's wound. It was this sight that had particularly upset her. It was no time for the dogs to start behaving like animals.

Harriet could not say what had happened. She kept asking if Dotty had ironed Tiz's uniform, and replies that covered all possible permutations could not stop her.

Warren and Damian went in the ambulance. Their shock and concern were ameliorated by awareness that this was their first happening as a couple. Warren's mind had not grasped, let alone embraced, the fact that Harriet's possible imprisonment for manslaughter might clear their path. But an instinct that moulds had been broken by Fate co-ordinated well with the adrenalin.

The ambulance man advised Warren that the police would have to be informed. Warren was worried that they would go to the house and arrest Harriet before he got back. Fortunately, owing to the number of officers taking autumn breaks in the Cotswolds, there was no one to send to the incident, and the Territorial Support Group was already engaged by thefts from three antique shops in Dorking. The ambulance man told Warren that, if the police had not come, it would be a good idea if

Harriet presented herself at Epsom Police Station in the morning, preferably in the company of a solicitor.

Harriet and Tiz had fallen asleep in a clinch on the sofa. The Reverend Vince snored in a chair, his hand still on his whisky glass on the floor. Warren had brought Damian back to pick up his car. They both decided it was not a good idea for Damian to face Harriet at the present time.

Warren surveyed the slumped bodies with pity, moved by their refugee formations. But, as when the surgeon has just washed his hands, there was no time to be lost. He woke Vince first.

'Have the police been?'

'Huh? Oh – no.'

'Good. We have to get her story straight first. Do you know what that kid saw? The one selling crap out of a bag.'

'He didn't see what happened, I don't think. He just went in when Tiz started screaming. Is Dotty going to be all right?'

'Too soon to say. How are these two?'

'Not so good.'

Tiz and Harriet had woken up and untwined their stiffened limbs. When Tiz saw her father she burst into tears and ran into his arms. He sat down and took her on his lap. Over her sobbing body he mouthed the question to Vince as to whether she knew about himself and Damian. The Reverend shook his head at the prospect of adding this morsel to Tiz's store of knowledge.

Warren told her to go to bed, so that the adults could discuss the crisis. She refused.

'After all, I'm the one who found the body.'

'Don't talk like that, sweetheart. Dotty's not dead. She'll be fine.

'Mum said she didn't do it. She didn't. I bet that boy did it.'

'Mum said she didn't remember, which isn't quite the same thing. Now you're going to have to be a very brave girl and stick with Mum whatever happens. She hasn't been well. We have to help her all we can, OK?'

Tiz put her head on his shoulder. 'I want Mungo.'

'Sure, honey. We'll fetch him back. Right now we have to decide what Mum is going to tell the police.'

'How can she tell them anything if she can't remember?'

'That's a problem, sure. But she can't just go into court and say that. See, unless she comes up with some sort of explanation they'll have to believe she did it.'

They turned to Harriet. She looked as likely to deliver an explanation as a Fabergé egg. She sat on the sofa, her legs askew, staring at the TV screen. The Reverend Vince went and sat beside her and took her hand.

'I think we should call Ruth Rendell,' said Tiz. 'She'd know what to do.'

'Sweetheart, we don't want to get anyone else involved here. That's important. What we say goes no further, OK? Not the police, not Japh, Mungo, or your friends. Not one word to any of them, OK?'

'OK.'

'Now, Harriet, honey, you say you can't remember what happened. Like – nothing at all?'

Harriet shrugged.

'OK. Do you remember going into the kitchen?'

She nodded.

'You walked out of here and found Dotty in the kitchen, right? You were mad at her, weren't you? You were mad at her because you reckoned she knew about me and Damian. See, the way I see it, all that looks bad for you. If anybody finds out about – us. On the other hand, we're the only ones that know. Your only hope is self-defence. You've got to make it look like Dotty was threatening you.'

The Reverend Vince pshawed. 'How could you get anyone to believe that Dotty would threaten someone with a knife? She was so law-abiding, she wouldn't even answer back to a traffic warden.'

'Not in cold blood, maybe. But, hell, they were arguing. She was mad at Harriet and the knife was there. She could just pick it up and chuck it at her, maybe.'

'I know,' said Tiz. 'Dotty threw the knife at Mum. Mum caught it—'

'Oh very likely,' said the Reverend.

'She could! She's good at that sort of thing. She had to train as a juggler for *Annie Get Your Gun*, didn't you, Mum?'

'Yes.'

'Anyway, Mum caught it – and Dotty rushed at her like she was going to strangle her – and Mum just sort of held up the knife to – defend – herself—'

Tiz had just realized the full implications. Her skin went the colour of raw potato.

'It's OK, honey.'

'What were they arguing about?' said Vince. 'If we leave out you and Damian. It would have to be something that would make Dotty very angry with Harriet.'

'That's a point. If it came out about me and Damian, that would give Harriet a motive. At least, it would explain why she felt like murdering someone.'

'What about you and Damian?' said Tiz.

'I'll tell you later, sweetheart. It's nothing. It's OK.' Tiz got off his lap and sat beside Harriet. 'Let me think. The only other person who knows about it is Avelina, as far as I know. She won't talk.'

'Perhaps Mum happened to say the Germans should have won the war.'

'Don't trivilize the situation, sweetheart. It has to be something more personal. Say Harriet was going to kick Dotty out – after all she'd done for the family—'

'Mum wouldn't do that.'

'Honey, *we* know that. We're trying to make a plausible story here. Mum wouldn't do that when she's herself. But she's been under a lot of stress lately. The show – then the accident – Japh leaving home—'

'The false arrest.'

'The break-in.'

'Yeah. It's been a bummer of a year for her. Say she'd decided to take this offer for the house and move to Hampstead after all. Without Dotty. Dotty has no money. She'd have to go in a bed and breakfast. Could that make her lose control?'

'It's possible,' said Vince. 'But why would Harriet suddenly come out with it while Dotty was making ham and tomato sandwiches? The circumstances aren't plausible.'

'Well, you know Harriet. Dotty couldn't do a thing right some days. You know murders peak around two-thirty Sunday, when guys come home late from the pub. It's often something real petty that's the last straw. Maybe Dotty used butter straight from the ice box, or something.'

Harriet spoke. 'She did.'

'Well – there you go! OK, now we're getting somewhere. So Harriet gives Dotty flak about the butter. Now as I recall, we all said we didn't want the fucking sandwiches.'

'Nor did I,' said Tiz. 'I came down to tell her.'

'That's right. So Harriet goes on from the butter thing to make like Dotty's into this control-by-food thing, and she can't take it any more.'

'Mum thought Dotty had given me anorexia by trying to make me eat all the time.'

'That's it! That's great. A perfect excuse to get Dotty out of the house.'

'I haven't got anorexia. I just don't want Telly to get a saggy back.'

'Sure, sweetheart. OK, so Harriet lets Dotty have it – verbally, of course. Dotty flips. Q.E.D.'

'There's one problem,' said Vince. 'How do you explain what Damian and I were doing here?'

'That's easy. You came to watch the first episode of *Inside the Rubber Boot* with me. Damian's a family friend. He came on vacation with us. And so are you, in a way. You have this connection with the station now too. Vince, are you OK with this? It kinda depends on your co-operation. If you don't feel able to—'

'Lie?'

'I'll understand.'

'On one condition. That if Harriet gets off, you look after Dotty.'

'Of course. I would anyhow.'

'Then I'll do it.'

'This is crazy. There's no reason why you should.'

The Reverend looked at Harriet. 'Personal reasons.'

'Oh.'

'Not what you think.'

'But Dad, what if Dotty comes round and tells the police it was all Mum's fault?'

'Sweetheart, the bottom line is, it's her word against Mum's.

I know it's a gamble, but all you have to do is put doubt in the jury's mind. If it works, Dotty won't suffer. Like I told Vince, we'll take care of her. Now, this may sound kinda gruesome, but I think we should go block the moves, to make sure it's feasible. Vince?'

Tiz hugged Harriet. 'Who will look after me if you go to prison and Dotty's in the hospital? Will Carmen come back?'

Harriet could not speak, but hugged her daughter until Tiz feared for her eyeballs.

When Harriet appeared before Epsom magistrates, Dotty had still not come round. In view of the fact that she might be facing a murder charge it was decided that she be remanded in custody. She was to be taken to Holloway and had only a minute to say goodbye to the family, and a few friends who had come to support her. Tiz was very brave for her mother, and exhorted her not to become a drug addict while inside. She had confused fears that buggery might also be involved, but was not sure if women did it, so said nothing. When they were left on the pavement watching the van head off towards the A24, she broke down and cried, and cried, on and off, until they reached Avelina's house in Hampstead.

The sale of Abutilon was set in train. Mungo wanted to come home straight away. Warren and Puline agreed that he would be better off to stay in Australia until a date for the trial had been fixed. British Telecom was loaned to Appalachia for the use of their au pair, and became a great pet of the Au Pair and Toddler Group.

Avelina experienced a personal renewal as a surrogate mother. She was sensitive enough to withhold the full force of her alchemical zeal until Tiz began to trust her, and was satisfied that Avelina was not going to make her take up the oboe. She took her to Pour Les Autres and Fibbets for sludge-coloured clothes, before casually suggesting they could go to the theatre to see something suitable for children, like *Coriolanus*.

Warren had entrusted Avelina with the pastoral mountain of explaining to Tiz the relationship between himself and Damian. Avelina laid the ground with fulsome praise of Julian Clary. Tiz's reaction was not quite what Avelina anticipated. True, she was at first incredulous, repulsed – somewhat, but also resigned. There were several pupils in her new school who had two parents of the same sex. It was not, as she said, as if Damian were a typist with tits. Avelina, startled, agreed that it was not.

'I'm disappointed though,' said Tiz.

'That's only natural.'

'No, I mean I quite fancied Damian myself. It's going to be very frustrating if we all live together.'

Avelina, fresh from a biography of the Bloomsbury beauty who was seduced by her father's best friend, had to sit down.

Dotty recovered consciousness and was interviewed by the police. She gave them an accurate and fair account of what happened, omitting only the part about Warren's shaver. After being discharged from hospital she went to stay with relatives in Northampton to await the trial.

Tiz found that her integration at the new school was greatly helped by having a mother on trial for attempted murder. She was concerned about Harriet's psychological condition.

'Are you going to plead insanity, Mum?'

They sat holding hands across the table. The snow had smothered all natural light, deepening Harriet's sense that she had been buried alive.

'Darling, I'm not guilty, remember? I shouldn't have to plead excuses.'

'Oh yes. I forgot. You seem quite cheerful, Mum. I hope you're not pretending just for me.'

'Of course not,' Harriet lied. She could not tell Tiz that the sight of her was so painful now that she would have cancelled the visits, were it not that keeping up Tiz's morale was the only thing that kept her going. One day after Tiz had been on holiday with Avelina, to a villa on the Bosphorus, and she had not seen her for a month, Harriet was distressed to realize that she could hardly remember what her daughter looked like. In fact, when Tiz walked in to the visitors' room on her return, Harriet did not recognize her for a moment. She saw a tall, slender girl in narrow black jeans and a tattered green velvet frock coat, with gleaming chestnut hair in Baroque flourishes down her back. A girl of such unique and earnest beauty that Harriet gagged when she saw that it was Tiz.

'I wanted to bring you a calligraphy set, Mum, but they wouldn't let me. Is there an art room? Perhaps there's one there. You've got to use your time to develop new skills, Mum. I've brought you this article about a woman who makes a living out of sign painting. You could do that. See – it says she started it as a hobby, and so many people asked her to do things she's snowed under with work. Now I think calligraphy is good because it's not, sort of, creative torment or anything that might send you off the deep end again, but it's very – orderly. It'll help you feel you're in control of things. You should take your City and Guilds, or whatever. Now when I come again, I want you to have got all the info on courses and stuff. Do you think you could manage that?'

Japheth was rattled.

'This is great, Mum. It really helps my image at the club to have a mother banged up for murder.'

'I thought Dotty was all right?'

'Oh yes. Sorry. Attempted murder. Fine. What really happened, Mum?'

'Dotty attacked me.'

'U-huh. She never seemed the homicidal type to me, Mum. I suppose it was delayed shock from the Battle of Arnheim.'

'Perhaps it was.'

'Do they let you have baths in here, Mum? You look a bit shop-soiled.'

'Thanks, darling. The facilities are minimal, but yes, we do have baths.'

She could not tell him the state of them, or the fact that inmates peed in the sinks and did unspeakable things with their sanitary towels. She now knew there were lots of things that went on inside that never got onto *Prisoner: Cell Block H*.

Harriet's lawyer, Harvey Tetherington-Hornchurch, was frank.

'As you know, Mrs Funkel, the judicial system tends to come down rather hard on women who commit acts of violence. So

in the event of your being found guilty we could expect a stiff
sentence. On the other hand, as it's only another woman who
was attacked, they may not think it worth the expense to lock
you up.'

'One woman equals two sheep.'

'Quite. Now I want to go through the business with the knife.
You say Mrs Outwood threw it at you.'

'That's right.'

'With which hand?'

'Um – the left.'

'I'd cut out the "ums" if I were you. Was she holding it by the
handle or the blade?'

'I can't remember. The handle, I suppose.'

'Because the trajectory would be different, wouldn't it? If she'd
done a sort of Davy Crockett special from the blade – whooosh!
– then it could kill a buffalo at forty paces. But if it was thrown
by the handle, the trajectory would be less decisive. No more
than an aggravated toss, really. As you say you caught it, it's
important. You have to remember, the Crown will do its utmost
to show your story is incredible.'

'It must have been by the handle, then.'

'Good. Now the other important thing is to establish Mrs
Outwood as a dangerously embittered poor relation.'

'No, please don't paint Dotty like that.'

'Mrs Funkel, you cannot allow your finer feelings, admirable
though they are, to undermine your own case. We must do our
utmost to get you out. Think of your family.'

'Yes.'

'Now don't go getting upset. Leave it for court. Of course, I
can't promise to deliver the verdict. Far from it. That's the fun
of this job. You just sandbag your conscience and concentrate
on your prospects.'

18 ∫

Only about twenty reporters and photographers were waiting on the morning the trial began. A cabinet minister had fortuitously had an affair with his daughter, which had come to light over the preceding weekend. The attention of the press was distracted, and the airways fulminated with ministerial thoughts on the invasion of privacy, and the awful prospect of not being able to attract the right sort of person into politics as a result.

Harriet was disconcerted by Guildford Crown Court. She had pictured the Old Bailey of television trials, the menace of mahogany and brass fittings. Instead, the courtroom was flooded with light from on high, its pine veneer and vinyl borrowed from the house style of the modern library. The failure to reflect the grimness of its business only increased the latent menace. Worse, she was at arm's length from the family, who sat in two rows close to the Perspex showcase in which she took her place between two policewomen.

The jury reflected the trend away from white, middle-class justice. They included an elderly Sikh, a pregnant punk, a Chinese man in a flashy suit, a West Indian lady saying the rosary, a young mum type in jeans and a black man in a dog collar. They seemed as anxious to avoid Harriet's eye as she theirs. The judge, Mr Jeremy Mitsotakis, had had a good weekend, to judge by his mien. Harriet noted that, while the prosecution had turned out a tall public school boy in immaculate gown, Tetherington-Hornchurch's togs were torn and faded. She found the contrast comforting.

Mr Runciman, for the Crown, referred frequently to his notes, so that his utterances were separated by intervals long enough for a short nap.

'The facts of the matter are not in dispute.' Pause. 'On the evening of Sunday, 27th October last, Mrs Harriet Funkel, otherwise known as Harriet Dimdore—' Pause. 'Stabbed and grievously wounded Mrs Dorothy Outwood in the chest.' Pause. 'Piercing the lung. Mrs Outwood is a relative of the accused, in the degree of, I believe—' Pause. 'Second cousin once removed, by marriage.' The judge blew his nose. 'The Crown will seek to demonstrate, ladies and gentlemen of the jury, that this was an unprovoked attack. On a defenceless elderly lady who, although recently widowed. Had devoted herself to the care and service. Of the defendant's family and household. In order to enable the defendant to pursue her career in. The theatre.' He reminded the jury that the defendant had pleaded not guilty, which meant that it was their duty to decide which of the versions of the case was more plausible, a task that would lead to the inevitable conviction of the defendant.

Tetherington-Hornchurch was equally confidant, at twice the speed. He turned a trusting shimmy on the jury.

'Ladies and gentlemen of the jury, this is in many ways a very sad case. A "domestic", as the police would call it – disguising, in that brief, everyday word, the deep and, yes, sometimes murderous passions, jealousy and despair that, sadly, so often characterize family life.

'My learned friend has said that the facts are not in dispute. What is also not in dispute, is the fact that no lethal disturbances sullied the home life of Mrs Harriet Funkel until the arrival in their midst of Mrs Outwood. At Mrs Funkel's own invitation. It is perhaps stating the obvious, to point out that Mrs Harriet Funkel would not be in the situation in which she finds herself today had she not taken her – very distant – cousin into her home. Mrs Funkel's life was up to that point orderly and satisfying. A devoted mother, who always put the interests of her children before her career. A woman who, from the highest motives, invited her unfortunate relative into her life, a relative who, to her horror, revealed herself to be consumed, not only with grief, but with mordant jealousy and envy, which ultimately led to an attack on Mrs Funkel, from which she was obliged to defend herself. Ladies and gentlemen of the jury, when you have heard the witnesses, you will have no choice but to agree that it would be a travesty of justice to compound the suffering that Mrs Funkel has already endured, as a result of her good intentions, by bringing in any other verdict but that of not guilty.'

Dotty had bought a cherry red suit for the occasion, with shoulder pads on which one could perch a hawk with ease. She had lost weight and had her hair cut in a chic short back and sides. She looked younger and smarter than Harriet had ever seen her, like a gutsy divorcee with a job at the Citizens Advice Bureau. She was, nonetheless, very nervous.

Mr Runciman, with some assistance from the judge, elicited a brief account from Dotty of the events of 27th October.

'Now, Mrs Outwood—' He stared at the desk for some time. 'You say you had a bit of an argument with Mrs Funkel. What was that argument about?'

'Well, Harriet – Mrs Funkel – was mad at me because – because I'd known Warren – Mr Funkel – was having an affair, and I hadn't told her.' Dotty sweated. This was sailing perilously close to the matter of the stolen shaver.

'Mr Funkel was having an affair, you say? And how did you know that?'

'Someone told me.'

'Objection!' Tetherington-Hornchurch was on his feet.

'Sustade.' The judge had got a cold. 'The jury will desregard what the widness has just said.'

Dotty looked confused. That was the truth. What was wrong with it?

'However, you were – discussing family matters.'

'Yes.'

'Apart from the putative affair of Mr Funkel, what was the general trend of the conversation?'

'We were – er – talking about the children leaving home.'

'Did you say anything of a provocative nature about the children?'

Dotty blushed. 'No, I don't think I did.'

Mr Runciman pressed the point that they had been having an innocent conversation about the children when, without warning, Harriet had gone bonkers and stabbed her. He then moved on to the nature of Dotty's role within the family.

'Could you tell the court how you came to be resident in the household.'

Dotty did so, becoming tearfully affected at the memory of Fin's death.

'You did, I believe, make several attempts to leave the household, did you not? And move into your own establishment?'

'Yes. But it was never convenient for Ha – Mrs Funkel.'

'And on the last occasion, when you had selected a suitable home, would you tell the court what prevented. Your moving into it.'

Dotty's lip quivered. 'I lost all my money in the Matterhorn International scandal.' A murmur of sympathy could be heard.

'And, as a result, you were destitute, is that right?'

'Yes.'

'Now, Mrs Outwood, how would you describe your relationship with your cousin, Mrs Funkel, prior to the incident?'

'Well, I've always been very fond of – Mrs Funkel. As far as the bees in her bonnet would allow. We got on pretty well, provided we avoided certain subjects.'

'Was Mrs Funkel satisfied with your care of the children? Particularly Tiziana, with whom you had most to do, I believe.'

'She thought I gave Tiz the wrong things to eat sometimes. You see, I believe in letting children enjoy their food, not get stupid phobias about cholesterol and that. But Harriet – Mrs Funkel – was always making her eat lambs lettuce and halibut and things. She went off her food altogether, of course.'

When Tetherington-Hornchurch rose he smiled upon Dotty.

'Now, Mrs Outwood, you say you were having a bit of an argument with Mrs Funkel when, for no reason at all, she took a knife, with which you had previously been cutting tomatoes, and plunged it into your chest?'

'Not for no reason at all, no. As I said, she was angry that I had known about – Mr Funkel's affair.'

'But you did not "know" of the affair, did you? "Somebody" told you. Remember you're on oath, Mrs Outwood. Are you prepared to repeat that allegation? Do you have witnesses? Photographic evidence? Times, dates, etcetera?'

Dotty could see a potential prosecution for defamation of character written all over Tetherington-Hornchurch. Her mouth was dry. 'Put like that, I suppose I wouldn't.'

'Very well. Now, you have claimed that the conversation which preceded the attack was of a non-combative nature?'

'Yes.'

'Is it not the case, in fact, that you made derogatory comments about Mrs Funkel's children, comments to the effect that she had failed as a mother?'

'I don't think so—'

'Did you not maliciously taunt Mrs Funkel about her husband?'

'No. It wasn't like that.'

'Did you or did you not say, "This family's days are over. Talk about an experiment that failed."?'

'I didn't mean—'

'Just answer the question, Mrs Outwood.'

'I – I may have done.'

'And did not Mrs Funkel then inform you that, as a result of this kind of subversive influence in the family, she had decided that they would not be taking you with them when they moved house, and that you would, consequently, have to find your own accommodation after all?'

'Eh? No, I don't remember her saying that.'

'And did you not then unleash a violent invective against Mrs Funkel, insult her professional capacities, her failure as a parent, the unfairness of her material wealth when it was you and your husband who had fought in the war, and not Mr and Mrs Funkel?'

'No!'

'And did you not then take the knife with which you had been cutting tomatoes, throw it with considerable force at Mrs Funkel, and then advance upon her with the clear intention of placing your hands around her throat?'

'No!'

'Objection!'

'Sustade.'

'Very well. You say Mrs Funkel invited you to stay with them after the death of your husband?'

'Yes.' Dotty was clutching her heart at the possible meaning of the Tetherington-Hornchurch scenario.

'Would you like some warder?' enquired the judge.

'Yes please.'

'Are you able to condinue?'

Dotty nodded.

'You stayed with the Funkels for a few weeks, and then returned to your home?'

'Yes.'

'And then what happened?'

'They asked me to go on holiday to Cornwall with them.'

'Which you did.'

'Yes.'

'Did you pay anything towards the cost of the holiday?'

'Well – not as such.'

'Did you ever pay anything towards the household expenses?'

'Not in money, no.'

'So. What happened while you were in Cornwall?'

'Mrs Funkel got a phone call from her agent asking her to take over the part in that musical thingy.'

'*Wipers!*'

'That's right. She asked me if I'd stay on and look after the kids. Tiz mainly. I'd been on the point of leaving.'

'And this was despite the fact that they already had an au pair in residence?'

'Yes.'

'Why did you agree to stay on?'

'I didn't want to.'

'Why not?'

'I didn't approve of Harriet's – Mrs Funkel's carrying on.'

'What "carrying on"?'

'Well, the – young man, Damian de St Croix his name is, came down to the cottage. Mrs Funkel admitted he had a crush on her. And – and I saw them kissing.'

'So you assumed they were "carrying on"?'

'Yes.'

'Another affair, Mrs Outwood? How very over-stimulating for you. In what circumstances did you see them kissing?'

'He'd just arrived. It was on the doorstep.'

'So, a young man, who has a crush on Mrs Funkel, comes to the house and gives her a kiss upon arrival. And from this you conclude they were having an affair.'

'It was that kind of kiss.'

'Are you an expert? Is it likely that, if they were lovers, Mrs Funkel would have invited him on the family holiday?'

'I don't know that she did invite him. He came of his own accord.'

'Precisely. Did you see them "carrying on" at any other time?'

'No.'

'So why did you stay on?'

'Mrs Funkel said she wouldn't do the show unless there was a responsible woman in charge at home. And I must say I agree with that. It wasn't meant to be for long.'

'But why did you stay after Mrs Funkel had come out of the show?'

'I was all set to move, when I found out the bank, or whatever it was, that I'd invested my money in, had collapsed.'

'Ah yes. Matterhorn International. Incidentally, why did you sell your house, Mrs Outwood?'

'Mrs Funkel's mother wanted to buy it. As an investment.'

'Did you not *persuade* her to buy it?'

'No.'

'What would you say if I told you that I have here a sworn statement from Mrs Funkel's mother, stating that it had never been her intention to buy property in this country as she had just become engaged – to a judge, as it happens, your honour – but that you pleaded with her to take the property off your hands because you couldn't cope with it, and you could not face the prospect of living there alone?'

Dotty spluttered. 'It was her idea! It was! When she found out the house was for sale.'

'Really? So this is a false statement, is it? Did you not tell Mrs Funkel's mother that you could not face living alone?'

'Yes, that bit I did, but—'

'At any rate, your house was sold. And you invested the money with Matterhorn International.'

'Yes.'

'I believe you responded to a promotion by the company outside Sainsbury's in the North Downs Shopping Centre.'

'Yes.'

'Did it not occur to you that a so-called international company reduced to hawking its wares outside Sainsbury's might be a high-risk venture?'

'I don't see why. Anyhow, I went to their offices as well.'

'Did you check that the offices were paid for? No, Mrs Outwood, I put it to you that you deliberately risked your capital so that you would become permanently dependent on the Funkels. Your motives may have been pathetic – that you could not face living alone – that you had become too comfortable in their well-appointed home – but, nonetheless, that is what your motive was. After all, we only have your word for it that you lost your money, don't we?'

'It's the truth! It is, your honour. I'm sure I could find the papers somewhere.'

'Address yourself to the jury, Mrs Oudwood. Mr Detheringdon-Hornjurch, whad is the purpose of this line of enquiry?'

'Your honour, motive is the *sine qua non* of this case. I am endeavouring to establish that Mrs Outwood, far from being the innocent, self-sacrificing old lady that the Crown has presented, was in fact a manipulative exploiter of the Funkels' hospitality, and it was the threatened withdrawal of that hospitality that drove her to attack the defendant.'

'Very well. Bud do id withoud intimidading the widness.'

'My apologies, your honour.'

Dotty, who could not remember which one the defendant was, appeared unaffected by Tetherinton-Hornchurch's game plan, which at this point included relaxing his attack, and smiling once more on Dotty.

'Mrs Outwood, you said you got on pretty well with Mrs Funkel, apart from her "carryings on".'

'Yes. We used to have quite a laugh in the beginning, when she wasn't in a stress all the time.'

'She seemed "in a stress" more often as time went by?'

'You can say that again.'

'You mentioned that you found it wise to keep off certain subjects. What were those subjects?'

'Oh, you know – the government, and capital punishment and that. I agree with that chap from Basildon – I could pull the lever myself. And she nearly burst a blood vessel if we got on the subject of immigration. I mean, Harriet – Mrs Funkel – is one of those armchair liberal types who never see a black man unless they've been given jobs on the television by people like her. She should try living with my sister-in-law in—' Her eye fell on the jury. 'Er – Peckham.'

'Thank you, Mrs Outwood.'

Mr Runciman staged an epic pause when the Nottingham Knocker mentioned that Harriet had had a knife in her hand when she opened the door. He was asked to repeat it several times. But Tetherington-Hornchurch forced him to admit that he could not describe the knife, therefore he could not say whether it was the same knife that had been used in the attack.

'How would you describe Mrs Funkel's mannner when she opened the door?'

'She was a bit, like, spaced-out. Sad, sort of. But she was very nice. She said she'd give me some money.'

'And did she?'

'Well, she went off to get it, from the kitchen, I think.'

'Could you see into the kitchen?'

'No. The door was only open a bit.'

'Could you hear what was said in there?'

'Yes, but I wasn't really listening, like, because I didn't expect anything to happen.'

'Of course. Did you see Mrs Outwood, the lady who was stabbed?'

'Yes, she came downstairs. I saw her go into the kitchen just after Mrs Funkel. She looked like she was holding something. With both hands, to her chest like this.'

'Could it have been a knife?'

'Dunno.'

'Go on.'

'They just started talking.'

'Quietly? Earnestly?'

'Sort of in low voices, like they didn't want nobody to hear.'

'Could they have been having an argument?'

'Yeah, like under their breath. Then I heard one of them shout "What about me?" Like that.'

'Do you know which of them shouted that?'

'No. Like I said, I wasn't concentrating. Besides, the radio was on.'

'And then?'

'Then I heard a bloody great clatter. And the dogs were barking.'

'When did the dogs start barking – before or after the "clatter" you described?'

'Er – before. Yes, definitely before.'

'How were they barking?'

Mr Runciman was outraged. 'Your honour, this is a court of law, not an animal hospital.'

'Dank you, Mr Runciman. I doe where I am. Mr Detheringdon-Hornjurch?'

'Your honour, the witness, though young, has a lifetime's experience of living with dogs. It is my contention that the dogs began to bark when they saw their mistress being attacked by Mrs Outwood.'

'Very well.'

'Thank you, your honour. Now, Mr Habgood, in your esti-mation, were the dogs barking in panic, aggression, growling, yapping? How would you describe it?'

'They were growling at first. After one of the ladies shouted. Then barking like in panic. Yeah, like they was scared. Then they suddenly shut up.'

Tetherington-Hornchurch asked Warren straight out if he had been having an affair. Warren was prepared, and had taken Valium, so answered 'No' with great firmness. As to Dotty's influence on the household, he said that Harriet had shown great forbearance with Dotty, despite their differing views. She had not really needed Dotty, as they were always provided with excellent au pairs, one of whom was now their daughter-in-law. On the night in question, Harriet was very tired, and worried that there might not be room for Dotty in their new house.

'Did you ever observe antagonism between Mrs Outwood and your wife?'

'That's kinda hard to answer. They argued, all right. About politics, and stuff. Dotty – Mrs Outwood is kinda feisty. If she didn't agree with something she'd, like, have a blow-out.'

'And how did you get on with her?'

'Great. No problem. Until she told me that Harriet – my wife – was having an affair with this guy she met on the train. It was nonsense, of course. I play golf with the guy all the time now.'

'That was Damian de St Croix and the "carrying on".'

'Right.'

'Do you think she was deliberately trying to turn you against your wife?'

'Well – I didn't see it in those terms at the time.'

'Mrs Outwood is a rather distant relative of yours. How is it that you had such a close relationship with her that it seemed natural that she should share your home?'

'Oh, that's because when I first came to England as a student she was the only person I knew in the London area. I lived with her as a lodger for a while.'

'Were there any problems then?'

'Not at all. She didn't want me to leave, as a matter of fact. But I wanted to be nearer the city.'

'She didn't want you to leave.'

'That's correct.'

'Would you say she had developed a strong attachment to you?'

'Well – I guess.'

Mr Runciman managed a smile as he asked the Reverend Vince to confirm that he was a disc jockey and self-employed vicar.

'I prefer the term radio presenter.'

'To what – disc jockey or self-employed vicar?'

'Disc jockey.' Titters from the court. 'And I am not a vicar, which is an official of the Church of England.'

The titters stopped.

'How would you describe your. Pastoral activities, then?'

'I'm an informal group leader.'

'But you do lead. This informal group. In a chapel, and wear. Ecclesiastical garments while doing so?'

'Yes.'

'How long have you known. Mrs Funkel and Mrs Outwood?'

'I met them together. About two years ago.'

Mr Runciman asked him to describe the events of the 27th October.

'When you saw Mrs Funkel sitting at the table, did she say anything?'

'She asked if Mrs Outwood had ironed her daughter's uniform. She was in shock.'

'Are you a doctor as well?'

'No.'

'So that is not a professional judgement. Of Mrs Funkel's condition.'

'It is a common-sense judgement.'

'Did she claim that Mrs Outwood had attacked her?'

'Not at that time, no.'

'Thank you.'

Tetherington-Hornchurch assumed an air of grave respect to question the Reverend.

'When Mrs Funkel came to your chapel, was she interested in joining the group?'

'No. She had only brought Mrs Outwood, because she couldn't drive then.'

'Was this the only occasion on which Mrs Funkel brought her second cousin once removed by marriage to the chapel?'

'No. She brought her several times.'

'When you and Mr Funkel and Mr de St Croix entered the kitchen, and Mrs Funkel asked about the school uniform, you say she did not accuse Mrs Outwood of attacking her?'

The Reverend gripped the edge of the witness box. 'That's right. We kept asking her what happened. She was incoherent. Mr Funkel and Mr de St Croix went to the hospital, and I stayed at the house.'

'What were you doing at the house?'

'Warren – Mr Funkel – had asked us to watch a programme that he'd – produced, I think. He was nervous about it. We were there for moral support.'

'When Mrs Funkel told you of the attack, why didn't you call the police? Why didn't you anyway?'

'It sounds ridiculous now, but – it wasn't my house. I was just a guest. Besides I was too concerned about Mrs Funkel to think about it.'

'You knew both these ladies quite well. Were you aware of any antagonism between them?'

'No.'

Damian was called. Warren had drugged him too. He denied ever laying a finger on any member of the family. His account of the events revealed nothing new.

Harriet had chosen a dove grey suit for her appearance in the witness box.

Mr Runciman questioned her for an hour about her relationship with Dotty, but failed to dent her self-portrait as a long-suffering philanthropist who only had Dotty's interests at heart. Mr Runciman was rattled.

'Your patience, Mrs Funkel, given the alleged provocation, and the catalogue of catastrophes that occurred at the same time, was heroic, was it not? Rivalling that of Job in the face of his comforters?'

Harriet smiled wanly. 'I wouldn't want to push anyone off their pedestal.'

Mr Runciman gazed at his papers for ten minutes. 'You claim that Mrs Outwood attacked you after you told her she had to leave the family. Wasn't this a rather odd time to impart such sensitive news – late on Sunday evening when you were both. Tired?'

'It was spontaneous. She had been goading me about the children.'

'Why?'

'We had been arguing about my daughter's eating habits. I told her that I thought her influence on my daughter was very harmful and it was our decision that she should leave. She then became very abusive.'

'So you took the knife and stabbed her?'

'No, I did not.'

'So what did happen?'

Harriet was afraid the judge could hear her heart beating. 'She was screaming at me, "Bugger Tiz. What about me?"

Then she took the knife and threw it at me. And I caught it.'

'Indeed? That was very. Fortunate.'

'At the same time, Mrs Outwood charged at me, with her hands out – so – I thought she was going for my throat, so I—'

'Dake your dime, Mrs Funkel.'

'Thank you, your honour. I put the knife up – to defend myself – and the next thing I knew, she was – on the floor—'

'You are asking us to believe that you just happened to catch the knife and Mrs Outwood obligingly committed hara-kiri on it?'

'I don't know what was on her mind. I thought she was going to kill me.'

'Because she had thrown the knife at you?'

'Yes. I think anyone would have drawn the same conclusion.'

'Would you be prepared to. Demonstrate your knife-catching skills?'

'Pardon?'

'I said. Would you be prepared to demonstrate that. You can catch a knife at, what – ten paces? Here in court? Well. Perhaps outside.'

'I – I don't know—'

'Wod are you proposing, Mr Runciman?'

'May we approach the bench, your honour?'

'I think you'd bedder.'

Tetherington-Hornchurch was flustered. 'Your honour, if he is proposing what I think he is proposing, it would turn the court into a three-ringed circus. It's preposterous.'

'Your honour, the defence rests solely on this point. It is the only way the Crown can demonstrate that her story is a complete fabrication. She is an actress, your honour, it's all a performance. This is the only way we can discredit her evidence.'

'By throwing knives at her in court! Is your honour going to allow such a farce?'

'I'd make dem use rubber knives,' mused the judge.

'Even so, your honour, my client could not be expected to repeat a feat achieved in a moment when her life was at stake.'

'*Au contraire*,' smirked Mr Runciman, 'in a very real sense, her life is at stake now.'

'Hmm. Unfordunadely for your client, Mr Dederington-Hornjurch, it would look very bad if she refused to dake the dest now it has been suggested. I dink we owe id do her do allow her do prove her innocence.'

'But – your honour—'

'Adjournment undil domorrow do make de arrangements.'

The list officer chose to cordon off the area in front of the side entrance to the court, adjacent to the car park. It was windy and cold. The court officers, jury and counsel stood at one end, everyone else at the other. A sturdy policewoman of the approximate size and shape of Dotty stood beside a small table on which were three rubber knives. Some curious spectators on their way from the Bedford Road car park to the shops stopped to watch.

Tiz clung to Warren's arm, shivering with dread. 'This is so *cruel*, Dad. I can't bear it. She'll never do it. Look at her – she looks like a dog on Death Row.'

'Yeah, she's even dribbling. Doesn't anyone have a handkerchief, for God's sakes?'

After lengthy consultations with the Clerk of the Court, which clearly included the likelihood of rain, the judge gave the signal for action.

The policewoman threw the knife with venom towards Harriet, who lunged at it, but it passed her at a distance of some 1.2 metres. She managed to make contact with her fingers before it landed on a Vauxhall Corsa.

Mungo covered his face. 'This is worse than the semifinal with Germany.'

The policewoman looked put out by the inaccuracy of her shot and rolled up her sleeves.

'They should let Mum wear goggles,' said Tiz. 'Suppose it goes in her eye?'

'They couldn't do that, stupid,' said Mungo. 'She wasn't wearing goggles at the time. I presume.'

'Oh shut up.'

The second shot was aimed at Harriet's midriff, and if it had been real would have split her diaphragm. She caught it with both hands. Someone started to applaud, but was silenced by the judge.

The policewoman was none too pleased with her bowling average. The third knife flew towards Harriet's neck. She leapt forward, caught it by the blade, overbalanced and fell to the ground. The knife bobbled across the ground to Mr Runciman's feet.

The judge adjourned the court for lunch.

His honour summed up for four hours, in the course of which his cold cleared up. He reviewed the physical evidence in detail and dismissed it as inconclusive. The knife-catching test was subject to too many variables to draw the conclusion from it that Mrs Funkel could not have caught a knife in the exceptional circumstances of the incident. He ruminated at length on the background to the case, and the characters of the protagonists as described by their witnesses.

'You have heard counsel for the Crown opine that as Mrs Funkel is an actress, there is the strong possibility that her version of events is a fabrication – a part that she has schooled herself to play. There is no doubt that a person such as Mrs Funkel, accustomed to perform in public, no matter what personal troubles and circumstances prevail in her private life, is at an obvious advantage when giving evidence in court. If you believe this, you must also believe that Mrs Funkel did, indeed, stab her cousin in a fit of temper, and that the whole story about the knife is intended to deceive. It is up to you to decide if this is a credible possibility. The nub of the matter is this. You have been presented with two women, each of whom has been credited with conflicting characteristics. Until this incident, I think it is fair to say that both were of irreproachable character. Both have been presented as good-humoured and stoical under stress. Both have also been presented as subject to outbursts under stress. The balance of possibilities which you have to judge, is whether it is more likely that Mrs Funkel, a blameless and conscientious mother who took her husband's second cousin once removed into her home as an act of charity, suddenly developed homicidal tendencies, or whether Mrs Outwood, deranged by grief, embittered by childlessness and consumed by envy of her more affluent relations, attacked her benefactor in a fit of unpremeditated spleen.' He concluded with instructions on the conduct of their deliberations and reminded them that they could review the evidence at any time. The jury was then led away.

There was no verdict that day. The following day being a Friday, the judge informed the jury that if they did not deliver a verdict during the course of it, they would have to spend the weekend in a hotel. Half an hour later the parties were summoned from the cafeteria, where Warren and the family had been sitting at a table next to Dotty and her relations from Northampton. As they went out Tiz, who had been tormented by Dotty's nearness, ran back and hugged her.

'I still love you, Dotty, even if you did try to kill Mum.'

'Tiz, I didn't—' Dotty started to cry.

'Ssh. It's all right.' She lowered her voice. 'I know the truth. If it's any comfort to you. But it's your fault for bringing her to court. If she's sent away for years I'll never speak to you again, I'm afraid.'

'Oh Tiz, my pet—'

'Got to go.'

It was Not Guilty.

Dotty and Harriet were caught up in a mêlée in the atrium. Dotty became separated from her elderly escorts and pushed her way into the toilet. Harriet was watching her and followed. Dotty was on the lavatory. Harriet leaned against the door. She listened to the tinkling and rustle of Dotty's performance. The relief of escape allowed guilt to flood back, and memories of her old fondness for Dotty's spark and spunk and WI values. She must make some gesture – Dotty opened the door of the lavatory and started when she saw Harriet. She looked her age – old. Her special occasion make-up made a grotesque pudding of her skin. They looked at each other for a moment. Then Harriet lost her nerve and left the room.

* * *

Mungo returned to Australia. Tiz stayed with Avelina until Warren found a flat. After a decent interval, Damian moved in with them. Warren, true to his word, approached Dotty with offers of help, including a share of the profits from Abutilon. At first she refused. Eventually she had to admit that the fleshpots of Hampstead had more to offer than the bungalows of Northamptonshire. To Tiz's relief, she joined them as housekeeper, providing she had a bedroom at the opposite end of the flat from Warren and Damian.

Tiz lived with Warren during the term until her GCSEs, and moved in with Harriet for her A-Level years. This was a wrench, as Harriet had moved to Suffolk. When the moment came for Tiz to say goodbye to the friends she had made in Hampstead, the wounds of loss gushed open again, glistening and relentless.

Japheth could not reconcile himself to Warren's relationship with Damian. He was equally critical of Harriet's folie de cock-up, as he called it.

'Mum's such a bell end,' he complained to Semi, relaxing after a 6–0 win over Swindon. 'Only Mum could get herself attacked by a harmless old crock like Dotty. I mean, why didn't she convert part of the house into a flat for us? Then she wouldn't have needed Dotty at all. You could have looked after Tiz. She was crazy about you.'

Semi made soothing noises and stroked his head. ''Arriet did not love you when she 'ad the chance. But I will make all OK.' She twined her long limbs around his body, enclosing him.

Dotty flourished in Hampstead. She quickly overcame her fear that she would be mugged by cosmopolitan chic as soon as she stepped outside the door. Incredibly, there were no WIs in North London, but she joined the nearest Townswomen's Guild, where she took charge of plans for VE Day. She was seduced by pavement cafés, and became the mascot of some dodgy Armenians to whom she gave English lessons over kir and pastries. In the course of which, she picked up information which she subsequently passed on to the *Sun* by anonymous telephone call. Shortly afterwards, Yoevil and

Kean were released from a disused laundry building on the slopes of Mount Ararat.

Harriet retrained as a speech therapist. She refused offers from the tabloids for her story. It took a long time to become accustomed to living alone, and rural silence, which made the shades of Lloyd George Drive seem clamorous. For several years she was afraid that Dotty might be prosecuted in turn, and confessed all to her psychotherapist. There was one dread she did not discuss even with her therapist, because it was too chilling. That was the Christmas when she had been poisoned. Not by the food, by a person. With hindsight there was only one who had a motive.

By the time Tiz came to live with her she was reconciled to being the victim of circumstances, possibly of The Age. She never gave up the idea that Warren had succumbed to sexual fashion, and that he would one day come to his senses.

The Reverend Vince made a great success of *High Spirits*. He was promoted to wildlife and, later, public forum programming. He married the niece of a duke.

Tiz set about rehabilitating her mother in earnest. The first step was to buy a horse. She thought it would be good for Harriet to care for a living creature again. Warren had kept the dogs. British Telecom was long since too small. Tiz thought a black Arab mare would be appropriate compensation for the upheaval and, after all, what was good for her was good for Harriet. She also decided that Harriet ought to start acting again. Since Harriet felt ill and dropped things at the very idea, Tiz could see she had a job on her hands.

'Mum, I've made an appointment with this woman called Jill Freud. You know, she runs the theatre in Southwold. Now don't say anything. She's very nice and she knows you're not looking for a part. You need to mingle with your own kind. I mean, the people round here are all well and good, but they're all potters, aren't they? You could help backstage. They need all the help they can get. You know what the arts subsidy situation is like in this country under the present government. You will go, won't you, Mum?'

*   *   *

Japheth's last game before joining Paris St Germain was the final of the Twiglets Cup against Liverpool at Wembley. He gave Harriet plenty of advance warning that he would be playing. He had wanted her to go and watch, but on the day it clashed with a gymkhana, so she set the video instead.

Reader, you are an intelligent person. You know what comes next.

It was the forty-second minute of the second half. Japh was in the penalty area. Wiggins had stroked the ball out of defence and made a run for it, Liverpool's midfielders scattering like pus out of spots. A cross to Umbalogu, who crossed it again to Pill, drawing the goalie away from Japheth. The ball was briefly regained by Liverpool's Valpolicella with a wicked backward flip from the ankle, but Pill caught it on the left heel, scooted it through the legs of three Liverpool defenders straight on to Japheth's right boot, from where it rose in an orgasmic plume into the top left-hand corner of Liverpool's net.

'And the – citadel is – taken—' trembled the voice of veteran commentator Dennis Wildacre. 'And the twenty-three-year-old – former schoolboy from Sutton – scores what must be – a decisive goal—'

The roar of Tatters' supporters thundered round the stadium and up into the grey sky as Japheth acknowledged their ecstasy, and ran round the perimeter of the ground looking for his mother's face in the crowd.